Mary Haslehurst

Days forever flown

Mary Haslehurst

Days forever flown

ISBN/EAN: 9783337108632

Printed in Europe, USA, Canada, Australia, Japan

Cover: Foto ©Andreas Hilbeck / pixelio.de

More available books at **www.hansebooks.com**

DAYS FOREVER FLOWN

" *Voice of the Western wind,*
Thou singest from afar,
Rich with the music of a land
Where all thy mem'ries are,
But in thy song I only hear
The echo of a tone
That fell divinely on my ear
In days forever flown.

" *Star of the Western sky,*
Thou beamest from afar,
With lustre caught from eyes I know,
Whose orbs were each a star,
But, oh! those eyes too widely bright
No more eclipse their own,
And never shall I find the light
Of days forever flown."

PRIVATELY PRINTED

NEW YORK

M D C C C X C I I

*A*T the repeated request of many friends, these leaves from my Journal of 1891 are given, with no additions or alterations, and few eliminations; and although of little interest to others, and unworthy to be read, as they were written solely for the refreshing of our memories as years passed on, they are offered to those who knew and loved my husband, in the hope that a glimpse of the last and happiest months of his young life may be of interest to them. Perhaps,—wandering in the same direction at some future time, it may be a pleasure to know what paths he chose, what scenes of peculiar interest attracted him, and what unusual sensations and impressions were his.

As the writing of this journal was at his instigation, and was stimulated and sustained by his earnest entreaties and watchful care, that no day should be without a chronicle; and as he always sat near during the hurried times of writing, it seems as if his spirit and sentiments so pervade these pages, that they must have been unwittingly written for just such a purpose, as a "Memorial of Sunshine," to give the brightness from those happy months to those who loved him.

How blessed that through those wonderful wanderings we dreamed not of the shadow, so swiftly following our path of sunshine. As we stood, side by side, in those supreme moments, when marvelous beauty suddenly surrounded us on every hand, and our eyes seemed to behold the reflection of some heavenly grandeur, we did not realize how soon the Gates of Pearl would open for one of us, and one would stand in the light,—and the other in the darkness. There was no fear for us then, by day or night; life seemed too bright for shadows or sorrows,—and it is well that "we are led on, like the little children, by a way we know not."

The sun will not shine for us forever, the brightness of life cannot always be ours, for "into each life some rain must fall," but when "the days are cold and dark and dreary," we can look upward to the "Man of Sorrows," who was acquainted with grief, and backward upon our lives, and win calm and peace to walk "serene in sorrow," from the happiness which has been ours, and from the blessed memories which the Father hath granted us.

> " With grateful hearts the past we own,
>   The future, all to us unknown,
>   We to Thy guardian care commit,
>   And peaceful leave before Thy feet."

M. A. H.

Jan. 7, 1892.

OUR JOURNEY OVERLAND

ALTHOUGH superstition points to an un-
lucky ending for anything begun on this
day of the week, James and I had long
ago chosen it as our particular day for
going anywhere, and as James often said, "We
start everywhere on a Friday, and we always have
good luck."

After spending together, at home, the wedding
anniversary—

> " As it fell upon a day
> In the merry month of May "—

which chronicled seven years of happiness, we
started to-day, Friday, May 8th, for our anticipated
journey overland.

The day was without incident; the "Pennsylvania Limited" to Chicago passing through quite
familiar country, and being "an old story" to us,
we had little to marvel at, and nothing to attract
us, save the beautiful suggestions of the coming
Summer, which are ever a powerful stimulant to
thought and reflection. A little verse on the

prophecy of Spring, which Mamma wrote, recurs to me :

> "And so the tiny tender blade
> Whispers the promise God has made
> Of Summer sun,—the song of bird,
> The valleys green,—the grazing herd,—
> And from the trees, the slender shoot
> Foretells the bud, the flower, the fruit."

"The April winds are magical," and bring the beautiful blossom-laden month of May, and the dainty daisies with their hearts of gold, and the violets in their modesty;—sweet shy blue-bells, hanging their heads "as they wait for their lover;" and the glorious daffodils;—truly the Springtime brings a newness to life and expectation, which makes the world as attractive and entrancing, as if touched by a wand of magic. There seems a new brightness and joy in the sunshine, a new beauty in the buds and blossoms in every Springtide, as if we had not experienced the same sensations only a twelvemonth ago.

And so a journey begun at such a beautiful season is always full of hope and promise.

SATURDAY, MAY 9TH.

WE reached Chicago at 9.45 A. M., and drove at once to the Auditorium Hotel. It was a pleasure to return to the beautiful city which was once home to us, and after five years' absence, we naturally found numerous changes in the appearance of things. If "Architecture is frozen Music" Chicago is one glorious harmonious anthem.

After resting, seeing some friends, and dining, we went to see Mr. and Mrs. Kendal, in "The Iron-master," and James was much impressed by the fine acting of the English favorites. Through great rolling tears Jamie smiled at me, and said "Is this the play that Mother and Lizzie wept over? I don't wonder at it!"

SUNDAY, MAY 10TH.

THE day dawned for us about ten o'clock, and it was pouring and promised a wretched day. It was bright indoors, however, for our welcome to Chicago was so cordial and enthusiastic, and friends were with us all day. We went to Cousin L——'s to supper.

MONDAY, MAY 11TH.

A LOVELY, lovely morning. After breakfast, James went down-town to see his friends, with whom he was associated in business many years in the "West Countree." His welcome was more than he had ever dreamed it would be, and he was like a big happy boy, when he returned to tell me of it. Miss K—— came to see me at once, and invited us to dine with them this evening, and see Mr. and Mrs. Kendal again, which invitation we accepted, and had a most enjoyable time.

TUESDAY, MAY 12TH.

ANOTHER lovely day. After breakfast, James and I went down town on some important errands, but returned in time to see our good friend C. S.W., who lunched with us and was delightful, as of old. We missed so many callers to-day, for we went about five o'clock, with Cousins L—— and A—— for a delightful drive, through Jackson and Washington Parks, and to visit the site of the World's Fair.

Chicago impresses us more than ever. It is a marvelous city, with superb drives and wonderfully beautiful parks, and so many and so large, that the few little breathing spaces, in most of our eastern cities, seem nothing in comparison. We dined at the fine "Washington Park Club," of which Cousin A. is a member, and had a charming drive back to the hotel.

WEDNESDAY, MAY 13TH.

WE had a feast this morning in some home letters, and such a laugh over a "Clever Collection of C-ing-C-ong Comedy," an unceasing flow from the little Mother's witty pen. The first few hours of our winged flight from New York to Philadelphia, I amused myself composing a stupid affair about "cheery cottages, with creeping climbers, churches with chorus choirs, chuckling chickens, comely cows, captivating caterpillars, capering calves and such coarse, comic comedy, "sending it home from Philadelphia on a postal card, and calling it "Concoction

No. 1." Imagine our surprise to receive in answer from the Mother, " Careening cars, carrying certain characters 'cross country, in continuous course, cause continual commotion, constantly conjuring clever conceptions, carefully concealed in capacious cerebral chambers, and conspicuously conveyed on a convenient card, to one closely connected by conditions of consanguinity. The Concoction, a curious concern from its commencement, containing considerable and commendable commodities, will convince and convict, caress and cajole its contents as you will, constraining one to conclude its contributor was certainly ' C '-sick, or perhaps 'half c's over ' ! " `

James with C. S. W. went to visit Pullman to-day, to see the place where, five years ago, he gave up his business relations and interests. He wanted to see the friends there as well, and the three clerks whom he gladly gave a start in the business world before he left them. He had a most satisfactory visit ; every one was rejoiced to see him, and he was thoroughly pleased that he had gone.

My day was a full one, with so many calls, a delightful luncheon with the H's in their beautiful new home, and we made calls in the evening.

THURSDAY, MAY 14TH.

AMONG many visitors to-day was a young fellow whom James had taken into his employ when he first went to Pullman, and of whom he was always fond. He was so anxious to see James, and after paying me a visit, he followed him down to Mr. K.'s office, and saw him there. He told me that he remembered so well the morning he arrived in Pullman, and sat on his trunk outside James's store. James happened to pass soon after, and seeing this nice little fellow of thirteen years, stopped and spoke to him, and finding he desired employment, James took him at once into his store, "for he was such a smart little chap," as he often told me. This "little chap" is now a fine big fellow, and he told me to-day, "It was my fortune to meet Mr. Haslehurst that morning, for he has always been my ideal ever since in all I have done, and I have never felt for any one else in the world the regard I have for Mr. Haslehurst." I could "fill a small volume" with his praise for James, but I felt most deeply when he solemnly added, "He started me right in the world, Mrs. Haslehurst, and I owe my good fortune to his advice and example." That boy is right; he is a "true knight and matchless."

More calls, and all day! Such a cordial and hearty reception in Chicago pleases James exceedingly, and is more than we could have expected. As we rolled into the depot last Saturday morning, with so much anticipation in our hearts, I whispered to James, "I wonder if we will be glad we have come, or perhaps we have lost our places in the hearts of our friends, and we will be quite ready to move on next Thursday." We feel like children now, quite ready to cry, because we have arranged to start on to-night. Chicago was never so charming, our friends have showered upon us most lovely attentions, and we find them more attractive than ever.

At half-past nine o'clock to-night, with C. S. W. accompanying (and a large roll of magazines and newspapers, and a big basket of every conceivable kind of fresh and candied fruit, which his bounty had provided) James and I started for the Chicago and North-western Railroad Depot, where we took a train for the West,

As we reached the depot, C. S. W. exclaimed, " This road discharged four hundred and fifty switchmen this morning, owing to a strike, and have new hands on to-night." Little chills played tag up and down my spinal column, but I only smiled automatically. As we moved out of Chicago, I rolled up my curtain and looked out, and sure enough every switchman was accompanied by a policeman, with club upheld, and in the weird light of the switchman's lantern, and the green and red lights of the switch signals, it was anything but comforting and reassuring. We slept, however, in spite of danger, real or imaginary.

FRIDAY, MAY 15th.

ON the train from Chicago to Denver. Breakfast at 7.45 A. M., and after that, what a long day it was! I was ready for bed at 11 A. M. ! It was one of God's days of creation, without beginning and without end. We managed to procure stools from the porter, and sat out on the rear platform of the car, within the folds of the vestibule appliance, most of the day. We met a gentleman from New York, and we three sat together in our "Observation Car," the two gentlemen smoking, chatting, reading, etc. We discussed Theology and Theosophy, Darwin and Evolution, and then descended to conundrums and stories.

We passed through Iowa and Nebraska to-day. Iowa is a beautiful State to us, finely cultivated, and for miles and miles we seemed to be traveling through great farms; the ground was ploughed and planted, cleared of all rubbish, and stumps and stones, and one could easily imagine they were traveling through English country. Prosperity and contentment were in the very air, and if we could have seen the farmers and their families, I am sure we would have found them all well fed and well clothed. It was a pleasant journey to Council Bluffs. There we waited a half hour, while wheelmen went under the cars, other men on top, examining and cleaning everything for the rest of the trip. We saw sad sights among some emigrants; poor people, they are handled like cattle in transportation.

When we crossed the muddy Missouri and reached Omaha, our friend, seeing some wretched huts and hovels near our tracks, exclaimed in most ironical tones to me, " This is the aristocratic part of the town !" " No, sir, it ain't," exclaimed a man standing near, who looked as if he had never understood a joke in his life; " I've lived here two years, and the best part of the town is up yonder." Well, Omaha is a fine city no doubt, but from the railroad it is singularly uninviting.

We hurried along through or into Nebraska, and as we came to the prairies, we were filled with interest to see the beautiful clusters of fine trees, the pretty farm houses and barns gathered under these trees, and lovely verdure everywhere. Gradually the trees diminished in number, and in nearness to one another, the houses were fewer and poorer, and finally there were no trees at all, and such parched and dry lands, such desolate and dreary deserts, and the huts and shanties looked as if they would tumble into heaps of rubbish, if their owners sneezed. Then the prairies became rolling and sandy; hills of sand had formed by the side of the tracks, where protective walls and fences had been erected, and as we went further, into Nebraska, the desolation was dreadful, and the degradation was in keeping with the rest. We saw ranchmen on their horses, sometimes shooting, at other times galloping across a limitless, undivided country, without road or anything to guide one, save marks at intervals of wheels and hoofs. The herds of horses and cattle were near the tracks, by hundreds and hundreds; and such deplorable, dispirited animals, looking like whipped dogs; they made our hearts ache, they seemed so dejected and forlorn. Even the cows (and I never did like cows), made me feel pity for them. They move like snails across the prairies.

Of course there are places in all this dreary desert that surprise and interest one. Corning, Nebraska, is a lively little place, with electric lights, a cable-road, and showed signs of genuine thrift. But these places of size and activity are few and far between in Nebraska. Grand Island was wide-awake and stirring, and when we asked what made its success and prosperity and growth, they told us "There's a big beet-sugar factory here."

SATURDAY, MAY 16TH.

ALTHOUGH we were conscious of long waits in the night, and visions of Indians with tomahawks and knives were in my dreams, we did not know until we awoke on Saturday morning, that a burning bridge had delayed us three hours and a half. A queer resignation comes over one, when he is in a fix and there is no help for it, and so Jamie and I settled ourselves, to wait indefinitely for breakfast, oranges and bananas, from the bountiful basket presented to us when we left Chicago, quieting the most acute pangs of the long enforced fast. About ten o'clock a porter's welcome voice rang through the car, and announced that "this train will stop ten minutes at La Salle (Colorado) for breakfast." Everybody braced up at the mere mention of such a thing, and visions of something, at least edible, wandered through our empty and benumbed craniums.   It was pouring hard when La Salle was reached, and a low one-story shanty, with a counter across one end, was the "breakfast room."   Mudlike coffee was sold to the weary traveller, with sandwiches, and although Jamie was among the first to leave the train in search of something tempting, the sandwiches had given out before he reached the counter.   Dirty and distressing it was, a little house set down in the wide weary waste, and the only thing attractive there, animate or inanimate, was a great big good-natured Newfoundland dog, who wanted every one to pet him,—but we could not eat him!   We returned to our fruit basket, with a " Thank God, we have this," and after our appetites had been appeased, having seen some weary and tired people in the emigrant car, I went there with my basket and attempted to feed them.   When I asked one nice looking woman, who had evidently seen better days, if she would have an orange, she answered, "Oh, yes, indeed I will, and I'll pay you too, how much is it?"   After explaining that they were given to me, and I in turn desired to give them to her, she hurriedly added, "But I always like to pay for what I have." Next I passed the basket to a young mother with a baby on her breast, and her big-lipped, stupid looking husband said "How much, Ma'am?"   My single word " Nothing" must have produced the desired result, for they accepted and devoured in silence. I then visited a poor young woman with two wee babes, and left my basket and its diminishing contents to her to distribute.

On reaching Denver at half past eleven, we drove to the hotel where President Harrison had stopped, but as it was not yet open for regular guests, we went to "The Windsor." We felt the high altitude of the city greatly, which is at an elevation of five thousand, one hundred and ninety-six feet, and it produced a depressing effect at first. It seemed as if our heads would surely leave our shoulders, they felt so light. "Was it the air," does any one ask? Unkind, unfeeling mortals!

SUNDAY, MAY 17TH.

THEY say they seldom have seen such a rainy day as yesterday, in Denver, and that five months may pass now, without more rain visiting the city.

To-day has been lovely. This morning the mud was ankle deep, but it has dried rapidly and was really dusty when we drove about the city in the afternoon.

Denver is a wonderful city. There are fine buildings and fine dwellings, some really palatial homes, but altogether the city impressed us as a great big town, overgrown and provincial. But the street-car system is marvelous. Cable-cars run in every direction, north, south, east and west, around curves, passing and crossing tracks of other lines, and making one dizzy by their rapid movements. The city seems like a great æolian harp, for every car must sound a gong at crossings, and they ring in every key of the chromatic scale.

We saw all parts of the city, Ex-Senator Tabor's residence, Grant Street, Lincoln, Logan and Sherman Streets, Colfax and Pennsylvania Avenues, etc., as well as churches of all denominations and creeds, and much of real interest. While a marvelous city in growth, power and prosperity, Denver attracts us less than any city we were ever in. Perhaps we are not yet in tune with the western spirit and enterprise, but I think we are fair in our judgment and criticism.

Everybody here is from the East, even the bellboys and maids and the porters. To-day our porter said "I'm from Boston M'am, I had the asthm-y, and had to come here, but I'm cured now."

MONDAY, MAY 18TH.

WE are thoroughly satisfied with our knowledge of Denver, as a long walk this morning added to our acquaintance with this western city.

It was beautifully bright in the early part of the day, but a mist and heavy clouds obscured our view of the mountains, which our geographical bumps told us surrounded Denver. When we turned on our homeward tramp, the clouds had all rolled away, and there before us were the snow-capped Rocky Mountains. They were most majestic and wonderfully imposing to us, and we stood spell-bound with admiration. A great range of dark stormy mountains surround Denver, and behind, peeping between the dark summits, are the great monarchs, beautifully and dazzlingly white. The highest peak we saw to-day was Long's Peak, over fourteen thousand and eighty-eight feet high. They are so near heaven, it seems as if they must reflect the glory of the Great White Throne.

TUESDAY, MAY 19TH.

WE were glad our lucky star had aided us in deciding to leave Denver to-day, for before we were astir, the hotel was noisy with the newly arrived representatives from Louisiana and Texas, for the Trans-Mississippi Congress. Before we were out of our room, while we were dressing, two noble specimens were assigned to our palatial apartment, but as we strongly objected, they went away. While we were at breakfast, we hired the chamber-maid to abide in our room, and guard our goods and chattels, and while she was getting fresh linen for the bed, the blooming Southern representatives walked in, deposited their "where-with-alls" and dusters, and began "a tub" in the bath room. They were cut short in their exercises by the return of our fair hired damsel, and were ushered out until we should start. They left their bags reluctantly, fearing we might "take them by mistake."

We left Denver at 9 A. M., and before we had

pushed our way out of the city, we were speechless. The great mountains of the Rockies stood out in bold relief, and such grandeur in their size and shapes, with the ever-changing fleecy clouds passing over them, made a picture against the sky never to be forgotten. The rocks and scrub-oaks were literally black in the shadows made by the passing clouds, and they stood out in such boldness against the white snow mountains in the background. It was a perfect day, and a perfect vision of wonder and surprise to us. Our trip from Denver to Colorado Springs was one long exclamation! Jamie and I, as usual, sat on the rear platform of the train, on comfortable stools provided by the porter.

As we left Denver, the great snow-monarchs seemed to form a half-circle about us, and as we hurried along, the view was ever changing, and presenting new and interesting sights. Looming up against the sky, we would see great rocks, with every kind of broken outlines, representing castles, animals, etc., and finally right before us, stood a great wall of rock, hundreds of feet high, exactly like photographs I saw not long ago, in one of our magazines, of the homes of the cave-dwellers of Mexico. As we hurried along, on what western people call a fast train (going twenty-five miles an hour), we were deeply impressed by the queer rock formations, along the plains and prairies on our left, and in the great mountains on our right. Some huge piles of stone, hundreds of feet high, terminated in a flat square top, making the whole mountain resemble a cone decapitated. I exclaimed once, in the presence of a fellow-traveller : "These must at one time have been volcanoes, they look just like extinct craters." "And they are," came the answer from my better informed companion. On top of some of these mountains were formations of rock, like the castles on the Rhine, as picturesque and beautiful, and of one of them I was able to take a photograph. Some rocks took the form of animals,—one near the railroad represented perfectly a huge elephant,—another was poised on a high pinnacle, and resembled an eagle.

It is wonderful to ride over these road-beds and fine railroads, and realize that all these miles of road, through the wild prairie lands and deserts, have been laid mile by mile, by men's hands ; and it is remarkable to see how all the obstacles of nature have been overcome by the brains of men. The country through which we passed was cultivated, and looked rich and fertile, and the ranches seemed prosperous and well-cared for.

What interested us greatly were the little towns of prairie dog mounds. These little animals move along in great numbers, and some hillsides were fairly peppered by the little pointed sandy hills.

Colorado Springs we reached at twelve o'clock, after a three hours' ride from Denver, and were most agreeably pleased in our first view. The town itself, numbering between ten and twelve thousand inhabitants, is prettily laid out,—the streets are very wide and the houses are exceedingly picturesque. Many people, who cannot live anywhere else in health, can live here, consequently many wealthy families have gathered in Colorado Springs, and as their surroundings accord with their means and taste, the town is exceedingly attractive. There are no tall buildings,—the hotel, "The Antlers," is the highest in town, and it is such a fine hotel, beautifully furnished and most comfortable. The whole city impresses one as a prairie town, with the exception of the grand mountains in the background. The stores are good, presenting novelties and attractions, and they have fine public buildings as well. One remarkable thing in these western towns is the great use of electricity. Nothing but electric lights are used everywhere, and electric cars go in all directions.

WEDNESDAY, MAY 20TH.

ALTHOUGH cloudy this morning, we determined to start out about ten o'clock for a drive, to begin to see the points of interest about this pretty little place. We had a good driver, a light wagon with a covering over our heads, and armed with mackintoshes and umbrellas, we started. We drove through Colorado City, which is ugly and flat, and has absolutely no charms, save its close proximity to the great rocks and wonders, rising so unexpectedly out of the plains, and called the

"Garden of the Gods." The great entrance, with its red sandstone and white rocky mounds, presented an imposing spectacle, as we first saw them during a drive through Colorado City to Manitou. Manitou is five miles from Colorado Springs, and is at the foot of a great mountain range, all its roads being up and down hill and wonderfully picturesque, with the little shops bordering them, and the pretty little houses for summer guests perched up on every conceivable pinnacle and corner of rock. It reminded us of a foreign watering place, but, of course, is not so large or so well patronized. We climbed one winding road to the famous Iron Spring, which James tasted and pronounced "good." We then retraced our steps, and the plucky little horses began an ascent, we little dreamed of at the start. We climbed up and up between two high mountains, over a road cut from the solid rock, with huge perpendicular cliffs towering up each side of us, and the driveway fenced in to prevent falling to the depths below. We were then climbing the celebrated "Ute Pass,"—the mountain pass used by the Ute Indians, and later by the people of Leadville during their mining excitement. The rocks are full of iron and copper, and the pink and green coloring was picturesque. Suddenly, and without warning, the driver turned directly at right angles and we began a climb, up, up, up, until we seemed in the very clouds, and as if we were hobnobbing with all the majestic summits of those wonderful mountains.

We curved around, until we had driven about half an hour, and had climbed to an altitude of over eight thousand feet. We were then at the mouth of one of the greatest wonders in Colorado. Travellers who have visited the Mammoth Cave in Kentucky, say these grand Caverns of Iron Mountain, Colorado, are small and insignificant in size, but they were of the deepest interest to James and to me. Outside the cave is a little hut where you register your name, pay your admission, and hire a guide. They give each visitor a lamp with a reflector, which you carry, and when our lamps were "trimmed and burning" we entered the cave.

The story says that a young man, named Snider, was one day hunting on the top of this mountain, and seeing a small opening among the rocks, where the snow was melted away, began to investigate to find the cause of the snow melting more there than at any other spot. He soon discovered warm air coming from the hole, and after digging awhile became convinced that he had found a cave. A visit next day proved that he had made an important discovery, and for four years he kept his secret, until he had obtained a right to the land. This happened in 1881, and in 1885 the "Grand Caverns" were opened to visitors. Twenty-five thousand people visited them last year; and at one dollar a head, who would not discover a cavern? I do not know how to describe our trip through these five under ground chambers, with their wonderful prismatic colors, their ribbon and pencil stalactites and stalagmites, their great ceilings formed of rocks weighing tons and tons, which seem ready to fall any minute. We entered by a long black spooky passage first into a "Grand Hall," they call it, three hundred feet long, and from fifty to one hundred feet high. Up among the great arches of the roof, where a ladder was placed to aid the ascent, was a guide with a lantern and a rod, playing on a natural organ, formed of huge stalactites of ribbon formation, which contain true musical scales of "F" and "G." He played "We won't go home till morning," and one other tune, and then sounded the most beautiful, rich, deep-toned chimes I have ever heard, on some pencil stalactites. The ribbon formation is thin and follows the surface to which it grows, like a ribbon caught by a pearl edge. The pencil stalactites fall in cone shapes. No one can imagine how queer it all was, and this wonderful music soared upwards in such volumes of harmony, in such rich crescendoes that it seemed uncanny and more than mysterious. The ceilings and walls are covered with rainbow colors in great waves, which our lamps enabled us to distinguish plainly, like mother-of-pearl in some places and great opals in others. The formations are remarkable, taking the shapes of carrots and beets, and of a great ham. Some of the walls are like delicate coral. The Bridal Chamber is beautiful. It has not been open to the public long enough to be smoked by the lamps, as some of the others are, and it is beautifully white. What seemed so strange to me were the great white stalactites, among the darker ones, of pure cream-white alabaster. Some were in the shape of huge candles, as purely white as snow. In one place it was quite wet and dripping, and when I asked the guide what made it so, he said, "No one knows why, or from where the water comes." The alabaster is still adding its white deposit, but as it takes many years to form the thickness of a sheet of paper, it takes a century to add one inch.

One passage had a dome one hundred and ten feet high. We saw a gate up at one place, and the guide told us that about eighty feet further in, the passage terminated in a bottomless pit. They have never been able to hear a stone touch bottom, or lower anything into it to touch or measure the depth. I noticed a board platform, and was standing on it, when the guide said, "Under your feet, now, is a channel we hope to explore next winter, over one hundred feet deep, which is pure alabaster, and magnificent." I jumped ten feet away, and shuddered; the mysterious influence of the place had begun to creep over me, and I exclaimed, "Please don't move too fast, guide, for if I lose sight of you, I shall scream," and most reassuringly he answered, "You might scream for a month, and no one would hear you." Another year they hope to light the caverns with electricity, and although it will enable people to see all parts of the cave better, it will rob it of its uncanny and mysteriously weird effect. It is so unusual as it is now.

When we came out of the Caverns we found it was raining hard, but we were well equipped and did not mind it an atom, and drove to the Barker House in Manitou, where we had dinner. About half past two o'clock we started for Colorado Springs, driving through the "Garden of the Gods," which is a collection of most wonderfully formed rocks, placed in the most remarkable positions, without rhyme or reason, without relation or likeness one to the other, and how they came there, and by what process formed, makes one fairly faint with conjecture. Some are of red sandstone, almost terra-cotta, others near these red ones are white, like granite, and remembering that behind, or in the background, is Pike's Peak, in a perpetual snow mantle, you can imagine what a beautiful picture these form. Queer resemblances were found to animals and people. The turtle, alligator's head and mouth, whale, porcupine, anvil, toad, bear, sheep and seal are all wonderfully formed in great isolated rocks, which stand out in relief against the sky. Three great rocks amused us greatly; one represented a man's head and bust, with a military hat, near it stood a woman in a cap, and between the two was a funny pile of stones, an exact counterpart of a fat jolly bald-headed baby. They are named "Punch, and Judy, and the Baby."

GARDEN OF THE GODS.

One part of the Garden of the Gods is called Mushroom Park. It is composed of huge mushrooms of stone, perfect in every detail, and so numerous and colossal, that a human being feels like the hundredth part of an atom of matter in this wondrous world of stone. I do not believe an atheist could go through this country without believing in the existence of a God. We are deeply impressed by all these natural wonders, and believe we see daily evidences of the rounding and moulding, in these volcanic masses, of the great ice covers of the earth of many centuries ago. The work of the ice artist is visible in isolated boulders, for how else could all these wondrous rocks come to be, in such prairie places as we find them, if they were not carried to their resting places by the glaciers. One can see the water marks, the great ridges formed by the cutting ice, and it must be deeply interesting to one well grounded in scientific lore.

THURSDAY, MAY 21ST.

ABOUT six o'clock this morning, our room being dark, I jumped up to find out what time it was, and to look out of the window to see what signs we had for the day. Everything was enveloped in mist, and rain was still falling. I went to sleep again, feeling we were in for a rainy day, and in a measure I have not been disappointed. About eight o'clock a most beautiful sight awaited us. The mountains, as well as the foot-hills, were (and are yet) white with snow, and seemed to be as near as our balcony. They are grand, and every one says it is a most unusual sight for this time of year. As I write they seem close to us, and one has such a feeling of chumminess with them. It snows at intervals, and is too windy to venture out to-day.

FRIDAY, MAY 22ND.

BREAKFAST about nine o'clock as usual, and a mean-looking cloudy morning greeted us too. "We're in for another day in the house," Jamie exclaimed; but as it did not rain after breakfast, we went for a good walk. Toward noon it cleared, and after lunch, Jamie and I took a most lovely drive to North and South Cheyenne Cañon. We drove across the plains for a long distance, and then right up between two magnificent mountains, and as it was brilliantly clear, and the peaks were all snow-covered, it was a most interesting drive.

North Cheyenne Cañon is a very narrow gorge between two great grand mountains. The road winds up beside a most beautiful babbling brook, twisting and turning at sharp angles, and constantly surprising one by new and unusually picturesque views. We saw here formations of rocks we had never seen before. Very different they were from the wonders in the "Gardens of the Gods," and yet only five miles apart, and James and I were deeply impressed by their grandeur. They assume more castle effects than individual forms, and are like great fortresses on the hill summits, some having magnificent turrets and watch-towers, and presenting the most amazing variety in architecture. These huge piles of stones are like plum-puddings hardened into shapes, that is, they are full of little and big stones, cemented together by a substance like batter, and hardened and shaped into serrated forms, and of course this form and deposit points most conclusively to the glacial period. But these great ice forces were artistic in their manner of sprinkling the earth with wondrous formations, for no artist could have done such marvelous work in the picturesque placing of these masses of stone. Some towered hundreds of feet above one's head in great walls, with strata formed lengthwise, sidewise, and every other wise ; others stood like colossal sentinels, magnificent and majestic in their might. We were spell-bound, as we turned sharp corners, and came suddenly upon new visions of splendor.

South Cheyenne Cañon is different in aspect from North Cheyenne Cañon, although so close together in the mountains. It is wilder, and has more solid walls of rock, hundreds of feet high, but fewer isolated pinnacles. Here we had the pleasure of fording the same stream four times each way, eight times in all, and it was real exciting, for owing to the recent rains the stream was full, and running with great force. We felt some alarm at the first ford, but at the second we began to enjoy it, and to watch with interest the hub of the wheels disappear under the water.

SATURDAY, MAY 23RD.

OWING to the extreme cold last night, we did not open our window, but trusted to the ventilator to air the room. About five o'clock this morning, I awoke nearly suffocated, and Jamie hearing my groans, arose to open the window. "Come here quickly, May, and see a beautiful sight," and I hurried with all the energy I could demand at that early hour, and joined my white-robed spouse at the window. It was a beautiful sight; all the valley lay in shadow, the foot-hills were nearly black, and only a tiny gas-light in one cottage near showed any signs of life. Pike's Peak, however, and the high mountains near, were silver, then golden, as the rising sun touched them with glory, and made them stand out alone, above all the dim shadow in the valley, and all I could think of was the glory of Heaven itself, kissing the mountain peaks with a morning blessing. If an angel had hovered in mid-air, it would have seemed in keeping with that silent grandeur. I felt over-powered and crept back to bed, very glad to have the opportunity to close my eyes and keep that picture with me for a little while; Jamie, on the contrary, went flying about the room, vowing he was " wide-awake and rested. I never felt better in my life, May; Colorado air does agree with me," etc. As I failed soon to audibly appreciate

32

these comments, Mr. J. W. H. jumped into bed again, wishing "it was time to get up." He soon showed signs of sonorous breathing, while I lay quietly wondering the why and wherefore of certain things in nature.

We woke again at eight, to find a most exquisite day before us, and we at once decided that a morning drive would be just the thing, but as we could not get our favorite driver, we fortunately postponed it until the afternoon. We drove five miles over the " Mesa," which means a "Spanish Plateau," and a fine view was obtained of the country in every direction,—the mountains on the left and hundreds of miles of rolling prairie on our right, made a beautiful picture. We drove to "Glen Eyrie," the residence of General Palmer, built in a cañon, with a natural fortification, as impregnable as a fortress. It is surrounded by beautiful scenery, and although a fine residence, it must be too shut in to be inspiring and always attractive. We took some photographs there, which we have since been told was strictly prohibited, but "where ignorance is bliss," etc. We have the photographs, and they have the law.

We then thought a sunshiny view of the "Garden of the Gods" would pay us for a second visit, so we drove there, and just before entering at the great red gates, we saw a dozen or more little children coming towards us on burros, or as they call them here, " Rocky Mountain Canaries." I stood up with my camera, they clustered round us, and were much excited over having their pictures taken.

The "Garden of the Gods" interested us anew, and at the "Balanced Rock" Jamie and I left the carriage, and I climbed up on the rocks to take a photograph of James and the big rock. The sun went under a cloud just then, and while I waited for it to peep out again, along came a carriage with a lady and gentleman in it. They stopped, and as the lady jumped out the man shouted to me, "there's *a party* who would like to have her picture taken too." From my rocky elevation I accepted the proposition, and the lady went and stood as cosily as you please next to Jamie. Either James was not entertaining enough, or she grew tired of waiting for the sun to shine, for she suddenly decided not to tarry longer, and away she went.

James went this evening with our good friends, Mr. F. and Mr. R., to the "El Paso Club," the freedom and courtesies of the club having been extended to him for two weeks. They treated him royally, and did all they could to tempt him to remain longer in Colorado Springs. ·

I spent a delightful evening with Mrs. R., a most intellectual, charming woman, and her experiences were most entertaining to hear, as she had lived in many strange countries, and at one time in Brazil, by invitation from the Emperor to her husband. Her son, a lad of thirteen, has become a special friend of ours, and is so clever and bright and com-

BALANCED ROCK.

panionable. He has a fine face, a broad intellectual forehead, and a large expressive nose. My theory is, that people with big noses always amount to something intellectually. They are not great because their noses are big, but their noses are big because they are great. Is that a distinction without a difference?

To-day, as we drove to the hotel in the sunshine, over the entire road arched a most beautiful rainbow. It was raining out on the praries, and we had the beauty without the clouds.

SUNDAY, MAY 24TH.

JAMIE says Colorado Springs agrees with his body and his conscience as well, and he wanted to go to church this morning, which we did. We had a good walk to and from the church. We did not know which church to attend, as the Presbyterian, Baptist, Methodist, and all, seemed flourishing and attractive outwardly, but we finally decided on the Congregational Church. The minister, Dr. Gregg, formerly of Hartford, preached a sermon exactly suited to our needs. It was on the " Religious Life in the Church and in the Home," and was excellent.

In this hotel, there is the funniest porter we have ever seen. He is a great, big, good-natured colored man, and has a most original way of announcing the departure of trains east and west. His voice has most remarkable acoustic properties, and reverberates all over the house. As our room is directly over the office, we are amused a dozen or more times a day, by this peculiar musical chant. The stage rolls up to the door, and simultaneously rings out:

"Rio Grande North to Den - ver, All aboard!"

"Chicago, Rockland and Illinois. { First stop, St. Joe, Missouri. } All aboard!"

MONDAY, MAY 25TH.

EARLY this morning, before five o'clock, I was up to take a survey of the weather, to see if we could hope to leave Colorado Springs, and begin our long journey "across country." It was pouring, with an evident determination to keep it up all day, and I awoke James, and prepared his mind for another delay. After a late breakfast, James donned his mackintosh, and armed with an umbrella walked about the town, and seemed happy and resigned. We lunched by invitation with " The Bachelors " to-day. Eight fellows from the East live together at " The Antlers," and we were finely entertained by them. They all had taken James and me for bride and groom,—the third time so far on this trip! This evening we spent by invitation with Mrs. R. again.

Jamie hopped up about five o'clock this morning, to have a peep at the weather. Pike's Peak stood out clear and bright, flooded with sunshine, and the entire Dutch army could have been clothed in the light ethereal blue. We soon began to make ready for our start, but before eight o'clock it had clouded over again, and seemed as unpromising as ever. Out of the three hundred and sixty-five days of the year, sunshine has usually blessed Colorado Springs for three hundred and twenty-six days, and "the oldest inhabitant" has never known such an "uncertain May."

As Jamie was restless, we determined to start at 11.55 A. M. for the West, which proved a wise decision, and we have blessed our guiding star ever since, for we could not have had a lovelier time, or have met a jollier party. Our friends came to the train to see us off, and we left Colorado Springs, with many kind wishes expressed for our trip.

At Colorado Springs, two couples besides ourselves boarded the train, and were all consigned to sections in the same car. In the car was a fellow who attracted James at once, he reminded us so forcibly of our good friend W. B. ; and these two couples, this young gentlemen, and James and I, were all crowded together on the rear platform of the train, and were soon friends, and we all kept together for several days, and had a royally good time.

The first interesting place we saw after leaving Colorado Springs, was Pueblo. We had dinner here, in the Railroad Hotel, and we thought it poor enough, but later learned to know it was a fine repast. We then passed through a most uninteresting country, with nothing but great mountains of gray stone, covered half-way with sand, gray sand, reddish sand, and straw-colored sand, and presented all kinds of fantastic shapes. At first we were interested, it was so different from all that we had seen before, but after several hours of it we grew unutterably weary. Some of these formations interested us in one particular; the rocks were in great strata, and in different colors,—copper, iron and sandstone, and formed some wondrous effects. But this region was so barren, nothing grew on the hillsides, not even sage brush, and the valleys were forsaken and doleful. Once in a while a cabin would be visible, and a few weak lonely horses or cows, but all seemed in keeping with the dire surroundings, and the poor animals looked as if they had been fed on stones.

About half-past three this afternoon, a general stir among the passengers was a sign that we were approaching something of interest, and we all gathered on the back platform (where we sat most of the time for the next three days), and saw the "Royal Gorge" as we passed through. It passeth knowledge how man ever overcame such obstacles in nature, as were presented to us in this royally

"Royal Gorge." A stream on one side of the track, rushing and hurrying along, with a great wall of solid rock rising hundreds of feet, nay thousands of feet, straight up into heaven on each side of us. They say the rocks rise three thousand feet on each side of the track. It is like a miracle to pass through that gorge. It seemed unearthly, as we twisted and whirled around the sharp and narrow curves, and looked up so far, to catch a glimpse of God's heaven. At first we were filled with wonder, at the marvelous engineering skill and genius, that had planned and executed so gigantic an undertaking; then an awe and silence stole over us, as we stood face to face with such wonders of God's creation. The summits of these walls of rock were pointed, rounded, in squares, turrets and spires, and the change in the color of these great expanses of stone presented prismatic tints, which no brush could imitate. Fiery red, terra-cotta, blue, then almost white, would appear in waves of color, and not one tiny bush or shrub to break the great breadth of rocks. It was a magnificent trip through that gorge, and one never to be forgotten. My words seem so poor in describing this grandeur.

We hurried along after leaving the Royal Gorge, through a very beautiful and fertile valley, and were rejoiced to see grander snow mountains on our left than we had seen before. We were nearing Salida, and were steadily going higher and higher, as the altitude of Salida is seven thousand and fifty feet.

We reached there at 5.35 P. M., and found it a very small town, formed of cheap houses and homes, a railroad centre merely. They told us the hotel "Monte Christo" was first-class. It is over the station, and a noisier, more disagreeable abode is hard to imagine, but we will have to be satisfied with much worse before we reach home, I fancy. As soon as we had obtained a room and deposited our traps, James and I started out to see the town, and take a few photographs. The mountains were magnificent. Salida is situated in a semi-circle of great mountains, so white with snow as to be almost too dazzling to look at. We were spell-bound with admiration.

We walked up the main street, which was filled with remarkably smart shops, but every other window presented whiskey bottles; in other words, every other store was a saloon. The night before our arrival, a hotel and five saloons had burned down, and the ruins were still smoking, but it was no loss to the little town. We hurried back to the supper-table, then took another walk with our friends.

WEDNESDAY, MAY 27TH.

W E had a wretched night, and longed for daylight. Long before five o'clock, we were too nervous with the noise of the trains to stand it longer, so we were up and out, and what a pleasure awaited us! The sun had touched all the hills and mountains, the snow looked like gold, and as we

SALIDA.

stood watching and wondering, we counted twenty-five great snow monarchs, so beautiful and inspiring they were, and reminded us in shape of the elephants at Barnum's circus, as they have stood with their backs to us, only they were snow from tip to tail, and colossal.

We found a native of Salida willing to talk and give us information, so we chatted until after six with him. He was a rude specimen, and was brought nine months before to Salida, so sick with consumption, he nearly died on the way, but now he is able to work on the railroads, and is as robust and well as any one. He told us that they seldom had real wintry weather, only in February, March and April they had some cold, but never any snow, except on the mountains which caught all, and kept it from falling into the valley. Colorado is a wonderful State, the scenery is grand beyond words, the climate is a blessing to scores and scores of invalids, and its mineral and mining products are rich beyond question, and make millionaires of many men. Oh, that we knew "the receipt for that popular mystery!" Colorado interested us so much and made Jamie so wonderfully better, that we think if he ever feels badly again, we will fly to Colorado Springs. When you come to real distance, it does not seem far from home.

At 7 A. M., in a queer, narrow-guage Pullman sleeper, we began our ride for the day. Mr. and Mrs. H., Mr. and Mrs. V. G., Mr. H., Mr. F., James and myself, took possession of the back platform. Jamie sat in the middle, right down on the platform, with his feet hanging over and resting on the coupling. Mr. H. sat on one step, Mr. F. on the other, Mrs. H., Mrs. V. G. and I on stools in between, and Mr. H. standing back of us, and in this fashion we went through or over the "Marshall Pass." How can I describe it! We began our ride, going through a most beautiful cañon, the rocks rising so far above us on each side, and the trees, grasses and shrubs being really beautiful. As we sat there, little dreaming what was before us, some one looked up the hillside and said, "Why there's another railroad right up above us." Perhaps we're going up to that," answered another. "Impossible," ejaculated a third. Pretty soon around a most beautiful horseshoe curve we turned, and Jamie exclaimed, "By Jove! we *are* going just where we thought we could not." Then our calmness vanished, and we began to watch and to wait for more glimpses of road and rail, and were in Wonderland before we knew it. Creeping like a snake up the side of the mountain, we would look ahead, and see a cutting through the rocks, outlined against the sky, and soon we would pass through that very opening. We ascended so slowly, so steadily, winding and twisting, turning almost at right angles sometimes, crossing trestles and bridges, through which we could look from our back seats and see hundreds of feet down. Gradually all signs of vegetation began to cease, trees became scarce, except the poor, tired evergreens, some looking too tired to live, others as if they had died an awful death. We began to get into the snow regions and to feel so familiar with the snow-capped mountains. Such views as were ours, for as we looked in every direction, we could see such wonderful scenes, valleys, mountains, white and black, villages nestled in the valleys, and we absolutely grew silent in admiration. Great snow-drifts began to surround us, snow-sheds began to bother us too, but these were short and we were soon through them. At last, as we neared the summit, 10,852 feet in altitude, we went into the clouds, and were surrounded by such a damp vapor, just like fog. We could see the clouds as we approached and went into them. The summit was reached at a quarter past nine, and then we rested there a little, while the brakes were carefully examined to see if all was safe for our ride down hill. While at the top, and in the snow-shed, we were nearly frozen—our hands and feet tingled, and we had to stamp about to keep warm. We had much merriment, snowballing each other, for we happened to stop right beside a snow mound, and had quite a jolly time. Mr. F. had not seen snow for ten years, living as he does in Galveston, and he was quite funny as he frisked about in his linen duster, making snow balls. It grew so cold during our downward journey, that we spent the rest of the morning inside the little car.

At Gunnison, at half-past eleven o'clock, we had dinner, and how hungry we were! After leaving Gunnison, we were told that at the next station, Sapinero, an observation car would be attached to the train, to take us through the Black Cañon, and we all gathered in the top-less car, with plain board seats. We then had fifteen miles of such magnificence, that Jamie and I are powerless to express our impressions of it. The Royal Gorge was grander, more colossal and majestic than the Black Cañon, because its walls of rock were in great vast masses; but the Black Cañon was to us more impressive, although much narrower, and the rocks stood in great solitary piles, forming cathedrals, castles and needles, while beautiful waterfalls seemed to tumble down from the very skies themselves. The rocks at times entirely surrounded us, and as I looked ahead at the little puffing locomotive, as it skipped along, now over a bridge, and then as if right against the solid rock, I exclaimed, "Surely, there is no way of escape for us, we are rock-bound in reality."

We were creeping along the bank of the merry little river Gunnison, which added greatly to the beauty of the scene, with its rapids and pretty falls. We wanted eyes on all sides of our heads for that lovely wonderful trip. As we finally crept out of the cañon into the fields and country again, they appeared tame and commonplace, in contrast to the beauty of the rock and rill which we had just left.

We stopped at a little village called Cimarron, where Mr. F. had to leave us, much to our regret.

After leaving Cimarron, we settled ourselves on the back platform of the car, little dreaming of the beautiful afternoon trip we had before us. Everybody had spoken enthusiastically of Marshall Pass and Black Cañon, but no one had said a word about the country further on. With two engines again, we began to climb another steep mountain, going around curves by the dozen, each of which rivaled, in beauty and wonder of engineering skill, the famous horseshoe curve in Pennsylvania. It was amost as fine a pass as the Marshall, and wonderfully rich in scenery and grand effects, and we were much impressed by it. The descent was especially beautiful, as we came down into a most fertile valley, the hills about were covered with rare and delicate wild flowers. Pink tinted the hillsides for miles, then yellow and white would alternate, and great bushes and shrubs of color would add their beauty to the scene. Suddenly the lovely valley was left behind, and we hurried along through a dry and parched country, so sandy and gloomy that only sage-brush was visible, with now and then a little courageous daisy or blue-bell, to relieve the monotony, and cheer the weary traveller.

Right in this glaring sand desert, our train was side-tracked, to let a train to the East pass, and we had several minutes to wander about. What a God-forsaken country it was, so parched and dry for want of water.

Montrose was reached soon, and there the wonderful circle of mountains, which surround Ouray and Silverton, appeared most majestic and grand. From Montrose to Grand Junction was a pretty trip. The country was full of fine and flourishing ranches, and cows, horses and sheep all seemed to prosper and to enjoy life. The ranches did not look over-attractive to me, but they were strikingly beautiful in contrast to those we had viewed before.

We arrived at Grand Junction, at a quarter past seven o'clock, and although we had been informed that Grand Junction and the hotel were worse than Salida, we were so tired we almost did not mind the unwelcome anticipation. So many people left the train at the depot, that Mr. H. hurried off and reached the " Brunswick " ahead of all travellers. Our names were first on the list, and in consequence we had the best rooms in the hotel, which was not saying much after all. Mr. H. told the clerk that we were bride and groom, and that he was best man, and had to arrange everything for us. Mr. and Mrs. H. and Mr. and Mrs. V. G. were indignant, because the four were offered one room, with two beds, and the clerk was much surprised when they would not accept such an arrangement.

Our little party had our dinner together, and imagine our consternation when, after a bowl of soup, our empty stomachs were asked to choose between "mutton, beef and *brains!*" So the waiter in his shirt-sleeves recited his lesson. After dinner we took a walk to see this little one-horse town, and to our surprise, we found it was quite an enterprising little place, with street cars, one or two large fine buildings, and some good stores. A very rough set of men were on the streets, and lots of cowboys. We saw a fine-looking cowboy, as handsome as a picture, finely dressed in his buckskin trousers, large Mexican sombrero, and elaborate jacket, all of which looked so new and shining. His face was a study for an artist, but it was such a bad face, and I wove a little romance at once, about that young boy, and I imagined the sorrowing mother weeping over her handsome wayward son. He is one of many wild boys, I suppose, who are sent away from home "to sow their wild oats."

SALT LAKE CITY AND THE MORMONS

ABOUT four o'clock this morning, we were up, and ready in a half hour to start for the depot, breakfastless, however. Last night, Jamie and Mr. H. ordered as fine a lunch as Grand Junction could get up, for us to take along, and have for an early break-fast. Imagine our dismay and emptiness, when we reached the train, and found that no one had remembered to bring the breakfast. We hired a man to run and get it, but our train cruelly moved out of the depot, before his return. To steam out of a station at 4.40 A. M. and leave a breakfast behind, is enough to spoil the temper of an angel, especially as we could not have breakfast until we reached Green River, at half-past eight o'clock, nearly four hours later. Then, to add to our discomfort, no one was up in the Pullman Car, and we had to crowd ourselves into a seat car, not a chair car, like ours in the East, but a car with seats, and narrow at that. How James and Mr. H. were "raked over the coals," for forgetting that breakfast.

After leaving one station, we missed Mr. V. G.,

and no one knew where he was. We were beginning to get anxious, when, through the stillness of
the car, sounded a regular war-whoop, and turning,
we saw our energetic friend coming towards us, in
great glee, with his right hand on top, and his left
hand under a great pile of sandwiches. The bread
was in inch-thick slices, and seven sandwiches made
a pile, never to be forgotten! But where had our
friend found these "loaves and fishes?" A woman
in the emigrant car had heard Mr. V. G. sigh:
"My kingdom for a sandwich," and had volunteered
to make what was needed for us, from her little stock
of provisions. Oh, that some one had given that
pile a little poke in the middle, and relieved Mr. V.
G.'s hands of the pressure between! But he was
jubilant and merry, and so happy over his little surprise, assuring us that "the woman was so nice and
clean," and his heart was nearly broken when James,
after the first bite, opened the window and threw
his sandwich out. Mr. H. slipped out on the platform, to "fully enjoy his'n"; but I—I choked mine
down to the last crumb, to atone for the short-com-
ings of the two boys. When we reached Green
River, we nearly embraced each other, in our joy at
the sight of food.

Thursday, May 28th was a hard day. We passed
through most uninteresting scenery, across prairies
and desert lands, so dry and white and parched—
across one big mountain, to be sure, but everything
about it betokened loneliness and gloom. Even the

names of the stations were depressing—"Solitude"
was one, "Rest" another. We had to wait till
nearly three o'clock for dinner, which we had at
Provo.

As we crossed Utah, and approached Salt Lake
City, we were impressed by the barrenness and dry
parched land on every side. Then followed such
loveliness—fertile ground, beautiful trees. Lake
Utah added to the scene, and the circle of snow
mountains capped the climax. The snow was so
purely white, and ran down the sides of the mountains like great veins. We saw to-day, as we crossed
the country, row after row of charcoal pits,
which looked like great white bee-hives. We were
also much interested in the white-covered wagons,
crossing the prairies, drawn by cows and oxen, coming along at a snail's pace, carrying a family oftentimes, with all their worldly goods and possessions.

Brigham Junction was the beginning of anything
of a Mormon flavor in our journey. We reached
Salt Lake City at half-past four, and a happier set of
people surely have never arrived, since the time that
Brigham Young, or Joseph Smith, brought their fol-
lowers over Emigrant Pass, into the valley of the
Salt Sea.

Soon after arriving in Salt Lake, we were comfortably located at the "Hotel Templeton," and then
James hunted all over the town for flowers, for Mrs.
V. G., whose second wedding anniversary was to-
day. No flowers are grown in Salt Lake City,

none can be had, except when brought from a distance, and to James' regret, he had to return empty-handed.

At half-past seven, all our little party met in the parlor, as Mr. V. G.'s guests, to dine with him, as "his anniversary spree." He had a private room, and had a very beautiful dinner. What amused us all were the sudden transformations, in each and every member of our little party. We had been for three days together, in travelling clothes, and, it was laughable to see the look of surprise on each face, and the side glance of scrutiny, which each bestowed on the other, when we thought no one was looking, as we appeared dressed in our best. After our fine repast, we took a little walk about the city, as a digester, then separated for the much-needed rest.

FRIDAY, MAY 29TH.

A LITTLE before ten o'clock, James, Mr. H. and I met at breakfast, in the sixth story dining-room. We have a table, in a corner of the room, which commands a most fascinating view in every direction. Salt Lake City is surrounded by snow mountains, which never fail to add the greatest possible charm to every view. The sunsets surpass in beauty any mountain sunsets we have ever seen. The mountains fairly glow with splendor, then turn a vivid violet, then almost black, while the sky retains its fire and glory, and mysteriously casts everything in shadow.

We sallied forth, after our morning meal, to present our letter of introduction to Col. W., the Superintendent of the "Zion Mercantile Co-operative Institution." He received us in his private room, was cordiality itself, and has done much for our enjoyment ever since. He asked if we would like to go then to the Tabernacle, that he would gladly go with us, and we accepted joyfully. Before going there, we went to see Brigham Young's homes, and saw what they call "The Lion House," where his surviving wives now live together, and also the " Bee-Hive," where his family lived. Both of these places we see daily, from our room in the hotel, also the new Temple, the Tabernacle, and Assembly Hall.

The Tabernacle, Temple, and Assembly Hall are in one large enclosure, surrounded by a high wall, with gates on the north and east. On Sundays both gates are open, on week days only the north gate. We found an entrance into the Tabernacle, by one of a multitude of doors, and were soon inside the great building, which is two hundred and fifty feet long, by one hundred and fifty feet broad, with seating capacity for eight thousand, without crowding, for ten thousand under pressure, and room for four thousand to stand. One great arch forms the roof, without pillar or support. There is not an angle in the entire building, not a corner, to echo or retard sound, and the acoustic properties of the vast building are marvelous. At the request of our friend, we walked to the farthest part of the gallery, and stood a few minutes. A man, near the pulpit, took a little white pin, and holding it not more than two inches above the railing, about the pulpit, let it drop. We could hear it distinctly. He then rubbed his hands together slowly, as one does without apparent noise, and it was distinctly audible where we stood, two hundred feet away. To our great delight, Col. W. told us that the organist happened fortunately to be in the building, and would be glad to play for us." Joy unspeakable! The organ is the largest in this country, and was built of Utah timber, and by native talent. It is a wonder, such sweetness of tone and richness of quality, such great power and strength. We sat in the gallery, and listened to a most beautiful organ recital. I always shiver when music pleases me, but I had genuine fever and ague then, and shook like a leaf. After leaving the tabernacle, we visited the Deseret Museum, a place of much interest and many curios.

Salt Lake City is situated twenty miles from the great Salt Lake, and after luncheon, our little party went to Garfield Beach, which is on the lake. After a forty-minutes' trip by rail, we reached the lake, a vast body of water, with mountains all about it. It is a wonderful place, so barren and dreary, for no trees or vegetation grow near its shores; they cannot live there, it is so salt. No birds or insects can live near it, not one living thing is in its water, save the smallest little black bug, about the size of a pin-head, so small one can hardly see it. Great rocks pile high on the shore, and the waves dash over them, leaving a white coating of salt.

"Garfield Beach" is composed of a pavilion, bath-ing-houses, and a lunch stand. There is excellent bathing, and they say it is remarkable, and every one is sorry that we did not try it, for the water buoys one up, and no one can sink. In splashing over the face, it leaves white spots of salt, which one must rub off. The water is one-fifth salt, and we took some up in our hands to taste, and found it decidedly briny.

After returning to the hotel, we received a call from Mr. J., a gentleman to whom James had a letter of introduction, but which we had not yet an opportunity to present. He heard from Col. W. of our arrival, and—true Mormon hospitality—he had called at once. We also found, on our return, beautiful roses from Col. W. and a book of poems, of which he had spoken in the morning. We had a most interesting conversation on the Mormon religion, for he is a strict Mormon, as is also our other friend, Mr. J. There is so much to tell, that I must take it in order, in a section all by itself.

SATURDAY, MAY 30TH.

EXQUISITE weather,—such lovely air, sky and views beggar description. At eleven o'clock, Mr. and Mrs. J. came in a handsome cart, with a beautiful pair of horses, to take us to drive. We had a lovely drive. We went all over the city, and out to the garrison, at Fort Douglass. We reached there just as the soldiers, and their fine band, were returning from the cemetery,—it being Decoration Day, and it was a beautiful sight, for, of course, crowds of carriages followed them. The garrison is composed of young officers, graduates,—only three are married, and they are there with their brides. It is lovely and very gay there.

Salt Lake City is wonderful in some respects. When one knows that the entire valley and foot-hills, on which it is situated, were once barren, parched prairie land, with nothing but scrub-oak, to relieve the glaring sandy soil, and then sees the beautiful city, with magnificent streets, and hundreds and hundreds of fine shade trees, it is a wonder, and cannot but provoke admiration. The early settlers came across the country in wagons, drawn often by cows, and were three or four months in coming. When this site was chosen for a settlement, the families of these people had to live, for months, in these miserable wagons, until the men could bring timber from the mountains, and build their houses. The land had to be irrigated, that it might become fertile and bear crops, and so much labor had to be expended to make this barren plain habitable. Trees had to be planted regularly, every man and boy turning out, one day in the year, to plant them. It was not safe, in those days, for men to go alone into the cañons for timber, on account of the many wild beasts, but they would go in companies, and in this way, little by little, the streets were planted on each side with trees, that have grown wonderfully fast, and formed such beautiful arches of grateful shade. The box-elder is a favorite tree, but the poplar is magnificent in its growth. As far as the eye can reach, in every direction, these straight slim trees are visible, standing in regular rows, like a company of a regiment out on drill. Their foliage is darker than the other umbrageous trees, and consequently forms a fine contrast in light and shade. They delighted us, these straight-laced poplars, although they seem chary of their shade, and fairly hug themselves, with their leaves and branches.

The streets of Salt Lake City are one hundred and thirty feet broad, and the houses and homes are, many of them, as handsome as we can find in our largest cities. The blocks are very long, and when the city was laid out originally, there were eight blocks to a mile. But people speak of these blocks, not as so many feet, but as so many rods. Our friend Mr. J.'s house is on one of the finest streets, yet within one block of a cañon, so one can imagine how near the mountains are, all about the city. From our window, we looked upon finely rounded green mountains, outlined against the sky, covered with brush, but not a tree to be seen.

This morning I asked the maid, why she had not

brushed the things I had asked her to do the night before? "Well," she answered, "I'm taking banjo lessons, and my teacher came last night, and I could not very well be excused." This gives a suggestion of the sort of maid-servants to be had in Salt Lake City.

SUNDAY, MAY 31ST.

TO-DAY has been such a bright, beautiful Sunday, but the sunshine seemed ten times stronger than in our eastern cities, and the glare of the sun, on the white sandy soil, is very trying in Salt Lake City.

James and I had our breakfast in our room, and did not appear in public, until we met Mr. and Mrs. V. G. at lunch. Then we four went to the Tabernacle, to service.

Salt Lake City is divided into twenty-two wards, and each ward has a Bishop or Pastor, and a chapel, where services are held morning and evening, and the people of each ward attend their respective chapels. But every Sunday, at two o'clock, there is service in the Tabernacle, over which the "President of the Mormon church" presides. The services to-day were especially interesting to all, as it was the "Annual Report of the Young Men's Improvement Association." A speaker from each ward was heard, and instead of one service in the Tabernacle, there were three to-day, and we attended the two o'clock service. The great edifice was literally packed, hardly one more could have been accommodated. It was a wonderful sight,—a great sea of faces of men, women and children. Little babes in arms were in great numbers also. The chorus, filling all the seats on each side the great organ, numbers over three hundred. All in Utah are musical,—it is the great talent in that territory, and a taste for music is nurtured and developed, and produces marvelous results.

The service opened by a song, then someone offered a prayer, then an address was delivered. Soon after the commencement of the address on "Self-Culture," a still small voice was heard, but we could not hear what was said. The speaker halted; all was silence while these few words were uttered; then a number of men arose, and began to pass the Bread of Communion. The speaker continued, and during his entire address, the plates of bread were passed—back and forth through those long rows of seats. Everybody partook, even the tiniest babies had a piece of the Bread put into their mouths by their mothers. No head was bowed, no prayer in silence offered, but all looked about as if nothing had happened, and they were merely being refreshed. The lecturer continued his discourse, when suddenly and once more there was a moment's silence, then the ushers began to move about with urns and cups, which were filled with water. Every Mormon, in that vast assembly, partook in the same seemingly unappreciative way, and then each child had some of the water also. As one usher approached the pulpit and the lecturer, he thrust the cup into the speaker's hand, and he immediately paused and drank. The solemnity of our beautiful service was not seen or felt, and I could not think that the sweet communion, which comes to us in our silent worship, could come in this way, and I wondered how these people could "take and eat," without bowing the head, or offering one little prayer.

A letter was read from one of the President's Councilors—a man named Joseph F. Smith, who has been in exile, since the law abolishing polygamy was enforced, for he had too many wives. He said in his letter that "Joseph Smith, the Prophet, was as truly a messenger from God, as truly inspired, as great a teacher and prophet, as Jesus Christ was," and much of a similar nature. It was a rambling, ranting letter, but listened to as attentively by that great audience, as if a message from Heaven.

Then President Woodruff, a man over eighty-five years old, made an address. We sat over two hours in the tabernacle, with tired and crying babies, on our right hand and left, before and behind us, and we were only refreshed, when that magnificent organ and chorus rang out, in great volumes of glorious sound.

Joseph Smith, the prophet, was the one who claimed to have found the lost tablets, through inspiration from heaven, which made polygamy permissible. All their freedom, in many marriages, dates from this licentious old fraud's sage and wonderful influence, over a readily convinced people. They say, whenever Brigham Young saw a nice attractive-looking young woman, and was beginning to tire of the previous wife, he used to go into the mountains, and come back after a while, and tell the young girl's parents, that he had had a revelation from heaven, telling him he should marry their daughter. It was a law of heaven, and must be obeyed, and so the girl became one of his wives.

In the early days of polygamy, the first wife could regulate the marriages of her husband, as her consent was necessary. In the latter days, however, the old rogues used to get married, on the quiet, and not wait for the consent of any one.

As I sat in the Tabernacle, all that I had learned of the Mormon religion passed rapidly through my mind, and impressed me with not a little weight and interest. But the polygamous side of the religion caused me no end of amusing thoughts, and each man I eyed with suspicion, especially if he sat "with his sisters, and his cousins and his aunts," and I could not help wondering which was number one, and which number six, and if they lived "at swords' points" with each other, or were at peace in their united love for their lord and master. I marveled at the wonderful strength of character those women must have possessed, who had such experiences.

A lady friend, a Mormon, told me that "the present trials of the men, caused by the recent strict laws, are only just, in proportion to the sufferings born by brave noble women in the past." I asked "how a man could choose between all his wives, and take one away from the rest, and live with her alone and only?" "Oh, the law regulates with which wife a man must live," answered my friend; "a man must take his first wife, whether she is the most attractive to him, or not. If he takes any other wife, he is liable to imprisonment. If a man's first wife is dead, however, he can then choose from his other wives, but he must be married to her by a minister, although he may have a large family of children, by that very wife." One gentleman, whom we saw, was in a sad predicament. When the law was passed, he was living with two wives, his first wife having died. The poor man could not live with either of these wives, because if he chose one, he made his other marriage illegal, and their children ceased to be his the moment he married the other wife. To be true to both, and to be able to care for, and be a father to all his children, he lives alone, and his two wives live together.

The liberty allowed by the Mormon Church, in taking a number of wives, has been terribly abused, and is keenly felt by the younger element in the church, and only the older men of the early days have many. Of course, every one is descended from some enormous household, and as children always reverence and love their grand-parents, so they always speak most kindly of them, and most apologetically. While chatting one day in Salt Lake City with a friend, thoughtlessly I asked her if there were many in her family. " Many!" exclaimed her husband; "as her grandfather had more wives than Brigham Young, there are naturally a great many in her family." "But," added my friend, "my grandmother was the *first* wife!" A strange thing, but the first wife was always treated with the utmost respect, by all the other wives, and their households. The law now prohibits a man from ever seeing his former wives, and if a man can be caught calling upon them, he can be fined and imprisoned.

The hard part is in disowning the innocent little children, who have been so unfortunate as to come into the world, under these trying circumstances. The Church provides a home for such mothers and their families, who are so uncomfortably deserted and unable to support themselves, but, as a rule, the deserted wives live together, and are sadder and more miserable than widows.

They say "Children are Utah's best crop." A childless woman, in the Mormon Church, is considered a disgrace to her family.

Brigham Young was a devoted father, and was constantly in the midst of his modest little flock of fifty-two children. He could not remember all the Marys, Susans and Kates, so they each had a number, and were "registered stock." There is now standing the school house, which he built for his own family, and where they were all educated. He left each an inheritance, at his death, of thirty thousand dollars. Brigham Young had nineteen wives.

Polygamy tended to the development of inconstancy, to speak mildly, and to a lack of concentration of affection, most damaging to home and happiness. The women of Utah were, in the olden times, quite like the women of to-day, and their sufferings must have been intense, as they bore it because it was their "religion,"—the inconstancy of their husbands,— and had to smother the jealousy and heartaches, and find pleasure in the love of their little children. The sympathy, and companionship, and love, of mother and child in Utah, is most touching and true. The mothers seem to have lavished all their affection upon their little ones, as the only beings in life, entirely and fully their own.

When walking with Col. W. to the Tabernacle, on Friday, we had a short talk on religion, as the Mormons believe in it. They believe in Jesus Christ, in the Holy Ghost, and God, in the Trinity, as we do. They believe that God is a Merciful Father, that He does not willingly punish any of his children, but that we bring punishment upon ourselves, by our own acts. They believe that God was once upon earth, that He knows our temptations and trials, but by His wonderful power He became our Saviour. They believe that we have all existed before, in some other sphere, and as spirits, and their greatest religious fervor is in preparing for the life to come. The truly religious look upon this life, as merely a place of preparation. They believe in a resurrection of the body, as well as the soul. They say this body returns to the dust, from which it was made, but our spiritual body will be the exact image of our earthly body; in other words, they believe in the resurrection of our body, without the earthly element. They have perfect faith in inspiration, and usually at their services, the President is inspired to call upon some member to speak, and that person considers it a "Divine Call," and speaks sometimes for one hour, sometimes two, as he feels impelled. The Church is governed by a President, by Twelve Apostles, and the Chosen Seventy, all of whom sit up in front of the organ, on raised sofas of red plush—the President occupying the highest. One thing Col. W. told me has impressed me more and more, as I have thought of it, day by day, that is— that we have a Mother in Heaven, as well as a Father. It will startle one at first, as it did me. The Mormons believe that, as "God is great in wisdom, and power, and might, so He is great in providing Himself with all that is best, and so He does not live alone in His greatness, but He has a wife!"—Don Carlos Young, one of Brigham Young's sons, thus expressed it to me. The idea was revolting to me at first, but after reading a little poem, which Col. W. sent me, it was so prettily expressed, that Jamie copied it, to insert in my journal. It is, of course, the one idea of happiness to Mormons, the possession of a wife, and so they cannot think of God in Heaven, as a lonely solitary Power. The Mormon religion savors of the Theosophists' faith, but it is in form more like the Quaker, in their belief in divine inspiration, and in their order of service.

INVOCATION
OR THE
ETERNAL FATHER AND MOTHER.

O MY Father, thou that dwellest
  In the high and holy place,—
When shall I regain thy presence,
  And again behold thy face?

In thy glorious habitation,
  Did my spirit once reside?
In my first primeval childhood,
  Was I nurtured near thy side?

For a wise and glorious purpose,
  Thou has placed me here on earth,
And withheld the recollection
  Of my former friends and birth.

Yet oftimes a secret something
  Whispered, "You're a stranger here";
And I felt that I had wandered
  From a more exalted sphere.

I had learned to call thee Father,
  Through thy spirit from on high;
But, until the Key of Knowledge
  Was restored, I knew not why.

In the heavens are parents single?
No: the thought makes reason stare:
Truth is reason: truth eternal,
Tells me I've a mother there.

When I leave this frail existence—
When I lay this mortal by—
Father, Mother, may I meet you
In your royal court on high?

Then at length, when I've completed
All you sent me forth to do,
With your mutual approbation,
Let me come and dwell with you.

By Eliza R. Snow, widow of Joseph Smith, the Mormon
Prophet, and afterwards one of Brigham Young's
nineteen wives.

Copied by J. W. H., June 4, 1891.

MONDAY, JUNE 1ST.

A LOVELY morning, cool and almost too bright
and sunny. After a late breakfast, I went
shopping with a friend, and when I returned, I found
that James had been with Mr. J. all the morning. His
hospitality and cordiality are most flattering to my
husband. After lunch, armed with my camera, we
went with Mrs. J. and her daughter to Brigham
Young's grave. To-day is Brigham Young's nine-
tieth birthday,—he has been dead fifteen years in
August. On his birthday, his children and grandchildren cover his grave with flowers, and the gate
to the burying-ground is unlocked, and strangers are
admitted. When we reached there, some visitors

moved away ; and while arranging the camera for a photograph, through the gate, and across the green lawn, walked five little children,the oldest about ten years, the youngest about three. They all carried flowers,—some in the form of wreaths, others bouquets. The thought flashed through my mind, what a chance for a picture ; it was so unusual a circumstance, and seemed made on purpose for me, for those five children were Brigham Young's grandchildren, and had come to lay flowers on his grave.

Afterwards I met one of Brigham Young's daughters,—a very pleasant, well-educated lady. She spoke of her mother's care and hardships, in crossing the plains, in a little wagon, when she came to Salt Lake,—of the long four months' trip, etc., and it was most interesting to hear.

In the evening, James and I went with the J.'s to Salt Lake Opera House, to see the "Lilliputians." We had a box, and spent a most delightful evening. The little actors were as cute as possible. The theatre is small but wonderfully pretty, and was built years ago, by Brigham Young, the centre light in the ceiling having been made of the wheel of the wagon, in which he came across the plains, with lamps hung around the edge, and in the middle. It is now replaced by a fine electric flower piece.

Brigham Young was a born organizer and despot, and he ruled his little kingdom like an emperor, in undisputed power and might. The people loved him, his word was law to them, and no matter how

down-trodden they were, his magnetic power carried all before him, and no one thought of raising a
voice against his edicts.

TUESDAY, JUNE 2ND.

A NOTHER bright day, and another drive with
our friends; in fact, most of our time is spent
with them, in their charming home, or driving.

They say the dusty season in Salt Lake City is a
most trying time and experience, but it comes later
in the summer. We think it is terribly dusty now ;
our boots and shoes are constantly white. Outside
all the front doors of even the finest homes, are
feather dusters, to use for the boots before entering
the house.

WEDNESDAY, JUNE 3RD.

L OVELY weather; in fact, every day seems lovely
here. Again, before eleven, we were driving
with Mr. J. We had a delightful drive, and are
becoming so well acquainted with the city, and so
interested in the wonderful growth of the trees.
The streets all have wooden gutters, through which
water is kept flowing, as nothing will grow, neither
trees nor grass, without this constant irrigation.
Lawns are regularly watered morning and evening,
as all would dry up if it was not done. Salt Lake
City did not impress me favorably at first, and if
James had felt like it, I should gladly have moved
on last Saturday. I am so thankful we did not ; for

the more we see of the city and its people, the more delighted we are that we have remained, and come to know both so well. The Mormons are greatly misunderstood. Of course, their religious views, differ widely in many points from ours, but we were glad to hear, from the Mormons themselves, just what they believe.

In Salt Lake City is the funniest little house we ever saw. Long ago, a young man lost his lady-love, the night before they were to have been married, and it changed his entire life, making a "crooked stick" out of a youth of bright promise. The lover is an old man now, but he lives entirely alone with his memories. A long curl of golden hair, and a sweet little wedding gown are his treasures. His house is the tiniest place imaginable, white as white-wash can make it, and as clean and shining within as without. The queerest part of it is, that all his choicest goods and chattels are put about the little place, on the *outside*. He thinks, for some unknown reason, that his sweetheart's spirit will not come into the house, so he has little chairs and a sofa, oil paintings, etc., yards of American flags, mosses, shells, and every conceivable thing outside, on the roof, the sidewalk and everywhere. The people of Salt Lake so honor this poor old man's sentiment and sorrow, that no one ever molests or destroys a thing. It was very pathetic to us. It seems sad that the one affection of a man's heart, should not be for its noblest development, and stimulating to the highest and best in character. Why should love, even deep and abiding, dwarf one, and make such gloomy shadows and sad lives?

FRIDAY, JUNE 5TH.

BEFORE we had finished breakfast, Col. W. called to ask us to accompany him, after lunch, to view the new Temple. Soon after he left, our friend Mrs. J. came for us to drive again, a little earlier this morning, for some one else had taken us yesterday, before she came. After a delightful drive, and lunch, James and I went to see the new "Temple." No one is admitted, usually; but Col. W. had obtained a private permit, and Don Carlos Young (one of Brigham Young's *fifty-two*), took us all over it, explained everything, and we came away full of religious points and principles, which I will add to this chronicle, in a Coda.

We did what few Mormons have ever done, and very few ladies; we climbed to the tip-top pinnacle, up stairs of stone at first, then wooden steps, climbed ladders, crawling through dark rooms where we could only feel our way, and finally, our climb was crowned by a most magnificent and glorious view over all the city, across to Salt Lake, the snow mountains rising so majestically all about the beautifully shaded city. It was an awful climb, but as James said, "it paid,—didn't it, May!"

We were nearly tired out before we were back at the Hotel, and then the packing had to be done, as we were to leave Salt Lake City, in the wee small hours of the night, for San Francisco.

After dinner, when all was in readiness for our start, we went with the J.'s to the delightful Musical Festival in the Tabernacle. It was a wonderful sight to us, that huge auditorium absolutely packed with human beings. The organ was in magnificent tone, and the chorus was so huge and so mighty in number and voice, that our ears did not seem one-fourth big enough, to fully appreciate that volume of wondrous harmony. It was magnificent! Some native talent was astonishing and marvelous. Myron Whitney sang well, and Miss Emma Thursby's voice was angelic,—both having come from the East, to grace the occasion. Miss Thursby sang as if inspired, and her audience was spell-bound, and not a note was lost by that music-loving assembly.

The musical feast was too soon over. James was never so enthusiastic,—in fact he was deeply impressed. At eleven o'clock, we were out in the open air again, and much interested in watching the mass of people disperse and disappear, in every direction. Where they all came from and went to, was a wonder to us. We went to our friends' home, expecting only to make a short call, but a dainty supper for the travellers, we found prepared; and it was long after midnight, when we hurriedly returned to the hotel for our luggage, to take the 2 A. M. train for San Francisco.

We left Salt Lake City at 2 A. M., but in reality

we left Ogden one hour before we reached there, for we arrived at Ogden at 3 A. M. by Mountain Time, but left there at 2 A. M. by Pacific Time.

SATURDAY, JUNE 6TH.

ON the train, going to San Francisco, across the most uninteresting portion of God's World! We were over twenty-four hours in crossing the Great Desert, and it was awful, such barrenness and doleful scenery, such weary wastes of woeful misery, and dust—like pepper—covered everything, for we were crossing the alkali plains. It was a most wretched day !

James and I sat together, on the back platform of our train, as it was too warm to stay in the car, and we were too tired and too dusty to care much for anything.

We saw plenty of Indians, in paint and feathers ; and one woman attracted us exceedingly, as she carried her dear little pappoose on her back, the little black head just peeping out from its awful wool wrapping. Another Indian woman was as handsome as a picture, and her rich dark cheeks were each painted with a fine white cross, put on in spots like beads.

SUNDAY, JUNE 7TH.

JAMES and I slept as well on the train last night, as we have lately at the hotels, where we have been. There was a general shake up and earthquake motion, which we do not find in hotels, but we were unusually comfortable. We had a miserable breakfast this morning, at Sacramento; but the waiter said, " Will you have coffee, or tea, *Miss*," which produced a well-fed satisfaction within my breast, in spite of the lack of proper provisions.

The ride, until after twelve, was truly delightful. Before we reached Sacramento, we had passed through a most beautiful country; and they say from Reno to Sacramento, passing through the Sierra Nevada Range, is a charming trip. Our train, unfortunately, went through the interesting part, during the very early morning hours, and we missed seeing it. The " Fast Mail " from Salt Lake City, takes thirty-five hours to run to San Francisco.

From Sacramento to Oakland, the country was like a beautiful flower garden. The marsh-lands and meadows were full of long reed grasses, and wonderful stalks of salmon-pink buds. On each side of the track, bordering it for miles, were great bushes of yellow wild flowers, so plentiful and profuse that, as we looked back from our seat on the back platform, the long straight track for miles, sometimes without a turn, seemed one golden pathway. They made the roadway look like some drive through a garden full of flowers. Between the rails, creeping over the sleepers, and peeping up everywhere, nodding so pleasantly and merrily as we flew over them, were millions of morning-glories; and all the buds and blossoms waved so cheerily, by means of the commotion we created in the air, of course, and seemed to bow and say, "Welcome to our flowery State." Some sandy hills were brilliant with orange-colored bells. We were soon creeping along the shores of the Sacramento River, but the flowers never forsook us, and came with us to Oakland Ferry, where we left the train of the Central Pacific, and took the boat for San Francisco. At Belencia, thirty-two miles from the City of the Golden Gate, we had to cross the river by boat, as we used to do at New London. James gave much pleasure, by taking a photograph there of our engine and all the train hands; and I never saw a happier crowd of men, and especially when James took their addresses, and promised to send each one of them a picture. As the train left the boat at Port Costa, the engineer and switch-men all raised their hats to me, as I stood on the back platform, and James was so much pleased and gratified; but we laughed heartily as we realized, by our satisfaction, how little it took to please us.

We saw many vineyards on our journey to-day, notably the Zinfandel Vineyard. Oakland impressed us as a very pretty place, and the sail from Oakland to San Francisco was delightful, as the boats are large and fine. There were many officers on board to-day, and we learned that three men-of-war had come in last night, and lay at anchor near our boat, and they had received orders to start at once for Chili.

We landed at San Francisco at noon, and drove at once to the Palace Hotel, and were soon taken to a very pleasant room; but one look at the bath-tub was enough for James, and he asked for another room, with better and fresher appointments, for nothing seemed so attractive just then as a clean tub of hot water; we were so travel-stained. While we were waiting for room number two, in came our good friend Mr. H., who had left us in Salt Lake City, and gone on to San Francisco. Poor fellow, he had taken a young lady to the boat with him to meet us, and reached there two minutes too late, so followed us to the hotel. He asked us to go to the parlor to meet his friend, which I did, dirt and all, and had a very pleasant call.

After ablutions and a dainty lunch, served in our room, and a good long nap, James and I prepared for dinner. As James was dressed first, he went downstairs to get a little idea of places and things, and was to return in a few minutes for me. Mr. H. came to the door to speak to James a moment, and I had just said "You'll find him down in the office," when I heard a colored man say "this is your room, I think, sir," and there stood James laughing heartily. "Well, I never was in such a hotel," exclaimed the poor fellow, "it's as much as a man can do to find his way about." Then he went on to tell us, that he had mistaken the floor and gone to the wrong door, which a dear little lady opened and shut as quickly. "Then I had to get the bellman to bring me to my room," he laughingly added. One cannot imagine, in their wildest moods, such a monstrous place as this Palace Hotel. It is larger and finer than any hotel we have ever seen in America, or on the other side of the water. Handsomely appointed and furnished, with halls luxuriously provided with innumerable sofas, etc., palms to decorate, and everything in such perfect order and cleanliness everywhere, the Palace Hotel is certainly not mis-named. Our room is on the second floor, and is "No. 946." The dining-room is finished and furnished in white and gold, and the *cuisine* is excellent. After a good dinner, we came to our room and spent a delightful evening, reading and writing.

SAN FRANCISCO AND MONTEREY.

MONDAY, JUNE 8TH.

SAN FRANCISCO! A breakfast in our room, then, at 11 A.M., Mr. H. came with Miss B. (the young lady he came West to see, who called upon me yesterday), and we four wandered out, first on errands, then pleasure. It was a most lovely day, but so *awfully windy*, which is San Francisco's chronic state, at this season. The Trade Winds begin to blow about 11 A.M., and woe to the big hats and parasols! Our first errand was to carry our Kodak to the agent here, to be developed. Then we called on Mr. J.'s business agent, who offered to go with us, in the afternoon, at 2 P.M., to the best shops in "Chinatown." We went into some of the stores on errands, had lunch at a restaurant, called "Maison Doree," and at 2 P.M. Mr. S. met us, and we went to Chinatown.

Chinatown is a part of San Francisco, directly off the main shopping street. We are only about six blocks from it here at the Palace Hotel. We walked along Kearny Street, for about five or six blocks, then suddenly turned to our left, and walked one block, up a steep hill :—the City is all hills, and we were in such a queer, unusual place,—the shops and streets outlined with Chinese signs, in great gilt hieroglyphics, looking most picturesque and unusual. The narrow streets were filled with quite American shaped houses, but the balconies were hung with banners and great Chinese lanterns, and were very showy and dressy. We walked a little through the streets and alleys, but soon began to visit the merchants in their neat shops. I thought we had seen Chinamen in our eastern cities ; but here we saw hundreds and hundreds of these solemn-faced, cleanly-shaved Celestials, in their long queer dark-colored shirts, or coats, their unsteady and uncomfortable looking shoes, their long pig-tails and cleanly-shaved foreheads. Half way back, towards the top of the head, Chinamen are closely shaved, giving them such tremendous foreheads, and one queer peculiarity of their faces is, that there is but little degree or difference in their foreheads —at least, I mean, it would be hard to tell where the forehead ends, and the nose and eyes begin, if it were not for the eye-brows (which no high-born Chinaman ever allows to grow). I have studied their faces quite closely, and find the lack of expression due mostly to this straight forehead and nose ; but they are an interesting people—keen, shrewd, sharp at a bargain, and cunning as witches. The high-class merchant is a fine specimen of man. Generally clean and neatly dressed, with wonderful dignity and solemn manners, no one can help but admire him; but one cannot help noticing the lack of frivolity, and utter absence of wit and humor. He seems heavy and solemn, as if life was a serious problem, and must be met with appropriate dignity, and silent struggle. Their language is a sort of chop-stick medley, a mixture of musical and unmusical sounds and groans.

Mr. S. took us to see many of them, and we were at once fascinated with their goods, and Chinatown. Everything in Chinatown is "two bit-te" (or 25 cents), "four bit-te" etc., and soon one gets to talking pigeon English unconsciously. We saw some little things, and asked the price, "Him cost four bit-te." Pretty soon I heard James ask "Well, what does him cost,—other him" pointing to some other article. Everything is "him." I don't believe the Chinese language has any but the masculine gender. If you don't like a thing you say, "Him no good, me don't want him." But we found some Chinamen who could speak English most wonderfully. One man spoke so well that we complimented him, and said "You speak English as well as we do." He answered: "Why, you flatter me, ladies," as polite as a Frenchman. But before we left the store, we had bought something, and told him to send it to the Hotel, at once, "I assure you, Madam, it will go surely, without f-a-i-l-i-n-g-s!"

They eat at queer times, some time in the morning, and again at four or five in the afternoon. As

you go through Chinatown, in the afternoon, you will
see red curtains hung up at the store-door, at 4 or 5
o'clock; that means "don't come in, we are eating."
In one store, the Chinaman was showing us something, and, being evidently cross and hungry, he
said, "Come to-morrow, me eat now," and we had
to go; he wouldn't show us anything more. Mr. S.
took us into one shop, when they were eating. In
the back of the room, around a bare table, sat six
Chinamen. Bowls of rice were before each one, and
one large dish of some savory something, in the
middle of the table, was the common property of all.
They fished in the centre dish with their chop-sticks,
sometimes all at once, snapping the chop-sticks together, until the ends hit some big bit, and they could
spring it over to the pursed-up lips. Then, holding
his rice bowl under his chin, so that, standing opposite, I could not see his nose, the Chinaman shovelled
the rice into his funnel-shaped mouth, at the rate of
"a mile a minute," with his chop-sticks. We do
not wonder that their mouths grow, as if they had
been born whistling, for they always hold the mouth
like a funnel. No women eat with the men, nor
have we seen any women in any of the stores,—
native women, I mean. Old hags are on the street,
and some very fine looking Chinese girls, but most
of these are the bad class of women. Really high-
class women are scarce in Chinatown, and what few
are there, are seldom seen. To-day we saw a little
girl of the high class, walking on the street in China-

town, followed by a maid,—a rude, coarse Chinese woman. The little girl was gorgeously dressed, in beautiful and tiny shoes, green trousers embroidered elaborately, a beautiful bright colored tunic, and a silver headdress, with ornaments dangling over her forehead, and long streamers hanging way down her back. She was a beauty, for Chinatown. We were in that fascinating place, until after five o'clock; then James and I came to our room. Miss B. and Mr. H. left us,—we dressed, had dinner, listened to the orchestra, which plays twice a week in the Court of this hotel, wrote my journal, and retired.

TUESDAY, JUNE 9TH.

AFTER a late breakfast, Mr. H., James and I wandered out to buy a little birthday remembrance for D———, and we found a fine silver store, Shreves,—where the daintiest novelties were to be seen. As we walked along, we were irresistibly drawn into Chinatown again. We became so interested there, and were on such pleasant terms with Sing Fat, Fong Sang Lung, and others, that it was two o'clock before we left there. We then went to see the films of our Kodak, to choose the good ones and hurry their completion. We had the merriest time possible over them, as the photographer said, "they were the best set of amateur photographs that he had seen in a long time—and a fine lens you have," he added. We then had a little lunch, and at four o'clock were back at the Palace, and after writing a short letter home, and having a nap, we dined at "table d'hote," with Mr. and Mrs. V. G. In the evening, we went through Chinatown— "the correct thing to do." We had an excellent guide, who took us everywhere, and "what we saw in Chinatown" will be written to-morrow.

At a quarter past eight o'clock, we assembled in the court, on the first floor of the Palace Hotel, to meet our guide, who was to take us through China- town. Our party consisted of twelve besides our- selves, our friends Mr. and Mrs. V. G. and Mr. H. and Miss B. among the number. We followed our fleet-footed courier through Kearny Street, until we reached the hill, which led us up into Chinatown. This particular and peculiar quarter of San Fran- cisco covers a space, fourteen blocks square, and is a more crowded place than any similar space in any large city. There are 50,000 Chinese in Chinatown, they say, and one would think there were five times that number, to see the swarms of children and men in the streets.

Our first point of interest was a Chinese Mission, maintained by the Baptist denomination. The little chapel was good but plain; but over the chapel was a school-room, divided into classes by partitions, and these little spaces were full of Chinamen, learn- ing to speak English, which an old white-haired man, and several nice-looking ladies were trying to teach these Celestials. Some of the scholars were

little boys, but most of them were men.   I, spoke
to a few of them, looked at their books, and asked
one about the American history he was reading, and
he spoke English very well.   Finally I came to a
dear little Chinese boy, and talked to him, and when
I left him, he spoke to me and said "Good-bye,"
which seemed to be the only word he could say, and
his effort proved a source of great amusement to
the older men about him.   One seldom sees an old
man among these Chinamen ; we have seen but one
in all our visits here.   They say Chinamen go to
these schools purely to learn English, for business
purposes; and although the Baptists think oftentimes that they have converted some, after learning
English, they almost always return to their old
faith.

We next visited "Chinese Dr. Wong' Woo." His
office is a shop full of herbs and drugs, and when
we went in, two men were grinding herbs.   They
sold us a pill, which is the size of a marble, and then
is covered with wax, making it as big as a lime.
They showed us a queer little frog-like animal
thoroughly dried and stiff, and they take the oil
from this little hide, and rub on joints of patients
who suffer with rheumatism.   The Chinamen in
this office were very coquettish, and flirtatious, and
as we made it a point to speak to any of them, who
could understand us, wherever we went, we had
quite a laugh here.   One man brought us some
kind of a root, and offered it to me, but not know-

ing whether it was poison or not, I was afraid to try it, until he commenced to eat some himself, when it seemed reasonably safe.

We visited several markets, where the most revolting black flesh meats were sold as choice morsels. In every market may be found eggs, which are brought from China; but they cover these eggs with a queer kind of black earth, before sending them over, to preserve and keep them fresh, and the earth is so strong, that it eats through the shell and makes the entire egg like ink, and most disgusting. Nothing in these markets looked tempting. The Chinese never season their food; but chicken, duck, or whatever meat they have, is cooked without butter, pepper or salt, and is consequently very unsavory to American palates. We saw a dismal basket full of gristle and bone, hanging up in full sight, and learned that these dainty morsels were highly prized feet of chickens. Such queer-looking joints, —some as black as your hat! They say they will not eat American-raised goose, but will eat all other American things. " Pigs they adore ! " When a Chinaman dies, the people are so terrified by death that they run away, and the friends generally hurry their dead to the cemetery, as fast as possible. They take all kinds of things,—roast pigs and all kinds of eatables, and leave on the grave, and they say their graveyard resembles a picnic-ground.

We visited a " Josh House." These houses are their temples, where they come to worship. A passage and stairway lead to it, and both walls are covered with Chinese figures, which we thought was a Chinese wall-paper; but the guide told us that they use the walls of these passages, as a directory of names, of the members of that particular Josh House. The Chinese language is a language of signs and symbols, and certain sounds mean certain things. For instance ⊙ (a circle with a dot in the middle) some time ago, stood for the sun, and the dawn was represented by this same sign, with a horizontal line drawn beneath ⊙ which was the sun above the horizon. Now both are modified into a figure or symbol, and a sound represents that particular figure. It makes one curious to know where the Chinese ever found their guttural grunts and groans. It impresses James very much, to think that this religion of theirs has lived so many more hundreds of years than our own, and it holds them so strongly, and makes the Chinese just as sincere worshippers, as our own religion does, even better in many instances. The Chinese are afraid to do anything that they have been taught their gods forbid. In this temple, we went behind a gorgeously carved and gilded screen, and were initiated into the mysteries of their religion. One great ugly looking god, all decked out in rings and gilt and fine colors, sat high up under a kind of canopy, and is considered their Supreme God; but whenever he displeases them too much, they go in a mass and take him down, destroy him, and put up a new god, or Josh.

In front of him sit four minor gods. Three were pleasant-faced images, all sitting like tailors or Turks, with crossed legs, but the other was the "Red-faced Josh," and the people fear him greatly. On the altar, in front of these gods, were two little frames, with three small tea cups in each, and these are filled each day, as they evaporate, with fresh tea, that the gods may never get thirsty. Then, in great brass urns, full of ashes of former sandal sticks, are put little sticks of sandal-wood, which are always kept lighted, to keep evil spirits away. When they go in to worship, they always put a little lighted stick in a jar, over the threshold, before worshipping. On the extreme left of the altar, in a corner, stood the funniest little figure, dried like a mummy, dressed in a reddish gown, and holding in his hand a big palm leaf fan. This we were informed was the "Good-spirit Devil," and on the floor before him stood a tin-pan, in which was a great quantity of ashes. They told us that the Chinese have an idea that, if they go before this God, and burn something that represents their characters, they will be safe from the evil in the world. If they do not perform this service, the world is supposed to rob them and ruin their characters.

A Chinaman, for a small fee, went through his form of worship for us. He knelt in front of the altar, then prostrated himself three times, striking his forehead on the floor, then he muttered away to himself in their peculiar monotone, bowing his head

at certain stated intervals. After much of this kind
of worship, he took two small pieces of wood, shaped
like half-moons, and threw them into the air, to try
his luck, and see if the gods heard his prayer and
were inclined to look favorably upon him. If these
two pieces of wood both fell with the flat side down,
he would have very bad luck; if both flat sides turned
up, his luck would be moderate; but if one was up
and one down, nothing better could be desired.
Our Chinese worshipper was rewarded by the last-
mentioned good fortune; but he did not stop here.
He next took a wooden jar full of flat sticks of
wood, quite long and narrow, each of which was
numbered, and shaking them three times and pull-
ing them, he began a gentle but steady motion,
with the jar clasped in his two hands. Slowly,
steadily, but resolutely he shook them, until one little slim stick began to push its head a little higher
than its neighbors, and gradually progressed in its
upward motion, until it came out of the pack, and
dropped on the floor. It was strange, but as we all
surrounded that queer little Chinaman, in silence
and wonder, as he knelt before his altar, he turned
to us, and singling me out of that little party said,
"That is your fortune, Lady." He then looked at
the number on the stick, turned to a book of refer-
ence and read my fortune:—it was good luck, and
something we could not understand about Chicago,
but he added, "You will be mich, and have luck,
big-ee house, much gold, and come Chinatown

again." Mich means rich, and James hopes his prophecy will come true.

One queer thing interested us very much. On almost every corner in Chinatown are fruit venders, who look so dirty, and their fruit so uninviting, that I wonder they ever sell anything. One fruit-stand on a corner is kept by a father and three sons. Over the stand, built close against the cornice of the window, and entirely out of the way, is a little cupboard, fenced in with sides, not bigger than our bathtub at home. A small ladder leads up to a door in one end, and in that "band-box," as tourists call it, sleep that father and his three sons. They are four full grown people. The last man in or up, pulls up the ladder. You cannot imagine how crowded the Chinese live, like sardines packed in a box. One queer place we visited was not as large as the pantry at Sunny-Slope. It is the home of an old woman named Annie, and her queer shriveled up husband, and around the wall hangs every article they own in life;—a little stove, a bed and a chair, compose their furniture, and the entire place is over-run with cats and dogs. The dogs gave us a dismal bark as we approached, but the cats were two deep every where,—on the bed, on every little niche and box, cats,—nothing but cats, a full dozen, or more!

We went to a Chinese pawn-shop, and to a barber shop. The Chinese need barbers, and go regularly to them to have their cues braided, their foreheads shaved; even their nostrils and ears are shaved also. When you see a man with blue braid tied in his cue, he is in mourning for some relation, and when he wears blue trousers also, he has lost all his relations. We went to the theatre, but no play was being given. Men are the only actors, and take the part of women characters marvelously, they say. During a performance, the furniture for the different acts is all placed together, on one side of the stage, and when a man wants to play that he is rowing a boat, he goes and selects a pair of oars from the pile, and springs across the stage, moving them as if he was in a boat. Everything is very primitive,—they have never advanced one step with the improvements of the age, in those things. All the actors live with their families, *underground*. Under the theatres,—(there are only two) there are subterranean passages, with only room enough for a man to stand upright; and on each side of the passages, live the actors, or stars, with their wives— always underground and in the dark. We saw many of them, as they were having vacation, and two had the most exquisite faces; really beautiful they were. One was the highest paid and finest actor. He receives three thousand dollars a year, and is considered *very* rich. His wife was having her hair dressed, when we went in, and they always put a kind of paste, as black and sticky as tar, all over their hair, to make it stiff and shiny. In their small room underground, they pointed with great pride to their Marriage Certificate, framed and hanging on the wall, as they were married by American rites. This actor had the dearest little daughter I ever saw, so sweet and refined looking;—high-born people they are. She sat on one of the beautiful ebony chairs, inlaid with pearl, which are common everywhere in Chinatown, and with a little oblique-eyed cousin,—both in their quaint costumes, they sang for us. We fairly wept! Two sweet little girls, not five years old,—little Lin Moy and her cousin, with their feet pinched into tight bands, that they should not grow, sat and sang to us with their dear little voices, and in the purest English, "Nearer, My God to Thee," and "Jesus loves even me." They go regularly to the English school for girls. I could have loved those sweet wee ones,—they were little angels.

In striking contrast to that scene, was our visit to a hermit. It was a most awful experience! We wandered through several streets, following Mr. L., when suddenly he turned into the darkest spookiest alley imaginable. The draught was too strong to allow anyone to carry a lantern, if we had had one, so we all filed in a single column up this narrow alley, so narrow that we could touch each wall with our elbows. No one felt very brave, and our perfect horror can therefore be imagined, when the guide suddenly sang out, "Get up there, you drunken white-trash, get out of the way,"—lighting his cigar-lighter, which gave one sickly flame, and then as if ashamed to show such a sight, sput-

tered and went out. "Come right along, ladies,"
came a reassuring voice from the pitch darkness,
"don't be afraid, only a drunken man, keep close to
the left wall"; and like a flock of sheep, no one
being able to see one inch ahead, or one another,
but holding on for dear life to whatever piece of apparel we happened to catch, in our Blind Man's Buff
parade, we marched forward. We had been
through Murderer's Alley, Rose Alley, Sullivan Alley, and many dark, dirty, villainous places in Chinatown; but this was the vilest and worst of them all.
Even James said afterwards, it was entirely too
spooky for him ! We finally reached the object of
our search, and the picture will never be effaced
from my memory. By the aid of the little cigar-
lighter, we stepped into a wretched hole of a place,
as dirty as absolute filth could make it ; and sitting
in one corner, close to the wall, his head bent so
low we could not see his face, sat—what they called
—a man ! When a Chinaman looses his cue, disgrace comes upon him. This poor creature had no
cue, his hair grew in a mass all over his head, and
had not been combed for years, if appearances do
not deceive. His poor ragged clothes hung in
great tatters from his shrunken shoulders, and one
shoulder was bare. The guide said,—"This man,
ladies and gents, is deaf and dumb. He has been
here in this one position, for ten years. A poor
man, like himself, living near, brings him food occa-
sionally. He has committed some awful crime, or

done some deed which I cannot find out, but it must be something awful, for none of his own people will come near him," etc., etc.; but I noticed when that guide said " he has committed some awful crime," even in that dim light, a tremor shook his entire body, and he was having more than his just punishment in this world,—even then. No one can make me believe that man is deaf, or cannot understand!

We saw a magnificent restaurant, furnished throughout with lovely ebony and pearl chairs and tables, — beautiful, exquisite. The House has many balconies, and all are hung with lanterns, Chinese banners, and all kinds of Chinese toggery. They give magnificent banquets here, but mostly for the fast set. Some streets or alleys in Chinatown are full of questionable places. They have no windows, and the doors are grated. Little spaces in the walls have gratings over them; and once upon a time, a pretty face used to appear behind these bars,—but these times are past, as the law forbids that procedure now. We visited one house, which has so many inmates, that they call it the Palace Hotel. Six hundred and seventy-five men, women and children live in this one house, crowded in so closely, it would make one sick to see them. Opium dens were in great numbers, and it became a familiar sight to see men asleep, overcome by this powerful drug. Some showed us how it was smoked, and it was quite interesting, but not so unusal as I expected.

The " High Binders " is a society like the Mafia, of Italy, composed of the worst characters among the Chinese. Their buildings have been seized by law and done away with, and their society, it is hoped, has become a thing of the past. They are a terrible set of lawless ruffians, and bring fear to Chinese and Americans alike.

There are so many things about these queer people, that are unusual and interesting, that I feel as if I had not chronicled one half of all we have seen and learned of them.

One thing I forgot to mention; the Chinese, in Chinatown, take the bleached bones of their dead, back home to China, and bury them in their own cemeteries there.

We visited the Chinese Dungeon, also, and it reminded us of the tales told of the prisons and punishments of the Inquisition. Punishment and sentence are pronounced, by one among them, given authority by the Home Government.

We were back at the Palace Hotel, about midnight, and were quite well satisfied with the knowledge we had gained, of the wonderful little world in Chinatown.

WEDNESDAY, JUNE 10TH.

WE were too tired to be up early this morning, so James and I took breakfast and lunch together, at twelve o'clock, with our good friend Mr.

H. Miss B. joined us a little later, and we four went out for a walk in the afternoon. It is a great pleasure to James and me, to have two such congenial spirits with us, as are these two young people; and we like both so much, we are hoping their fondness for one another is prophetic. We had dinner together, then sat in the easy-chairs in the Court, and chatted until quite late.

THURSDAY, JUNE 11TH.

SAN FRANCISCO is the queerest City to us, in its strange weather. To day is damp and dismal,—a fog is over everything, and a little mist is falling; but it is the only bad day we have had, in at least three weeks. It is lovely to have such weather.

San Francisco is not attractive to us, except in a few ways. It is quite cold here, which is of course delightful, when we hear of our loved ones, in the East, melting with the heat. Every night since we came here, we have slept under two heavy blankets and a spread, and warm clothing has been a necessity to us. I sit in our room and shiver often with the cold. The other attraction to us is the flowers. Such roses, pinks, and sweet-peas! Men and boys stand by the dozen, in the streets, with their flower baskets fairly laden, with the most glorious bunches of color,—great pink La France roses (five for a quarter, or " two bits," they all say), violet and dark blue sweet peas,—great bunches of corn-flowers,

Jacque roses in plenty, and all so cheap! Jamie buys me flowers every morning, and never pays more than two bits a bunch. This morning, he brought me the most glorious La France roses, with beautiful foliage and long stems, and a bunch of the daintiest pink and white carnations,—cost, only ten cents for them all, imagine it! James says "I could fill a big packing box full, for two dollars, but it would cost too much to send home, or I would try it." The poorest people have flowers, and it is really remarkable to walk along the streets, and notice the glorious bunches carried by the poorest of the poor. Everybody seems to love them, and to wear them. The colors are more brilliant than at home, and I suppose it is the peculiar brightness of the sunshine. The sun is dazzlingly brilliant in these western states,—it nearly blinds us. Another thing which interests us in San Francisco, are the cable cars. They run so fast and so close together, with four separate tracks on the main street, on which the Palace Hotel faces, that it is all one's life is worth to cross the street. I fairly fly across when I have to go, and expect to be run over yet. As Mr. H. expressed it, "You can run for the stern end of one of those cars, and missing it, you will run right into the bow of another." They run like mad all over the City, and cover distances so fast, and go so thoroughly all over, that few people keep horses and carriages here, and not one stylish turn-out have I seen, since we came here.

One thing San Francisco entirely lacks, is a good restaurant. There is no Delmonico, or Brunswick here, only what we would call second-class places. The best people patronize them, however, and as one " wants to do in Rome as the Romans do," we have gone to them, and been much surprised at the good things, and more surprised at the prices (of which I will write later). This hotel is certainly magnificent; the finest and largest hotel we have ever seen at home or abroad. It is built around a huge courtyard, with balconies about, on each floor, and on four sides. Easy chairs and sofas line these balconies, and make a most delightful place to sit, at any time of the day or evening, but especially on Monday and Friday evenings, during " Concert hours." The halls of the hotel are huge and well kept, the elevators are many,—the bell-men and porters, and chambermaids, are the best to be had.

This morning, James decided that we would rest and do nothing, as it was disagreeable and rainy. I went to my room and to the table in the bay window, and wrote as fast as I could on my journal. About half past five, we decided to go out for dinner; so "we three,"—Mr. H. having joined us,—went to a place across the street, kept by a man named Swain, and then the question arose, " what shall we eat?" "Oh, anything," I said, " only don't ask me to order." Just then a sign on the wall attracted us,— "French dinner, 50 cents." "Let's try that," I suggested. To be sure, the service and appointments

were not like Delmonico's ; they filled the glass water-pitcher on each table, from a big tin pail, and we ate with rather thinly plated spoons, but it was a most remarkable repast for the price.   James and I then took a very short stroll up Market street, and re-turning to the Palace, we made Mr. and Mrs. V. G. a short call.

The Kodak photos came to us to-day, and we have looked at them a dozen times already.   They are so good, and Mr. V. G. is so pleased, that he has borrowed over a dozen of the films, and will have more struck off for himself.   He is a good friend of " the Duke " as he always calls Jamie.

FRIDAY, JUNE 12TH.

L OVELY in the morning, dismal and foggy at noon, but clear in the afternoon.   We were invited to go with Miss B., her father and sister, and Mr. H. to visit Leland Stanford's celebrated stable at Palo Alto :—we were to start at ten o'clock, but I felt so miserably this morning, that James would not let me go, and he sent a note to make our excuses.   We spent most of the morning in our room, receiving a visit about two o'clock, from our kind friends, who told us they had given up the trip to the stables, because we could not go with them.   Then these two dear friends told us, what we had been most anxious should come to pass, that they were engaged to be married.   The symptoms of Cupid's work had been very evident to

James and me; and our own sweet experience made us feel that we were competent to judge, in such matters. We rejoiced, when told that Mr. H. would wait awhile, and take his bride home with him; and James and I are to take the "bridegroom elect" away with us, to Monterey. How little James and I thought, when we left home, that we would have a part so soon in a love affair! It is truly a delight to see young people so much in love, and I do hope heartaches may be spared them forever. We are glad to be of aid in such happiness, however; but James often says, he wishes he could be sure, that all our friends could have the sweet and blissful happiness and contentment, that are ours. Few are so blessed, and few are more thankful than we are. Surely a married life like our own, with its perfect trust, and love, and confidence, is a bit of Heaven on earth, the highest and sweetest and best of all God's blessings to His children.

A package arrived from home this afternoon, while we were sitting together, and of course I opened it at once, and began to peep into the two boxes. Suddenly an envelope slipped out, and "M. A. H." seized it with a hug, for it was all her own. Opening it, I found a tiny envelope, enclosed in which was a great yellow velvet pansy, with its sweet heart full of gold, which I know had grown right by the Library window at home. With it were some verses for me, which I began to read, when James called to me "read it aloud, May, don't be

selfish ;" so, while our two friends and James listened, I read the sweetest of verses ever written, by
a mother to her daughter:

"ONLY a pansy blossom,
    Plucked by a gentle hand,
      To send far away,
      To loved ones, who stray
    Across this broad, beautiful land.

A modest plebeian flower,
Of lowly and humble birth, —
    Yet in its short day,
    And in its own way,
It gladdens the face of the earth.

Look into its heart, where the yellow
Is deepened, as if by a blush,—
    And a dark, heavy shade,
    A wall round it has made,
To hold it, and keep it,—for hush

Now, while there is no one to listen,
And softly 'twill whisper to you,
    How, with tenderest care,
    A treasure to bear,
It has hastened the long journey through.

For lips, that are aching and longing
To press themselves close to your own,—
    But now denied this,
    Have planted a kiss
Deep down in its heart, where alone—

Close in the embrace of the petals,
Held in by the dark wall around,
   Securely it lies,
   As onward it flies,
And there, all unharmed, may be found.

So, just for a moment, pray hold it
Close up to your own fair warm cheek,
   And into your ear,
   While it nestles near,
A message of love it will speak.

And if to your own lips you press it,
You will think of one far, far away,
   Whose love you may miss,
   So she sends you a kiss—
With a prayer, that God bless you each day.

Only a pansy blossom,—
A plain little everyday thing,
   That never has guessed
   How it might be pressed
Into service, my message to bring."

I could hardly read it through, for I had such a time swallowing; but I thought it was my love for the writer, which made every word sink deep into my heart, for it was written entirely for me, without a thought that any other eye would ever see it, or ear hear it. But, when I finished, every one was so silent, that I looked up enquiringly; and the three were in tears. "My gracious, that would melt a heart of stone!" said Mr. H. "Mother is an angel!" stammered James. "It's beautiful!" and

Miss B. could say no more, but put out her hand in silence for the letter, and the little golden heartsease. She took the little pansy and looked at it so lovingly, and then, as James and Mr. H. left us, we had a sweet heart to heart talk, and were firm friends from that moment, and forever, I hope. I wished that the little mother could have looked into my room, in San Francisco, at that moment, and realized the mission of the little flower.

After dinner together, and an enjoyable concert, it being Friday, and Concert Night, at the Palace Hotel, our friends left us and we retired.

SATURDAY, JUNE 13TH.

LOVELY weather again. James and I took breakfast and luncheon together, as we awoke quite late. After writing a little, Miss B. came with Mr. H.; we wandered out, and as usual drifted into fascinating Chinatown, hunting for embroidered gowns. Fong Lang Lung was most anxious to please us. We know these Chinamen so well now, and they have taught us to say in the Chinese language "How do you do," "Thank you," and "Good-bye." The first sounds as if it was spelled "Noo-lah." Thank you sounds like "Tar-tare," and good-bye is "Ten-or." Mrs. V. G. was told in Providence, at one time, to say a certain Chinese word, whenever she wanted to particularly please any Chinaman; therefore, whenever a Chinaman came for her laundry work, or whenever she spoke to any Celestial on the street, she would say it, thinking it was some specially polite greeting. After months of practice, and much wonder why she made no impression, because of her fluent use of the Chinese language, she was told one day, that she should not use that expression, as it was a genuine Chinese oath.

These Chinese merchants are so funny, and yet so serious. Only once have we been surprised by any unusual brilliancy, and that was to-day, when we expostulated about the price of a gown, and the Chinaman's answer made us laugh. "Well," he said, "it must be higher in price now, because, you know, the 'McKinley bill'"—but his sentence was never finished. So the McKinley bill had reached Chinatown too! We took our camera to this interesting quarter to-day, and one Chinaman escorted me to a side street, that I might try to take a photograph of some tiny tots there. He gave them candy and they were pleased; but when they saw me with my little box, they ran away like mice, and huddling close together, with their faces hidden, they cried pitifully. It made my heart ache, and I called to them not to be afraid; but the poor little things, the more I said, the more they cried, because they could not understand me. One funny little specimen was too young to be afraid, and stood looking enquiringly at me; but the moment his father spied me, he snatched up the little fellow and ran into the house. We did not have much luck to-day, but we intend trying again, when our guide will go with us. The Chinese are like the Indians ; they are superstitious from ignorance, and afraid to have their photographs taken. They think you have taken some advantage of them, when you obtain any likeness of them.

SUNDAY, JUNE 14TH.

WE slept late this morning and did not go out to church. After lunch, I wrote in my journal, willing, however, to drop my pen at any moment, if James desired to go out, but I was quite pleased to remain indoors for one day at least. We thought at first we would take a drive in Golden Gate Park, but it was so awfully windy, dusty and cold, that we postponed it. Mr. H. came in for about two hours, but left us at five o'clock, and I have been writing ever since. I never knew such long twilights ! It is brilliant sunshine, until nearly half past eight.

Miss Emma Thursby called on us yesterday, with her sister, but I was out. Jamie sent her some flowers this morning. Sunday morning is the great flower morning, and I had three of the most magnificent bouquets sent me, I have ever seen. One is over twenty-two inches in diameter, and more than one could carry. It is composed of white, tea, and red roses, beautiful pink carnations, heliotrope, maiden's hair fern, mignonette, and dusted all over with the most delicate little white flower. The other two are more exquisite, yellow roses in the middle, surrounded by maiden's hair fern and pink carnations and heliotrope, make a sort of raised centre. This is surrounded by a band, five inches deep, of pansies, solid, and numbering about three hundred pansies, at the least calculation. They are all dark purple ones, with a yellow heart once in a while; and around the edge, against a fern border, lie the delicate white feathery flowers and pink carnations again. It is a dream in color! Nothing was big enough to hold them, so "Whiskers" the colored man, brought me three silver pitchers, and my room is a flower garden. When we came up from breakfast and opened our door, James exclaimed: "It smells just like a funeral!"

There are two colored bell-men on this floor, one named Charles, who is devotion itself to us. He asked me to take his photograph, and he was as pleased as the Chinese were horrified. The chambermaid asked me this evening, if we had been married long; and when I told her, she exclaimed, "Oh my! we thought you were bride and groom! I told Charlie the other day, that I had a bride and groom in 946, surely, because the husband was always sending her flowers and lemonade; and we were all wondering how long it would last."

MONDAY, JUNE 15TH.

THIS morning we were up soon after seven o'clock, breakfasted about eight, and were ready for guests in our room, at nine o'clock. Miss

B. had ordered two Chinamen to come to our room at that time, with Chinese gowns for her selection, as it was more convenient for her, and for us.

Later, Miss B.'s sweet sister, Ivy, with Mr. H., James and myself, started for Chinatown again. James was specially anxious to get some photographs with our own camera there, and so we had planned to meet our guide, that he might pilot us up and down alleys, where we would not go alone; and he had as much trouble in getting subjects for us to photograph, as we would have had ourselves. While the guide had gone to try and persuade the little girl, who sang for us the other night, to let us photograph her, Ivy and I wandered around the corner of the street, a very little way, waiting for James and the guide to join us. Ivy stood near me, when suddenly a swarm of Chinese men surrounded me, at my back, and on each side; and when I spoke to them, and pointed to my little detective finder, they crowded around me and looked at it eagerly. One or two Chinamen walked in front of the camera once or twice, and did not discover it at first, but when they did, you never saw men disperse more quickly. They are afraid to have their photographs taken, and yet they were full of curiosity to look into my funny black box. No power on earth could persuade them to let me take their pictures. Our good friend "Louie," a Chinaman at Fong Lang Lung's shop, was the only sensible man among them, and he agreed willingly to have his photograph taken. James and the guide would stand in the street in front of me, and I was therefore hidden; but whenever a little child came along, or a woman, and stood in full sunlight, they would step aside, and I would snap my picture. It was awfully exciting work, and I was quite in a tremble when we had finished. I took at least fourteen in Chinatown. We did not succeed in taking buildings,—the streets and alleys were too narrow and dark.

We reached the Palace Hotel, at half-past one o'clock, then had luncheon, after which James, Mr. H. and I went out to inquire about our trip to Monterey. We were back at four o'clock, then I wrote my journal. James and I spent our evening on the balcony, on the second floor of the Court, with our friends, Mr. and Mrs. V. G., and were also joined by Mr. H. and Miss B.; and the concert was delightful.

TUESDAY, JUNE 16TH.

WE have been painfully tired of San Francisco for several days, and have felt that we have had enough of large cities, for awhile at least, but we have been waiting a few days to know what our good friend Mr. H. would decide to do. Finally, yesterday, James and I grew desperate, and decided we would go to Monterey, or rather to what people call " Del Monte, Monterey," to distinguish it from the little village of Monterey. We arranged for it, and Mr. H. then decided to go with us, to our delight.

We left San Francisco to-day, on the 2.30 P. M. train, and our trip to Del Monte was a lovely one. It was terribly hot, however, between 85 and 88 degrees,—the first really hot day we have had. I had heard of the lovely trip to Del Monte, of the beautiful country-places of California's millionaires,—of the wonderful trees, which only grow in this portion of the United States; but when we first started out, and flew rapidly over salt marshes, with flat, uninteresting country about them, I was wonderfully disappointed. Soon, however, as if touched by magic and a fairy wand, the country changed, and such beauty I never saw. It seemed as if all California was haying,—for the country, for miles, was all covered with golden mounds,—in regular rows sometimes, like soldiers,—then again a hill-side would be peppered irregularly. It seemed to me that Dame Fashion, in originating styles for this summer, must have travelled in this country, so spotted over with little button hay-mounds, and in that way received the inspiration for our summer fashion of dotting waists and sleeves all over, with jet or gems; and nature had in this instance the start of fashion, and had "set the style."

The hills, on which the harvest had already been reaped and garnered, were most exquisite in the sunshine,—like old-gold plush, and making the lights and shades most velvety and deep. Every

once in a while, great twisted trunks of trees, sometimes singly, sometimes in groups, would add their
beauty to the scene, with the most marvelous dark
foliage, so dense sometimes as to admit no light
whatever. These darkly beautiful trees, against the
golden hill-side, made wonderful effects; and all
along the views were changing, filling us with wonder and delight. The great dark giants are indigenous to the coast in California, and mostly to
Monterey County, and are called "Monterey Pines."
Their "Live Oak" is a variety unknown to us in
the East, and also indigenous to this quarter of the
globe. It is a lower tree than the pine, with twisted,
knotted trunks and feathered foliage, not so dense or
dark. At times, its branches are hung with a queer
"greybeard moss," which drapes itself gracefully
from branch to branch. Great groves of these two
trees made beautiful views, and especially with the
remarkable golden background. Vineyards were in
great numbers,—some were so full and rich, others
seemingly just planted, and vegetable gardens,
which were a pleasure to the eye, so finely kept and
so fully grown. We saw some magnificent residences—and such luxurious homes without, made
us long to look within, for the surroundings were
gorgeous. The growth of vegetation is remarkable
all through this State,—much more wonderful to
us, than the most glowing accounts ever pictured.
Even at the railroad stations, the great palms and
cactus plants were all about, on the platforms, in

little flower pots, and such wonderful vines covering telegraph poles and everything else—roses
in vases and on bushes, nasturtiums in brilliant colors, all so beautiful and attractive.

We were three hours and a quarter coming to
Del Monte, and therefore reached here at 5.43 P. M.
Our first view was enchanting! Luxurious bushes
and fine trees, picturesque walks as well, commence
from the very station ; and all this was enhanced by
some stunning equipages, little donkey carts, etc.,
for the richest people of California come to this
" Heaven upon earth." James was fairly wild with
delight. He went down to be shaved, shortly after
we arrived, and he came flying back and said, " I
came near telegraphing mother that we had reached
Heaven,—I never saw such beauty, May," etc., etc.
It is the loveliest spot, in every possible way, that
I can dream ever could exist. I have never seen
such perfect beauty. After getting dressed and
dining, Mr. H., James and I walked out about the
hotel for an hour or more ; then we strolled to a
cunning little club-house, so picturesquely placed in
a beautiful grove of trees, where every game, from
Ten Pins to Pool, is played by ladies, as well as
gentlemen.

WEDNESDAY, JUNE 17TH.

HEAVEN is undoubtedly more lovely and glorious than we mortals can picture, or paint to
ourselves, in our highest moods, more inspiring, and

exalting and beautiful; but, Del Monte is as near my ideal of beauty, natural and artificial means combined, as any spot on earth that I have ever seen, or any ideal or picture I can make in my mind of Heaven. We have seen the "Garden of the Gods," beautiful in name and actual splendor; but Del Monte is so exquisite, and delicate, and dainty, that one feels as if the sky had opened and let down a little of its choicest charms, and gathered them all together in this one place. It seems like the "Gate of Heaven," and makes one pause in awe and wonder, at the beauties of Nature, and the riches of her boundless store. "You cannot describe Del Monte," a *near* neighbor and travelling companion of mine has said; but its beauties have sunk so deep into my innermost heart, that I must try to describe, to the best of my ability, a little of the hotel and its surroundings.

"El Monte," or "The Forest" was the name of a hotel, standing where the new one is now, which was burned down two years ago; and Del Monte, "Of (or in) the Forest" is the name of the magnificent new structure, which is one of the most delightful hotels we have ever been in, in appointment and service. The building itself covers six and a half acres, and is so huge that, from the end of one wing of the hotel, to the end of the other wing, is one third of a mile. It is built with many piazzas and doors, many, many windows,—in fact some passages are all windows. It is beautiful within, with "all the comforts of home," and heavenly without. About the house—on every and all sides—in every available nook and corner, are plants, flowers, great trees, of different kinds of palms, dates, banana trees, foliage beds of rare and marvelously beautiful designs, in such variety of figures, squares, rounds, oblongs and circles, that one is bewildered and confused, one minute declaring, that there never was such an exquisite Turkish rug in plants, only to turn and find another of such greater beauty, that adjectives and superlatives grow scarce and weak, and one becomes silent (perhaps for the first time in life). Out of every window, in whatever direction one looks, beautiful and rare flowers are everywhere seen, in novel combinations; and as I have said before, all colors seem intensified in this warm southern climate. About every doorway, along the railings of the balconies, hanging with hundreds of blossoms, are climbing rose bushes, so full and large and big, that one stands to count the roses, only to move on the next minute, realizing what a hopeless task it is. Red, pink, and white roses, great big ones, filling the air with the most exquisite perfume, and clinging so lovingly to every post.

Soon after breakfast this morning, James, Mr. H. and I wandered out on the grounds. One hundred and eight acres are under cultivation, and hundreds of Chinamen, and others, are every day at work, keeping lawns, beds and walks in perfect order. Such trees! Cypresses, with their tall straight trunks, and deep-toned foliage (like the evergreens), Monterey pines, so high-toned and aristocratic, and the short, stubby and thick set Live Oaks, with their feathery foliage, make the grounds of Del Monte most beautiful. Hundreds and hundreds of these trees, are every one covered thickly, about twenty or thirty feet up the trunk, with the most luxurious growth of ivy. Jamie said, at least a score of times, " What wouldn't Mother give for just one such vine, to coax, and watch, and tack up." Dear boy! his enthusiasm knew no bounds, and he grew absolutely worn out exclaiming. In the grove about the house, there is the most beautiful rose garden, with thousands of plants, and hundreds of varieties of roses, all named for Rose-study. Another garden is full of all kinds of cactus growth, and is most weird and strange. Queer things, with marvelous shapes and wonderful growths, and awful names, are so many, that it needs several visits to see and appreciate all. All through the grounds, among the trees, are great beds of creeping vines, myrtle in flower; and all the beds and borders are overflowing with such quantities of flowers, and such marvelous blending of colors, that each view one has, is a picture in itself. Tennis courts appeared every once in a while, as we walked,—made courts, surrounded by high wire fences, and these fences are overgrown with vines—poppies, forget-me-nots, daisies, heliotrope, forming borders all about the enclosures. Swings for children, rustic vine-covered benches for lovers, sunny seats for sun-bath invalids, and a "Maze" to tempt people into its embrace, and then make them "swear a blue streak" before they can get out.

"We three" approached this marvelous terrace of pine hedge, cut in such beautiful arches, with hedge vases, urns, etc., and as we peeped into its high-walled walks, I said "let's go in a minute." Woe betide the wicked spirit that tempted me that day! Three innocent, unsuspecting mortals entered the evergreen portals, and amused and curious, wandered along a straight, narrow path, walled in with hedges. Turning a corner, we came to another long way, parallel with our first promenade. Idly, we continued on, coming now to a queer, short little turn, then a corner, and so on, always between the same green walls, until we felt wearied by the monotony, and decided we had had enough. Signs faced us at every turn,—"Do not break through the hedges." "What lunacy," I exclaimed to my companions,—"who wants to crawl through hedges?" but how I longed to break through rule and hedges later! "Let's go out," James calmly called. We turned to retrace our steps, but they would not retrace, for somehow, or other, the corners we had turned, and the long, straight aisles, had all moved, and such funny little short walks were ours now. Mr. H. had dragged his cane in walking along, I had noticed, and he now owned up, that he had done it on purpose to guide us, in making an exit.

But some other fellow had had the same dreadful idea, and dragged his cane also ; and soon we missed our trail and were lost, absolutely. We were very, very hot, and *some of us* were getting a bit anxious and excited, for it seemed hopeless, and dinner hour was approaching. Suddenly James exclaimed, "Here's the way—we haven't passed that barbed wire before—come along this way ; " and we went along that way, and after a tramp we came right into a bench, and the end of that aisle ! All this time we could hear voices in some hidden path, and once in a while, we could see a light dress move along, but merriment had melted, and solemn despair reigned. We continued to wander and wander, and seemed to be revolving about a hollow square, but although we knew it was " The Centre," we could not get there. We were standing still and quite silent outwardly, no matter what was going on inwardly, when a man and a maiden approached us. Formality had fled, and I gasped out, "Will you please tell us the way out ? " Imagine our despair, when the young woman answered, " We've been hunting it for a half hour, and we can't find any way to get out." " Thank you," we three hopelessly gasped. " Let's make a grand effort, now," chirped Mr. H. We solemnly filed in line, and after the second turn, we walked into "The Centre," which we had not been able to reach before. Seats surrounded the square, and we sank down, exhausted. Suddenly in walked our couple,

THE MAZE.

—it was their *ninth* entrance,—they would always turn up there, when they were trying to get out. Flying along the sandy paths, we met constantly the same sad man, tearing along as if an evil spirit was after him We asked him pleadingly, if he knew the way out. With his teeth tightly set, he whistled out "can't find it," and away he went, as mad a man as you could ever find. James and Mr. H. were just beginning to suggest taking off coats and vests while they rested, but the ninth entrance of the other lost babes restrained them. Joining forces, we five began to wander again, leaving with regret, after all, as we hated to leave a certainty for an uncertainty, as we had found the centre, and were still in doubt about the entrance, and way out. James and Mr. H. made up their minds that there was some rule about it all,—that either all left hand turns, or vice versa, was sure to do something, —so leaving marks in the sand at crossings, we marched ahead, and after ten or fifteen minutes, perhaps less, we saw the daylight coming in, and like the Pilgrim Fathers when they landed on Plymouth Rock,—we each said a little thanksgiving in our hearts, I am sure. We heard the mad fellow tearing about, as we were coming out. Oh, what a maze that is: people have been caught in there for hours sometimes,—lost their dinners and tempers, and yet all came out alive. It was an adventure, and one that makes us roar with laughter, now it is over; but we wanted to warn everybody, after that.

A little visit to the Club-house, and some cooling lemonade refreshed us all, and we went afterwards to see the green houses and have a chat with the gardener, by which we profited, as he gave us much information. Flowers are exquisite here, some bloom all winter in the open air.

THURSDAY, JUNE 18TH.

EXQUISITE, beautiful, lovely, and such a day for the drive we took! We breakfasted at nine-twenty, then started at ten o'clock, in a comfortable carriage, for what Del Monte people call "the eighteen mile drive." It was a drive never to be forgotten, as it took us, for ten miles or more, along the shore of the great Pacific Ocean ; and as we gazed at the beautiful surf, and watched the great waves roll in and dash so high, we realized, for the first time, that we had absolutely crossed our Continent, from ocean to ocean, and were gazing toward Japan and China, with nothing but the open sea between us and those marvelous countries. It made me feel queerly, for a few moments, and I just stood still on those great rocks on the shore, and thought to myself, "Can this be I, or am I dreaming; and am I really not here, but only imagine that I am?" But that philosophy of the Germans would not satisfy me then, and I took a good breath of the Pacific Ocean salt breeze, and—was myself again.

Our drive, at first, was through the old Mexican

town of Monterey; and the guide-book informed us, that "Monterey was the capital of California, when the territory was acquired by the United States, and it is the place where General Fremont first raised the stars and stripes, and took formal possession of the country." Many buildings still stand that were built by the Mexicans, and queer, quaint structures they are, dingy and old, but interesting in their antique style of architecture. We saw one enclosure where, in olden times, the inhabitants used to have bull-fights, for their amusement and recreation. We saw the house where General Sherman lived, when stationed here; also where General Fremont camped, and tried to protect—something.

We drove for miles, through the most interesting country, and finally came to Pacific Grove, a summer resort and bathing-place. "The Church of Aunt Mary" amused us greatly, on account of its unique name.

We had the funniest old driver we had ever chanced to meet,—a queer, quaint man of over sixty, but with a fresh and ready wit, really amusing. His name was Alexander Early. "Queer name, ain't it?" he said, when he told us. "Do you see that little house?" he added, after a while, as we passed a pretty, modest little cottage, with a wealth of color and radiance all about it, in the glorious flowers. "Well, in that house lives a woman, who came across the plains with me, over

thirty-nine years ago, as steerage on an ox team."
"Steerage!" I gasped; "what difference could be
made, coming across the plains, between cabin passengers and steerage?" "Cabin people rode,—
steerage walked," he answered. As we passed
through the beautiful woods, just outside Pacific
Grove, a fence ran across the country, and a gate
allowed drivers to pass along. "What's that fence
for, driver?" I asked. "To divide Pacific Grove
Methodists from cattle!" was the answer; and just
then as two pretty young girls passed on the road,
he exclaimed, "Look at those destroying angels!"
Then ·he told us, in his own queer way, out of
the side of his mouth, about a passenger he had
once, "who shaved as all them Boston fellers do,
way down to his collar. Well, this Boston chap
could ask more questions than anybody I ever met.
Says he to me, 'Driver, how old is that tree?'—
thinkin' he'd stick me. 'Two thousand and six
years old,' I answered. 'What,' say he, 'how do
you know?' 'Well,' says I, 'a naturalist come out
here six years ago, and said it was two thousand
years old, and I reckon it ain't stopped growing
these last six years.' That nearly fetched him; but
pretty soon he said, 'Is the Carmel Mission built
on the water, driver?' 'No, Sir,' says I; 'can't
build no such stone structure on water, not in my
time.' 'No impertinence, driver,' says Boston; 'I
mean *near* the water, of course.' 'Within a half
mile, Sir,' I answered. That feller slowed up a

PYRAMID POINT.

scrap then. Travellers are awful fresh, sometimes,"
Alexander added. The full wit in these items or
scraps, from a four hours' drive, bountifully sprinkled throughout with them, is lost, when the manner, and enjoyment of his own jokes, cannot be pictured. He was quite inimitable.

After driving through the loveliest of pine woods,
most picturesque and beautiful, we came suddenly
out into the bright sunshine, right on the shore of
the great Pacific Ocean. Our drive continued, for
ten miles or more, right by the ocean,—the great
rocks rising about us, and the breakers dashing high
in surf and spray, making a white, thick outline
along the beach, as far as the eye could reach. Our
first glimpse of the ocean and rocks was, perhaps,
the grandest of all, as the waves come in six different currents, and the meeting point makes a grand
picture. It is called Pyramid Point. "When we
reach a fine place, driver, I want to take a photograph," I said. "Well, ma'am, this is the boss
place,—the first starter," he answered; and I
jumped out with my Kodak.

The trees on this drive are magnificent! It is the
only place where the Monterey Cypress trees grow,
in great numbers. They are most picturesque, tall,
with dense foliage, but quite flat on top. This is a
marvelous country for trees and palms. The Monterey Pines; and the Live Oak, with the Cypress,
made our drive most unusual and picturesque. I
was anxious to get a picture of a real good specimen

of the Cypress, and when I told the driver, he said, " I've got a tree all picked out for you, just ready, it's been sketched, photographed and painted, until it's pretty nigh worn out." I photographed it,—or rather Mr. H. did, with James and myself standing near. It is called the "Lone Tree." He gave the reins to James once, and jumped out of the carriage like a boy of sixteen, instead of sixty, and came back to me, with a branch of the Cypress, with cones, so different from other cones ; and as he handed them to me, he said, " When we only have one lady along, we have to treat her well ; but when we have more than one, we let the gentlemen look after them."

One sight of unusual interest to us, were the Seal-rocks, where the sea lions live. They are near the shore, so one can watch these sea-monsters quite closely. Law forbids any one from shooting or kill-ing them. They were thickly settled all over the rocks, where we saw them basking in the sun, their great wet shiny bodies and little heads, looking most strange and uncanny. We saw them fight, and heard them bark plainly, and were much interested. There were several hundreds in sight. They weigh two thousand pounds, sometimes. Further down the coast, we saw the leopard seals, with their striped bodies and queer heads, and the driver said, " Those leopard sea-lions don't bark or make no racket, but are high-toned, and don't associate with no other seals."

Some trees make shapes and forms of animals ;

and two great cypress trees, on that shore-drive, made the exact representation of an ostrich, with long slim legs and slender arched neck. We also saw a Buffalo Ranch, where that already scarce animal is being raised and bred. One beautiful sight was a hill, at least one mile in length, and quite high, covered with ferns, beautiful in form, and not one coarse one among them. It made me think of papa and mamma, and their love for the wild flowers and ferns. They would absolutely grow frantic, in this country of brilliance and beauty. The Trade Winds have much to do in shaping the trees. The wind bends the trunks of the young trees, and as the old adage says "As the twig is bent, the tree inclines "; so as one travels through the country, it is very easy to see from what quarter the wind has come. Fields are covered with trees, oftentimes, which bow all in one direction, as if doing homage to some unseen God or Goddess. Such a field we passed on this drive, and Alexander Early said: "A lady asked me why all the trees were bent in one direction," and I told her "cause they had a *lean* on the property."

One more item; then endeth the chapter on A. Early. As we passed through a lovely grove, the perfume of the pines was delicious ; and as we breathed it into our lungs, with an "Ah, how good it feels," and an "Oh my," some one said, "How good this must be for consumption." Alexander Early said, "Yes, that reminds me of one of those

Raymonds from Boston, who asked me once if this was a good place for consumption. I told her no, because I had been here ten years and I hadn't got it yet." The drive was a most enjoyable one, and it was over nineteen miles, for we had taken a couple of extra views ; but it was none too long.

FRIDAY, JUNE 19TH.

A BIT cloudy when James, Mr. H. and I went to breakfast soon after nine, but after that the clouds cleared away, and it was loveliness itself.

About eleven o'clock, we three " chums" walked to the little funny horse-cars, with rope-traces on the horses, and rode to the Natatorium, a fine establishment on the sandy shore of the Pacific Ocean, or Monterey Bay, as it is properly called. It is a huge building,—glass sides and roof, with warm water tanks inside,—some colder than others,—to suit every taste and desire ; and about these clear fresh-looking tanks, full of salt water at different degrees of temperature, are the most magnificent palms and plants, of all sizes and variety, while hanging from the ceiling are fine baskets, full of vines ; and an air of a tropical climate is everywhere. It is a most unusual bathing establishment ; and it seems as if bathers should wear satin and silk suits, to harmonize with the luxurious surroundings. There is always a bathing master in attendance, who gives swimming lessons ; and it was remarkable to see some little tots, who could not stand upright, because the water was over their heads, swim about, tread water, and move all over, like little fish. Outside these tanks are dressing rooms, for those who bathe in the open ocean ; and we soon left the tropical tubs, for the seats outside, and watched some fine swimmers, both ladies and gentlemen. About twelve o'clock, in company with the young bride and groom from Salt Lake City, whom we met in the Maze, we came back to the fascinating Club House, had lemonade, then wandered through the beautiful grounds again, to fully impress them upon our memories,—then we came in to lunch. After luncheon, and a little chat on one of the many piazzas, I left the " two boys " and came to do a little packing in my room—then wrote this journal, while Jamie packed his "traps."

This morning, in our walk, we passed the Maze, and hearing some voices within, we stopped to listen. " Poor things " exclaimed Mr. H. " lost as we were ; " and the merriest laugh rang out from that labyrinth of green : the poor lost people had heard us, and evidently felt encouraged to think they were not alone in their affliction.

UP MT. HAMILTON TO THE LICK OB-SERVATORY

SATURDAY, JUNE 20TH.

FROM Monterey to San José. At the unearthly hour of half past four o'clock A.M., James and I awoke, in anticipation of the order we had left at the office last night, to be awakened at 4.45. We arose, dressed, breakfasted at half past five, and at three minutes before six o'clock, James, Mr. H. and I stepped into the "bus" and were driven from lovely Del Monte, to take the train for San José. Our trip of two hours and a quarter, to San José, was quite uneventful, but pleasant, but as we had so recently gone over the same road, it was not so novel or entertaining. We went at once, on arriving at San José, to the new Vendome Hotel, a very prettily situated and comfortable little place, which, however, was quite tame to us, coming so directly as we had from Del Monte. But at night, when we returned again to it, unexpectedly to ourselves, it seemed a palace and paradise. After sitting a couple of hours on the piazza, and listening to a band, consisting of three pieces, who play morning and evening, James, Mr. H. and I jumped on an electric car, and went to view the town. We found it a remarkably wide-awake little place, fine stores, nice goods, and quite inviting and pleasant. What impressed us most in San José, was the wonderful growth of the palms. Along the streets, by the side-walks, they are planted in rows, palms by the hundreds, like real trees, giving such a tropical air and style to the streets. We had a lunch at a quarter to twelve, and at half past twelve we were sitting with our hand baggage on the piazza, waiting for the stage to take us, and many others, up Mt. Hamilton. At least a hundred people drove up that mountain with us, in private carriages, etc., that day. It was a magnificent day, not a cloud to be seen, and full moon at night; and (as we learned later) it had been foggy, rainy and unpleasant for the last three Saturdays; and as that is the only public day, it was too much to resist, and many drove up. At the Observatory, one of the Professors remarked, within my hearing, that "they had done no work for a week, in the Observatory, as they had been enveloped in a dense fog." Our "good fairy" had not deserted us. James and I had engaged the box-seats with the driver; but finding the seats inside the coach filled with ladies, I suggested that Mr. H. and I exchange seats, which we did, and fortunately for me,—at least going up, for the sun was so hot, it nearly broiled the two poor fellows. We had a very dusty and a terribly hot drive, starting as we did about one o'clock, and driving through a most beautiful country, with very little shade. But it paid us well, and will stand out in our memories always, as a delightful experience.

California is the most beautifully fertile country I have ever seen, and not an inch of ground seems uncultivated. Our drive, at first, was through the famous Santa Clara Valley, and it was like driving through a beautifully cultivated park, with such well kept prune ranches, cherry farms, and pear groves, such a luxurious growth of every kind of fruit, apricots, plums and everything good, making one long to stop and have a picnic, in among the trees. But we did not stop: we drove on and on for about six miles; and then we began to climb the hills, creeping round the mountains like snails, but going steadily higher and higher, slowly, inch by inch, but surely. We finally crossed one range of hills, then came into a beautiful valley, as shady along the road-way, as the path we had just left was sunny and barren of trees. The Buck-eye bushes were white with blossoms; and as they are as long as our horse-chestnut blossoms, only thicker and denser, it was a pretty addition to the green of the trees. Wild lilac was plenty,—in great white bushes —in fact, the flora on that drive, was really beautiful and wonderful. Finally, about half past four o'clock, we reached a place called "Smith's Creek," where all stages stop, change horses, and feed passengers. Some people remain here also over night, so as to break the drive, and rest. We intended to do so; but one glimpse of the house and surroundings, one meal in the spacious (!) dining room, settled our minds, and decided us in our doings. Rather than stay at Smith's Creek, we decided to drive back to San José, and run our risk of getting bed and board. As the four stages, with four horses each, came thundering up to the hotel (we were in the lead), an army of attendants came flying out of the house, each armed with a feather duster and brush, and everybody was brushed, pounded and thoroughly cleaned before we could enter "Smith's Creek Palace Hotel," as I named it. As soon as we were in order, we three chums marched boldly into the dining room. *The Dining-room!* The laundry at Sunny-Slope (a bit longer perhaps, but no wider), is palatial to that dining room. We had a very frugal repast, not enough to give us proper nourishment, but all we could get.

At Smith's Creek, we could look straight up and see the Lick Observatory, and by a trail, it was just two miles; but by the road, it was seven miles, and took us nearly three hours to crawl up. Our road was wonderful,—marvelous,—cut from the sides of the hills, and winding, twisting, turning, in the most graceful curves, through the most beautiful country and land, and giving us views, unsurpassed, of miles and miles in every direction. As far as one could turn the head, to the right, or to the left as well, a view of wondrous beauty was visible; the only spot, not actually calling forth the most enthusiastic praise, being directly at one's back. James was an enthusiast in every sense of the word. He would call out to me every other minute, saying, "Isn't it grand! Did you see anything like this even in Switzerland?" In those seven miles, the road turns three hundred and sixty-seven times; and gradually we reached the summit, and drove up in front of that marvelous structure, in all its massiveness,— the "Lick Observatory." Mt. Hamilton is about five thousand feet above the sea level, and we had come twenty-seven miles, the driver said, to see it; (but the miles in this country are equal to about two each in the East). It is built of brick and iron, the base being painted a dull red, and the domes, one on each end, are white, and can be seen for miles, with the naked eye. It is a fine structure, full of every manner of electric appliance, and every new and old invention, for the study of science,—a comfortable library for the professors, who number about six or eight, I believe, with their attendants, making about twenty in all, on that lonely mountain.

James Lick, the founder of this observatory, was a very poor lad, in a country village, and loved, unfortunately, a miller's daughter. His request of the miller, for his daughter's hand, was denied him, because he was poor. He made up his mind to prove himself worthy of his sweetheart; and, leaving home, he went to California and settled in the

Santa Clara Valley, near the foot of Mt. Hamilton, obtaining employment, and finally becoming interested in a mine near, which made him, in time, a very wealthy man. He built a mill, far surpassing the one owned by the stern old miller, finished in California woods, and then wrote to the miller, to invite him to come and visit him, and to ask again for the hand of his daughter. The story says, the daughter had not been true to her lover, but had married;—and James Lick remained a bachelor all his life. I asked some one, who seemed to be posted, why James Lick left his money for an observatory : for, if he was a poor man, and had had but little education, how did he come to feel an interest in scientific research ? The answer was this : When a boy, he had known a monk whom he admired greatly, who was always studying the heavens, through a little telescope he possessed, and it was from him that he first learned of the glory of the heavens, and the need of means to study and learn. James Lick died an eccentric old bachelor, and after willing the immense sum of money for the building of the observatory, and a fund for the maintenance of professors, etc., he requested that his body be placed under the great telescope, in the great dome, where it now rests. We reached there about half-past seven, and at once began to look about. The view of the surrounding country was beyond words to describe, as we looked nearly a hundred miles in every direction, across to California Bay, and to the coast range of mountains. As we peeped over the stone wall on the edge, looking down, we could see over two thousand feet, straight down the mountain side, into the valley. Jamie and Bert were annoyed by the great crowd of people, waiting in the Grand Dome, to look through the great telescope of thirty-six inch diameter, so they went outside, after looking at the moon through the smaller telescope; and by so doing, they saw one of the finest of sunsets, and gloried over me in their glee. Bert did hunt for me, and took me to see the last fading remnants of its glory; but I was too late for much. We were nearly two hours in the great dome, sitting in the dark, waiting for our turn to view Saturn, with his rings and satellites. At last our chance came, and we stepped into the charmed mystic enclosure, and approached the great wonder in the scientific world, the powerful lens. When it came my turn to look, I climbed the ladder up to the little eye-hole, and then held my breath, as I viewed Saturn, with his rings and six satellites. Surely, " the heavens declare the glory of God, and the firmament showeth His handiwork." It was a wonderful view I had, that one-half minute, but it is indelibly impressed on my mind. It was a glimpse into the mysteries of that attractive science of astronomy, of which I know so little, and which makes one hunger for knowledge, and a keener insight into the glories of the heavens. I did not wonder that those learned men would sacrifice everything,—

home, happiness, comfort,—to stay on that mountain peak, to study and learn of the heavens. I also looked through the smaller telescope, which has no mean lens, but is, of course, inferior to the greater monarch. I saw the moon through that, and was much interested. It was too full, to see the volcanoes and mountains, but I could see a portion of it very well. I had a minute then, and could not help asking the professor in attendance, "if there could ever be a telescope, powerful enough to discover life on the other planets, if there is life on any of them." He answered "We have never had a telescope yet, strong enough to discover life on any planet." When we emerged from the dome, we saw the electric key-board, where at twelve o'clock every day, "Pacific Time" is flashed to many places, also the self-registering barometer and water-gage, etc. The entire building is full of photographs of the moon, at different periods and quarters, and of all kinds of heavenly bodies; and I learned that it takes, sometimes, ten hours to take a photograph of the heavens. Imagine it! At ten o'clock, our passengers were, with difficulty, gathered together, stowed away and sufficiently wrapped; and we began our descent of Mt. Hamilton, in the most radiantly beautiful flood of moonlight, I have ever seen. If the "Moon and I" had arranged to be out the same night, we could not have done better. It was a superb night; the moonlight was white, and seemed to give color to the trees and grass. As we followed the winding road, flying along like mad around the curves, we had so slowly crawled up, in the afternoon, we could see the distant hills plainly. They were a delicate gray mass against the sky; then against them in turn were the foot-hills,—a dozen shades darker, and more distinct; and then in the foreground, the great trees and their clearly-cut shadows, made a picture never to be forgotten. It was a glorious drive! It took an hour to reach Smith's Creek, and at 11.15 P. M. we had a light lunch there. We then drove until 1 A. M., when we changed horses, and drove on, reaching the Vendome Hotel at 2.30 A. M. *Tired?*—We had reached the superlative degree of that word! *Dusty?* Words are poor to describe our condition, as to cleanliness! The drive down, however, had been well worth the dust and fatigue, and was glorious. We sang,—to keep awake,—told stories and conundrums, and finally lapsed into an ominous silence, which was made visible, by nodding heads, and wabbling bodies.

On reaching Vendome, Bert tried to register us, and nearly fell asleep during the process. At that unearthly hour, rooms were assigned us, and we fairly rolled into them, and were in bed in quick haste. How James and Bert roared, as we walked into our room, and they had a good look at me by gaslight. With my rubber coat and cape, and my little fur shoulder wrap over it, my poor wreck of a tin-pan hat, stuck back on my head, and my hair hanging in a regular fringe, I must have presented a sorry sight; and the boys laughed hard enough at me, to make me right angry, if I had not been so tired. All Bert could do was to wave a good-night, as he grabbed his "grip" and was shown to his room.

SUNDAY, JUNE 21ST.

NO one of our little party appeared, or showed any signs of life, until noon, to-day. Then we came from our rooms, looking as if we had been on an awful spree, but were trying to brace up. A luncheon and breakfast combined, and at half-past two o'clock, we took the omnibus for the depot, and the 3.05 P. M. train for San Francisco. While waiting for the train to start, Bert and James smoked out on the platform, and when I looked out a little after and finally joined them, I found a Chinaman conversing with them. He had come to them and spoken, said he had seen us all in Chinatown, and proved to be one of our friends there,—Ah Fung by name. Somebody in San José had seen a Chinese funeral, a couple of days before we arrived, and they said it was very singular. The Chinamen rode in carriages, but they made an unearthly noise, with gongs and bells, and acted as if they were possessed of evil spirits. They have a great fear of death, and generally hurry their dead to the cemeteries, as fast as possible. During the drive to the grave-yard, all of them throw little colored pieces of paper out of the carriage windows, in every direction ; and the more they can scatter in this way, the better for the dead, for each piece of paper has nine holes in it, and their theory is, that the Devil must go in and out each hole; and the more they can distribute, the more work the old fellow has to do, and therefore cannot catch the mourners, before they have buried their dead. They have a regular chase with the Devil, which shall first arrive at the cemetery.

We were rejoiced to reach San Francisco again, for, although, as a City we do not like it, it was a bit like home to us, this time. The porters, bellmen and waiters, all welcomed us ; and as James said, it was pleasant to have somebody to speak to you, and welcome you back. We found letters from home also, and after reading them, dining, etc., we went to our room and had a quiet, undisturbed evening, writing my journal, and James reading.

MONDAY, JUNE 22ND.

WE could not think of leaving San Francisco, without seeing the Golden Gate Park, and the famous Cliff House; and as the winds are high in the afternoon, James, Bert and I started at ten o'clock, for a drive, first taking my camera to have the films developed. We drove through the Park to the Cliff House, which is on the Pacific coast. Golden Gate Park is pretty in some parts of it, but it is young yet, and does not begin to compare with our Eastern parks. It has many obstacles to sur-mount, for it is built on sand-hills, and is also swept, at this time of year, by the destructive winds, which dry up everything, and make sad havoc with trees and shrubs as well. But, giving it every benefit of every doubt, it is an unattractive place to us.

After leaving the Park, we drove along the beach to the Cliff House, which is, as its name implies, built on a cliff over-looking three huge rocks, on which live the celebrated sea-lions. These are the attraction, of course, and we spent a long time, watching the great monsters, and studying their ungainly and awkward movements. Eleven hundred sea-lions live on these rocks. They chose this spot many years ago, and are true to it, never deserting their home. They are creatures of habit too, always going to the exact place on the rocks, which they have had before, which, if occupied by an intruder, is quickly fought for. Some of these sea-lions are tremendous! Four huge fellows are "monarchs of all they survey" on these rocks, and they weigh from fourteen hundred to two thousand pounds. We saw three of them;—Brigham Young, one is called, and another Ben Butler; the latter is a re-markable likeness. They have real battles, and bark like dogs, when angry. After watching them some time, we drove up still higher, to view the private residence and grounds of Mr. Sutro, called "Sutro Heights." It is a marvelous place, beautifully laid out, with flower-beds equal to Del Monte in design, but not so many, of course. The grounds are full of every conceivable kind of statuary, or "stationery" as a man told us. The views are extensive, and altogether it was a most original and unusual place, well worth seeing.

We reached the hotel again at three o'clock, had our luncheon, and then went shopping. In the evening, Miss B. and Mr. H. were with us, listening to the music in the Court; and after a little packing, we retired.

THE YOSEMITE

TUESDAY, JUNE 23RD.

SAN FRANCISCO to Berenda! We were up, and ready to see Mr. H. this morning, at nine o'clock, as he had promised to, go with his father-in-law, to Palo Alto, to see Hon. Leland Stanford's stables, and was therefore obliged to say good-bye to us early. James and I felt badly about it, as we have shared the same fate for four weeks, and we have enjoyed Mr. H. wonderfully; he has done so much to make us happy, and has been a delightful travelling companion.

After breakfast, James went on errands, to see Mr. S., get tickets, etc., and I went out "shopping" for a few necessary articles. I was back at half-past eleven, then packed, and at 2 P. M. I was ready to start,—had a bite of lunch, sent a scrawl, added to a line from Jamie, to the three at home, and at half-past two o'clock "we two babes" started out alone, for a trip to the Yosemite. We went to the Oakland Ferry, crossed, and took the train there. On the boat, we saw two young men, who went up the Mt. Hamilton trip with us, and although we did not know them well, we were glad to hear they were bound for the Yosemite too, for it was some one to talk to. As we turned from speaking to them, we saw a little German bride and her big German husband, who had sat at our table at Del Monte, and to whom I had spoken once or twice. Four familiar faces,—and in a strange part of the country, among strange scenes and people, familiar faces are a blessing. James and I had the drawing-room, but a warm wave seemed to have found and decided to accompany us, and we were remarkably uncomfortable, during the night. James slept but little, and I managed to put in a few good hours.

We had rather an uninteresting ride. California has been delightful to us, in every particular, and in every trip, until this ride from San Francisco to Berenda. We had supper at "a railroad eating-room," The place is called Lathrop. When we reached Berenda, the car we were in was side-tracked ; and as the town of Berenda consists of a railroad depot, and a few houses, instead of being side-tracked in real Berenda, we stood all night out on a genuine Nebraska prairie, a most lonely, God-forsaken spot. No Indian or out-law molested us, and we had a quiet but very trying night, it was so warm.

WEDNESDAY, JUNE 24TH.

A T four and a half o'clock this morning, James Walcott Haslehurst was up, washed and dressed, and in his right mind ! I followed suit, as

the car was to start at five o'clock, and I thought it
would be pleasanter to dress quietly, than to a waltz
step. We were relieved to be up and out, and half
past five found James and myself sitting on the
back platform, as wide awake as we ever are at
home, at nine o'clock. The dust and cinders soon
drove us into our little room again, and we were no
sooner in and comfortably placed, than "Raymond" sang the Porter, and out we bounced, bag
and baggage. Raymond, thought I,—where is
Raymond? Surely that white house, covered with
vines, does not constitute the town of Raymond;
but it did. As I looked, two or three other little
huts loomed up; but with a thanksgiving in my
heart, that fate had spared us from the necessity of
eating our breakfast in any of them, James and I
approached the vine covered piazza, of what proved
to be rather a nice place, after all. In front of the
house was a platform, on which, in the most picturesque groups, the Yosemite passengers had piled
their baggage. It is not well to bring a trunk into
the valley, unless one comes for some time; so the
number and variety, the shapes and kinds and marvelous contours of those parcels, beggar description:
little and big, round and flat, neat and untidy, and
all in separate little piles, to be put into the coaches
before starting.

At a quarter past six, we all went to breakfast.
It was good, as such meals go,—nothing surprising,
but one could take enough bread and coffee, to last

for a few hours. Our repast was soon over, and at seven o'clock, sharp, two four-horse coaches came to the door, luggage and grips were stored away, passengers given their allotted places, and away we started, with as blazing and hot a sun, as one ever cares to have, pouring down on our unprotected heads. "Unprotected heads," does anyone exclaim? James and I were the only sufferers. The best seats, on such drives and such stages, are with the driver, and out from under cover, and we were considered fortunate indeed, to have secured them, a week ago. But we had such a dreadful morning, —nothing but awful dust, intolerable heat and real discomfort. This was not visited on our heads alone, for the people inside suffered as much from dust, as we did. We thought ourselves fortunate, however, in being outside, as whatever little stray breeze came our way, we were sure to catch.

The driver said, as we drove out of Raymond, that the drive to " Grant's "—the dinner-station,— was most trying and uninteresting,—and it was so in every sense. The country was lovely, but somehow or other, there was not much to interest one. One little encounter was quite exciting. Coiled up in the road, so that one wheel nearly passed over it, was a real big rattle-snake, about four feet long. One of the passengers spied it, and at once, driver and passengers, with sticks and stones, were out by the snake, trying to kill it. It was a lively young fellow, and showed fight from the first, evading his

would-be assassins very adroitly. Finally the
driver pinned him down with a stick; and then how
his poisonous tongue did run out, in energetic little
jerks, trying to hurt somebody. At last, his rattling
highness escaped his wooden pin, and jumped right
in among the warriors bold, and they all jumped
in turn about ten feet, in every direction. The
quick, active driver, with the strength of a Hercules,
gave one good blow at that moment, however, and
a limp, lifeless head was the result. Then the remains were brought, for inspection, to the stage,
and the rattle was taken from the end of the tail.
Twelve rattles were found; and if the theory is correct, that each rattle represents one year, his de-
ceased snakeship was just twelve years old.

This wild country is running over with animal
life. We saw squirrels by the hundreds, rabbits by
dozens, and quail, buzzards, lizards without numbers,
and even a wild cat (but a dead one, thank fortune).
One funny, unusual sight, was an old man on horseback, herding geese. He seemed the biggest goose
of the lot! One gets so used to strange names for
places, people, and horses, that they fail, after a time,
to impress one as anything unusual or peculiar; but
as we drove along this morning, and passed several
teams, hauling loads, the driver of our stage called
out to the driver of another: "Say, how does Jimmie Neversweat work now?" Poor little Jimmie
Neversweat—he was a poor, tired, worn-out little
animal.

Alexander Early used to drive a stage into this Valley, and all the drivers know him. When we asked our driver, Thomas Gordon, he said: "Know Alex. Early, gas-sy Alex. we called him." Then he told us a story, quite in keeping with Mr. Early's yarn to us. The pine trees in this Valley sometimes die at the top, and therefore present a strange appearance. A traveller asked Alex. Early, once, "why so many trees died at the top?" "Oh, the season's so short here, the sap don't have time to get up there," he answered.

As we drove through the country, this morning, we saw a queer wooden affair, running along for miles, and raised on stilts, to keep it at a certain angle. We, of course, were curious about it, and asked the necessary questions, finding out that this queer arrangement was a lumber flume, running for sixty-five miles through the country, to a saw-mill. The flume has a stream of water flowing through it, and the wood is tied in certain sized piles, and floated through. It was decidedly novel to us.

Well, as we crept over hill and dale, we tried to feel glad we were there; but a sigh would escape somebody, once in a while, and it was quite evident that no one was overjoyed, to be in such a dusty scrape. We reached a place—or rather a house— called Grant's; and then the honest convictions, of the souls of our passengers, found expression, and everybody wondered " if all travellers to the Yosemite had turned liars, from such afflictions and trials,

—if it was really worth so much discomfort—if there was really anything to see, after all." But, after as nice and tempting a meal as one could wish to have, we all took our places in the stage again, and went on. Nothing pleasant presented itself, until about four o'clock, when, after climbing by inches the highest of high hills, we reached the summit of the mountain, and were 5,600 feet above sea-level, and about four thousand above the valley. There we saw beauty enough to pay us for our long uncomfortable trip. We drove into such a forest of loveliness, with huge pine trees rising hundreds of feet, on all sides of us, with their great straight trunks and magnificently mottled bark. The ground was covered, each side of our roadway, with mammoth ferns, and a sea of huge collossal pine cones. A peculiar growth, like whiskers, but of strong wooden spikes, are all about the trunks of these pine trees ; and a bright vivid green moss clings most lovingly to these rope-like limbs, and sometimes covers them entirely. The contrast of this bright green moss, with the darker evergreen foliage, and the rich loam of the earth, made a picture never seen by us before. Then, after those seven hours of hot discomfort, we were glad we had come. When we reached Wawona, we found the loveliest and cleanest of little hotels, most attractively surrounded, and delightful as well, in food and lodging. After a good pounding, by the corps of attendants, who appear with a brush and duster, on arrival of every stage, we had dinner, then visited the studio of the artist, Thomas Hill, of Yosemite fame, whose medals of honor and reward, show well that his work is highly approved by judges of art.

A letter, written to the three at home, finished the evening, and before eleven o'clock we had retired.

The distance driven to-day was thirty-nine miles.

THURSDAY, JUNE 25TH.

A T 5.30 A. M. we were awakened and up, and although poor James groaned, "When will I get rested?" we had to be up and away at 7 A. M. It was a beautiful morning, exquisite in every way, except the heat, which was intense. We did nothing but go up and down hills, but such awfully steep places, where our road lay right on the edge of the deepest precipices. We could look hundreds of feet right straight down into the valley, over the tops of the highest trees, with such grand, such magnificent views for hundreds of miles. It was a wild, exciting drive, through the most beautiful wooded country, around curves by the dozens, when the four horses would go as if demented, or chased by some fiend. We forded little streams, crossed innumerable bridges, and had a glorious drive. Our only anxiety was in meeting teams or stages; then sometimes our hearts were in our mouths, for the roads were so narrow, and there seemed no place to turn out. One poor, lone man had to turn out for us, as the stage has the right of way, and as he sat in his little light wagon, he looked the picture of fright, and exclaimed, in an agonized way, "The bank's going from under me!" "Serves you right!" exclaimed our driver; "you should have waited in some safe place for the stages."

Our drive this morning was twenty-six miles, and we reached the Yosemite Valley at 1.30 P. M.

The Yosemite Valley is just eight miles in length, and when travellers first see it, it is from a height of about six thousand five hundred feet. As we turned a sharp curve, in descending Mount Chowchile, the Valley was seen suddenly; and nothing, that I can write, can give any idea of the impression that first view gives one. Never in my life, but once, have I felt so before; and that was, when we stood at the foot of Mount Blanc, and the clouds parted, and we saw the reflection of the setting sun, on that mountain of ice. Now, as then, words were gone; my tongue refused to articulate, and I could not even think. I felt as Moses must have felt, when the Lord appeared unto him on the Mount. I only looked, wondered, and admired, in awe and reverence, this great marvel of nature. Rocks of all shapes and tints, in most majestic magnificence, walled us in, as we descended into the Valley, with the most brilliantly bright falls of water, the most luxurious growths of trees, shrubs and flowers, and the grandest grandeur ever seen, on every side. It has been said, that "it is not easy to describe, in words, the precise impressions which great objects make upon us"; and I felt this then, and realize it more now, when I try to write of this entrance of ours into, and our first glimpse of, the Yosemite Valley. Actual objects, and places, like Chinatown, etc., one can picture and portray by word or pen, sometimes; but these great scenes, these wonders in nature, only sink deep into the heart, and defy pen or words, to picture or describe the impressions made. It makes one feel the presence of the Creator of all this wondrous beauty, in the rocks and rills, the mountains and myriad wonders; and the heart stands still, in silent homage to the Great God; and prayer and praise come intuitively to a thoughtful mind.

After dinner, or rather lunch, James and I came to our comfortable room in the Stoneman House, and after necessary ablutions, slept soundly for several hours. In the evening, we chatted with some fellow-passengers, sent a letter on its way to the three at home, and started early for the "Land of Nod."

FRIDAY, JUNE 26TH.

IN the Yosemite Valley! Breakfast is over here at 8.30 A. M., and James and I managed to scramble in, just at the last minute. Most of our companions had made early starts, on excursions, etc., but we were too tired for much sight-seeing to-day. It was too lovely to stay indoors, so Jamie and I took a walk, through the most beautiful woods,

STONEMAN HOUSE, YOSEMITE VALLEY.

along the Merced River. We came to such pretty bridges, made of huge logs, which tempted us to cross over to a lovely little island, surrounded by fine rapids. Still another log bridge, and another, enticed us along, until we had wandered some distance, and seen such dainty bits of views, such picturesque islands, fine trees, and dashing rapids, and real beauty, that we were well satisfied with our morning, and felt repaid for our exertions in tramping.

We spent a quiet afternoon and evening, reading, etc. I managed to write much in my journal, and we both felt better for the day's rest.

This far-away spot, in the heart of the Yosemite Valley, sixty-five miles in one direction, from the railroad, and ninety in the other, seems the place of meeting for all nations. The Antipodes appeared to-day, in one stage-load. One man from Scotland, another from England, one from Tasmania, one from North Australia, two from Calcutta, one from China, came to-day. Two are here from Mexico, one from Germany, and America is well represented.

SATURDAY, JUNE 27TH.

LOVELY day, and lovely at 5.30 A. M., when we arose, to be ready to go, at seven o'clock, to Mirror Lake, to see the sun rise *in* the lake. Mirror Lake is about a mile from the hotel, and at that hour in the morning, it is as calm and smooth as a genuine mirror. Every mountain is reflected, as clearly as it is seen above the lake, and it is an exquisite sight. Groups were scattered along the shore, gazing at one rocky reflection in the water, called the "Old Man in the Mountain." About a quarter before eight, an ominous silence showed that all were intently watching a little rim of light, that was creeping along the edge of this rocky projection. It seemed a halo of radiance, and deepened and deepened, until all at once, Old Sol made his appearance, reflecting such a brilliant blaze, from the depths of the water, that one could look but a moment at him,—his light was as intense as an electric light. It was a most unusual experience. We then returned to the hotel; but the rest of the party separated on different excursions.

One trip is to Nevada and Vernal Falls, another to an immensely high point, called Glacier Point. Both trips must be made on horseback, or mule back; and although James and I had planned to do both, when we finally came into the valley, a peculiar nervousness came over James, and seeing his condition, I could not urge it. The trails are very steep, and make some people so dizzy, that they have to be blind-folded in coming down, and James said he felt he could never even reach the top. We spent a quiet morning, an opportunity I seized for writing; and after lunch, at 2 P.M. we took a carriage, and a good guide, and drove all over the valley, down nine miles below the beginning of the valley, in the Cañon, saw all the falls, all points of interest, etc.,

EL CAPITAN.

and were gone four hours and a half. We had a lovely time.

We went first to Yosemite Falls. It is a very high waterfall, and is divided into three parts. The upper part is thirty-four feet wide, at the top, and drops 1,502 feet, without a single break. The middle fall is over 500 feet, and the lower 487 feet, making 2,550 feet of waterfall. It is the finest thing of the kind we have ever seen. There is another, in the valley opposite this, called Sentinel Fall, which is the highest in the Yosemite; it falls 3,270 feet, but is broken in its descent many times. We became familiar with the great rocks, El Capitan (3,300 feet above us), The Three Brothers (the highest rising 3,830 feet, above the valley), The Three Graces, Cathedral Spires, North Dome (rising 3,700 feet), South, or Half Dome (5,000 feet above the valley). They are superb, and all rise, as you see, over a half mile, and one nearly a mile, right up into the air, on all sides of us. There are many more, Sentinel Rock, Washington Column, Star King, and Cloud's Rest; the latter is 9,772 feet above the sea-level, and 5,780 feet above the valley. The delicate dainty waterfalls are many in number, and make such refreshing contrasts, with the great granite boulders. As we drove down the valley, the driver stopped near El Capitan, and asked us if we could pick out "The Lone Tree." Sure enough, there in a crack in the rock, 1,000 feet up from the valley, with no other trees near it, grows a cedar tree. It looked to us about *four inches* high; but it measures just 125 feet in height. We climbed up the trail, to the foot of Yosemite Falls, and were well repaid, for we were able to realize better the enormous height of the falls, and were able to get good and wet, with the heavy spray. After a drive to the Cascade Fall, and along a series of beautiful rapids, we came back, close to the beautiful " Bridal Veil Fall." It is the loveliest in the valley ! It falls 860 feet, without a break, and it is so coquettishly tossed and swayed, by every breeze that blows, that it waves and curves, in a most fascinating manner. About five o'clock every day, the sun touches it, in such a way, that it is all prismatic colors, and as the spray is tossed, the rainbow widens or decreases, rises or falls, at the caprice of the zephyrs. We sat in the carriage a long time, watching the picture. One minute, the rainbow would sweep across the rock, in a broad band of color, for a thousand feet or more ; the next moment, it would arch gracefully over the rocks, at the base of the fall, or perhaps spread upwards like a ribbon. It was exquisite !

I must not fail to mention the roads, through which we drove, the most picturesque ever seen. Overgrown with ferns, wild flowers, vines, the great trees themselves, with lovely green moss on them, the driveways in the valley are most beautiful, in their very wildness. We agreed when we returned, that of all our drives in Colorado, and elsewhere, none had surpassed, in wild beauty and grandeur, this drive of ours, in the Yosemite Valley.

A letter written home was the only incident of the evening.

BEAUTIFUL day, but it began very warm, and promised a regular broiler! James and I breakfasted at the very last minute, as usual, then sat on the piazza awhile, with the K—s, Mrs. J— and a party from Peekskill, then came to our rooms for a quiet morning, which I spent in writing my journal. About noon, we all congregated on the piazza, to see three stage loads, of hot dusty passengers, arrive. Gen. Schofield, and his new wife, arrived, with a little coterie of friends, also an English Baronet,—Sir F. and Lady B. After lunch, James and I again sought the seclusion of our own apartment, one reading, while the other wrote.

Yesterday, we were much amused, by a conversation I had, with our guide and driver, on the probable formation of this Yosemite Valley. Some scientists hold to the Volcanic theory,—that much has been split and broken, by volcanic action, earthquakes, and such forces. In fact, we know it all came to be, in the beginning, by these great forces. The greater number of scientists, however, hold to the glacial formation, to the rounding and polishing and cutting, of these great masses, by the ice action of later date ; and to me, this is the most plausible of any theory. There are positive evidences, on every side, of glacial action, and proofs positive, by terminal moraines, in this immediate neighborhood. It is as clearly the result of the Ice Age, as anything we have yet seen. Great rocks are piled upon one another; then, every once in a while, a tremendous boulder is isolated, in some green field; and the question arises at once,—how did that great mass get there? Oh, if some spirit, or power, could make these great rocks unfold their secret, and speak of the mysteries of their being! If a single stone would only confess its secret, and turn state's evidence on the spot, what a blessing it would be to science, and what a blow to some cherished theories and laws! But no: each little stone, however small, each blade of grass and tiniest leaf, keep folded up, within their breasts, the story of their birth; and the inquirer goes away, little wiser than he came. All bask in the sunshine, and smile together, in their silent splendor and happiness, and keep their secrets, until the Author of their being shall bid them speak. The waterfalls and cascades sing away the hours, but their language is one of sounds and sighings; and no student, of even the ancient hieroglyphics, has yet interpreted their little humming and murmuring songs. So we leave the beautiful Yosemite Valley, in its silent grandeur; but we feel wiser and better in our hearts, because we have beheld and pondered awhile, on these wonders of our God.

Our Sunday evening was spent on the piazza of the Stoneman House, in the pleasant company of the Peekskill party. Being friends of Mrs. Gen. S. before her marriage, she, of course, joined them here; and James and I met her, and were pleased with her simple girlish manners, and shall meet her again in San Francisco.

James foolishly went to the piazza, about five o'clock, to look at the thermometer. In the office, it was 84 degrees; on the piazza, it was 98 degrees, in the shade, and in the sun, 115 degrees. We nearly melted, after we knew how hot it was; but in the evening, it was delightfully cool and comfortable.

It is beautiful here; the Valley is exquisite, with its carpet of ferns, and wild flowers, and the great rock mountains, so majestic and wonderful, some so high, with their crowns of pure white snow—looking like a great white throne, waiting for its King.

MONDAY, JUNE 29TH.

AT half-past four o'clock this morning, the porter knocked on our door, and James and I were up in a twinkle, and dressed and ready for breakfast, at a quarter past five. It was hard to get up, but once started, it was delightful; and the earliest hours of the day are always so quiet and peaceful.

At 6 A. M. sharp, we were in our high seats by the driver, and started promptly for our long drive, which, for eight miles through the Valley, was ideal; —the birds sang a good-bye to us, and we were really sorry to leave. Some tourists were out, with rod and line, ready to catch fish, and bugs, too ; for we had a naturalist in our midst, from the Smithsonian Institute, who was collecting and preparing specimens, for classification. After driving through the ferns and flowers, our road turned suddenly; and for two full hours, the dear old horses pulled and tugged, panted and perspired, dragging the heavy stage-load of passengers, up a very steep hill, rising half a mile in five miles, such an incline as we had not been up before. Our drive of twenty-six miles, to Wawona, which place we reached at twelve o'clock, was most interesting and exciting. Our trip *into* the Valley was a little nerve-trying, as we had a driver we could not feel confidence in, and a man who made his horses too nervous and excitable. As we turned those dangerous curves, on the edge of the precipices, we were frightened by his carelessness, and really dreaded the drive *out*. It was such a magnificent trip, however, that we were sorry when it was at an end ; and we can look forward with pleasure, to coming into the Yosemite Valley again, with the same driver we had to-day,— Uriah Toby by name,—or as the children call him, " Maria." Owing to his skillful management, we turned those sharp curves, and flew over hills, and through the valleys, with only interest and excitement in our progress, and not one fear, as to our safety.

After reaching Wawona and having lunch, at 1.15

P. M. we started again in a stage, with Toby, to visit the Big Trees. It was broiling then,—the sun was at his highest, and was sending down burning bolts upon our already hot heads; but we were soon so interested in our surroundings, that we forgot the heat, and decided finally, that we would rather bake, in the process of seeing those giants of the Sierra Nevadas, than not to see them at all. The great trees of Mariposa County, grow in the highest altitude; and in our drive of eight miles, to the Big Trees, we went up 2,600 feet, bringing us to an altitude of between 6,500 and 6,600 feet. The Sugar Pines and Cedars, of the evergreen tribe, were tremendous, in the woods through which we passed; and we exclaimed, dozens of times, as some straight trunk raised its branches to nearly two hundred feet;—but when we saw the Big Trees,—the real live wonders of the forests, we could not find words to express our surprise and admiration. They silence one completely! As we drove along, these giant trees, with their red trunks, stood by our roadway, like huge monsters; and the "Three Sentinels" were our first introduction, to this peculiar specimen of forest growth, the "Sequoia Gigantea," which is more ancient than any other family of trees. Then, in groups of twos and threes, sometimes more, we met these giants, and were lost in admiration, as we gazed at trees which, scientists say, are fully 5,000 years old! "The Three Sisters" stood on one side of the drive, with "The

Big Brother" opposite. "Princeton," "Harvard," "Lincoln," "Washington," "The Faithful Couple," with "Brooklyn" and "New York" near, "Massachusetts" not far from "St. Louis," and so many gigantic giants surrounded us, that we were absolutely getting accustomed to their size, until we came to the greatest of all. "The Grizzley," it is called, or "Yo Semite," which means the same thing. We all left the stages here, to walk about this monster, which is thirty-three feet in diameter; and eight feet up from the ground, it measures one hundred and one feet in circumference. It stands two hundred and ninety feet high, and one of its branches is six feet in diameter. It is collossal, grand, magnificent, its trunk so dark and red, so massive and tremendous! Another great wonder is the tree "Wawona," *through which we drove.* When the Indians lived in these woods, they used to burn them out every year, to clear away the underbrush, so they could hunt better. Some of these huge monsters were badly burned, and Wawona was also damaged, so that, some one in authority, tried the experiment of cutting out the burned part. and making a drive-way through the tree. It is a grand success, and is a wonder! A four-horse stage goes through easily, and as the tree is twenty-eight feet in diameter, the opening accommodates not only the stage, but both pairs of horses, with the exception of the leaders' heads. The two tallest trees in the entire grove (which contains about six

WAIKINA.

hundred mammoth trees, four hundred of which are
marvels), measure three hundred and thirty-seven
feet. If any one will take a cord, and measure one
hundred and one feet, then place it in a circle, a little
idea can be obtained of the size of "The Grizzley,"
the largest of all trees. We all stopped at a little
log cabin, where the "Guardian" lives, for these
woods are carefully protected from fire and damage.
We found samples of bark and wood, cones of huge
size, and some curios. The strangest thing is, that
these huge cones are not the fruit of the biggest trees.
The huge trees have small cones, but the sugar
pines have the large ones. These pines have often
the bright green moss on their trunks ; and as the
moss always grows on the north side of a tree, the
Indians used them as their compasses, and guides.
They could always tell the points of the compass, by
the moss-trees.

While at this "Log Cabin," we all climbed up, by
means of a ladder, on to the trunk of one of the big
trees, which had fallen. It accommodated about
twenty of us, on the roots alone. It was huge!—A
great giant, named "Grant," stood near the cabin,
and somebody suggested that we should make a
circle, and see how many it took, to surround the
trunk of a moderate sized tree. Accordingly we
joined hands about the tree, and then, breaking the
circle, straightened out in a line, "to count noses."
Consternation showed on many faces, as our count
stood "thirteen." "How dreadful!" said some-

body. " Oh, dear!" exclaimed Mr. W., of Tasmania, to me, "that's bad luck; I wouldn't have had that happen for anything!" " What happen?" said I. " Why, there were *thirteen* of us around that tree." " No, indeed; there were fourteen of us in all," quoth I; " surely the tree counted for something, and made fourteen of us." We had a fine time there; then taking our seats beside Toby again, we had a flying trip down the mountain to Wawona ; and although we had driven forty-six miles, since six o'clock in the morning, and had been eleven hours in the stage, we were really sorry to think that our day was over. One thing I must chronicle,—it takes nineteen people, with arms outstretched, to encircle old Mr. Grizzley.

In the evening we chatted with our German bride and groom, Mr. and Mrs. M., of Mexico, and the Peekskill party ; and we went again to Mr. Hill's studio, where James presented me with two souvenirs, painted on the natural wood of the big trees, one of "Wawona" with the driveway, the other of Bridal Veil Falls, in Yosemite, both lovely, and Mr. Hill's work.

TUESDAY, JUNE 30TH.

NOTHING but awful heat to chronicle to-day. At 8 A.M. we started in the stage, for the dusty and disagreeable part of the Yosemite trip, the drive from Wawona to Raymond. It is thirty-nine miles, and takes from eight o'clock until half past eleven, when we stopped for luncheon at Grant's. Then from half past twelve, to half past five, it was dreadful,—so hot we could hardly breathe—but while everybody perspired and groaned, James and I had not one drop of perspiration, to moisten gloves or collars. We stopped at a little mining camp, to take on a mail bag (a place bearing the refined name of "Grub Gulch"), and seeing a thermometer hanging near, asked the man to let us look at it. It hung in the shade, but I saw, with mine own eyes, the mercury at 105 degrees. We were driving in the sun, and it must have been ten degrees hotter. When we reached Raymond, at 5.30 P.M. the thermometer stood at 108 degrees. We had our supper there, then took the train for Berenda, and in the car, the thermometer was 102 degrees, at 8 P.M. James and I felt as if we were burning up, inside and outside, but we were as dry as bones! Queer heat it was, not a drop of moisture in it.

The car for San Francisco, in which all our party were, goes to Berenda, where it is side-tracked until 3 A.M. when a Los Angeles train, going to San Francisco, picks it up. We had to leave the train and wait at Berenda, from 8 to 10.25 P.M., when a train, going to Los Angeles, picked *us* up.

Berenda consists of a station and nine houses, by actual count! When we left the train, the porter said: "There are generally lots of tramps about, you had better keep close to your baggage." We could not find chairs, or even a bench, so we took a baggage truck, put our things on it, James loaded his pistol, and we sat ourselves down to watch and wait, with the one mild man who was going our way.

Soon, down the tracks, walked a little party of our friends from the car, who came to pay us a visit. After a while, as the extreme heat made us thirsty, (at Berenda, the thermometer had been 117 degrees) these good friends carried me with them, to the car, (one remaining with James), and treating me as a guest, they entertained me accordingly. Then they escorted me back; and some of the gentlemen, Dr. B—— of England, and Mr. W—— of Tasmania, remained with us until ten o'clock, so our weary vigil was brightened and shortened. At last, our train came; we boarded it, engaged the Drawing Room, and were soon as comfortable as we have ever been, in any place, on such a warm night, and were too tired to stay awake, to comment on the heat.

SOUTHERN CALIFORNIA

AS James and I have comforted ourselves all along, by saying, " It is not half as warm as it might be," so we started out this morning, and although we kept hearing people groan, on all sides of us, and poor little children cry, we were remarkably comfortable. The thermometer performed some famous gymnastics, however, a record of which I kept as we went along.

We breakfasted at Mojave, a most God-forsaken place, at the entrance to the Desert of Mojave, and we had an awful meal. The thermometer we saw there, at half past eight o'clock in the morning, registered 98 degrees. In our car it was 99 degrees, and at noon, the thermometer stood at 100 degrees. Last night at Raymond, one queer thing was the amount of heat, which was communicated to every dish and spoon. I lifted a glass dish, full of nuts and raisins, and it was so hot I could hardly hold it; and every spoon and fork, and every dish and glass was *hot*, not merely warm, but burning.

We had quite a comfortable trip, in spite of the

heat. Nothing was interesting, for we came through a desert, whose only redeeming feature was the peculiar growth of cacti, or Yucca Palm. These large tree-palms grow in among the sage-brush, and are as large, oftentimes, as apple trees. They give a little variety to the dreariness, and are remarkable in themselves, but they have no real beauty, and only vary the monotony.

James made such an impression on all the train men to-day, that they could not do enough for him. He expressed a desire to ride on the engine, and the conductor promised he should; and he went, and had a glorious time, "The event of my trip," he exclaimed when he returned; "it was most interesting and exciting."

We reached Los Angeles at 2.30 P.M. and came at once to the Westminster Hotel, where letters from home greeted us, to our joy.

THURSDAY, JULY 2ND.

UP at about half past eight, to find the day bright and lovely, but warm already. After breakfast, James and I wandered about the streets, looking in shop windows, etc., until twelve o'clock, when we returned, I to write, James to read.

After lunch and a rest, James and I went out, at 5 P. M., for a lovely drive, all over the City of Los Angeles. The heat here disappears at sunset, and the nights are always cool and delightful. We chose a splendid time for a drive, for the lights and shadows were beautiful. Los Angeles is as pretty a city as one can wish to see. The houses are, many of them, really magnificent; but the full glory of the place is in the trees. Pepper trees, with their delicate dainty foliage, line the streets, with palms, planted in wild profusion anywhere and everywhere,—palms that grow like our commonest trees, before houses of every grade, the lowliest cottage having, before its door, the finest of palm trees, banana trees, and bushes, and shrubs. Rose bushes climb all over everything, even creep up on to the roofs of houses, and cover them oftentimes with such a luxurious growth of vines and blossoms. Rubber trees, as big as our chestnuts—only not so tall,—great magnolia trees in full blossom ; dates, fifty years old and older, and oh, such wealth of beautiful buds and blossoms! Los Angeles attracts us more than any little city we have seen, since we started. The buildings are large and imposing, the streets finely paved, and everything has an air of wealth and luxury. Judge Silent's place is a marvel of beauty. The driver said, in answer to our exclamation of delight, "If that place pleases you now, you should see it when all the flowers are in bloom—in mid-winter—then the air is almost sickening, it is so sweet from the flowers."

Of course we are here in the wrong season, for winter is the time for Southern California, but we think it better to see it now, and dream what it must be in winter, than not to see it at all.

FROM Los Angeles to Coronado. We were obliged to make an early start this morning, and were up soon after six o'clock, having breakfast at seven, and at half-past seven, we started for the train, which brought us to San Diego. Being the day before the " Glorious Fourth," a crowd was anticipated, and we were advised to reach the train in plenty of time, to secure good seats in the sleeper; (there are no chair cars here, such as we have in the East). It was a very bright day, and we had a very dusty and warm trip, until we suddenly came to the Pacific Coast, when it was lovely and cool, and has been so ever since. We passed through such funny little towns on our way—so Spanish in name and appearance. Many of the towns and cities are Spanish in language, the inhabitants having come from Mexico. Santa Anna is one, Sorrento (Italian flavor) another, San Juan by the Sea, Encinetas, Orange, San Fernando, etc. All are small villages, with most unattractive surrounding country, for the desert makes itself at home, even in Southern California, and in spite of labor and irrigation, the white alkali dust rises to the surface, and must be so discouraging to the people, who work hard to rid themselves of it. It has always been my idea, that all Southern California was fertile and beautiful, with flowers, vineyards and orange groves ; and our first introduction to the State was to decidedly deepen that impression. No more beautiful country can exist, than that between San Francisco and Del Monte, and no more fertile farm lands, fine orchards, flowers and fruits. The Santa Clara Valley, through which we drove to Mt. Hamilton, was ideal, not one inch, on hill or dale, uncultivated or uncared for. A veritable park it is, all that vast valley, and most beautiful. Of course, the further south we came, the more fertile we expected the country to be. Imagine our horror, when a regular Nebraska desert, a vast and dreary waste, confronted us on our journey to Los Angeles. It does not extend to Los Angeles, but within forty miles of it. Beyond beautiful Los Angeles, the desert conditions prevail in part, and especially barren are the lands near San Diego, along the ocean. But every farmer, and every humble cottager, has planted brilliant geraniums, which grow like trees, bright yellow daisies, pink asters, and all kinds of flowers, about the modest tumble-down homes;—vines crawl all over them, and the dreary surroundings are forgotten, in the flood of color, which make a pathway of beauty, through which the train passes. The approach to San Diego was very picturesque and foreign in aspect. The harbor is marvelously fine, one of the best on the coast, and the land rises very perpendicularly about the town, and makes a half circle of mountains, an artistic background for the pretty little city, which is built on a series of foot-hills.

We did not wait long, however, to admire San

Diego, but jumped into a Hotel Del Coronado stage, and were driven to the ferry-boat, a little one-horse concern, which soon carried us safely across to Coronado, which is a sand peninsular, curving around like Fire Island, or Sandy Hook. The Hotel is a mile or more from the landing, and the drive to it was a pretty one. There is a steam motor, as they call it, which flies all over the island, up to the Hotel, etc.; and the railroad is lined, on both sides, with magnificent great palm trees, placed about twenty feet apart, quite regularly planted, making an avenue of palms, through which the railroad passes. I counted for a while, then grew tired; but half way up, there were two hundred and thirty palms. I have never seen such tropical growth as is here in Southern California. The commonest flowers grow on bushes, almost like trees.

As we drove up to the Hotel Del Coronado (or Hotel of a Crown), we were greatly impressed by its magnificent dimensions. It is simply huge, and a magnificent structure, in a most attractive and artistic style of architecture. Gables, chimneys, balconies, appear in the most unexpected places, and in the most picturesque positions. It is built around a court, full of beautiful blossoms, just as Del Monte is, and is quite foreign; and the interior is beautiful, Fine rooms open one from the other, billiard rooms for ladies, writing rooms, beautiful reception rooms, a most elegant music room (the finest I have ever seen), with a daintily decorated and artistic stage, and pianos are everywhere. It is situated, like our Oriental, directly on the sea, and has just the surroundings of our beach hotel. A museum, containing fine specimens, a hot-plunge bathing house, cold ones as well, surround the Hotel in separate buildings, and make it attractive to all kinds of people. The dining room, which is beautiful, is made of Eastern oak, walls, floor and ceiling, and every inch of this wood highly polished. At dinner there is always music; four well-trained musicians play good selections, and make the dinner hour most attractive. The furniture of the dining room is unusually fine for a hotel. High oak chairs with tapestry seats, such as one would have in a home, with round and square tables, little and big, and fine china, good silver, glass and flowers on every table, make an attractive dining room. This room seats, without crowding, five hundred people; in "the season," it accommodates seven hundred. We were there out of season, but there were several hundred people then.

James and I did not begin to enjoy it, as we did Del Monte. At Del Monte, the Hotel is "as clean as a pin," and although not so gorgeous, it is more attractive to us. We were always out under the trees, and among the flowers. At Del Coronado, one walk about the grounds was sufficient, and then a person contentedly stayed at the Hotel.

After lunch, James, Mr. D—— (the German acquaintance of the Yosemite, whom we met on the train to-day) and I, walked about awhile; then, as I had a violent headache, we sat on the fine broad piazza and kept deliciously cool.

About nine o'clock, a gentleman came along the piazza, and asked some ladies, whom he knew, to come to the Music Room; they were to have some fun,—"a fight to the finish," he said. Turning towards us, he asked us to go also. James, Mr. D. and I went in, and enjoyed a funny performance. It seems they had gotten up a little merriment, at short notice. There was much musical talent on hand, so they began with a fine piano solo,—then followed duetts, trios, solos, recitations, etc. A right funny young man, with ready wit, announced the performers. "The proprietor had gathered together, at great expense, a fine lot of talented art-tistes, etc., etc.," this young man remarked. "The first piece on the programme, will be a piano solo, entitled 'The best I can,' by Moszkowski." Later he came on to the stage and announced, that "a celebrated artist had been prevailed upon to appear, but although highly talented, he was likewise modest and needed encouragement." Two bell-boys marched onto the stage, one with a music stand, the other with a table, and then in came another, carrying a child's hand organ, A fine looking man, in evening dress, walked in amid deafening applause, put his sheet of music on the stand; the announcer turned his pages, and in the most solemn and earnest manner, he ground out "Annie Rooney."

Once or twice his music fell off; he stopped, and with great seriousness found his place again. Finally his right hand grew tired, for he had played it over, at least six times,—his left hand was then exercised, and growing bodily weary, he seated himself on the table,—all done with great dignity and solemnity. It was quite funny. The last part of the performance was a miniature prize fight. Two diminutive boys came in, with their attendants, all in shirt sleeves, no collars or cravats, with towels to rub down, ice to put on their heads, a formidable black bottle, and all the requirements of a genuine ring fight. Arrangements were made, rules closely followed,—the Marquis of Tewksbury's rules in order, and as James said, " every detail of a genuine fight." How the audience roared with laughter! The Pacific, in its wildest moods, could not have drowned that noise.

SATURDAY, JULY 4TH.

A FOURTH of July odor was in the air, when we awoke this morning,—a sort of powder perfume and fire-cracker atmosphere, and the small boy had been up for hours, no doubt. Of course, the day was pleasant, for it always is pleasant here, at this time of the year, as no rain ever falls. A more even temperature cannot be found, than in Southern California. The thermometer seldom varies twenty degrees, all the year round, and snow is unknown, except on the highest peaks of the mountains.   No wonder palms and plants can grow and become trees, in a year or two.

James greeted me, when I joined him for breakfast, with the announcement that the warship *Charleston* was in sight,—had brought the Chilean *Itata* in, and was anchored just off the hotel.   Sure enough, there she lay, a fine picture and surprise for a Fourth of July morning, and a beauty she was, too,—so white in the sunshine.   Crowds of people came all day to Coronado, to see the " Keeper of the Peace," and the entire place was crowded from morning till evening.   We watched the ship and the crowds, sat on the piazza, and walked, and had a nap in the afternoon.

After dinner, although every available spot was full, we found a comfortable corner, and watched the fire-works, which were displayed from a private yacht anchored near, belonging to the Millionaire Spreckles, of San Francisco.   We were not altogether pleased, and were trying to keep our sentiments to ourselves, when a queer and strange appearance in the sky, like long tails of light moving mysteriously, attracted us.   Going down on one of the walks, we soon saw that the *Charleston* was taking her turn, at lighting up the heavens and earth, and was having Fourth of July celebration, with her electric search light.   In bands of light, then great flashes, sometimes in one spot, sometimes chasing each other in a circle on the sky, these great fingers of fire illuminated the entire horizon.   Two powerful reflecting head-lights could be seen on the ship, and from their intensely bright centres, the rays seemed to fly out into space, searching every nook and corner with its radius. As we stood there, one minute in darkness, the next in a blaze of brilliancy, we agreed that the *Charleston* had out-shone all fire-works, in her unusual and dazzling display. It was the most interesting thing to us, and we returned well pleased with our quiet Fourth.

MONDAY JULY 6TH.

WE left Del Coronado, soon after ten o'clock this morning, and on reaching the wharf, at San Diego, a carriage was awaiting us, to take us about the little city, and to the Old Mission. After viewing the business streets, banks, hotels and churches, we drove among the residences of the city, and found some really beautiful homes. In 1885, the population of San Diego was 4,000; to-day it is 30,000. It is a pretty little city, quite foreign in general appearance, but its chief charm is its exquisite land-locked harbor, which reminds one forcibly of the beautiful Bay of Naples. The land, near the water's edge, rises quite suddenly into a series of foot-hills, upon which the City is built, and finally terminates in a rolling Mesa, which runs for miles back into the country, until it meets the Old Mission Valley.

After seeing all the visible charms of this picturesquely placed city, we decided to drive to the Old

Mission, a sight every one must see, as it is one of the few ruins we have on American soil. It is now a lonely pile of stones, but stands in a glorious position, on a promontory, commanding a magnificent view in every direction. This tumble down cathedral was once the centre of life and activity, of that portion of the country, and was the scene of all the glory and splendor, that the people, for miles about, ever knew; and the old Mexican fathers were like emperors or kings, in their little domain, but ruled the people by love, rather than fear. This mission was burned down in 1769, but rebuilt in 1789. The land, for miles, about this old ruin, is cultivated and cared for, and at one time belonged to the Church. Opposite and close by, was the finest olive orchard we have ever seen.

Standing near the road, where our carriage stopped, was a queer tree, which I should have called a willow, if I had been asked. After James and I returned from our climb, among the tumbling walls and stones of the Old Mission, our driver told us of this remarkable tree, which his priest had often declared to him, was the only one of its kind in America. It is said to be a cutting of the tree, from which the Crown of Thorns was made, which was placed in scorn upon our Saviour's head. James and I, at first, naturally doubted such an assertion, for it seemed preposterous to our American minds, that such a thing could be hidden so far in the wilderness as it is, away from all eyes, and be

OLD MISSION.

really what it pretended to be. A close examination, however, brought us to the conclusion that after all, we had never seen any tree like it, any where in all our wanderings. We sent a request to the people, in the little house near, on whose grounds this remarkable tree grows, for a small branch of it, and our desire being granted, we were able to examine it closely. Delicate slim branches this tree had, slender and pliable and easily twisted into shape, and its little lace-like leaves grew, according to the mathematical law of leaves on their stems, but covered completely the most marvelous thorns, as sharp as needles, pointed and piercing, and appearing at every angle, and so staunch and strong were they, that a big pull was necessary to tear one from its position. Stripping the leaves from their places, and twisting the branch into the shape of a crown, the needle-like thorns stuck out in every direction, and convinced our minds, that, if not a cutting from the actual tree, from which Our Lord's Crown of ignominy was made, it was without doubt the same species of growth, new to our eyes, which was used by the soldiers of old, in those days of Our Lord's sorrow and anguish.

Although bountifully covered with dust, we drove away from the Old Mission, quite satisfied and pleased that we had visited it, and next turned our attention to " Old Town," as it is called, or North San Diego. We had several miles to drive, through fertile and well kept farm lands.

Old Town, or North San Diego, we found to be a
most complete wreck, of a once prosperous village.
The low Mexican adobes were numerous, but although interesting in their picturesque decay, the
entire place impressed one, as a deserted village, a
scene of activity and life once upon a time, but
dead and destroyed now. No people were visible
in the streets, or about the few houses, which
seem to be still used as dwellings, and not one living being did we see, until we stopped in front of a
long low adobe building, and at our driver's suggestion, knocked at the door. A sweet, lovely young
woman, a Roman Catholic Sister, opened the door,
and asked us to walk in ; and we learned that we
had reached one of the most prosperous Indian
schools, in the South. Over one hundred Indian
boys and girls are taught here, during the year, but
as our visit came in their vacation time, only thirty
were left, the others having gone to their homes, for
a visit. It was most interesting to see these girls,
averaging in age, from five to sixteen years, all so
bright, quick and intelligent. Sister Octavia, as we
afterwards learned, the Lady Superior of this school,
showed us the sewing, mending, and other work of
these girls, who are trained in womanly and household duties, and are clever indeed in all branches.

After we had spoken to " Cloudia," " Juanita,"
" Letitia," and many others, the Lady Superior took
us into a room in the house, where an altar was
standing, which, she told us, was the room where

Father Gaspara lived, when Ramona and Alessandro came, that dark night, after their journey through that wild cañon, and told their sad story of their love and misfortunes.   Mrs. Helen Hunt Jackson's narrative and portrayal of the sufferings of these peculiarly interesting people, has made Southern California familiar to many minds, and no one can have read her sweet story of Indian life, without recalling this incident.   As she writes—"On the opposite side of the way, in a neglected, weedy open, stood his little chapel, a poverty-stricken little place, its walls imperfectly white-washed, decorated by a few coarse pictures, etc."   To this little one-room abode, the outer walls now covered with boards, our mild-voiced guide led us, and we stood within the little chapel, where Ramona and Alessandro were made man and wife, by the black-bearded priest, Father Gaspara.   A tiny chapel it is, with an altar at one end, and *ten* pews for the congregation, and probably there was plenty of room to spare, at every celebration and service.

A queer little place it is, but one of interest to us, for it has been a haven of rest to many a weary wanderer, besides Ramona and Alessandro, and was also where Father Junipero Serra, with his wonderful strength of character, and marvelous endurance of hardships and discouragements, had begun his work, so many years ago.

Sister Octavia sent for the Indian girls, whom we had seen in the school, and they came to the little chapel and sang some of their Latin chants. It was pathetic to us, to hear these fresh young voices singing their Ave Maria, and to realize how short a time had passed, since they had been brought from their homes in the wilderness, and taught these sacred things. James was much moved by this singing, and as we sat in that tiny chapel, we felt as if years were passing in review before us, as we pictured to ourselves all the happy hearts, and sad as well, that had stood before that sacred altar, and received the blessing of their priest. After seeing the priestly vestments, James asked the privilege of photographing that little gathering; and standing beneath the "Old Bells of 1802," which are at one end of the little chapel, James photographed the Lady Superior, and thirty Indian girls.

As we drove away from the little group, the children waved us a good-bye, and my noble, thoughtful husband exclaimed, "What a beautiful work that is, May, to rescue those girls from their wandering life on the plains, and teach them to be noble women in the world. No wonder Sister Octavia's face expressed such calm and peace, that must come into the heart, and face as well, when one gives their life to such a grand work."

TUESDAY, JULY 7TH.

AT six o'clock we had breakfast, and at half past six, we started on our trip, from Del Coronado and San Diego, back to Los Angeles. It was as pleasant a journey as possible, but it was very warm, and made us apprehensive about our afternoon. Before we left Los Angeles, we arranged to have a carriage meet us at the depot, on our arrival to-day, to take us immediately into the beautiful country, surrounding the city. On reaching Los Angeles, "the chariot" awaited us, and sending our small baggage to the Westminster Hotel, we started at once into the San Gabriel Valley; and what a scene of beauty it was! For miles and miles, we drove through beautiful orange groves, the deep heavy foliage of the short stubby trees, making a fine contrast to the golden fruit, still hanging in some groves. An orange grove in blossom, has the most powerful perfume ever known, which pervades and fills the air, until everything seems saturated with the odor, as if the entire country was decorated for a marriage feast. It must be a veritable paradise in this valley, in the winter season, when the woods and meadows are carpeted with every variety of blossom, every tint and hue mingling and blending in harmony and exquisite beauty, and all watched over by the serious, solemn Sierra Madre Mountains, with their snow-clad peaks and yawning cañons. No wonder invalids, by the hundreds, fly to the protecting arms, and mild climate, of the San Gabriel Valley in winter, for surely no more beautiful place on earth is to be found, this side of the tropics. Great avenues of banana trees, palm and date trees, fig and plum and apricot trees, the Eucalyptus, in their slim stately style—in fact, the San Gabriel Valley, of ten miles wide, by thirty miles long, is one series of beautiful and wonderful drives, through orange groves, vineyards, wonderful cactus growths, avenues of feathery pepper trees,—and such hedges ! Pomegranate hedges in rare beauty, with the blossoms en masse in the richest of color, which the Southern sunshine seems to have kissed and glorified, with a new radiance. The fatigue of our early start and journey, was forgotten, in the midst of this entrancing restful beauty, and the first part of our drive brought us, about two o'clock, to the lovely hotel San Gabriel, where we had an excellent luncheon. We had seen, in our drive, the oldest grapevine in Southern California, a mammoth tree and stem, as large as some of the trunks of our chestnut trees, at home.

It was also our good fortune, to see the famous San Gabriel Mission, which was founded in 1771, but placed in its present position in 1775. Some of the bells still hang in the old belfry, and were most picturesque, and we admired them, but they were deaf to the piteous plea " Ring out wild bells."

After luncheon, we drove to the famous Raymond Hotel, at Raymond, and such a magnificent hotel it is, with such walks and drives about it, such glorious shrubs and plants, that the entire place was fascinating to us, until we turned and saw the view; that beggars description ! In the soft mellow light of that southern climate, and the approaching twilight hour, it was a dream of such wonder, a vision of

radiant and perfect proportions, that, as we feasted
our eyes on all before us, a calm and restful peace
stole over us, and we seemed in paradise at last.   In
the distance, the Sierra Madre mountains were violet in color, then the orange trees, in their regular
stately rows, with now and then a tall palm, or date,
or eucalyptus tree, so clearly outlined against the
mountains and sky, and then, perhaps, a fine villa,
with its shrubs and plants and rose bushes, until the
scene before us was too beautiful to describe, and
can only be remembered as a complete and perfect
whole.

Pasadena, with its entrancing beauty, attracted
James more than any city we have seen, in all our
travelling, and a dozen times, he exclaimed, "A little
home here would just suit me, May; it would seem
as if we had gone to Heaven, in reality." Pasadena
is a paradise on earth; a new joy was in the sunshine, a new life seemed to touch and beautify the
flowers, and all smiled with a radiance and beauty
most contagious.   We felt it even in our drive
through the streets; we saw it in the open and attractive homes, and we drove about, for a long time,
and did not wonder that people chose this beauty
spot for a home.   Oranges grew on the trees, right
along the streets, and when we exclaimed that we had
never picked an orange off a tree, our driver drove
up to a well-laden tree, in front of a fine villa, and
began to take all the oranges within reach.   James
and I were horrified, and forbade any further pillage,

but when we were well on our way toward Los Angeles, the golden fruit in the bottom of the carriage "tempted me, and I did eat." Never has an orange tasted like that orange, perhaps, because "stolen sweets are best"; but my gratification soon tempted James to join me, and our only regret was that we had not allowed our driver to take more.

We reached the Westminster Hotel about eight o'clock, had dinner and retired, well satisfied with our day in the beautiful San Gabriel Valley.

WEDNESDAY, JULY 8TH.

WE left Los Angeles to-day, at noon, and with some regret, for the city is really beautiful, and James and I felt we could spend several weeks here very pleasantly, if we could spare the time.

Our trip to-day was quiet and uneventful, and pleasant, as we passed through the monotonous Mojave Desert, during the night. We have become so used to sleeping cars and travelling now, that we are quite contented, when en route, and really enjoy moving along and seeing our great and glorious country; and we are proud that we are Americans.

NORTHWARD OVER THE SIERRA NEVADAS

WE reached San Francisco at noon to-day, and found it very warm, but quite like home, or perhaps I should say, *more* like home, than any place in this far away country. California impresses us in every way. It is a wonderfully beautiful State, magnificent in every respect, and is so large. We have travelled in California, nearly 2,000 miles, and we have yet nearly 500 miles to cover, going north to Portland. The distance from San Francisco to San Diego is 608 miles; but when James and I first planned to go there, we thought the journey would be about equal to a trip, from New York to Utica. We blushed, when we learned how ignorant we were. Coming over-land, we travelled over 3,000 miles, equal to a trip to Europe.

We were much amused at the News Agent, on the train, who electrified us, by singing out, as he sauntered through the car, "Travelling caps, and *Neuralgia combs!*

WE were sleepy this morning, and, as usual, had a late breakfast. We had planned to go, at half-past ten o'clock, with F. J. to Chinatown, to buy his wife a gift ; but I was delayed in going to my room this morning, by meeting friends from Salt Lake City, and later by meeting Miss Thursby and sister, and the Rev. Dr. B., of Brooklyn, in the corridor. About eleven o'clock, however, we started (James, Mr. D., F. J. and I) for Chinatown. We stopped at Liebes' celebrated fur store, to see the beautiful furs, from this part of the world, and Alaska, etc. Mr. H. (a friend of F.'s) was very kind, showed us very choice skins, took us to the cellar, to examine rare furs, see the process of curing and treating; in fact, we had a regular lecture on the subject, and acquired much information. Then ho ! for Chinatown.

Of course we visited Fong Sang Lung, Kim Woo, Hon Wing, Sing Fat, and many others; and Mr. J. was as much interested in his visit, as when he went there first, many years ago. We spent several hours, in wandering about, and picking up a few odd trifles ; then happening to be near a Chinese restaurant, we walked in. To follow the old adage, " While in Rome, do as the Romans do," while we were in Chinatown, we did as the Chinamen do,—we took seats at a big round table and ordered tea. It was a beautiful restaurant—the ceiling and side walls were covered with Chinese hieroglyphics in gold, gold scrolls hung on the walls, the partition between two divisions in the room was of carved wood, very artistically and beautifully carved, then covered with gilding, and in every little window space was stained glass. The furniture was ebony, inlaid with pearl, beautiful chairs and tables. The restaurant was up two flights of stairs, and had balconies, with flower-pots all along the edge, full of Chinese plants, dwarf oaks, etc. It was an unusual place. The tea was good—but the variety of sweetmeats they brought us, the sugar-coated cake, with pink Chinese hiero-glyphics on it—the nuts, preserved citron, cherries, etc., were too much for me, so I ate a nut or two, drank my tea, and spent the rest of the time taking a mental inventory. We finally wandered back to the civilized stores, did a few necessary errands, for our Alaska welfare, then we came to the hotel, and I wrote a letter home. I found some lovely roses waiting for me, from Miss T. We had dinner at a quarter past seven, F. and Mr. D. dining with us, and after dinner, we went with Mr. and Mrs. V. G. to Chinatown, to see the theatre and play, as we could not see it when we were here before. Every-body said it was a thing not to be omitted, a sight well worth a trip to enjoy. We found the guide awaiting us at Kim Lung's, and through the dirty alleys, we picked our way to the back, and stage entrance of the Jackson Street Theatre. Crowds of Chinamen surrounded us, before, behind, on our right hand and on our left, for the theatre is their one recreation and amusement, and this was the only one open. Chinatown accommodates more Chinamen, than any known space, of equal proportions, in America.

After threading our way, in the underground passages, up the narrowest, steepest staircase, so narrow, everybody wiped down each wall, as he crept along, we emerged into the "Green Room" of the actors, a place about the size of our laundry at Sunny Slope, crowded and jammed with actors in their costumes, densely thick with smoke,—and such awful smoke too! Finally our guide waved everybody aside, and the crowd of celestials moved a tiny bit, for us to press our way through, and the first thing I knew, we came suddenly right out on the stage. We would have stepped back,—our natural modesty, of course, suggesting such a thing,—but no, we were not allowed to escape. A table was on the middle of the stage, two chairs by it—one on each side—and beside it stood two actors, going along in their queer performance, oblivious of all else. Into one of these chairs, on the middle of the stage, they tried to put me. No indeed—I had come to see, and not to be seen; so I pushed my way back, against a solid wall of Chinamen. Visitors are all seated on the stage, and usually have comfortable quarters. To-night, however, the theatre was so crowded, the sides of the stage were arranged in tiers, for the Chinamen, and in front on each side, in a semi-circle, we finally were all placed. Across from us, sat the Rev. Mr., Mrs. and Miss B., all as engrossed and amused as we were.

The theatre was jammed, from the floor to the ceiling, not one place, in aisle or anywhere, that was not occupied. The men never sit with the women—the women are in two balconies, on one side of the house, unescorted—and such a medley! Some were quite aristocratic looking, highly-born, perhaps; others had huge, coarse features, but all were intensely interested in the performance. Not an eye wandered; no one thought of anything but that drama on the stage, and in some parts the women wept copiously, then hung their handkerchiefs over the railing to dry. Below, and in two other balconies, were the men, so closely packed, so densely crowded, and all smoking, and eating fruit—such an odor! As James said, he was as much interested in watching the audience, as he was the actors. When anything seemed pathetic, they were as solemn as judges; when anything amused them, they set up a Chinese howl, a genuine roof-raiser! But the stage, and the play!

When we entered, two women (men dressed as women), were performing. It seems, one woman was a widow, had lost her baby (we were too late to see the Chinese mother bring in a rag-baby and wash its face), and the other woman wanted her to marry again, which she refused to do. The older woman took a long broom-like whip, and whipped the widow, to the great grief of said widow, and delight of the house. Whenever any great emotion was being portrayed, a band—behind the table—accompanied the emotion, with appropriate selections; but if one hundred Scottish bagpipes had been let loose upon the audience that night, it would have been ten degrees below the volume and quality of sound sent forth. It seemed as if our ears would never be restored to normal condition again. The play continued; the widow's mother and father received her back to their home, in rather an unpleasant manner, and the father and mother had such a war of words about it, that the father killed the mother, that is he made a rush at her, *stepped hard on her toe*, and like a log of wood, she fell to the floor. A man stood near us, who went, as soon as the mother fell, and stuck a straight long thing under her head, like a *pillar*, but it was a pillow. She straightened out, then picked herself up and went away.

A Chinese play often lasts for *months*, and is carried along like a story. They have no scenery whatever, only represent what they desire with articles, Their voices are shrill and piercing, and their acting is automatic, wooden, as if they were on wheels, and were worked by strings, from beneath the stage. I never have seen such "pirouetting," such absolutely ridiculous performances! They seem a thousand years behind the times; and yet this is their choice, their recreation and amusement, and they are perfectly satisfied. We were there half an hour, and would not have left then, if the ponderous perfumes had not overcome us. It was most interesting, so serious and solemn, the spectators so intent upon the actors; and the actors were artists in stiffness and absolute awkwardness. Delsarte never could teach these celestials the poetry of motion. *They* move in angles; nothing beyond a straight line touches their sense of beauty,—even their faces betoken angularity.

We were worn out and weary, on our return, but well paid, by our visit to the theatre, in Chinatown.

MONDAY, JULY 13TH.

WE left San Francisco last night, at nine o'clock. We found our days were gliding swiftly by, and we had need of haste, as we must reach Tacoma, and go on board the steamer, for Alaska, on Thursday night.

The Mt. Shasta Route, to Portland, had been much praised, by travellers we chanced to meet, and pronounced grand and magnificent, and we naturally anticipated it; but we were little prepared for the beauty, which has greeted our eyes, all the way to-day. From San Francisco to Sacramento, we passed in the night, but having been through that country before, we lost nothing. After leaving Sacramento, in the early morning hours, our road followed closely the banks of the Sacramento River, which ran through a most beautiful and fertile valley. After

Redding was reached, and breakfast over, our feast of delight really began, as we climbed among the mighty mountains of the Sierra Nevada range. Slowly, and with difficulty, as the grade is severe, we crept around curves and sharp cuts in the rocks, passed over bridges and trestles, through a dozen or more tunnels, and in a short distance of eighty miles, we crossed the tortuous course of the Sacramento River, eighteen times. From a beautiful broad band of blue water, at the city,—bearing its name, with so much life and energy manifested on its surface, as if it had come a long way to do a great work,—we followed the Sacramento River, up to its source in the mountains; and it diminished in volume and brightness, to a ribbon of grayish color, and twisted, and tumbled, and turned, as if its narrow boundaries were irksome, to the energy beneath its waters. Its river-bed lay between banks of such forbidding nature, as if a great river of lava, from Mt. Shasta's depths, had poured down that gorge in the mountain, and hardened, and finally, in a fit of rage and despair, had split and divided into two lava banks, between which the river ran, on its way to the sea.

Our first point of interest was at the Soda Springs, now becoming so well known, for their fine mineral qualities; and in a little flock, all the passengers on the train, hurried to the rustic enclosure over the Spring, to refresh themselves with one "life-giving draught." Beautiful little streams of

water constantly coursed down the steep, rocky
sides and cañons, as we flew along; but a perfect
vision of loveliness was ours, when we stopped opposite Mossbrae Falls, as lovely as anything of the
kind we have seen, outside the Yosemite. Splashing suddenly and playfully out, into the sunshine, as
if it had just escaped, for the first time, from the
icy grasp of one of Mt. Shasta's greatest glaciers,
these "laughing waters" spring, from a bed of exquisite ferns and mosses, which wave and tremble,
under the pressure and spray of the cascade, as if a
new and welcome guest had just come to them, and
had not been their companion, for many years. A
luxuriant growth of these ferns, and mosses, and
grasses, have flourished so marvelously under this
constant shower of icy water, that the usual barren
rocks are nowhere visible, and are picturesquely
covered by this dainty fertility. Perhaps Robert
Southey had seen just such a sparkling stream,

> " Rising and leaping,
> Sinking and creeping,
> Swelling and sweeping,
> Showering and springing."

when he wrote " How does the water come down at
Lodore!"

The Castle Rocks attracted us next, with their
solid walls of granite, rising 4,000 feet above
the valley; and with their columns and minarets,
they presented a scene of marvelous beauty; but

every once in a while, through the great pine trees, so colossal and magnificent in their forest fortresses, we caught such dazzling glimpses of shimmering beauty, that we were breathless in anticipation, and powerless in awe and reverence, when finally, Mt. Shasta, in its whiteness, rose before us, "its great white dome of incandescent snow and lava crags" so impressive, as it stood outlined against the silent blue heavens. Mt. Shasta is called, the key of California scenery, because the Sierra Nevada Mountains, bounding the eastern portion of the State, and the Coast Range, bounding the western meet at Mt. Shasta, "making a mountain arch, of which the Great White Butte is the keystone.'

Words fail to give expression to our impressions, of the solemn repose, and stately grandeur, of this mountain giant. The snow-filled crater, of this once fiery mountain, and the lava gorges, now the bed of numerous glaciers, shone like silver in their silent beauty, and made the great peaks surrounding it, so black, and bare, and desolate, stand forth in wondrous contrast. But how small all those grand mountains seem, how insignificant, as Mt. Shasta raises its cloud-crowned cliffs, two vertical miles above the surrounding country!

Right in front of this ice fortress, twelve miles from its base, which, in the clear air, seemed a distance of only a mile, at the little village of Sissons, we stopped, and had time to enjoy this grandeur;

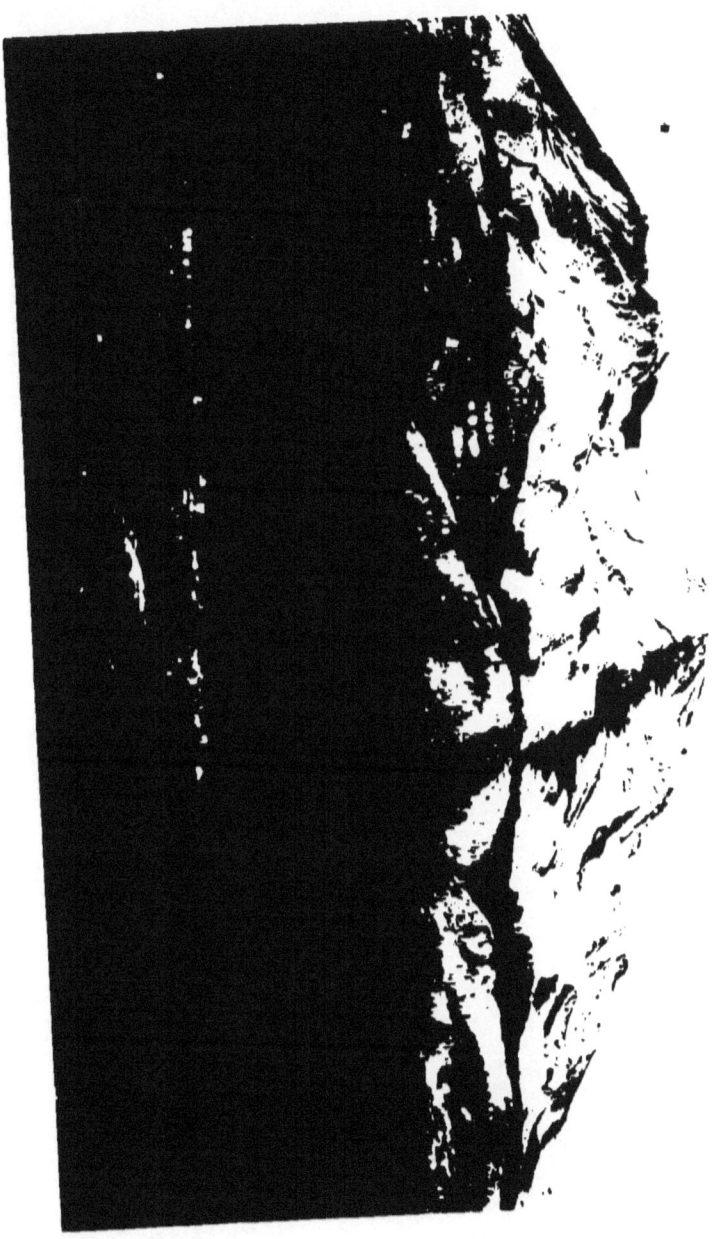

MOUNT SHASTA.

and as we rolled away from the place, the five volcanic cones of Muir's Peak, added to the charm of
view.   We passed through Strawberry Valley, and
Shasta Valley, and soon crossed the state line, between California and Oregon, and began to climb
the Siskiyou Mountains, which form a natural line,
between the two states.   This ascent is a wonder of
engineering skill, and although the Royal Gorge,
and Marshall's Pass, in Colorado, had charmed us,
here we were dumb in wonder and amazement!
Such marvelous skill in building a railroad, where it
seemed only the fleetest-footed animals could hope
to climb—such twistings and turnings, tunnels bor-
ing into the very hearts of the forests, disturbing
roots of those stately and venerable pines, and carrying us higher and higher, into the mountains.
Such views as were ours! James' exclamations
were constant, and he seemed as deeply impressed
as I was.   The scenery was indescribably magnificent, for as far as the eye could reach, the great
snow-monarchs soared up into the heavens, and we
seemed encircled in their icy embrace.   Extending
north, for hundreds of miles, stood the Cascade
Range; to the west, we could see the Siskiyou and
Coast Mountains; sparkling lakes, fertile valleys in
all their loveliness, rivers, and splashing springs,
deep solemn gorges were before us, awful cañons on
every side, forests of pine and oak, and a more wonderful, ever-changing panorama, of magnificent
grandeur and variety, cannot be imagined.

"Speech was given to man, to conceal his thoughts," seems true indeed to me, as I strive to express the impressions, made upon our minds this day. It is a hopeless task, to attempt to portray such inspiring and up-lifting emotions, which bring one into harmony with the best and most beautiful, in God's world of wonder; and it seems to me, sometimes, that in just such experiences as these, we are given a little suggestion of that higher and better life; as if the veil, which separates our mortal life from the immortal, was for a moment parted, and a single God-given emotion sent—to fill our souls with a rapture before unknown; and we have a foretaste of that glorious hereafter,—a glimpse of that Better Land, toward which we are all hastening.

TUESDAY, JULY 14TH.

ARRIVING at Portland, at half-past nine this morning, James hastened to " The Portland " (which is a very fine Hotel), as I was feeling quite sick, from our incessant travelling of late. A good day's rest restored me, however. While I stayed quietly in my room, James spent this exceedingly warm day, in hunting for a winter ulster, for the Alaska trip.

We met such charming people on the train,— Lord and Lady F. from London,—and their friends and travelling companions were equally delightful. They had just landed from a trip through Japan. James was much amused this morning, when the waiter brought "Mi-Lord" an egg, opened in a glass, as we often eat them. With a disgusted expression, and a genuine drawl, he ordered it from the table, and turning to James, he exclaimed,— "I haven't got used to eating eggs, *all messed up*, —you know."

WEDNESDAY, JULY 15TH.

ALTHOUGH we had seen nothing of this great City of the West, we were obliged to hurry northward to-day, and took the 11.45 A. M. train for Tacoma, promising ourselves another visit, on our return from Alaska.

Our trip of 144 miles, was one of exceeding interest, although so different from our recent journey. We followed the shores of the Willamette River, crossed the Columbia and passed through most beautiful forests, with such giant trees,—so straight and grand, one was constantly reminded of the days in the Yosemite, with the great pines there,—not the Mariposa Grove of monarchs, to be sure, but stately enough to challenge our praise.

We had with us, all the way, the snow mountains of the Cascade Range,—Mt. Hood, which keeps constant guard over the city we had just left, Mt. St. Helens on one shore of the Columbia River, Mt. Adams, Mt. Jefferson; and as we approached Tacoma, Mt. Ranier stood forth, in the glorious rose of the twilight, to welcome us.

There is a mythological legend, that long ago, in the prehistoric ages, Mt. St. Helens, and Mt. Hood, were firm friends, and stood side by side, in their glory and pride, presided over by certain gods. A serious quarrel occurred, between the gods of these two mountains, which set the whole mountain range in such a furious frenzy, upset so many tempers, turned calm and contented peaks and cones into fiery fiends, and caused such grave and terrible damage to the country about, that Mt. Hood, and Mt. St. Helens, were irrevocably doomed to be separated forever, and in heaviness of heart and with tremendous lamentations, and an upheaval of sighs and groans, these mountain companions were torn asunder, and the Columbia River decreed, to run forever between.

We reached Tacoma, about half past six o'clock, and went to "The Tacoma," a large hotel overlooking Puget Sound, and in full view of Mt. Ranier, or, as the people here prefer to call it, " Mt. Tacoma."

THURSDAY, JULY 16TH.

A BUSY day, preparing for our trip to Alaska. We went, in the afternoon, to view our abiding place for the next three weeks, and we found the *Mexico* a larger steamer than we imagined, comfortably appointed ; and we are quite ready to start on a trip, which offers such unusual attractions. A friend, whom we met in San Francisco, had just returned from this trip, on the same steamer we are to take, and her answer to our question as to whether she enjoyed it, would have been decidedly depressing, if we had not already brought our courage to the sticking point, and were little daunted when she exclaimed, "Oh, its pretty good, that is, if you like a *good dose* of scenery!"

About ten o'clock to-night, with as little baggage as we could arrange to take with us, we embarked on the "Pacific Coast Steamship *Mexico*," and as it was a superb moonlight night, we remained out on deck, met the officers of the ship, and learned a little of the trip we were just starting upon. The *Queen* is the regular excursion boat to Alaska, but the *Mexico* and *Topeka* are mail and freight boats, and go to the little, as well as the big, Alaskan ports, and to many of the out-of-the-way places. We are content with our lot thus far, and are anticipating much pleasure.

About half past eleven o'clock, I went to our cabin (the palatial proportions of which are eight feet long, by six feet wide), and began to arrange our things for comfort and convenience, when a deep-toned voice at my window sang out solemnly: "Lights ordered out at ten." I felt as if I had jumped back to my boarding-school days, and was subject to "rule and rod" once more, and the hours and regulations, which were all so quietly maintained at dear old Farmington.

FRIDAY, JULY 17TH.

ALTHOUGH we knew the *Mexico* was to leave her wharf, at four o'clock this morning, we were oblivious of the fact, until we were fast to the wharf at Seattle, our first stopping place. After a couple of hours there, we started again, and in a few hours more, reached Port Townsend, a little place of considerable shipping importance, but of no interest otherwise. We found this stop a bit tedious, and longed to be off, for new and interesting sights and scenes, but we wandered about the town, and finally contented ourselves on board our ship, chatting, reading and writing. The Olympic Mountains made a beautiful picture, and background for this little city, and Mt. Baker was regal, in its northern position and unrivaled splendor, as it stood alone in silent beauty.

SATURDAY, JULY 18TH.

A LOVELY day, a few showers at mid-day, but not enough to do any harm. We were tied up to the dock at Victoria, British Columbia, before

Jamie and I were up this morning. We left Port Townsend at four and reached Victoria at six. After breakfast, Jamie and I jumped into a carriage and drove up into the town, about three-quarters of a mile, and bought two steamer rugs, which we found we needed. We then drove about Victoria, and found it a very English looking town, with about 25,000 inhabitants, but very sleepy in appearance. They say it is an attractive summer resort, but we failed to see many points of attraction. There were some fine churches, a few fine dwellings, but they were mostly low and of inferior appearance. The Olympic Mountains, with their white caps, made a beautiful background for this little British town. We were back at the steamer, at half-past nine o'clock, and were off from Victoria, at 10.20 A.M., and had a lovely sail all day. It was like a trip through a colossal Lake George; everything was on a magnificent scale, so beautiful, and reflected in the water was every mountain and island, like Mirror Lake in the Yosemite. Jamie and I sat in silent comfort and asked the conundrum to ourselves, " Why were we like the luckiest of all vowels, the vowel *i*? Because we were in the middle of bliss." Nothing disturbed us, until a man went about the decks, ringing a fearful bell, and calling, "All to the Purser's office for table seats." A crowd immediately flew, but Jamie did not go at first, for we had been informed in the morning, that we were to be seated at the Purser's table.

We reached Departure Bay, British Columbia, at five o'clock. Jamie heard that the *Queen* (with Aunt Mary on board) was at Nanaimo, a little place three miles from Departure Bay; and although she was reported to sail at six o'clock, and we had only one hour in which to reach her, we determined to try it. Jamie felt really sick, with a neuralgic headache, but we flew along the wharf, across the little bridge, and along the beach, a half mile in all, to a house, which was store, post-office, livery stable and all. In perfect breathlessness, we asked to hire a driver, horse and wagon in hot haste, to reach the *Queen*, in double quick time. Inside of five minutes, we were seated in an old farm wagon, on the back seat, and a right good horse was tearing along, driven by the funniest specimen of a country green-horn. If he had leaned over too far, or pulled the horse up suddenly, he would surely have split his coat, from seam to seam, for he looked as if he was stuffed into it. We flew along those three miles to Nanaimo, and it was an exquisite ride. The road passes through the most beautiful woods, really lovelier than any I have ever seen, except in the Yosemite, and it lay between tremendous ferns, six or seven feet high, and growing *en masse*, close to the driveway. As far as one could see into the woods, between the great fir trees, the same mammoth fern thicket was visible, and huge trees of wild flowers, mountain lilac making the air almost sickeningly sweet. As far as one could look ahead, the same fern road-way invited us on, and it was lovely. Before we reached Nanaimo, we came from the woods into a clearing, and saw the little town lying before us, with its lovely harbor full of ships; and the *Queen* lay at her wharf, as true to her name as possible; but we expected every minute to see the great black smoke pour from her smoke-stack, and see her sail away. We tore through the town, over bridges, where fast-driving was forbidden; and " John Gilpin "was nowhere! Finally, we landed at a little hill, beyond which " the chariot " could not go. Jamie and I ran up the hill, rushed along the coal-tracks towards the *Queen*, and at last, as we reached the gang-plank, worn out by our rush (for it was four minutes before six then), I gasped out to a coal-man standing near, " When does she sail?" " About twelve o'clock to-night " came the answer. What a relief! If that information had only been ours sooner, we might have escaped the hurry and fa-tigue, and Jamie might not have had such a head-ache. Well, we were *there*, anyhow; now, how were we to find Aunt Mary? A boy's interest was so-licited, but the *Queen* was a large steamer, and we were at a loss to know how to find her. A gen-tleman came to our assistance, and to our inquiry for " Mrs. B.," he said " she is right here." Turn-ing and walking a few steps, we came face to face with her,—and I shall never forget her surprise. She was delighted to see us, and the pleasure was mu-tual, and we chatted an hour with her. We had a lovely drive back to our ship, meeting many of our passengers walking in the woods, and found that some people had tried to get conveyances to take them to Nanaimo, but we had *the only one in the place.*

SUNDAY, JULY 19TH.

TIED up to the dock, at Departure Bay, all day long; and such a dirty place as this boat was, until five o'clock this afternoon, from the dust and dirt of the coal. This is a great coal district; a large coal mine here gets out twenty-five hundred to three thousand tons a day, and this vessel, since last night, at five o'clock, has received four hundred tons.

After an eight o'clock breakfast this morning, Jamie and I came forward to our stateroom, wondering where we would spend the day. The sail which had been hung up forward from our room, to keep out coal dust, suddenly wavered, and a great cloud of dust came towards us. "Too bad," exclaimed Mr. Gray, the first officer, "the wind has changed, and we're in for it." Sure enough we were, for from that hour, the dust sifted all over the ship, on one side. We shut our room up tight, covered everything with papers and towels, and left it all day closed, and it was unharmed to-night. Jamie and I took our chairs this morning and went to the clean side of the boat, and sat for a while, but it grew cold, and Jamie was feeling very poorly with neuralgia, and threatened with lumbago, which filled him with alarm, but did not, somehow or other, frighten me. I began to take a mental account of the remedies which I had in my bag, but the probability of possible illness did not assume alarming proportions in my mind. As it grew colder, Jamie managed to meander around, with his back *on the bias*, and finally informed me that he had found just the cosiest corner for us both. Following my "lord and master," we wandered into the little smoking room; Jamie put his chair in a corner, I seated myself at a table near by, and we spent our entire day there, as comfortable and snug as could be; and I wrote letters home. At twelve o'clock, we went down to luncheon and then returned to "our retreat" again, where I wrote until half past four o'clock, when Mr. Gray came for my letters. We then came to our room to make ready for dinner, and tie up some pretty sweet grass, which Miss C. of Oakland, had brought me. Everybody has been off the boat, into the woods to-day, or else in little boats to Nanaimo, but James not feeling well, we have kept very quiet all day. The sweet grass is lovely; it consists of great big fresh green leaves, on a long stem. They gather it, make it into round green balls, hang them in the staterooms, and as they wither and dry, the perfume is very sweet and very strong.

After a good dinner, James and I came to our clean and cosy corner, and I was writing to-day's journal, when Officer Gray appeared, with the biggest ball of sweet grass that I have yet seen, and presented it to me. I felt quite complimented, as he had sent a man to gather it for me.

At 8 P. M. we set sail from Departure Bay, and right happy we were to be on the move again. We were all up on the hurricane deck, to see the start, and also to see the loveliest of sunsets. It was brilliant daylight until nine o'clock, and not dark then, only the moon began to be radiant and shut off the twilight. The sky was as blue, and the clouds as pink as shells, long after the path of moonlight on the water, had widened to a broad shining ribbon. This is a land of wonder that we are approaching, wonder in sky and sea, as well as on land; and a trip to Alaska is instructive, as well as interesting, teaching us of tides as well as of glaciers and ice-bergs. If the days are so long, and the twilights without end, one wonders why, and the very query leads to questions and research, and ends in knowledge gained, if only to be the beginning to paths of wisdom.

Jamie and I were right royally tired by half past ten, and glad to retire to our little shelves.

MONDAY, JULY 20TH.

GREY all day, no sunshine and very, very cold. After our breakfast, at 7.30 A. M., I did a lot of mending on my new ulster. Before I get through, I shall have made an ulster, for new rips come every day, but it is a good coat for all that, and a young lady on board said, she "knew we were from New

York, by the cut of our clothes." As I was dressed in a Tacoma cap, and a Portland ulster, I was amused. Afterward, I joined Jamie in our "cosy corner," but all our wraps were necessary to-day, as it has been very cold and disagreeably blowy. Mr. Gray had an awning put forward, to protect us a little from the wind. We slept all the morning, quite overpowered with fatigue, and after luncheon out on deck, we slept two hours more, until three o'clock, when Miss C. and Miss K. came, by invitation, and we had "afternoon tea," with my Chinese "Tea-basket;" and a third guest came before we had finished. After dinner, we did nothing but chat with Commander and Mrs. G., Senator and Mrs. D., until nine, when we had supper. We eat and sleep constantly. The passengers were reading novels on deck, until half past nine to-night,—such long twilights !

TUESDAY, JULY 21ST.

A GREY day; clouds have hung low over the mountains, just lifting once in a while, to give us a peep of some snow-caps, then nestling closely again, down on the tree tops. Instead of detracting from the beauty, I think the clouds have added to this scene of wildness and mystery, for they have been like thin gauze ribbons or festoons, hung in every variety of way. I say this "scene of wildness," because every hill and mountain, every island and shore line, is covered with fir trees thick

together, and so dense, one sees hundreds of trees
on a mountain, like one huge green covering; there
is no outline of individuality, or any marked feature,
to distinguish one spot from another, and not one
living thing to be seen. There is a sameness in
color to-day, because there is no sunshine to produce
a variety; but the sunshine is not needed, to show
us the beautiful outline of the islands, or the changing coast of the mainland. The islands cannot be
numbered, for every variety,—from a little round
tuft of rock and green, to a great big surface, half
the size of some of our Eastern States,—we have
passed during the last two days. It makes an ever
changing scene, as we steam along a narrow channel,
close to the shore, then out on a stretch of ocean,
the roll of whose waves sends timid hearts and unsteady stomachs to their little rooms. There is
only one stretch of sea-crossing, which is really very
rough, and that is Queen Charlotte's Sound, and
we made that yesterday. We have not been yet out
of sight of land.

To-day has been too short. We began by having
breakfast at half past seven; then, after attending to
a few " odds and ends," Jamie and I seated ourselves in our corner, to enjoy the morning, and before we were aware, the sea breezes had made us so
drowsy, we could not keep awake, and it was near
eleven when I opened my eyes, to find the wife of
Senator D., of Oregon, seated near us. She had
adopted our corner, and we were glad to have so

agreeable and handsome a companion. We chatted, and a very good article in Frank Leslie's Magazine, of August, 1891, on "A Trip to Alaska" was read, then twelve o'clock and luncheon. After lunch, Mr. C., the purser, Mr. C., the freight clerk, Misses K., D., J., of San José, Miss C., of Oakland, Dr. N., of Johns Hopkins University, Mrs. D. and a few others, all gathered in our corner, and we asked conundrums, until worn out and weary, when we dispersed for naps. I tried to write my journal, but my head was in such a state of commotion, from the ship's motion, that I could do nothing, so gave it up until we should come to Loring. Miss C. came, about half past four, and serenaded me outside my door, with a banjo and a song, very sweet and pretty. About five o'clock, "first dinner" was announced, and after it, as somebody at our table discovered that I knew a little about palmistry (they did not know how little that was), our corner was soon full of applicants for "a reading,"—thin and fat hands, artistic and practical. I read about two dozen, *very poorly*, too, but it pleased the little crowd, and especially Jamie, as I happened to "hit several nails on the head." I think twenty-five or thirty surrounded us ; it was as bad as in Chinatown with the camera.

At last, about 8 P. M., we steamed up to a miserable collection of little huts, about fifteen houses in all, and the Captain said, "This is Loring, in Alaska." A fish cannery is the industry of the place, where they can salmon; and some people who went ashore, say, "You will never eat canned salmon, if you once see the process!" Lots of people went ashore, but it was pouring—a regular Alaska down-pour,—and as I knew we should have another chance to land here, on the return trip, I came to my room, to get in out of the rain, and have been writing this journal. I am sitting in the tiny room, my door is shut and light comes only through a small window, and yet it is quite light enough to see to write; and it is 8.50 P. M., and a rainy night at that.

To-day we passed an empty Indian village, Fort Tongas, it is called on the map. The Indians return to it in winter. We saw many Totem poles, and the Indian graveyard. They put their dead under ground, but build little houses, and fences about the corpse, and it is quite an unusual sight,— a little miniature village.

WEDNESDAY, JULY 22ND.

AT five o'clock this morning, we steamed up to Fort Wrangle's dock, and tied up to the wharf. It was a damp, chilly, disagreeable morning, but we were up early, in order to see all we could at this Alaskan Port. Fort Wrangle, once upon a time, was a flourishing little town, being the nearest one, of any size, to the British boundary, and mines in the vicinity were in working order, producing activity and life in this small village. The river Stikeen opens up from Wrangle to the British possessions, and was the quickest path, in those days, from Victoria to the British mines. That life of activity and interest, bringing Fort Wrangle in touch with the world, is over now, as capital *for* the mines and deposits *in* the mines, have both simultaneously given out, and this little village has dwindled into a tumble-down wreck of a place, which was not much to boast of, in its palmiest days. From the wharf, broken-down huts, devoid of paint or embellishment of any kind, one story high, seem to be clustered about the curve of the shore, making a semicircle of civilization, most unattractive externally and swarming with Indians, of every age and size. Everything seems stamped with the motto " going to destruction," for houses are tumbling down, their supports seem insecure, and uncertainty is written on everything, in the little town of Fort Wrangle. Rubbish lies in every path, broken wharves, wrecks of once fleet steamships, tumbling shanties, and no one seems thrifty enough to put a nail into needy places, or clear away the piles of rubbish. In going about, we had board walks for a while, but then had to wander on the shore, covered with stones, and old shoes, and tin cans.

At ten minutes after six, Jamie wandered back into the stateroom, and I arose. He had been out to walk, having met Miss C., and gone with her to an Indian silversmith's, and bought me two tiny silver bangles, of dainty design and work. He hurried me as much as he could, and before seven o'clock, we were wandering up the wharf, poking our noses into the funny little shops, and finally we wandered into the silversmith's little out-of-the-way cottage. We then went through a long alley-way, up a little incline, and came to a neat little hut. As we approached, I could smell—a smell I shall not forget, —an odor of smoked and smoking herring! Oh, how these people,—their baskets and wares,—do smell! By a stove, stood a young Indian boy, cooking the small red fish,—opposite, at a table, sat Indian Charlie, eating his fish like sticks of candy. Nothing else was before him,—absolutely nothing,— *that* was his breakfast! The room was small, but it looked clean. It was papered with daily newspapers; once in a while, an illustrated weekly shone forth conspicuously. In one corner stood a bed, clean and white and nicely made, and on it lay a bundle of flannel, on pillows. In another corner, on the floor,—on some kind of mattress,—*in a pink dress*, but under a sheet and blanket, lay a young Indian woman ; and by her side was a plate, with the sticks of unappetizing herring on it, for her to eat. This young woman was just a mother,—and the bundle on the bed, was the two days old Indian baby,—a little round roll of fatness. James marched into the room, and straight over to the bed, as if he was an old friend of the family, and he called to me, to come and see the little baby! It was a dear little dark-skinned Indian, and was·fighting with its little fists, like a born warrior. When a child is a year old, the first winter, the mother takes it to the river or bay, and puts it in the coldest water to be found. If the child lives, it is hardened, they say, by this process; but if it dies, it was too sickly for earth. After viewing the infant, we wandered about again, and met a white man, who took us to see an old war-boat, used always in war, and carrying forty or fifty men. It was cut from one log, and had long pointed bow and stern, like gondolas. As we passed through an old building to go and see it, we came suddenly upon a dog, —I thought it was,—and although chained, I was not afraid, and put out my hand to pat his head. He growled fiercely, and I jumped back fortunately, for it was a wolf, and he was quite ferocious toward strangers. The owner came and held him, while I passed, and said, "Well, he might do no harm ;—he tore the minister's clothes all to pieces last time he called !" On all corners, sat groups of old women and children, in their queer crouching positions, bent shoulders, thick bright blankets and brilliant head handkerchiefs. Their faces are stupid and express but little, their skin is like a hide, and very dark. They rub in paint of red shades, or else blacken the face, all over sometimes, again only in spots, with stove blacking, or a gum of one of their trees.

We came back to the ship for breakfast, which we

swallowed in double quick time ; then in a flock, we all wandered out again, around the shore to where the totem poles were the finest.   These Indians at Fort Wrangle get trees from the forest, take the bark off, and carve—rudely, to be sure,—their family history upon these poles. They are their family trees, their badge of heraldry, historical record of their own brave chiefs; and they set them up in front of their houses, usually placing on the summit, some monstrous animal, with huge wide-open mouth, or all eyes, which means something, that I could not find out.   These poles are called " Totem poles," and are usually five or six times as high as the house.   Some are painted, some seem all eyes, which they vary with different colors.   They also place them about their graves, and they are most unusual, and very interesting.   In Longfellow's beautiful poem, we read of this peculiar characteristic of these Indians :

> " All these things did Hiawatha
> Show unto his wondering people,
> And interpreted their meaning,
> And he said ; ' Behold, your grave-posts
> Have no mark, no sign, nor symbol.
> Go and paint them all with figures ;
> Each one with its household symbol.
> With its own ancestral Totem ;
> So that those who follow after
> May distinguish them and know them.'
> And they painted on the grave-posts
> Of the graves yet unforgotten,

Each his own ancestral Totem,
Each the symbol of his household,
Figures of the Bear aud Reindeer,
Of the Turtle, Crane, and Beaver."

We saw five or six very fine ones. Two were in
front of the house belonging to a nephew of the
Chief—" Shakes " by name, and he asked us in and
up one flight of steps (for this was a new and modern dwelling), to see a totem pole, of small dimensions (carried on all state occasions by the Chief),
one thousand years old. He also showed us a queer
hat, five hundred years old, worn by many Indian
chiefs. It was like an inverted pan, made of wood,
painted a queer blue, and on it was a monster,
spreading all over it, with outstretched claws, and
tremendous shining eyes, in a bronze color. On top
of that was a queer little thing, which stuck up like a
chimney, and waved when a man walked, from
which hung tails of fur.

James and I had a pleasant time, and were returning to the ship, when Mr. C., the clerk, a good-natured
fellow, came running after us, to say they had persuaded Katashan to put on all his fine toggery, and
come out for me to photograph him. Of course,
we were delighted and hurried back, and as soon as
we came in sight of the door, there stood the Indian
in full regimentals ; and a study in color he was. A
Chilcat blanket, full of yellow wool and great black
eyes, covered his shoulders, and the straw-colored

fringe hung nearly to the ground. On his head was the old hat, and in his hand the showy totem pole, and he was a picture indeed. After he had disappeared, his little son came up and asked if we would like to have him sing. He was a little chap, and too cute for anything. He had been taught in the Indian school, which is doing wonderful work among the little people. "Thumpkins he can dance alone," and similar ballads, were his stock in trade, and very cutely he sang them too, then bowed very low, and *at once* passed round his little straw hat. He was bountifully rewarded. We soon had to hurry back to the steamer, as we were to leave Fort Wrangle, at 10.30 A. M.

Our trip all day was lovely, through exquisite scenery, bountifully supplied with snow mountains and numerous islands, most picturesque and beautiful. I sewed a bit before lunch, and after lunch, in the delicious cool crisp air, we slept and *nearly froze*. After dinner it was very cold, so we sat in our cabin reading, until we began to approach Point Ellis; then we went on the hurricane deck, and watched the man throw the lead and take soundings.

Point Ellis consists merely of a cannery, belonging to Mr. E., who was a *Mexico* passenger; and the *Mexico* went out of her course, to take the owner to view, for the first time, his property. We left him there, and will go after him later, on our return trip. As we were rounding into the Bay, near Point Ellis, Miss C. said, "Isn't it light for nine o'clock?" "Nine o'clock!" I exclaimed, "you're crazy; it can't be more than seven, if it is that." We immediately took out our watches, and sure enough it was nine o'clock. It was as bright as it is at home at five.

The view here was perfectly beautiful. The foreground was full of lovely wooded islands, of numerous shapes and sizes, then a band of blue water, behind which, the great ragged peaks of the mountains rose, boldly outlined against such a sky as one seldom sees,—the bluish grey of the rocks on their summits, contrasting strangely with the great white snow patches on them; and, over all, a pink glow was thrown from the sunshine, which deepened into rose, then red, purple and all shades of violet; and all was reflected in a mirror of water below. We stood in a speechless trance, spellbound by such beauty. The sunshine lasted until after ten o'clock, then a radiant twilight came down upon us, and at eleven o'clock, I could see plainly, sitting outside my own room door, as I wrote a letter to the three at home.

We had much fun to-day, watching whales, which came so near the ship, we could see their great heads and shining bodies plainly.

THURSDAY, JULY 23RD.

ANCHORED at Douglas Island, Alaska, 10.30 P. M., in bright daylight and on deck.

Although half past ten o'clock, it is bright daylight, and I am sitting outside my stateroom, writing in the twilight of this Alaskan day. It is a queer sensation to have the daylight linger so long ; it quite upsets one's ideas of the proper order of things, and makes going to bed seem almost a sacrilege. The sun set about half past nine to-night, and the beautiful rose-glow on the snow mountains was simply heavenly, at a quarter to ten o'clock. Now, as I write, without exaggeration, it is as bright as it is at home, at seven o'clock in summer. The mountains have a golden glory all behind them, and it is beautiful, although uncanny and mysterious, to one accustomed to darkness at the "proper hour." They say, to-morrow night, it will be still later when the sun goes down, for we start out in a few minutes now, to go further north. I must say, this long twilight is simply fascinating, and makes one forget fatigue and every care, in the cheerful and continual blessing of the sunshine. It covers the entire scene with a glow and a glory, which make all beautiful. Last month, the days were longer, but gradually, month by month, the days shorten, until, during the winter, the sun departs about two o'clock in the afternoon, and although not inky black until six o'clock at night, lamps are lighted about 2 P. M. Doleful it is then !

We were up this morning at the usual hour, had breakfast at half past seven ; and it is simply astonishing how much one can sleep and eat, on shipboard. A trip to Alaska is "a life on the ocean

JUNEAU.

wave," without much wave about it, just delightful and ideal, and as unusual as it is easy. After break-fast Misses C—, J—, D—, K—, N—, and I, sat awhile together, then I came to my room to finish a letter home, which I wanted to mail in Juneau. Dinner at twelve o'clock, or rather luncheon, and then about two o'clock, we were nearing Juneau, the largest city in Alaska, and naturally, everybody was on deck, and all on the "qui vive" to see this spot. We had travelled miles and miles, without a single sign of civilization, and now we were approaching a *big* city. At the foot of some very high mountains, nestled close to the water's edge, stood Juneau, a city of a few hundred inhabitants. Houses were many, with but one story, and usually one room in them, and although some, high upon the hill, were more palatial in appearance, they were only moder-ately beautiful, that was all. We went on shore as soon as we could, and everyone made a rush for the stores marked "curios." Etiquette was forgotten, in some instances, and a person's natural selfishness stood out "in full feather." Jamie and Miss C. made a mad march for "souvenir spoons." Everybody is spoony in these trips; in fact, the fad is an epidemic, in a violent form.

Of course, Juneau is hilly, and the best street is on the side of the hill. There are nice stores here, —a fine drug-store, good provision stores, fur shops without number,—and baskets of Alaskan weave in every form and variety. We saw a funny sight on a street corner. Under a sheltering roof, by the side of a store, sat a dozen Indian women, crouching down on their haunches (for Indians never use or possess chairs). They were sitting back against the wall, in a row,—such filthy, dirty old hags, that one felt like keeping a good distance from them. In front of them were china cups, filled with all kinds of berries, which they expected we would buy. They wear always moccasins, an old calico skirt, blankets pinned about the neck and falling from the shoulders, and handkerchiefs over their heads. Yellow, red, and bright green, are their favorite colors, and in contrast with their dark skins and black hair, are very picturesque. A group of Indian women is generally a study in color, of the highest tints. Some of these women were young, some were old, but all wore innumerable silver rings, sometimes on every finger, and bangles of silver by dozens. There is no Indian woman poor enough, to go without her silver ornaments. One curious custom among them is, that they paint their faces with vermilion, and rub it in, until it is a brilliant red. As I said before, the most revolting habit is painting the face black, which is a very common custom, and we saw many at Juneau blackened, and shining, as black as a coal everywhere, except rings around eyes and mouth. They do it for three reasons—to protect the face, sometimes, from the sun when canoeing, again for beauty, but mostly, as a little Indian boy expressed it, "When she wants to cry a good deal, cause she lost her papa"—in other words, as a badge of mourning. When a woman marries, she has her chin pierced, as we do our ears, and has a silver piece put in it. It is called a labret, and is the mark of a married woman. It is like a cribbage marking pin, only made of silver, larger and longer, and even in size, and sticks out of the lower lip, or the chin under the lip, about an inch. One woman we saw at Juneau, had not only a labret, but she had a silver ring put through her nose. You see dozens of these people, on the corners, and on the wharves, all offering goods for sale, and at big prices too. They live in huts, always close together, and as they have no fear of dirt, you see it in every variety and form, in Indian villages. One walks into an Indian village at first courageously, and with interest, but feels like *crawling out* as soon as possible. We visited the little village, or settlement, near the wharf. In a door-way, crouching down, sat a young mother, with a ten days old baby in her arms. We went near and looked at the diminutive scrap, and *never in my life* have I seen such an atom, in the form of a baby. An ordinary sized orange would be large, in comparison with its head, and its hands were like birds' claws, as some one expressed it. I do not believe it measured more than twelve inches, "over all" (as they say of a ship). I tried to get the mother to let me take her picture, with her baby, but she cried and went into her house. After strolling all over town, trying to get some lemonade, or apollinaris, or something, which we could not do, we wandered back to the ship and rested, for we were to have a long evening. Dinner at five o'clock, then we mustered up a little crowd and went on shore, up to an Indian tent, to see a War Dance by the Indians, in their native dress, paint and feathers. It was a disappointment, no doubt, to the Indians, that so few people came to their unique performance, but some did not think it worth "one dollar admission," and only about a dozen of us were present. Behind a miserably dirty curtain, on a little raised stage, sat the Indians, and in their shrill harsh voices, they chanted for about fifteen minutes, before we were allowed to see them. We, in the meantime, were seated on boards and benches, in the middle of a medium sized tent. At last, Yash Noosh, the Chief, in a checked suit of brownish tint, and a straw hat, gave the signal, and the curtain was drawn aside. About half a dozen Indians, in brilliant paint, with Chilcat blankets and feather head-dresses, with numberless ermine tails hanging down behind, and queer war-spears, began to tip back and forth, from heel to toe, and then jumping and see-sawing on their toes, and keeping time to a queer melancholy chant, as weird and doleful as it could be. They kept this up for a while, then the curtain came down, and a recess was taken. Another dance exhibited other war-garments, queer trousers of buckskin, bright woven blankets, new attitudes, and new tunes, and quite

unusual and different from the first. The performance consisted of a series of these dances, very strange
and picturesque, and ended in a " Medicine Man's
Dance." The Medicine Man was trying to expel an
evil spirit from his patient, who lay quite still on
the floor, and the physician and attendants made the
most unearthly noise, screaming, howling, beating a
drum, and doing enough to kill any sick man from
sheer exhaustion. All the time, the wonderful doctor was sitting down on his haunches, and hopping
around like a toad, while another attendant kept
throwing feathers all over him, and in his face also.
The performance ended with this Medicine dance,
and while we would not go one block to see it again,
it was well worth one visit, and we were glad we
had gone. Among the performers was a tiny boy,
whose reddened face and black lines, over nose and
cheeks, enlisted the interest of all the audience.
He teetered back and forth on his little toes, to the
great amusement of all. He was dressed in a little
fur coat, and was too cunning for anything. After
one dance, this diminutive scrap came tumbling
from behind the curtain, in a flood of tears,
stopping every few steps to rub one poor little toe,
which a big Indian had stepped upon. His red
paint and black, were getting hopelessly mixed and
streaked. One of our party took the little fellow,
and sat him in our midst, and as she did so, she exclaimed, "Oh, how I would like to wash you, you
dirty little thing!" He was almost better than the

performance. All the while these Indians danced, it seemed as if they were waxing more and more angry, and one could easily imagine that they could commit any number of atrocious deeds, after such agitating performances.

At eight o'clock, the *Mexico* steamed off from Juneau, across the bay to Douglas Island, a couple of miles only, and we remained there from nine o'clock to twelve, when we set sail for Chilcat Canneries. On Douglas Island, we were much interested, for the richest mine of gold in the world is there, turning out a million dollars worth of gold a year; and there is no sign of any lessening for years to come. It is the Tredwell Mine, owned, it is said, by D. O. Mills, and other capitalists.

At 9 P. M. in an army, the passengers marched up the pier, to the buildings of the mining company. We were specially invited, by a young friend of Miss C.'s who was here, and had influence, to go with about twelve, in a private party, so we went through the Tredwell Mine, with a former superintendent of the mine, who took us everywhere, except into the room where the gold is poured into moulds. That is a forbidden place to all, as the immense yield of the mine is kept secret. We saw the two hundred and forty stamp mill, where the ore is put into the crusher, the quicksilver slabs over which the gold is washed and caught, the concentrator, or a vertical shaking slab, where all gold, that escaped the first slab, is caught and separated from the soda; then that dust is put in fires and baked, and again put in tanks, and a solution of acid thrown over it, which separates the last remnants of gold, from the common stuffs. We went everywhere, even climbed up a steep place, and looked down into the mine, saw the shutes, down which the ore is thrown into cars below. It was a most interesting experience. At 9.45 P. M. we came out of the mine and enjoyed the exquisite sunset, with the lovely pink glow on the snow-mountains.

We saw some icebergs to-day, not large ones, to be sure, but a little taste of what we are to see later. The glaciers, on the mountain sides, were beautiful to-day.

Miss K. gave me a pretty drawn work hand-kerchief to-day, and Miss N. brought me some lovely wild flowers at night.

FRIDAY, JULY 24TH.

WHEN we awoke this morning, we were anchored off the Chilcat Canneries, and found ourselves unable to go ashore, even if we desired to do so. The wind is very strong to-day; the tide is low, and as there is but little to see, we are not sorry to be obliged to stay on our ship. It is a lovely place to anchor, for the views, in every direction, are grand and magnificent. As we stepped out of our stateroom, to go to breakfast this morning, we looked right into the face of a tremendous blue glacier, on the shore opposite. It is a wonderful sight to me, these great frozen rivers, so majestic in their silent grandeur; and in the sunshine, the variety of blue and green ice crevices, give a marvelous effect to the entire surface. Near the ship, is a queer formation of stones and boulders, in piles and layers, which is said to be the terminal moraine of an ancient glacier. This huge glacier before us is called "Davidson's Glacier." The story is told, that a man some time ago, grew discontented with his work for Mr. Muir (of Muir Glacier fame), and rather than stay with him, he determined to cross this dangerous ice-flow, and reach his home on the bay, where we are now anchored. He was fourteen days in doing it; and although he had two extra pairs of shoes with him, he reached his destination bare-footed. He had coffee and biscuits with him, —fortunately met and killed a bear, on his way, and had many and thrilling experiences. Some days he would creep for only two miles, then find some gorge or crevice impassable, and have his steps to retrace, and a fresh beginning to make.

This morning, after breakfast, I was standing near the pilot-house, taking a view of our surroundings, when a gentleman joined us, and began to speak of the two missionaries, we are to leave in this desolate spot,—a young man from Princeton, and his new wife. I was at once interested, as being in the forward part of the ship, these facts had not reached my ears. I went aft to see them, and had a long chat with the brave young people. They have left home, a father and mother over seventy years old, to come and teach these Chilcat Indians. The Chilcat tribe numbers about three thousand, and are the most powerful tribe in Alaska. They are the most warlike too, but these young people are devoid of fear. I had a most interesting chat with the young wife,—long enough to satisfy myself, that she little knows what she is undertaking. They are truly in earnest in their work, but have little realization of the desolation and loneliness, they are about to enter. It is said, if the Indians are friendly, they nearly live with the whites,— come in crowds into one's kitchen, and sit on the floor for hours, saying nothing,—only watching. If the lady of the house goes into any other room, they go along, and at any and all hours of the day, Indian faces may be seen, pressed close to the window pane, watching every movement. The Indians here are more easily taught, than the ordinary Indians of our Territories and Western States. They claim they are of Mongolian descent, and are more intelligent. If these two young missionaries are favorites, in the new home to which they go, they say, the Indians will, in time, make a great feast for the newcomers, and with fitting ceremonies, adopt them into their tribe, and give them Indian names. While I chatted with brave Mrs. W., I found she was quite unprepared, for the common ordinary aches and pains, which mortals are heirs to, and did not fully appreciate the ninety miles of space, between her and *any* doctor; so I came into my room, searched through my bag, and could only find Jamaica Ginger to offer her, which she most joyously accepted. Such faith and self-sacrifice, as these people exhibit, such forgetfulness of pleasure and comforts, of home and family, in the service of the Master, makes one stand still, and wonder in silence, at the strength which such faith can bring, and at the bright cheerful heart, so full of hope and pleasure, even knowing the hardships. I know the discipline of pain, and I know one can accept the trials which come; but to absolutely go out into a nest of trouble and discouragements, to settle down in the midst of distresses, and keep cheerful and happy in hard work, expresses a strength of character, I am utterly unable to appreciate.

While we chatted, a lady from Montana joined in the conversation, and she was rich in experiences with the Indians of Montana. She told us of the lawless times they used to have, before justice had any voice in the administration of affairs, when the sheriff was the head of a band of robbers and thieves, all being road agents. Murder and housebreaking were common everyday affairs, and there was no redress,—one lost everything,—life was demanded at a moment's notice, and no voice was raised in complaint, for the safety of the people, for some time. Finally, right was might, and the downtrodden sufferers joined in bands, called "Vigilantes," and hung every out-law they could find, at a moment's warning. At last, they brought some out-laws to trial. This lady's cousin was just stepping into a stage, in this little settlement, which was to carry him to his home, when the people came, to beg him to stay and try their case, as the road-agents and sheriff had bought up all the lawyers in town; and this gentleman was a judge. He yielded, but there was no house or place for the Court room. Taking a farm wagon, and calling jurors, he stood up in the wagon and "held court." It was simply and quickly done. The man under arrest was a fine looking fellow, but a villain. He had murdered any number of innocent people, and his favorite method was to catch them on some high-way, bind them to trees, and then, as recreation between his courses at lunch, or between drinks, he would shoot at them, and watch and ridicule their agony. He would riddle his victims with bullets, which usually resulted in their deaths, but if not, he would dispatch them more brutally. This young man was tried and sentenced, to be hanged in an hour. In a most pathetic manner, he begged for more time, that he might write last letters to friends; and this lady said that her cousin felt sympathy for the fellow, and could hardly bear to be so cruel, but he knew that if he yielded one moment, the road-agents would rally and free their companion. One man in the crowd reminded the masses, of the little mercy ever shown by the prisoner, to any of *his* prisoners, and at once the verdict was changed to *immediate execu-*

tion. Of course this is only an incident, in the history of our Western States, in the early years of their formation. This lady says, in Montana now, and especially in Helena, whenever any robbery is committed, or any threatened assassination, boards are stuck up all over Helena, and all the newspapers print a mystical signal. It is " 3-7-77,"—and under this number, is always a skull and bones. No outlaw ever stands upon the order of his going, but departs at once, when this sign appears. It means,—as it counts,—" In twenty-four hours, you will be skull and bones." She said she saw the sign, only two years ago, in Helena. She also amused us, by telling of the Indians' love for dress, and the queer fancies the men take for peculiar articles. Sun-umbrellas are their delight. She saw an Indian, not long ago, in buckskin trousers, a bright red blanket, his hair braided, and amply hung with rattlesnake rattles, and over his head he carried, with great satisfaction, a *pink cotton umbrella.* A Sioux Indian went to visit a friend of hers, and having to ford a stream, the Indian took off his scanty supply of clothes, and hanging them on his arm, waded across. Instead of dressing again on the other bank, he approached the tents, with his clothing on his arm, and a blue-checked sunshade over his head!

While I was writing this journal, Mrs. S. came to my cabin door, to ask what I thought about getting a cow for the missionaries. It seems there are no cows near Chilcat,—no milk is anywhere to be had, and they cannot get butter or any fresh meat. Eggs are one dollar a dozen, and scarce and hard to get. A cow could be brought here, perhaps, etc. I put on my cap and went out on deck, to see what Jamie thought of such a plan, what he would give towards it, but he did not encourage it much,—in fact, I found there was much opposition to missionaries, as many in these parts have been said to be scoundrels and scamps, feathering their own nest, under the cloak of religion. But, despite the antipathy to missionaries, the fact stood unchanged, and the women on board appreciated the discomforts and deprivations, the young wife had before her, and longed to ease them a little, at least. The fact that she was a missionary was forgotten, in the sympathy of one woman's heart for another. But the little discouragements disheartened us, and we reluctantly gave it up. About half past two o'clock, I was resting in my "tiny boudoir," when Mrs. S. came again, to ask me to come and wave the missionaries off, as they were to go ashore then. I went out, but there was the usual delay, and while we waited, I chatted with a gentlemen from Lincoln, Nebraska. I told him of the desire that we had and he spoke so encouragingly, that I flew to Mrs. S. and suggested that we do, in those few minutes, all we could. In fifteen minutes, we had seen a dozen or more people ; all gave, and in less than half an hour, Mrs. S. stood on deck, with fifty dollars in gold in her hand, for the little wife. She called her into the saloon, and gave it to her; and for the first time, the tears came, and the poor woman wept. It was awfully pathetic, and we cried too. When she opened the envelope and saw the shining gold, she was overpowered and could hardly speak. The cow is to be called Mexico, at our request. Several heard of it later, and some came to me with their donations, and we sent more to her by the Captain. It seemed only right, to do a little for her, when we were all out on a pleasure trip.

Jamie went on shore, and into the Cannery, with Commander C. of the Navy, and had quite an interesting time.

After dinner little groups gathered in "our corner," and we had a right merry time. At nine o'clock, the sun was so high in the heavens, that Jamie took a photograph of us all; but we were laughing so heartily, I fear the photograph will not be good. The sun was blinding on the water then. About half past nine, the *Mexico* steamed from Chilcat to Pyramid Bay, to another Cannery, to discharge freight, and take on more canned salmon. Pyramid Bay takes its name from an island, just off shore, formed entirely of rocks, and in the form of a pointed pyramid, and it is interesting, because it is the terminal moraine of a once powerful glacier.

We all remained on deck, guessing proverbs, and having much merriment, until after ten o'clock, then we went down to supper. After supper Miss C., who has a glorious voice, sang for us, and we had some other good music, until half past eleven, when we *made* ourselves go to our room, but it seemed cruel and wicked, to go to sleep, and leave the twilight. It was light at twelve o'clock—mid-night —and the sky was blue, the clouds were rose-colored and purple, and it was heavenly! These northern nights are worth the journey to see, and to exper-ience the queer sensations they produce. I felt as if I was going to bed at five o'clock, and yet, my tired bones warned me, it was bedtime.

What a lovely trip this is! At first one has much to become accustomed to, discomfort, inconvenience and cramped quarters; and the first few days seem long. Then, as soon as the rough edges wear off, and one gets settled and learns to manage, a charm and fascination comes over one, and you float along from day to day, and wish the voyage was ten times as long; and each day we long to stretch, to its utmost limit. It is glorious, such a blissful rest!

SATURDAY, JULY 25TH.

THESE long days upset every one, and make regular hours a dream of the past, a remnant of the Dark Ages. Last night, no one wanted to go to bed, and it was not strange, for it was quite bright at twelve o'clock, at mid-night. Some people sat up, hoping to see the Northern Lights; but there were none to be seen.

Nothing to chronicle to-day, so far. We spent the morning at Pyramid Bay, anchored, loading with canned salmon. At noon, we moved back to Chilcat, but we hope to leave here, in a couple of hours now. I have "cleaned house" this morning, that is, straightened and arranged my room, as order is an absolute necessity, and I have been writing also, between chats with passing people. We have been watching the Indians in their canoes, which have hovered about the ship all the morning. A strong young Indian, with his squaw and pappoose, and three other tiny tots, paddled out to the ship, to try and sell some things. We had fun with him, offering to buy the pappoose, and he finally said he would sell it, for ten dollars. It is interesting to watch these people, *from a distance;* they are often good-natured and jolly, and what little English they can speak, they use in such an original choppy way, but they are too dirty, to have a nearer acquaintance safe or pleasant.

This morning, one of the men on the ship, went ashore with his gun, and a little while ago, he brought to show us, a bald-headed eagle, which he had shot. It was a fine fellow, and measured six feet from tip to tip of his wings. His great white head and claws were large in proportion, and it was an interesting sight.

It is delightful to see the improvement in Jamie's health. He has gained hourly of late, eats like a starved child, and is as full of fun as possible. The prediction about "our table" in the dining-room, is true, and we have the jolliest times imaginable.

We steamed over to Chilcat about noon, and stayed there until about four o'clock.   James went ashore yesterday, but not again to-day.   While at Chilcat Mrs. S. came to me, with a dish of the most beautiful strawberries I have ever seen.   Mrs. W., the missionary, had sent them over to the ship, to the ladies who had given her the cow; they were picked in the meadows and were wild strawberries, and were magnificent, and so large, with stout stems and a good flavor.   Strawberries grow marvelously in this country, as do all things: ferns are colossal, mosses are glorious, wild flowers are plenty in certain locations.   I saw seven strawberries on one stem, the other night, and the stem was as large as a pipe stem.   The leaves were equally large.

After dinner we all scrambled on deck, to see the Davidson Glacier, as we passed it.   It is a tremendous great ice river, three miles across its front, and for miles and miles, it covers the country.   The crevices were many and deep, giving] a dark blue, and oftentimes a green color to the ice.   It was most interesting, but seemed only grand in size, when we turned to see ten pure *white* ones, nestled close in the mountain's side; then we felt we had seen glaciers in their finest form, and they were the most beautiful pictures imaginable.

The scenery, from Chilcat to Sitka, is the most magnificent sight, one can ever hope to see, in this world.   After leaving Chilcat, we stood for hours on the hurricane deck, watching the grandeur.   It was sublime, ideal, such a sight as one wishes to hold forever in the memory. The mountains rose on each side of us, in great ranges, so high they seemed to touch the sky. Their base and sides were gray and dark, but the ragged peaks, in every conceivable effect, from round to pointed, ragged and sharp and blunt as well, were each and all covered thickly with pure white snow, which crept down to the dark sides in great rivers of white. The spaces between the mountains were full of great shining glaciers, icy and white; and all was in marked contrast to the dark angry waters, and the heavy rain clouds in the sky above us. We stood in admiring silence, until the rain drops fell upon us, and then went below, with the picture indelibly printed upon our minds, for it was a scene of awful grandeur, magnificent and inspiring.

SUNDAY, JULY 26TH.

NEVER was scenery more daintily picturesque and beautiful, than this morning. Through narrow passages, close to thickly wooded shores, in and out, between most exquisite little islands of rocks and trees, into enclosed lakes, for which there seemed no opening nor outlet,—until a gateway suddenly presented itself to us, as our bow was almost on shore,—the good *Old Mexico* has carried us on, and we became as enthusiastic, over the delicate outlines and profusion of beautiful islands, as we were last night, over the solemn grandeur of the great gray monarchs, with their snow covering and glacial deposits. The entire morning was one long exclamation of "Oh, how beautiful!" Islands, like little buttons, stood side by side, with great green emerald isles, all reproduced in the quiet water, so mirror-like in its reflection. Ducks were swimming on the surface, and at our approach, with a dive and a long streak of ruffled water behind them, they would disappear, only to rise up serenely, a half minute later, and with a shrill call, fly off to the land. Porpoises, too, were waltzing along, like pin-wheels, and racing with us. Finally a ring from the Captain on his bridge, quieted the engine; the good old ship's speed was lessened, and we seemed to float forward in silence. Somebody said, "This must be White Stone Narrows, the most dangerous pass on the trip," and then every one was on the qui vive, to see the ship pass the danger point, and enthusuastic over the marvelous dexterity, with which the Captain and his assistants, handled the big ship. Two buoys were placed, about two boats' length apart. We had to pass one on one side, and the other on the other, making a letter S, and we clung so close to one buoy, caressing it the entire length of our ship, that *somebody* suggested the conundrum, coined on the spot, "Why was the *Mexico* exceedingly improper? Because she had been seen *hugging a buoy!*" As we steamed out of these Narrows, where the great rocks and reefs stood out boldly, on each side of us, re minding one of the St. Lawrence Rapids, we suddenly rounded a point and saw, in the distance, Sitka, the Capital City of Alaska.

As pretty a picture as one cares ever to see, is this little town, situated at the foot of the great Mt. Verstoria,—the sides and top so green and beautiful, —beside and behind which are numberless mountains of pure snow; and opposite the little city stands, as sentinel, the extinct volcano, Edgecombe, with its great open cup full of snow. Islands without number, in picturesque confusion, stand between Sitka and the open ocean, and make an island barricade, like the links in a chain. As we approached Sitka, going beyond and in and out, among these islands, threading our way with cautious care, we were spell-bound, by the beautiful picture, this isolated little city presents. The ancient Russian Castle, now in such picturesque ruins, stands out in bold relief, against the green Mt. Verstoria and looks like the haunted house, it is said to be. It was once the residence of all Russian Governors, who were men of rank and title, and lived here in luxury and state, bringing their Court and state furnishings from Russia; and the stories told of their grandeur, of their Court, and doings, make one believe in the past greatness of Sitka, but also make one see how truly *past* is that greatness.

Once upon a time, Sitka had fine industries. A marvelous foundry here, was the one that fashioned all the bells, for the missions in Southern California, and sent its work to many large cities. Slowly, and

SITKA.

by the law which governs the rise and fall of nations,
Sitka began to lose power and people; and in 1867,
when America negotiated with Russia, and purchased Alaska, as a territory, paying " at the rate of
two cents per acre," the legends of Russian glory,
became the property of the American people.
Sitka is the brightest little place imaginable, and it
is hard to realize, that it is so remote from all civilization.

When we steamed into the harbor, between the
town and the islands, we were impressed by the
picturesqueness of this little city. In contrast to
the great Russian Castle, in its square box-like
architecture and remnants of brown paint, its brok-
en windows and tumbled-down ruined appearance—
stood the Greek Church, in about the centre of the
town. Its spire is bulging, like beads on a string,
set on end, an oblong one, then a round one, and
surmounted by a golden Greek Cross. Behind this
spire is a dome of ample proportions, and dome and
spire are painted a light green,—not a bit of yellow
in the green—pale but distinctly green. The rest of
the building is devoid of paint; or the incessant
rains, which visit Sitka, may have washed away
the less powerful colors. An old tradition says,
that whenever a ship is in sight, the ravens always
gather on the gilded cross, on the spire of the Greek
Church; and as we came nearer to the town, a
couple of great black ravens flew towards the cross.
Whether they really knew their lesson and direc-

tions, and were going to perch on that cross, is a question; only knowing the tradition, their flight seemed a coincidence. Barracks, a Court house, innumerable houses low and small, all curving along a cove of the sea, form the little city.

The *Mexico* reached Sitka at eleven o'clock; but we were obliged to anchor off shore, as the steamer *Queen*, the excursion boat, had come, out of her regular order and time, into Sitka this morning, and occupied the dock-room. A disgusted set of passengers we were; for the *Queen* swallows up at every port, all the choicest of curios, and we had rejoiced that we were to reach there first. The *Queen* only remained five or six hours at Sitka, however, and was to move at 2 P. M. by Sitka time, three o'clock by our watches, as Sitka time is one hour earlier, than we are on shipboard. We could not wait, however, until that hour to go ashore, so small boats were put off, and we went about one o'clock, fifteen at a time.

As we landed at the dock, we were charmed at the outset, by the aspect of things. Before us, was a large green parade ground, on one side of which stood the Government Buildings, the long stairway leading to the lofty Castle, and some trees. Under the trees, along the wharf, in front of the buildings, sitting closely together in rows, were the Indian women with their wares, all of their own make. Baskets of every conceivable design and color, silver rings and bangles, wooden totem poles, basket

bottles, etc., etc., and everything in the most picturesque confusion. The coloring of their dresses,
blankets, and head-handkerchiefs, their dark yellow
skins, contrasting strangely with their dozens of
silver bangles and numberless rings, and the little
children in brilliant colors, all presented a picture
of wonderful combinations. It was interesting to
walk along, and look at the rows of dark-skinned
women, to see the different degrees of intelligence,
and marks of industry, and their adroit manner of
displaying their things. Any Indian woman, or
every one, I should say, can speak enough English
to sell; they can all say, "two bits," or four, or six,
as the price may be, and some are so jolly about
it, and hold up their fingers to denote the price,
thus displaying the silver bedecked arms and hands.
They never undersell each other, and nothing
makes them more angry than to have people offer
them less than they ask, and yet bargains are sometimes gained by perseverance. James and I wandered along the row of Indians, really thoroughly
interested in them and their wares, and also in
watching the passengers from the *Queen*, who were
strolling along as we were, when we suddenly looked
up and stood face to face with Mrs. V— N——,
of Brooklyn. We have never been more than bowing acquaintances, but to meet any one from home,
in such a far-away place as Alaska, makes one feel
very friendly indeed, and we greeted each other in
the most enthusiastic manner. After a little, James

and I grew interested in looking at trifling souvenirs of Sitka, and we wandered from one little group of Indians to another. Then we remembered our letter to Mrs. H. of Sitka, which a friend in Chicago had given us, and we found Mrs. H. lived in an entire house, all to herself, which is a mark of superiority in Sitka, as most of the people live in rooms over stores, or in cabins,—even the officers and their wives. We found the house without difficulty, and were received by a little lady, in a very pretty room, full of the most curious of curios. Her welcome was most cordial, but as we soon found she had two cousins on the *Queen*, who were to sail away in a very short time, and who were then visiting her, James and I left for a while, and went to the Greek Church.

This church is still maintained by the Russians, and although there are but few full-blooded Russians now in Sitka, many of the people attend that church. (The other chapel is Presbyterian.) We entered the front door, were received by a young man, who politely requested each to deposit fifty cents in a contribution box at hand, which is used for the attendants on "Tourists' days," etc. We then entered the church proper, which is small in size, but large in rich possessions. No man or woman ever sits during a Russian service, so there are no pews or seats anywhere visible. Two huge white columns supported the dome, and made a fitting frame for the beautiful altar before us. With three or four steps leading to it, was a kind of Reredos, or screen, formed of beautiful paintings, the middle part having golden-bronze gates full of lovely pictures, four of which were set in ovals and represented the four Evangelists,—the two middle ones were to represent the Annunciation. There were three in each door, and one peculiar feature and effect was produced by a silver mantle (of genuine ore) over each picture. The heads and hands of the figures were uncovered, but all the rest was covered by exact representations of the paintings underneath, but made of pure silver, and all the shades and folds were most carefully wrought. No idea can be obtained from a word picture, of the singularly unique and beautiful effect this produced. On each side of this door were similar paintings, but almost life-size, one of the Virgin and Child, the other of Jesus Christ, and both were covered with a full-length silver covering. St. Michael, being the Patron Saint, was represented twice, once in a gorgeous gold covering. Three of these paintings in panels were on each side of the middle door, four with their glorious draperies, and two without, but all were really marvelous works of art. Before these paintings stood and hung beautifully wrought Russian silver lamps, and all produced a grand effect, and were so decidedly foreign to anything we expected to see, in such isolation. On each side of the main altar were smaller sanctuaries, with rare gems in beautiful paintings, sent by royal Russians, one conspicuous for its frame of rare and precious stones.

In the left hand chapel is a head of Mother and Child, said to have been painted by Raphael,—it is exquisite. The tenderness in the Mother's face, the beauty of the eyes, reminds one forcibly of the Sistine Madonna, and lingers long in mind and memory. This gem has also a silver covering, most curiously fashioned, but exquisite,—head-drapery and shoulder covering of silver, with gold wrought in, and a huge golden halo. It is the loveliest thing of its kind that we have ever seen. There are also many costly works of art and ivory carvings several hundred years old.

Behind the golden gate in the centre, we were told, was the "Holy of Holies," the most sacred spot to all Russian men, but between those portals no woman is allowed to enter. The usher kindly opened the doors, which are always thrown open at service, and allowed us to *peep in*,—just a look at the Holy Place. It was a room with altars and accompanying fixtures, but brilliantly glorious in silver and golden laces and decorations, more beautiful than can be described. Vestments of the priests were to be seen, of gold and silver cloth, with tapestry colors woven in such gorgeous glory, that it seemed cruel to have it all so hidden from the world. A head-piece, worn at service by the Russian Priest, was one mass of jewels; one huge emerald cut in the shape of a cross, set in the front, was grand and magnificent. This little church is rich beyond compare, in glorious Russian richness, and is so strange and out of place in its setting, for Sitka seems quite unequal to such grandeur and beauty.

When a couple are married in the Greek Church in Sitka, they come to the church door and knock, and the door being opened by the priest, the groom makes his wish known. Approaching a little raised platform in the centre of the Church, the bride and groom stand upon it, sometimes for an hour or more, all the time the bride wearing upon her head a *beautiful crown*. If the crown is too big, as often happens, the best man is obliged to hold it over the bride's head. The service is long and tiresome; at its finish, the groom approaches the figure of Jesus Christ, touching the toe with his lips, and the bride approaches the Mother and Child.

After dreaming in silence a little while, in a corner of the Church, and allowing our thoughts to run riot and revel in the ages past, when happy and sad Russian men and maidens attended this choicest chapel, Jamie and I wandered out again, into the crooked little streets, with the log-huts and cabins, the houses of more modern comers, and the relics of Russian Architecture.

Hearing the whistle, which announced the *Queen's* departure, I went again to see Mrs. H. while Jamie returned to the ship, and when I left her an hour later, she insisted that we should call for her after dinner, and she would take us through the Indian quarters, or the Rancherie, as it is called. About six o'clock, therefore, we went again to the house, taking a few friends with us, and we all went to the Siwash, or Indian settlement. It is situated right on the water's edge ; the houses are of moderate size and appearance, and are built in rows, and quite closely together. We were at once interested and curious about the numbering of the houses, and questioned everybody, to know why one house was numbered over the door, in huge figures " 100," the next house " 200," the next " 300," and so on. Mr. H. explained it to us and it is a most curious reason. The numbers increase one hundred each time, until one thousand is reached, then they jump one hundred each time, also, and the why and wherefore is just this. A census was taken some time ago, and it was found that often in *one* house *of one room*, ten families live, with the multitude of children always accompanying. They allow ten numbers to each household, or to each family under one roof, and registered them " A, the father, B, the mother," without recording their names, and allowed for eight children in each family. One hundred numbers were therefore allotted to one mansion ! No one, without seeing, can form any idea of the swarms of human beings living in cramped and crowded quarters, such as we saw in this Siwash village. Mrs. H. took us into many houses, which were all built alike. A square of stones and ashes, in the centre of the only room, forms the rallying point, around which all gather. There is usually a fire burning, and crouching figures, rolled in blankets, about it.

The roof is always a little open, and much smoked and blackened, as the smoke and soot rise and cling to it. Fish, split open and drying, are always hanging from the beams, and add another perfume to the well-scented air. Around this central square is usually a raised platform, on which are all the wearing apparel and property of the different families. No curtain divides one apartment from another, no partition or division of any kind, but all are huddled in together, like sardines, and delicacy of feeling or modesty, in the slightest degree, is never visible nor thought of. The fathers and mothers and the children live together like a cat and her kittens, with just about as much care for personal and household cleanliness, as a feline animal would have. Of course, there are exceptions in every case, and marked exceptions, especially where civilized ways and means have been shown these people, but I am now speaking of the Siwash people, in their natural and unchanged ways of living. Rude, rough bedsteads, without pillow or mattress, are sometimes seen, but they are not large enough for all the family, and most of them sleep on the floor. We saw a girl of fourteen—a mother then, with her tiny babe in her arms—and it was a sad sight. A funny sign over the door of one house, amused us all immensely—it was this: "Elisha Ltahin, Head of a large Family of Orthodox Christians." No one knows exactly why this Indian put up that sign, but he is very proud of it, and it is really a curiosity! Mrs. H.

surprised us by saying, that these Indians are often really clean, and that they are never known to steal. She never locks the door of her house, except at night, and in winter often finds a half dozen women in her kitchen or sitting room, when she returns from a walk, getting warmed up. Blankets are their measure of wealth, and an Indian is worth so many blankets, rather than so many shares of a certain stock. They put *all* their money earned in trading, into blankets, which are packed in chests in their houses, and are the pride of their hearts. When a man wants some cash, he *pawns* some blankets, which he never redeems as a rule, but he does not *sell* them, oh no, that would hurt his pride, and his family honor! In some houses into which we went, we saw a dozen or more huge blanket chests in the corners, a sign of wealth. If a ransom is ever demanded for a life, or a fine to satisfy any law of theirs, it is often paid in *blankets.* One Indian woman in Sitka, has accumulated such wealth, that she owns a trading-ship, they say, and has saved twenty-thousand dollars. She leads a wicked life, but she rules the town! There is decided " caste " in these little settlements, and Emeline Baker is said to be the queen of this " Rancherie," and is acknowledged as " Princess Thom." She is fat and fifty, lame and ungainly in her fleshiness, and as homely as can be imagined. Of course, we went to her house to see her collection of wares, which were for sale. James made a great impres-

sion on Princess Thom, and she sold him a most remarkable ring from her index finger, and her smiles
and coquettish airs set us all into fits of laughter.
She was stiff in her prices, and knows how to get
and keep the mighty dollar, but we had much fun
at Princess Thom's. After walking to the end of
the village, as we passed the home of the royal
princess in returning, she came prancing out to
offer James another ring she had, and invited him
into the house again. The coy princess had changed
her dark stuff dress to a " Mother-Hubbard " of the
brightest yellow; a deeper yellow handkerchief
covered her head, and some other brilliant colors
were visible. Instead of being "a dream " in yellow,
she represented a genuine nightmare!

Almost as numerous as the children in this village, were the dogs; there were big dogs and small
dogs, fat dogs and lean dogs, and all were as ugly
and wolf-like, as any I have ever seen. They are a
pest and a nuisance, as they follow one, and are so
creepy and uncomfortable. Some were quite ferocious, but seemed brave only until an umbrella was
raised, or a foot stamped; that always upset their
courage, and sent them flying in all directions.

These Indians are peaceful now, and never give
any trouble to the residents, but about seven years
ago there was an uprising among them, which was
put down providentially. They became angry over
some imagined injury from the whites, and were in
war paint for several days, and finally attacked the

residents of Sitka, who resisted them for a time, by barricading themselves in their houses. One morning, hope of battling longer was about given up by the white people, and without doubt a general massacre would have resulted, if a war ship had not happened to put in an appearance that very morning, for coal or water. The Indians have immense respect for a gun ; they fear the business end of such articles, and as soon as the ship appeared, they disappeared into their huts and were as docile as kittens. The Government keeps soldiers in Sitka now, and a small war-ship is most of the time anchored here, and manned by clever young officers. The *Pinta* is stationed at Sitka, and we were invited on board, an invitation which James accepted.

I wish I could describe the queer Indian canoes. They are cut from a tree-trunk, hollowed out by the Indians themselves, without rule or measure. They give them long over-hanging and slender bows, and sterns as well, which make them quite like gondolas and decidedly picturesque. Nothing is more strange than to see these long slender canoes glide along through the water, with their brilliantly decked occupants, crouching in the bottom of the boat. At almost every place we have stopped, these canoes have gathered about the ship and presented such varied little pictures of Indian families and Indian life.

Mrs. N. one of our *Mexico* passengers had known, many years ago, the Russian Princess Maksoutoff, the first wife of Sitka's last Russian Governor. She died early in her life and was buried in the little graveyard in Sitka. For the sake of old times, and their friendship, Mrs. N. visited her grave, and was horrified to find it one mass of weeds and brambles, the beautiful tombstone having been carried away some distance from the grave, and it hurt Mrs. N.'s feelings so much, that she had men clear and cut the bushes and weeds from about it, replace the stone, and left it in good condition. It was a sweet noble woman's heart, that prompted such an act of kindness and respect, and we love our fellow traveller for her quiet tribute of love to her old friend.

Sitka was pronounced to-night by all, to be a most charming little place. It is a marvel in many ways, —in its remote situation, so far from all civilized portions of the earth, in the midst of wildness of land as well as of people—and yet it holds up its head proudly and bravely, and seems as happy a place, with as contented a set of people, as one can find anywhere.

Sitka, with its greatness in the past, its legends of romance and love, of blood-shed and glory, with its relics and treasures in true Russian gorgeousness, is the most fascinating little spot we have seen in our entire journey. It seems entirely out of the commonplace, and is unique in itself and unusual and foreign in many respects. One could easily spend a month here, with pleasure and profit, and our friends urged it so strongly that we would have remained, had we been a wee bit prepared for it. They promised camping and hunting, glimpses of exquisite scenery, but although sorely tempted, we could not stay.

MONDAY, JULY 27TH.

W E were up early as usual, this morning, and soon on shore, for Sitka was too attractive for us to resist. We were able to photograph a little, as the sun produced a glare and semi-shine, good for photographers. Jamie, Miss C. and I wandered about the shops until about ten o'clock, then James went to the *Pinta* with Capt. Coffin, and I took a long walk with Mrs. and Miss N. and Miss C. to the wonderful Mission School for boys and girls of Indian parentage. It is a remarkable institution, for the Indian children are taught not alone studies, but trades and occupations. Many of the young Indian boys do all the building, and do it remarkably well. We were much interested in the fine-looking young fellows in their uniforms, and feel that the Sitka Mission is really a fine institution. This is the one in which Mrs. Shepard is so interested, and in large letters over a door of one building is " Elliot F. Shepard Training School." We also visited the little Museum, full of most interesting curios, really remarkable relics and antiquities. The pleasantest part of the morning was our walk to Indian River, about a mile and a half. It was through such an ideal country, so natural and wild, so full of ferns, and exquisite trees, and views, really most picturesque and delightful. I had to leave my companions at the Mission and hasten to the *Mexico*, for James and I had asked Mr. and Mrs. H. to lunch with us at twelve, and we had to be on hand. They came, and we had a lovely visit with them, and were right sorry to leave them. Mrs. H. brought me as a souvenir, a most unusual and unique wooden "potlach spoon" and Jamie was delighted. After luncheon Mr. H. walked with us to the Indian Ranch, and we took a photo of the "Orthodox Family of Christians,"—at least of the remarkable sign over the door.

Mr. H. told us that he and some of the officers had put a stop to many of the atrocious habits of the Indians. One was that, whenever a man or woman was dying, they would place them in a corner against the wall, and putting a piece of wood between their teeth for them to bite on, during their last agonies and struggles, the heartless people would go on preparing for the burial. A lady on the *Mexico* told us of an experience a naval friend of hers had, when officer on a vessel stationed at the Fiji Islands. An old Chief was ill, and he was on his way to inquire for him, when he met the Chief's son, who said simply "Father's dead!" Walking to the house, the officer entered and saw the Chief laid out in state, but still breathing. He expostulated with the son, and tried to show him that his father was *not* dead, but that he still breathed. "Oh well," said the youth, "he may breath but his soul left the body long ago." The Chief was carried to the grave prepared for him, and buried, *while he still breathed!* Two of his wives were strangled to death at the same time, which was their custom then, for a chief had always to have company for his soul, as well in death as in life.

The *Mexico* sailed at two o'clock. Princess Thom was on the wharf, and remarkably radiant in colors and avoirdupois, a spectacle which made the amateur photographers particularly lively,—Jamie among them.

We had a very quiet afternoon. We took a rest in our chairs and enjoyed the beautiful scenery. It was exquisite to-day, just such scenery as we had coming to Sitka—lovely wooded islands, beautiful little lakes, snow-capped mountains, and the narrowest of passes.

TUESDAY, JULY 28TH.

POINT ELLIS was reached again, and our anchor cast, at a little after five o'clock this morning. We expected to reach Glacier Bay at that hour, but it was so stormy last night, the Captain decided to come here to-day, and give the weather a chance to change. Jamie and I did not know the change of plan, so this morning, when we anchored, it awoke me, and I jumped out of bed to see where we were in Glacier Bay. My eyes were not half awake, and I imagined that I saw ice-bergs in the distance, which proved to be rocks in the mist and rain, for it was a stormy morning. I jumped back on my little shelf after that, and slept heavily until seven, and when we learned later that we had come to Point Ellis for the canned salmon, we were surprised. Our day in Glacier Bay is "*the day*" of our trip, and as sunshine is needed to make the sight perfect, the Captain is most anxious to have a little sign of clearing, before going there. We anticipate it like children, and although the dangers are many, it gives spice and flavor to the experience. On the last trip, a big ice-berg took eighteen inches off the *Mexico's* bow, but the damage was soon repaired, and the trip enjoyed.

This morning I came at once, after breakfast, to my cabin, to have a good long morning with my writing, but soon I began to have callers, and until lunch time I was not alone. Senator D. brought me a few posies,—Mrs. N. came to chat awhile,— Mrs. S., of Summit, also Miss J. and Miss E. in turn, and after luncheon, and a little call on Mrs. C., I came to my room again. Nothing, of course, has happened to chronicle to-day, thus far. Everyone on board is resting, or reading, to recover from our long enjoyable day in Sitka, which was as exciting to all as it was fatiguing, and now the unavoidable reaction has struck the ship, and all are resting.

Dinner at five,—then we gathered in groups and

had a merry time. About twelve came to our corner, and as we had only one cabin chair, and two steamer chairs, we had to offer seats to some of our guests on the floor. Down on the deck,—all like tailors,—sat our company, and we sang "rounds," and had the jolliest of jolly times.

About nine o'clock to-night, we began to approach Killisnoo, a "Herring Fishery Oil Manufactory." We were all anxious to get ashore, for every Indian village attracts travellers, even having seen so many already,—so, as soon as the gang-way was lowered, although the tide was high, and we were to climb down at an awful angle, we scrambled ashore, to see all there was to be seen in Killisnoo. There was much to smell, for the refuse of the herring, after all the oil is extracted from it, is prepared for a fertilizer, and those articles are never choice nor pleasant. The Indian women, true to their trading instincts, had tumbled out of their homes with their wares, and were in selling trim when we arrived.

These villages consist of a couple of dozen shanties,—no house of size or ambitious inclinations being visible. The cannery, at Killisnoo, is the industry which holds the village and its hundred or two Indians together. We wandered through the dirty lanes, stamped our feet at the miserable wolf-dogs, which infest Indian villages, and saw little new or of interest, until we came to the house of the Chief,—" Saganaw Jake," as he is called. A little broad-shouldered Indian, very thickly set, but

KILLISNOO.

with such crooked legs that he was made lame by them (by constantly tripping over his own toes), was in his house, entertaining some of the *Mexico* passengers by his number of uniforms. It seems he was such a bad Indian that some of the naval officers took him, some years ago, to San Francisco, where he was tried and confined in prison for one year. He has killed scores of people,—Indians and whites—and held undisputed sway after his brother, who was really the Chief, and had a similar experience with the Navy. He held such a power over the Indians, that the Oil Company realized that they must acknowledge his authority in some way, so they made him a policeman, and he holds that position undisputed and alone, as unique as any curio in Alaska, for Indian policemen are not many in number. He wears a big bright shield, with " Indian Policeman " on it, in big letters. His peculiar fondness is for uniforms, and officers visiting here on vessels, and others, have given him uniforms of different naval degrees, and land regimentals as well. When a steamer is in Killisnoo, Jake dresses up a dozen times a day, and parades on his crooked legs down to the wharf, to be admired, and keeps it up until all his numerous uniforms have had an outing. As we were there in twilight, he did some rapid work, changing his effects in his house, while an admiring crowd stood by to watch him. We were on hand, and were much amused by the soldierly air with which he donned his cap and

epaulettes, and moved about to " show his shape."
Most of these Thlinket tribes are well developed
from the waist-line up, having broad shoulders and
good chests. Their legs are frequently dwarfed, in
both men and women, which comes from sitting,
hour after hour, and day after day, in their canoes.
We went outside Jake's house, and were much interested in a peculiar carved ornament over his door.
Over the door is a window, and above this window
is a carved wooden eagle's head, and spreading from
it are huge wings, made to represent feathers. Below the window is the tail, also in pieces like feathers. The window forms the body of the eagle, and
they say this is the only eagle in Alaska, "with a
pane in its breast!"

It spreads outside the roof line, and seems as if
it could stretch its wings and fly right away, with the
house and the Chief as well. In the Indian or Chi-
nook language, a Chief is called a *Tyee*, and an
island is called *Illahee*. On the back of Jake's house
are these verses, written for him by a white man at
Killisnoo, and cut out of wood.

VERSE 1. By the Government's commission,
And the Company's permission,
I am made the grand Tyee
Of this entire Illahee.

VERSE 2. I am sung in song and story,
I've attained the top of glory,
As Saganaw I'm known to fame,
Jake is but my common name.

To-day several ladies, asked Mrs. Willard,—the missionary,—to tell of her life among the Indians. I went to hear her, and was intensely interested. She has now a mission school at Juneau, but came on the *Mexico* from Sitka with us. She came to the mission work in Alaska ten years ago, and although a terrible tirade has been made against the missionaries, in some of these ports (as some have been unquestionably bad, and under the cloak of religion have done all kinds of outrageous things), I feel sure Mrs. Willard has been a marvelous exception to the rule, as she seems a woman of great strength of character. Quiet, dignified, calm, not at all prepossessing in appearance, yet she impresses one deeply, when she speaks of the experiences which have been hers. Ten years ago, she came with her husband to the very mission at Chilcat, in which we felt an interest early in our voyage, because two of our passengers were left there for the mission work. When she went there, there was not one white person near her, not one soul but Indians, and they were the war-like Chilcats, the most troublesome tribe, even now, of these people on the Alaskan coast. They were in quite a fury when the Willards reached them, as they had had a long fight with a neighboring tribe. The Chilcats number between two and three thousand now. They are separated in five villages. The Willards selected their site for the mission buildings in the centre of these five settlements, and while they were building the husband and wife went to visit the villages. One chief refused to admit them to his village, but they were bold and brave, and did not stop, but went on and were received after all, by His Highness. A great storm (more severe than any storm known in that vicinity before or since), visited that part of the country, the first winter the Willards were there, and the " Medicine Men," the men of power in the village, told the people, that the gods of the earth and air were angry, because these white people had come into their midst with their new God, and they must kill them. The " Medicine Men " are the priests of the villages, but the Indians believed then, in no God, except gods of anger, and gods to fear, and fear in its most terrible form was their only natural emotion. These Medicine Men were listened to attentively, *as long as their hair was long*, but the minute a man's hair was cut off, he was lost until it grew again, and the worst punishment that could happen to a Medicine Man was to lose his hair. They wore all kinds of charms about their necks, and all over them, and their work was to frighten away evil spirits, and when they used to dance over their patients, they would put on a mask, and then roar and plunge about the sick one, throwing charms at him, and making passes, until the spirit was supposed to be driven out of the patient. Most usually the patient died! Mrs. Willard said these Chilcats were so against them, that they kept provisions or any food from them, and the dire results make one almost sick to write. The poor woman had her limbs paralyzed, from her waist down, and one of her husband's arms became useless,—and to crown all, her little girl was very ill. All the time the Indians were making their lives a purgatory. They had been fired upon,—the Medicine Men and Chiefs had threatened their lives, and all kinds of hardships had been theirs, through which, Mrs. Willard said, they were carried miraculously, by a power unseen, and not tangible, but ever by their side. The Indians have a law, that if a life is taken, one must be given in compensation,—if a man is killed, according to his rank, lives are demanded. For instance, if a chief is killed in battle, four men's lives are demanded from the enemy in return. They have a caste and a standard, and it is as unchanging as the laws of the Medes and Persians. Mrs. Willard used to visit the sick, and take gruel and medicine to them. The Medicine Men saw their power slipping from them, so they would meet Mrs. Willard, on her walk to and from these people, and shaking their fists in her face, tell her she would be killed if she continued such acts,—that if one person died, they would demand her life, etc. She continued her work, with supernatural courage. After years among these Indians, the Willards gradually gained their affection, were adopted into their tribe, were most cordially treated and loved, and even now, when Chilcat Indians come to Juneau, they always visit the Willards, and beg " father and mother, to come home to Chilcat." But after many years among them, in their school, a Chief's child died, and then the Indian affection had a test. The lives of Mrs. Willard's little son and daughter were demanded, as a recompense for the death of the Chief's child. The old Chief himself held out against this demand for a long time, but the other Chiefs assembled and demanded it, for the pride of their tribe was in danger, and their time-honored law could not be insulted. At last, the father of the child demanded the two lives as his right, but the Willards held their own, and kept calm, and soon moved away to Juneau. She told us many interesting items of the queer lives of these people, of their wealth, etc. The rich Indians give sometimes, great feasts, called "Potlaches," which cost them thousands of dollars. At these potlaches they give quantities of food, and throw hundreds of blankets among the guests, which the guests immediately reduce to tatters, tearing in strips, and throwing over themselves, and over the ground. This constitutes great liberality, and is their idea of a good time. The more they destroy, the grander the feast, the greater the Chief, and the more successful the potlach. The poor Indians often gather up the broken strips and make themselves clothing out of them.

We left Killisnoo at 10 P. M.

THERE are some days in life, which defy the cleverest pen to describe, or picture, when one feels dumb and speechless, and the sensations and emotions are too many and unusual to portray. Such a day in our lives was Wednesday, July 29th 1891. It was the day chosen by the Captain for our trip into Glacier Bay, to see the greatest glacier known to scientists, the Muir Glacier. It is the acme of enjoyment to all travellers in Alaska, and the most unusual portion of the trip, in every sense of the word. Usually the steamers approach the Glacier until within a half mile in front, and then anchor off the side, in thirty fathoms of water. The Muir Glacier is said to be grand beyond measure ; it is three miles wide across the front, and one solid mass of ice coming to the water's edge, and it breaks off in great masses every little while, making the sound of roaring cannon, and producing disturbances of unusual features in the Bay. Its water front, or terminal moraine, is between three and four hundred feet high, and full of wonderful deposits. People are landed a half mile from it, and are able to walk to it, and over it, if they wish. It is the most wonderful sight imaginable, but—*we did not see it !* It nearly broke our hearts, but we were compensated in the end, and now feel that we have had two experiences never before allotted to Alaska tourists.

About half past four o'clock this morning, I was

aroused by an awful thump on the ship's side, followed by another, and another, until I began to awake to the realization that we were at last in Glacier Bay, and in the midst of ice-bergs. I jumped down from my shelf, opened the door, and peeped out; and such a scene as greeted my eyes! A dozen or more fine ice-bergs surrounded our ship, and the dear old *Mexico* was pushing her way along, like a veritable snail. Just then Mr. C. the freight clerk, whose room is next door, knocked hard on the partition, according to promise, and Jamie awoke also. I could hardly see, I was so sleepy, but I realized this was a day with few parallels, in our lives, and we could afford to lose sleep, rather than one moment of such an unusual experience. Jamie was of similar mind, so we were up and dressed soon after five o'clock, and out on the hurricane deck. We found lots of fellow passengers and slowly, little by little, others came, until most of us were on deck. It was bitterly cold, and icy, damp and penetrating; the sky was gray and overcast—the mountains on all sides were a deep misty blue—but the scene before us beggared description! I looked in every direction, and was dumb. Not a single word came at my bidding, and I shivered and shook, from the intense cold, as well as from the impression of the marvelous scene before us. Coffee was to be had below, but I was glued to the spot, and Jamie went and ordered the hot drink with toast, brought to us on the hurricane deck, where we stood and ate in silence.

Around us, before, behind, on each side, was ice,—
great ice-bergs,—so tremendous that our ship
seemed but an atom, a speck, to their wonderful
size. As far as the eye could reach, these mountains of ice were to be seen, in such magnificence,
in such wondrous shapes and colors, that I shall
not be surprised, if I am considered extravagant
in my description of them. At first the bergs were
fewer and with distance between them, but the
crystal clearness of the water doubled each monster, and we could only imagine the depth below
the water-line. The mountains also were exquisite in the water mirror, and the gray light made
the ice-bergs a glorious white against the sombre
background. Little by little, the ice closed in upon
us ; the good old ship buried her nose in it, pushing it aside, scratching against it, and splintering
her bow dreadfully. Two hours' steaming only
registered five miles covered, and we were then
twelve miles from the Muir Glacier. We could
see it in the distance, in its awful grandeur, and
the snow mountains surrounding and encasing
it, in a radiant white circle. It seemed very near to
us; its wall of ice looked mountain high, and so
strangely distinct, but a traveller who had three
times seen this wonderful sight, told us we were
viewing a mirage. Often much ice is encountered in
the passage through Glacier Bay, and only the last
trip, the *Mexico's* bow was taken off eighteen inches
back, and water came into the hold. Never but

once, however, had our Captain seen such a sight; only once had he ever been obliged to turn back. Slowly the ice closed in upon us; the great ice-bergs encircled us, and seemed to hold us fast in their embrace. The old ship shivered and shook—she pressed her bow against the· great obstacles—she pushed, twisted and tried to advance one inch, but to no avail. We were truly bound tightly in, by the wonderful ice. Commander C., who had been to the Arctic Sea, on the *Alert*, in search of Greeley, said this scene was as truly like the Arctic Ocean, with its bergs and ice, as anything he could possibly imagine, and we were having an experience which few people, except explorers of the Arctic regions, ever have. We fully realized it. The ice impeded our progress; not one inch could we move without imminent danger, and the engines were stopped, and we lay quietly in our cradle of ice for a couple of hours. The scene before us was magnificent, and swallowed up all worry and fear we had, or might have had, if we had not been in the seventh heaven of bliss and ecstasy.

The great bergs towered on all sides of us, in such marvelous sizes and such remarkable shapes. Some were like several houses in one mass, and reflecting the most wonderful colors. As far as the eye could reach, there was nothing but wondrous ice and snow. Some ice-bergs were a brilliant green, others as if a bag of blueing had been poured on them, the blue was so intense, and these colors were reflected in the queer gray water, which is invariably the result of glaciers, and denotes the proximity to one, wherever it is met. It is caused by the sediment of matter, deposited in the water by the glacial action. On these ice-bergs, imbedded often in the ice and snow, were huge boulders and coal, rocks of all sizes and colors, carried along for miles and miles by this ice river, and brought from—goodness knows where! Some of these ice-bergs were like mushrooms, glorious in size and pure white in color, forming marvelous contrasts with the greens and blues. Between these floating mountains of ice, were smaller masses, crowding together, heaping up in little piles, and chipping and tumbling about, but slowly and with dignity, for the whole harbor or bay was covered as solidly as if the pieces had been glued together. The most beautiful thing of all was the delicate musical hum of the ice, as it cracked, and creaked, and knocked together. It was a positive song, as rhythmical and harmonious as an orchestra could make it, with a distinct melody of sweet sounds. As it thumped against the sides of the ship, it hummed away to itself so merrily and cheerily, and seemed to sing something about "not going home until morning," or "Forever and Forever." The big pieces seemed more sedate in their measured metre, but the little cakes of ice danced in their glee over their prisoners, and were tremulous in their treble clef. As far as the eye could reach, great ice-bergs towered to the sky, and seemed to threaten, with numerous fingers of ice pointing upwards, dire disaster and calamities great, if the old ship dared try a step more, or persevere against their great glorious fortress of snow and ice. The ice-song went on, in single voices, then in great and grand choruses, a little metallic ring making it different from any oratorio or opera ever sung, and yet never surpassed by any Musical Festival, or Bayreuth Carnival. It was a song of the ice witches, a wild weird harmony, with such soft and mysterious crescendos. I felt such supreme and unusual emotions, as if I had been transported to another world, where language and life were so new and strange,—as if a door had opened to some "Kingdom Wonderful" and I had been allowed to stand on the threshold and look therein.

While the dreamers dreamed, and gazed off upon that Arctic scene, consultations were being held by the careful officers of our ship, and it was decided unsafe to push our way any farther into that river of ice-bergs, all of which seemed so cold and inhospitable to our approach. Before we turned our bow homeward, a small boat was lowered from the ship, that our ice supply might be re-inforced, and the only way the little boat could go ahead to the bow of the *Mexico*, was by the two sailors jumping out on the ice, pushing the ice a little away with boat hooks, and then dragging and hauling it along. The men walked about the ship as if on land. Great cakes of ice were pulled up, a strong net of ropes slipped under, and by a pulley and ropes from the yard-arm in the bow, several small ice-bergs were taken on board, to keep our provisions good for the rest of our trip. The tide changed, after a couple of hours of waiting, and cleared the ice only a little bit from our bows, but enough to allow the good old ship to swing about, and go an inch at a time towards clear water. Cautiously and carefully our capable Captain carried us along, but the five miles took us about three hours to cover. It was one constant feast of unusual sights and scenes, and we spent our entire morning flying from one part of the ship to another, as exclamations of delight would reach our ears. Finally, worn out after five hours of this enjoyment, we had just settled ourselves in our chairs for a rest, when Mrs. C. came to me in quite a fever of excitement, and said, "Come quick, and bring your camera!" I ran after her, and as I reached the other side of the ship, I saw the picture she desired me to catch. In between the great cakes of ice, and the ice-bergs, like a veritable atom of life, came a little tiny canoe, with an Indian, his squaw and pappoose! It was bitterly cold and raw, but way out in that sea of ice, as fearless as a lion, came the seal-hunter, in his light frail craft. Sitting in the stern was the woman, her pappoose in her lap, rolled so much in heavy cloths it was hardly visible. She paddled very rapidly. In the bow sat the Indian, and in front of him was a queer square sail-like arrangement, behind which the seal-hunter

crouches when he approaches a seal. The little
canoe was covered with white, and all this is done
to make the small affair resemble a cake of ice, as
much as possible, and surprise the seal. The canoe
approached our ship bravely and steadly and the occupants seemed so pleased to see us. We all gathered to see them, Miss N. lowering on a string a
pretty and bright head-handkerchief for the squaw,
which gave much pleasure to the poor woman.
They paddled along for a while by our side, then as
we all saw a seal, we told them of it, and they turned
and went in search of it, and the last we saw of the
little canoe, it was pushing its way along in the ice,
and seemed a mere speck in the distance. Sometimes those hunters are out, for two or three days, in
their boats, seal-hunting. Just as we were coming
to clear water, we met the grandest ice-berg of our
morning. It was as long as our ship, which is two
hundred and seventy-five feet in length, and was
fifty feet high, and it went sailing by us like a magnificent ice-palace, of grand and colossal proportions.

After reaching clear water, we steamed at usual
speed and reached Juneau at 7.15 P. M. Although
it rained hard we went on shore, but having seen all
before, in sunshine, we did not do much, except look
into the stores. As we returned to the ship we saw
a genuine Medicine Man. He was tall and dark,
wore high rubber boots, and a brilliant striped
blanket covered him from neck to knee. His face
was as hard and stern and as ignorant as a brute's,

and I would like to apologize to the brute for the comparison. What interested us most was his head. His hair was long, and probably it was against his religion to ever comb it, for it hung in ropes, like great cords, it was so matted together, and it was caught and tucked under his blanket. I never have seen such a dreadful head in my life. Medusa, with her myriad snakes and serpents, would be a fascinating picture to the dirty, unwashed, uncombed heathen Indian.

THURSDAY, JULY 30TH.

WE remained at Juneau all night, and about eight o'clock in the morning, we steamed over to Douglas Island for the Treadwell Mine, gold. My own eyes feasted on the small parcels of gold brought on board, which amounted to *ninety-thousand dollars*. It was good to look upon. About ten o'clock, the dear old *Mexico* steamed away from the wharf at Douglas Island, and we started for Taku Inlet, for the Captain was bound to have his passengers see some glaciers, and in Taku Inlet are two fine ones, not so grand as the Muir, but very fine and to some more beautiful, because of the purity of the ice. We had a most exquisite sail into this little paradise, into this Inlet of wooded shores and glorious grandeur. Finally, about twelve o'clock, we were nearing the Taku Glacier, and were to approach through the sea of ice-bergs to its front, when the channel having shifted, owing to glacial deposits, high and dry on a sand-bank went our bow, and we were grounded. We rejoiced all day over this fact, and called it "our good fortune," for we had to remain until high tide to get afloat again, and high tide was at 9 P. M. A whole day in such magnificent scenery, a whole day in Paradise!

Around us on every side were the most majestic mountains, every one with a crown of crystal snow, every one with such glorious outlines, such ice-cut rock sides, such green foliage near the water's edge, that the picture was one exquisite vision of color, a veritable mosaic. We lay in among ice-bergs without number, in a basin of beautiful outlines, encased and surrounded by a circle of grand hills, whose variety of form against the blue sky, made an impression upon us never to be effaced. Down the mountain sides tumbled breathlessly a multitude of silvery streams, and once in a while, a glorious mass of brilliant red, informed us where the snow-flower was growing. Toward our left hand, in beauty and grandeur, stood the great Child Glacier, but a mile of mud and stones deposited by the ice, made a nearer acquaintance quite out of the question. In front of us, about three miles away, in most inviting beauty, stood the pure and exquisite Taku Glacier, in such radiant glory in the sunshine that it was a feast to stand and watch it. Between us and the Glacier, as well as on our right hand, and forward, were innumerable ice-bergs, more beautiful, if that could be, than any of Glacier Bay, more individual and characteristic.

Although no boats had ever been sent to the front of this Glacier, although all the sea-faring men said it was fool-hardy and dangerous, and the people were taking their lives in their hands, three crowded boats started out after luncheon, and rowed in and out between the ice-bergs, to the front of the glacier. We watched these three boats until they were tiny specks in the distance; we lost sight of them many times, and for an hour or more could not find them, they were so hidden behind the ice. The greatest danger was in the fact that huge pinnacles were constantly being deposited in the water, breaking off from the glacier, and when these masses fall they produce disturbances in the water, which oftentimes overturn huge ice-bergs, and make much danger for any boat, especially a small one. These boats were terribly crowded, and Jamie and I were not alone, in refusing to imperil our lives in such a crowd. We remained on deck all the afternoon, most enthusiastic and excited over the scene before us, for it defied description, and words can never tell what a mysterious charm came over us this day. We could do nothing but absorb and drink in that grandeur. After four hours' absence our three boats returned, enthusiastic in the wildest terms over their experience. Some poor women had been in hysterics over the trip, and came home used up and worn out and in tears, but most of them were anxious for us to see the same wonderful sight. Mr. Gray, the first officer, had asked us in the afternoon, why we did not go, and when I told him it was because of the crowd that we were afraid, he promised to take us there himself, and in perfect safety, and after dinner, and sending one boat-load of twenty people off with two sailors, Mr. Gray took Jamie and me, with seven friends and four sailors, to see the great sight.

We pushed off from the ship about 6 P. M. and rowed directly toward the Taku Glacier, threading our way in and out between the great bergs, and oh, how great and cold and awful they did look to us, in our tiny boat! It was then that we appreciated the size and height of those terrible ice mountains, the beauty and magnificence and grandeur of those marvelous churches and palaces and cathedrals of ice. A great arched berg, raising its head so proudly and gracefully, resembled a swan of colossal proportions, another was a great bear, and all the animals in the animal kingdom were faithfully represented there. We rowed around a great white snow berg, with such tremendous perpendicular walls, such slabs of snow ice, that it seemed impossible to realize, that such a weight could be buoyed up by the water, and came to a transparent castle of glorious blue, like a gem, a veritable turquoise, as if it had just dropped from God's blue skies. Next we would see a huge ice-berg, whose overhanging top made beautiful ice-grottos, far surpassing in glorious beauty, the famed " Blue Grotto " of Capri. Next to this a transparent ice-berg of pure clear ice, then a deep green one, until one was bewildered, and the

mind could grasp no more.   As we crept by inches
between the ice-bergs, we were crawling *over* them as
well, as vigorous thumps on the bottom of the boat
informed us.   " Easy boys," sang Officer Gray to
his sailors, " we don't want to go to the bottom
here in such ice water."   " Is there danger? " quoth
I. " Yes indeed, but we'll be careful," was the reply.
Was I nervous?   Maybe! a little at first, but the
novelty of the experience, the beauty of the scene,
the great and glorious ice, finally absorbed and swallowed up all fears, and I felt as if I was in Heaven
at last, and if I was tossed into that water, I could
not be far from God's Great White Throne.   We
went within an eighth of a mile of the front of the
glacier, and there we lay for a while to watch and
see.   Oh, how beautiful it was !   Rising two and
three hundred feet, right from the water into the air,
in pinnacles, turrets, spires and columns, in blue and
white and green ice, was this great frozen river, in
exquisite purity and whiteness.   Some points and
pyramids were divided by tremendous cracks and
crevasses, which produced the most marvelous
shadows, such deep colors, that it made one creep
with fear, to see such unfathomable depths.   As we
sat in the boat and feasted our eyes upon that marvelous miracle, in the last rays of the setting sun, it
was a glimpse of Heaven in reality, a sight which
grows more and more impressive, as I think of it day
after day.   It was the mysterious wonder, the one
great unexplained query of all that night, as to the

age and meaning of those rivers of ice; their historical records imprisoned in the stranded boulders and floating ice-bergs, could not be fathomed ; they held their secret fast, in their silent beauty. Our row back to the ship was even more beautiful than our row to the glacier, and it was with regret that we reached the *Mexico*, after 9 P. M. We returned, thoroughly imbued with the emotions of the occasion, and in a spirit of exaltation and ecstasy, of awe, wonder and of praise. "Ye ice and snow, Praise ye the Lord," had been fulfilled to the letter of the law, and we were in tune with the anthem.

FRIDAY, JULY 31ST.

OH, how we slept last night! Not a sound did we hear this morning, not even the great rising bell, until Tom, our *chambermaid*, knocked on the cabin door, with hot water. I jumped up then with my eyes full of sticks, and a big wish in my heart to remain for an extra snooze. Breakfast over, we put on our ulsters and heavy things (for it was very, very cold), and went up on the hurricane deck, for we were nearing one of the narrowest passes of our trip. Wrangle Narrows is a dangerous passage, and requires great skill to go through safely, but Captain Hunter is equal to anything, and no one can be timid with such a safe, reliable captain at the helm. The passage is most beautiful, winding in and out between thickly wooded banks, and giving us glimpses of the greatest beauty and variety. The men casting the lead were of interest too, and their weird calls " By the *mark*-five," "and the *deep*-six," emphasizing always the words underlined, were like Greek to me, until I learned that all odd numbers were accompanied by the word " mark," and all the even by " deep." They have such a clever adroit manner of swinging the lead back and forth, until it is in proper form to turn in circles, and this gives it carrying power, and takes it flying out beyond the bows into the water.

We enjoyed the morning chatting, as we had lots of company in our cosy corner. About half-past one o'clock, we began to see Fort Wrangle in the distance, and were all on the *qui vive* when the *Mexico* reached the wharf. The Captain gave us only an hour this time, as we had been here for much longer when we first came, so we jumped off the ship in quick hot haste, Miss C. and I in the lead. We had ordered a souvenir spoon, and having very little confidence in the Indian's word of honor, we were anxious to reach his hut before others should persuade him to sell to them. We two fairly tore through the village, between the little huts and through the alleys, and on reaching Indian Charlie Gunnak, the silversmith, we found our fears were without foundation, for our spoons were carefully put away, waiting for us. We then strolled about the place, walking along the beach in the wet, for it was sprinkling and real damp Alaska weather, and we found another Indian who wanted to sell us something. The entire village turns out on steamer days, and as most of the village consists of Indians, the houses are lined and outlined by these crouching figures, with their bright yellow, red and green head-handkerchiefs and their showy blankets, and their baskets and skins of animals, spread out before them to sell.

We were bound to see the Chief's house this time if we could, the "Chief Shakes," who was away fishing when we were in Fort Wrangle before. He lives in a typical Indian house, but the one room was large and had three tiers about it. The lowest part or square is where the fire is usually built; around it are two steps, or balconies, on which the Indians lie on fur skins, and eat, smoke, or sleep. Still higher is a raised shelf-like balcony, running entirely around the room, on which are put the rude board bedsteads, tables, etc. Shakes was at home, but was very different from my idea of a real chief. He is short and does not impress one very deeply, yet he is their Chief, the Chief of the Wrangle Indians, and has great power among his people. He is wealthy and displayed with great pride his collection of curios, which consisted of relics of years and years, some having rather interesting legends associated with them. The Shakes family have a tradition, that a big white bear jumped out of Noah's ark, swam to Alaska and went to Shakes' great, great, great, great grandfather for food. The grandfather mentioned is said to have fed and housed the bear, who lived in peace and gratitude with the family for years, until his death. The skin is shown by Shakes, with great pride, and he told us to-day that the skin and head were about eight hundred years old, showing the Indian idea of the date of the deluge. He had many robes, shirts and blankets, worn at different times by his ancestors, and these were elaborately decorated with pearl button designs, men's faces made with them, eyes, nose and mouth being very expressive and lifelike! He had numerous hats, such as Kadishan showed us, with bronze dragons and ermine tails hanging, innumerable totem effects, carved and painted figures, wonderful carved horns, some most unusual curios, and all were heirlooms and priceless. Outside his house were two totems. One was wonderfully fine and old, in fact, only the old Indian villages have these totem poles; the other represented the historical bear. The sides of the pole were covered with bear foot-prints, as if the bear had climbed up the pole, and on the top was a carved wooden bear crouching. It tells its own story, the fable of the bear from the Ark, and makes the family history of Shakes branch and tribe of great antiquity.

We were as much interested in these totem poles, seeing them the second time, as at first; in fact their originality and unusual appearance were more impressive to-day than before. Nowhere else in the world are these totems to be seen; they are unique and one of Alaska's charms. We left Wrangle about three o'clock and steamed around a short distance, only fifteen minutes' sail, to Labouchere Bay, where a cannery is situated, and where we took on more canned salmon. No one went ashore, as there was absolutely nothing to see. Jamie napped and I took the little opportunity of quiet and repose to write. After dinner, it was cold, so until we started I sat inside my cabin door and wrote a little more. By snatching odd unused minutes, my journal is kept, for I cannot spare the time when there is anything to see or enjoy. About seven o'clock, Miss N. and Miss K. came to my door, to tell me there was music and dancing on the hurricane deck, so Jamie and I went up, and it was such a jolly evening. A young fellow had come aboard at Fort Wrangle, who played the banjo, Miss S. accompanied on the guitar; Capt. Hunter is a musical genius and had his violin on deck, another man had a violin also, and the dancing was quite spirited. We had the jolliest time imaginable, for we all know one another well now, and congenial spirits always flock together, consequently " our crowd " is a right royally jolly one.

About 8 P. M. we moved out of Labouchere Bay, and every one was deeply grieved because one of the ship's dogs had been left at Fort Wrangle. Around to Fort Wrangle we turned, to find the missing favorite "Texas." Capt. Hunter has two huge Newfoundland dogs, who never leave him, and whose devotion to our Captain is truly touching. Everybody on the ship is devoted to Texas, and Jeff Davis. Owing to some mistake Texas was left, and no one could be reconciled to make the rest of the voyage without him. Up to the wharf the big *Mexico* steamed ; lines were thrown out and made fast, and a boatswain sent on shore to find Texas. No one else went ashore but every one watched for the dear old dog. Soon, down the long wharf came the great black fellow, running like mad, and when he saw the ship, the Captain and the people, I thought his tail would wriggle right off, it waved so rapidly. No gangway was put out, but he was helped into a port hole, and as soon as he was on board he rushed for the Captain, who stood on his bridge. The meeting between the Captain and Jeff and Texas, was really touching. Jeff ran up and kissed Texas, and Texas could hardly do enough to express his gratitude to his master. He jumped all over him, licked his hands, and expressed his thanks as no words could have done, and it was truly wonderful to see the love that noble old dog was trying, all the evening, to express to his Captain.

We had the pleasantest evening of the voyage. Mrs. N., Mrs. C., Miss C., Dr. N., Miss N., James and I sat together until half-past nine o'clock, then we went for some supper. When we went down, it seemed wicked to eat and leave such beauty, for the scenery was magnificent and the sunset glory was radiantly exquisite. Gold, liquid and pure, with filmy violet and rose tints strewed over it, with a reflection of such shimmering beauty, that it seemed almost unnatural, was the picture we saw. Ten minutes after ten o'clock, when we came up from supper, it was still beautiful and bright as day.

We were just parting for the night, when some one told us there was music in the Captain's cabin. Going to his room, we found a crowd assembled as audience, and inside the room were a few fellows with pleasant voices, singing glees, old-timers some of them—but always good. It was a pleasant ending to a most lovely day.

This morning we saw as many as twenty eagles, on one bank of Wrangle's Narrows. They were big fellows, with white heads. On Tuesday last, one of the engineers went out into the woods again, and when he returned came to my door and showed me his prize. He had shot a big bald-headed eagle, and we measured his wings from tip to tip, and he measured seven feet eight inches. He was a monster.

SATURDAY, AUGUST 1ST.

WHEN we awoke this morning, we found it raining dismally, and we were anchored in the beautiful land-locked harbor of Yaas Bay. It is a beautiful spot, wooded to the water's edge, and the ferns and mosses are exquisite. There is a cannery here, and we are doing a great salmon business, this dear old *Mexico*, and we must lie here all day loading. There is a salmon wheel here, and we anticipated seeing it, as the fish are caught on the paddle of the wheel, as they pass through the stream, and are thrown on shore. But, although some people ventured on shore, they found the mud ankle deep, and were unable to reach the wheel. Jamie borrowed a big pair of rubber boots, and started off, but he went into mud almost to his knees, although he succeeded in seeing the wheel. We have had a quiet day,—good to most of us, for we were tired. I have sat in my cabin, with my door open, most of the morning, while just outside sit an army of people, all scraping horn spoons. It is an epidemic and has struck everyone on board, except Jamie and myself, and we expect to succumb soon. The horn spoons made and used by the Indians, from the horns of the mountain sheep, are very old, and after scraping down with glass and sand-paper, are capable of being highly polished, and although it takes great elbow exercise, each one tries to outdo his neighbor. As I write, the scrape, scrape, scrape, makes a regular song, an opera in sand-paper rhythm, and such groans and sighs as come from the spoony crowd! Oil is rubbed in, rosin is used, and a real dirty operation it is, but everybody is working like a day-laborer. The workers sit in little groups, and such merriment as it all provokes. I wish some time that I could put down all the jokes and fun. We think something of having a "horn-spoon photograph," and as no one will be allowed in it, unless he can give a certificate that he has scraped, at least five minutes, we must get to work and qualify for office. I saw Mr. S. in Fort Wrangle yesterday, with a paper bundle under his arm, and as everyone asks everybody else what they have bought, and what they have paid, I said to Mr. S., "Been buying photographs, I see." "No, I haven't," he answered, "that's a pane of glass and sand-paper, for I'm going into the spoon business."

This afternoon Miss N. and Miss K. came to my room, and we all copied Captain Hunter's record of the nautical miles of our trip. Outside the door sat Jamie and several others. About half-past three, I made "tea" in my little Chinese basket, and entertained the crowd. We had lots of fun and merriment, and kept it up until dinner time. Just before going to dinner, Mr. C. gave me a beautiful spoon, a light-colored horn one, and beautifully polished, his own work. I was much pleased.

After dinner, we all put on our rubbers to go ashore at Loring. It rained, of course, as it does much of the time in Alaska, but we all went ashore armed with umbrellas, and marched in Indian file, up to the one store in this cluster of two dozen little huts. The door was locked, and a man standing near said, "the man will open the store after he has finished his supper." There was independence for you, a little piazza crowded full of people, about seventy-five in all, standing and waiting for Loring's

one merchant to finish his supper! I could not help
expressing surprise at the man's utter indifference
to the almighty dollar. He came at last, and opened
the store, and we all tumbled in *en masse* and
divided as our tastes led us. Some small boys
wanted candy, so we waited about fifteen minutes
for them to be satisfied, and for the one store-keeper
to come our way. After a look about, Jamie and I,
with a young lady from Pasadena, went with Mr. E.
into the Salmon Cannery. I had not been into any
such establishment, and James thought I should see
one before leaving Alaska. Every one advised me
not to go, but I did go, and I'm glad. I saw the
salmon taken, and heads and tails cut off, split,
cleaned, and then thrown on a table, and cut into
pieces. The machine was not working, but I saw
where the pieces of salmon are put in, where the
can comes down in a shute, and is filled, and then is
pushed by steam in a little channel, to have a top put
on. It is then soldered, and put in hot water, boiling water, where it remains forty-five minutes. A
hole is then made in the can, to allow the air to escape, and it is at once soldered again. It is then put
into " coolies," they are called, and placed in a retort,
where they stay one hour, at a temperature of 240°.
They are washed immediately in cold water, and
then put in a trepanning bath. Labeling and packing come next, and then the process ends. It was
really interesting to me and I was glad I went. They
fill about forty-eight thousand cans a day, each can

containing one pound. Chinamen are the workmen, and this Cannery at Loring is one of the best paying fisheries in Alaska.

It is interesting to watch the salmon in the water. They jump several times their length, up, out, and over the water, just as one makes a stone skip along the surface. They put nets out all about the mouths of the streams, and at Chilcat we saw the men hauling the net, and were much interested in watching their process of handling.

SUNDAY, AUGUST 2ND.

WE left Loring last night, and when we awoke this morning, we found it was raining again and was cold and damp. We were sailing through most beautiful channels and sounds, and were a little vexed that the rain followed us so persistently, when, turning a sharp point in our course, we saw the most glorious sunshine ahead,—and out from under the low hanging clouds, which had hovered about us all the morning, and had veiled the mountains from our sight, we steamed into such radiant sunshine, with blue sky above us and blue water under us, and the dividing line between sunshine and shadow was as distinct as if it had been cut with a knife. With the sunshine came our spirits, and we fairly jumped for joy. The views were exquisite, and we were enjoying them, when our attention was suddenly arrested by a most unusual appearance of the water. To all reason, we were sailing in *blood-red water*,—the bow of the *Mexico* cut its way through really bright red waves, and left curling tracks behind of the same marvelous hue. It was thick,—one could see it plainly,—like a substance dissolved in water, but still retaining its body. (But can a substance be *dissolved* and still retain its body?) " We scientists " went to the Captain, to solve the question why this water was so red and thick, and the Captain *thought* it was salmon-spawn, swept out by the tide. Another suggestion was, that it was a low form of animal or vegetable life, the same that produces the phosphorescent light in the water. To prove this theory, Dr. N. had a pail full of this queer water reserved until night, and taking it in the dark, into our cabin, proved that it was the red variety of that vegetable life, which produces the light in the waves.

At 11.45 A. M. we approached Metlakahtla, an Indian village of remarkable and civilized development. We anchored off the little settlement and after dinner we went ashore in small boats. Having no wharf to approach, we were rowed on to the beach, and having a heavy load, of course our boat stuck in the sand and some feet of water lay between us and the beach. As quick as lightning, our gallant Third Officer was " afloat " in the intervening space, with his high rubber boots, and approached the bow of the boat where Jamie was sitting. In an instant, off to the shore went my dearly beloved, on the back of a strong fellow, one of the sailors, and was landed high and dry on the beach "in a twinkle." How everybody roared, and how relieved we ladies were, when we were informed that the same method of transportation was not necessary for us. A board was brought and stretched from boat to shore, and we scrambled across on that—in fine style.

Metlakahtla is a model Indian village, and all to the credit of one man, who has given his life to this great work. Mr. William Duncan lived in England, and was a smart, energetic young man. One stormy night he went to a missionary meeting, and as only nine persons were present, it was suggested that the meeting be postponed. Another suggestion, however, carried the vote, which was that the nine brave members of that little gathering be rewarded by a service then and there. It resulted in one of the little band leaving the gathering, with a verbal vow to give his life to the missionary cause. In 1857, this young man—William Duncan—came to British Columbia, going among the Indians at once. When I asked him if he would tell us a little of his life,— if he had a hard time at first, etc.,—he would not reply, except by a nod of such solemnity that I hesitated to press my request. Once, while talking to us later, in his office, he took a little book from his book-shelf, and opening to the frontispiece said, "Where is the lady who wanted to know how I was treated, when I first came among these people?" and when I identified myself, he handed me the

book and said, "That's the way they treated me."
Four or five Indians, in war paint and feathers,
were beating a man, bound hand and foot, who
was crouched on the ground, begging for mercy.

Later he told us a few incidents of his life. In
1858, when he reached these Indians, they were
hostile to all white people, and were the most savage
tribe on the coast. They were cannibals, and Mr.
Duncan said he " saw them cook and eat a slave at
one time, a woman." He was shot at, and every
means taken to dispose of him, and when I gasped
" How *were* you saved?" he answered, " Because I
was protected, and when the Indians realized that
some power unknown to them protected me, they
felt powerless, and gave up their repeated attempts
to dispose of me." He worked for many years
among them, and had done much good, when
the Bishop of the English Church reprimanded
him for laxity of church discipline, in service
and liturgy, and demanded form and ceremony,
instead of the simple services which Mr. Duncan
had found more attractive to the Indian's intellectual demand. Mr. Duncan remonstrated, and
finally, after many other disagreeable incidents, he
determined to seek liberty under the United States'
laws. Going to headquarters, at Washington, I believe, he asked for land in the Alaskan territory, and
his request being granted, he returned, going directly
to his new home. The Indians heard of his return,
and one by one followed the man whom they loved

and trusted. Mr. Duncan said, "One canoe-full after another arrived, sometimes fifty canoes in a day," for they determined to live with him wherever he was. His settlement of Metlakahtla dates from August 7th, 1887. It is a model village. He has taught the Indians to be self-supporting; they have learned trades,—build their own dwellings, churches, and school-houses,—have a cannery, a joint-stock company, the natives holding the stock, and receiving large dividends—besides several other industries which pay well; he taught them to play on musical instruments, and they are very proud of their band. They are the nicest set of Indians one can see anywhere, all *well* dressed and most orderly and civilized. They number nearly five hundred, and their village is a marvelous little place. They are all devoted church workers, and have put away their heathenish and idolatrous beliefs, regulating their little settlement by rigid and strict laws. No work is ever permitted on the Sabbath, and as we arrived on the Lord's Day, we had to wait until midnight for the freight of canned salmon, the *Mexico* had come to take away.

As soon as we reached the shore, we made our way to the little Church, but were too late for service. We were entertained, however, in listening to some young Indian men and women singing religious songs in English. All the young Indians here speak English. James was much impressed by a verse over the little plain wooden pulpit, which an

Indian boy had painted in huge bright letters, on the wall, and he copied it in his note book for me:

"Glory to our Lord and King,
Honor, majesty,
This the song the angels sing
Through Eternity."

We were especially interested in a lot of old white-haired men, who had such amiable faces and such a pleasant greeting for us. They could not speak our language, but they held in their hands, nevertheless, with great reverence, Bibles in the English language. I spoke to several old Indian women and they seemed to understand me. I was much touched by one old woman; she told me much in a moment and only by gesture. I said, " Do you speak English?" she shook her head—" no," and then taking hold of the end of her tongue, she looked sadly at me, and pointing to my tongue, shook her head—"no" again. Laying her hand on her heart, and pointing to my heart and then up to Heaven, she smiled and nodded her head—"yes." She told me so plainly, that although we could not speak the same tongue, we both loved the same God in Heaven.

Mr. Duncan took us to his office and showed us the sea-weed food of the Indians, which they gather far out on the rocks, dry thoroughly, and either stew or eat as bread. " Eat some," he invitingly asked. We all ate a little and quietly one by one slipped outside the little room, returning as seemingly un-observed, but to that little crowd, the moment's absence spoke volumes. We knew the short acquaintance with the sea-weed bread, was not all one's heart could desire.

MONDAY, AUGUST 3D.

WE slept pretty well last night, although I awoke when we left Metlakahtla at 1.30 A. M., and later also, when a little rolling of the ship, announced to me that we were making one of the very few sea crossings, and at half past five o'clock I heard the anchor lowered in Nichol's Bay. The morning was exquisite ; the sun was as bright and warm as mid-summer, and every outline of the shore and islands was so clearly cut, so finely chiseled and beautiful. All felt jubilant, for we have had so much rain. After breakfast, I interviewed an Indian woman, who had paddled out to the ship in a canoe, with her family and a dear old dog, whose company was not wanted in the family ark, and so he swam around and around it, in circles. Jamie and I chatted for awhile with friends, watching the Captain's caution in guiding the *Mexico*, from Nichol's Bay, through a wonderfully narrow passage, and as we steamed out into Queen Charlotte's Sound or Dixon's Entrance, we settled ourselves in our chairs, wrapped up warmly in ulsters and rugs, and decided to take a nap. The cool sea air and sunshine made us so drowsy, we soon fell sound asleep, and as our chairs were just outside our cabin door, and necessarily very close together, we proved food for amusement to our friends. Jamie and I were entirely ignorant of the part we were playing in the comedy, until we awoke, two hours later, to find we had been sketched, photographed and viewed, by almost everyone on the ship. They tell us that any number of cameras were snapped at us; a procession filed past us, to view the "sleeping beauties"; Captain George, the pilot, shouted and snored right in our ears; our artistic friends took sketches of us, and there we sat, Jamie and I, for two hours, perfectly oblivious of all this fun-making. How we laughed when we awoke, and how pleased we were when we saw the sketches and had them presented to us. As we went down to luncheon, so many said, "Had a nice nap?—I went around to see you," until I actually believe we were viewed by all. "Did you see Mr. B.'s sketch of you? It's so good," and another said "Isn't Miss N.'s sketch excellent? Your husband's mouth was wide open, and she has made it true to life."

About noon we steamed into Cordova Bay, and anchored opposite *one* building on the shore, to take on salted salmon. It is so queer to go miles and miles, to come to a tiny building like this, and then see barrels after barrels come out of a moderate sized shed, to be shipped. It brings us into the loveliest possible places, through narrow openings, into exquisite land-locked bays and is delightful to one *not in haste.*

Such exquisite scenery as we have enjoyed to-day! As we turned to come into this Bay, the mountains and islands were perfectly beautiful, reflecting all shades of green and all shapes of islands in the water, and we feasted our eyes upon it, as if we had not seen anything fine before. Many passengers went ashore, but we surmised that it would not be very attractive, and waited until someone should return and report. It was, as we thought, terribly muddy and dirty, and nothing at all attractive, except the woods, which were too wet for comfort. *Horn spoon maniacs* went on shore to hunt for spoons to polish, for the craze is so very strong that spoons have been in great demand. As I write, six scrapers surround my door, each expatiating on the superior polishing qualities of his or her spoon, and all accompanying their conversation by the most vigorous rubs and scrubs. The deck is covered with bone shavings, and sand-paper, and glass, and dirty hands and dusty dresses are the style. As one passes along the deck, in the stateroom doors sit young women and old, old white-haired men and boys, all scraping spoons. The craze has struck James; he is head over ears in shavings and bone-dust, and rubbing as if his life depended upon it.

Opposite our anchorage, and the only hut to be seen, save one small cottage near the " Salt-ery " (as it is called), is an Indian hut, with characteristic surroundings. As we steamed into the Bay, it was most picturesque. On the shore, to the right, was a tall rafter-like concern, covered thickly with bright pink salmon, split open and turned inside out to dry, and near the green of the trees it presented a fine contrast. Close to these brilliant fish were brown blankets, drying; shirts of white and red were also visible ; up under the trees sat the women with red handkerchiefs on their heads, and down on the shore were the little bare-footed children, crouching on a big rock, with three or four Siwash dogs roaming about. It is a very pretty picture, at a distance. We pass miles and miles of shore, where not one single soul abides; the wild animals possess much property here, and roam at their own sweet will. Eagles are plentiful, and almost unnoticed by us now.

A gentleman remarked the other day, in a dry way, "Well inhabited Alaska is! There must be at least one person to every thousand miles, in this territory."

To-night, or at least after a five o'clock dinner, as we came up on deck, Mr. S., from the East, met James and asked him if we would enjoy rowing with a party, to a very old Indian village, about five miles away. We were glad indeed to go, and to see anything unusual, out of the ordinary line of sight-seeing ; so about six o'clock the Third Officer and two seamen, took sixteen of us in a life-boat, to the deserted village of Klinquan. The row to and from the village was beautiful enough in itself to reward us, if the place had not been of interest. We rowed around beautiful little islands, close up to rocks, covered with wondrous sea-weeds and purple star-fish. The browns and tans of the sea-mosses, the color of the fish, the stones above, bare and gray, and above these still, the exquisite shades of green in the foliage of the trees, made the most exquisite rainbow effect in the water, for the red glow of the sunset furnished the brilliant colors needed. It was a beautiful little trip, and we felt like veritable explorers, approaching an unknown buried city. Quite enclosed by islands, and protected from the sea by a natural barricade, with a fine beach upon which to drag canoes, a band of the Hydah Indians have settled, some long time ago, in this little cove, and built themselves houses and homes, wherein they dwell. The entire village consists of about one dozen houses, and not one soul was there in this little town, when we visited it. Every house was locked or barred with wooden sticks, and not one living thing did we see, save an old and wild cat, which one of the sailors found and tried to catch. It was truly a deserted village, as all the inhabitants were away fishing and working. They return to this sheltered nook when winter comes. As we approached the little hamlet, an exclamation of wonder and delight went up from our boat like a chorus, for we had not seen a spot like it in all Alaska. Fort Wrangle had totem poles of great interest and antiquity, but here were totem poles by the dozens, and of most superior quality. As I have men-

TOTEM POLES — KLIN QUAN.

tioned before, these poles are the historical records of the family. Any family having enough history to erect and furnish a pole, is honored by all surrounding tribes. These totem poles belong, however, to an age that is passing swiftly along, for many customs of these people are being abandoned, as the Indians become better educated. Antiquity consequently, of tribe and people, is made known by means of these signs and symbols. Klinquan contains about twelve houses, and more than sixty totem poles of the most marvelous workmanship. Some carved trees were so huge, it was a marvel how they were ever conveyed to their present location, and even when brought and carved, how they were ever stood up and placed in the ground. They are carved in the most curious designs, in the most grotesque figures, and yet all most symmetrically done. Such huge eyes as the monsters have, such a queer arrangement of figures, such marvelous ornaments to crown the top. The Bear Tribe always surmounts each of their totems with a huge crouching bear, marvelously done. In looking up at one to-night, we discovered in each claw a good representation of a human face. An eagle, with outstretched wings, surmounted several columns, and an Indian with huge ancient hat, such as the Chief Kadishan wore, when we took his photograph, was several times repeated. One curious thing was, that on top of one tall slim pole, a cunning little figure of a man, was poised on one foot, on a ball, with the other leg and his arms outstretched, just like the figure of Victory, on the 14th of July column, in Paris. The question arose, where did these Hydah Indians get the idea for that figure? Was it wafted to them across the waters, or did the same genius burn in some Indian brain, as in the brain of the artist who designed the French model? It was a marked feature in that collection of totems. Some of them are mostly grotesque, others mysterious and solemn, and all stood about that collection of little huts, like sentinels on duty. We were much interested also in some graves, and the peculiar fencing about them. Around one chief's grave, was a high fence, and on each corner stood, what seemed to us, a white china milk pitcher. On examination we found that the pitchers were carved out of wood, and painted white to look like china. Queer little summer-houses were built over some graves.

The officer found a most interesting ruin of a house, into which we went. It was built like all Indian houses, with a square and two tiers around, and the sides of wood, two feet and a half deep, were most beautifully carved. We had much excitement in landing, and in getting away also. We reached there at half tide, and could not make a good landing, so the men held the oars together, putting one end on land, the other on the boat, and we crawled across that way. But our visit thoroughly paid us, and we decided it was one of the features of the trip.

Five people from our ship, had been to this same spot in the afternoon. Seeing a pole, with a queer box-like thing on top, they gave it a vigorous blow and down it came, with a crash. Imagine their surprise, when bones and dust came tumbling out and an Indian skull, with hair and flesh still on it, but dried like a mummy's skull. They left it, horrified at what they had unwittingly done, and sickened by the sight of the life-like head.

We reached the *Mexico* at 10 P. M.

TUESDAY, AUGUST 4TH.

WE were all much concerned last night, when we went to bed, over Baron Von B.'s non-appearance. He is a German, a magnificent specimen of a man, of glorious physical proportions, and an indefatigable hunter. He has been in Alaska hunting for some time, and we took the Baron and Baroness on board at Juneau. We left the Baron yesterday at Nichol's Bay; he was to hunt and then join our ship at Cordova Bay, and a young Indian was his guide. He did not put in an appearance until this morning at 7 A. M., when the *Mexico* was on her way to find him. It seemed he became interested, had shot two deer; his Indian guide lost his head and his way, and they had a dreadful time. The Baron was too heavy for the canoe, which was old and rotten, and they had to bail out the water every minute, and expected to go to the bottom, at short notice.

We left Cordova Bay as soon as he was on board,

and we have had a lovely sunshiny day, and a most exquisite sail. We had about sixty miles of sea to-day, but we had to ask when we were at sea, it was so calm and pond-like. Jamie and I slept in our chairs again this morning, but I kept one eye open, and watched photographers and sketchers, whenever they appeared.

After dinner, we all gathered on the forward deck, tied a ladder to a ventilator, and had a " living totem pole." We arranged our little crowd in tiers; all held horn spoons or some Indian curio in our hands, and had our photograph taken. Dr. N. and I were " photographers royal," but numerous Kodaks were snapped on us. We numbered about twenty in all, but our audience numbered nearly a hundred. We had a fine time, as we all know one another so well now, and we had the jolliest kind of an evening afterwards. We enjoyed the beautiful sunset and after glory, which lasted until nearly ten o'clock. It was " one of those heavenly days that cannot die." Then we went to supper, after which we assembled on the hurricane deck, sang rounds, and danced, and finally, seeing a steamer approaching, we all gathered together to give a song of greeting, which we shouted with all our might, as the stranger passed us. The phosphorescence in the waves, as we ploughed our way along, was perfectly beautiful, like melted silver, and full of bright and glittering stars, and made a wondrous light, like electricity.

EN route all day, with beautiful sunshine most all the way, although we had some fog in Queen Charlotte's Sound. The morning was not eventful ; Jamie and I had a nap again until luncheon, after which Mrs. D. and a party of six or more, settled themselves with us in our corner, and we polished and scraped spoons until about three o'clock, when Miss N. came to see me and we shut ourselves in my little room for a chat alone. Mr. McD., a most interesting man, who has lived for twenty years or more in British Columbia, as overseer of the Hudson Bay Company, is on the *Mexico*, on his journey home. He had interesting curios in his trunk in the hold, made by the Indians, three or four hundred miles in the interior, and offered to show them to James and me, but to no one else, except Miss K. (who was with me). We made a secret trip down, and he showed us some interesting things—Indian work on leather of porcupine quills, dyed different colors, blankets for his four dogs, who dragged him all over the snows in those Arctic regions, and he ended by presenting me with an interesting piece of work, made by an Indian of the Cascar tribe, who lives three hundred miles beyond Fort Wrangle.

Our evening was just like last night, only we did not sing *en masse*, but Miss C. gave us a treat with her lovely voice. This life is most fascinating to us, with its rest and perfect freedom from care, and there are so many interesting people on the *Mexico*, that one can hear words of wisdom, and learn something every day. One of our passengers is Mrs. A. who has made quite a trip in Alaska, staying more than two weeks in Fort Wrangle, and also in Juneau and Sitka. She is full of interesting Indian legends and folklore, and entertained us to-night by a little talk, as we all stood out in the bow, viewing the magnificent scenery. It was glorious to-night; the sunset was like liquid gold, and the rose and violet shades on the mountains, which assume such glorious tints in the twilight hour, were more radiant than ever. Our constant attendants, the snow mountains, have been left behind a little now, as we are nearing warmer latitudes, but once in a while, a great giant in white raises his head above the surrounding greenness, and gives us a look, as we steam along, and makes us long to turn again and hurry northward, for one more glance at those circles of great and glorious grandeur.

THURSDAY, AUGUST 6TH.

JAMES was up and dressed for breakfast, as usual, this morning, but as it was pouring hard, and was cold and damp, he did not waken me, and I was not conscious of much in the wide-awake world, until the big whistle of the *Mexico* announced that we had reached somewhere, and looking out of my window, I recognized Departure Bay. We had been steaming along for forty-eight hours and it was good to stop. We remained only until half past ten o'clock, long enough, however, to send to Nanaimo, for the ship's mail, as well as to send telegrams. Jamie sent one home, as being three days late in reaching Tacoma, we feared there might be some little anxiety felt by the three loved ones at home. Nothing to chronicle so far, except that our good friends, Mrs. N. with her daughter and son, have decided, instead of stopping at Victoria, to go with us to Tacoma ; then we five move along next week to Portland and take the trip on the Columbia River together. I wrote all this afternoon while James slept.

About seven o'clock to-night we reached Victoria, and at once some of our *Mexico* family went up into town. It was rainy and disagreeable, and we decided to wait until morning for our trip. We watched the people moving about, saw the " Steamer *Queen* " come in with her load of Alaskan travelers, and rejoiced that we were not of the number, for although much more palatial, she goes too fast to suit us.

This afternoon, as I came up from luncheon, Miss W., a clever women, offered me copies of Mr. Duncan's little paper, called *The Metlakahtlan*, printed in Metlakahtla. In one tiny sheet of November, 1889, was a letter by Mr. D., and the preface says, " Having been frequently asked to give some explanation of the peculiar carving, found among the natives of this coast, I think it well to insert in *The Metlakahtlan*, the following letter, written last summer to a friend in Washington." I have just copied the letter, omitting a short paragraph in the beginning. I have copied it, because it seemed to give such a good idea of the carving and use of the totem poles.

In this letter, Mr. Duncan tells of the operations of the silversmith, in making silver spoons out of silver dollars. He says, "the designs they cut on the spoons, are peculiar to the carving and painting of the Indians in this country, and are symbolical of the curious crests or totems (as they are sometimes called), which seem to have been adopted in far back ages, to distinguish the four social classes, into which each band is divided. The names of these four classes in the Tsimshean language are, Kish-poot-wodda, Canaddo, Lack-a-boo, and Lackshkeak."

" The Kish-poot-wodda, by far the most numerous hereabouts, are represented symbolically by the fin-back whale in the sea, the grizzly bear on land, the grouse in the air, and the sun and stars in the heavens."

" The Canaddo symbols are the frog, the raven, starfish and the bull-head."

" The Lackaboo takes the wolf, the heron and the grizzly bear for totems."

" The Lacksh-keak, the eagle, the beaver and the halibut."

"The creatures I have just named, are however, only regarded as the visible representatives of the powerful and mystical beings, or genii, of Indian mythology, and as all of one group are said to be of one kindred, so all the members of the same class, whose heraldic symbols are the same, are counted as blood relations. Strange to say, this relationship holds good, should the person belong to different, or even hostile tribes, speak a totally different language, or be located thousands of miles apart. On being asked to explain how this notion of relationship originated, or why it is perpetuated in the face of so many obliterating circumstances, the Indian points back to a remote age, when their ancestors lived in a beautiful land, and where in a mysterious manner, the mystical creatures, whose symbols they retain, revealed themselves to the heads of the family of that day."

"They can relate the traditional story of an overwhelming flood, which came and submerged the land, and spread death and destruction all around. Those of the ancients who escaped in canoes, were drifted about and scattered in every direction on the face of the waters, and where they found themselves after the flood had subsided, there they located and formed new tribal associations. Thus it was that persons related by blood, became widely severed from each other; nevertheless they retained and clung to the symbols which had distinguished them and their respective families before the flood;

and all succeeding generations have, in this particular, sacredly followed suit. Hence it is the crests have continued to mark the offspring of the original founders of each family."

"As it may interest you to know, to what practical uses the natives apply their crests, I will enumerate those which have come under my own notice."

"First. As I have previously mentioned, crests sub-divide tribes into social clans, and a union of crest is a closer bond than a tribal union."

"Second. It is the ambition of all leading members of each clan, in the several tribes, to represent, by carving or painting, their heraldic symbols on all their belongings, not omitting even their household utensils, as spoons, and dishes, and on the death of the head of a family, a totem pole is erected in front of his house by his successor, on which is carved and painted, more or less elaborately, the symbolic creatures of his clan, as they appear in some mythological tale or legend."

" Third. The crests define the bounds of consanguinity, and persons having the same crest are forbidden to intermarry; that is, a frog may not marry a frog, nor a whale marry a whale ; but a frog may marry a wolf, and a whale may marry an eagle. Among some of the Alaskan tribes, I am told the marriage restrictions are still further narrowed, and persons of different crests may not intermarry, if the creatures of their respective clans have the same instincts. Thus a Canaddo may not marry a Lacksh-keak, because the raven of the one crest and the eagle of the other, seek and devour the same kind of food. Again, the Kish-poot-wodda may not marry a Lackaboo, because the grizzly bear and wolf, representing those crests, are both carnivorous."

" Fourth. All the children take the mother's crest, and are incorporated as members of the mother's family, nor do they designate, or regard their father's family as their relations. A man's heir and successor, therefore, is not his own son, but his sister's son, and in the case of a woman be-ing married into a distant tribe, away from her rela-tions, the offspring of such union, when grown up, will leave their parents and go to their mother's tribe, and take their respective place in their mother's family. This law accounts for the great interest which natives take in their nephews and nieces, which seems to be quite equal to the interest they take in their own children."

" Fifth. The clan relationship also regulates all feasting. A native never invites the members of his own crest to a feast; they being regarded as his blood relations, are always welcome as his guests; but at feasts which are given only for display, so far from being partakers of the bounty, all the clansmen, within a reasonable distance, are expected to con-tribute of their means and their services gratuitously, to make the feast a success. On the fame of the feast, hangs the honor of the clan."

"Sixth. What I have just written reminds me to add, this social brotherhood has a great deal to do with promoting hospitality among the Indians, a matter of immense importance, in a country without hotels, or restaurants. A stranger, with or without his family, in visiting an Indian village, need never be at a loss for shelter; all he has to do is to make for the house belonging to one of his crest, and which he can easily distinguish by the totem pole in front of it. There he is sure of a welcome, and of the best the host can afford. There he is accounted a brother, and treated and trusted as such."

"Seventh. I may mention too, that the sub-division of the bands into their social clans, accounts in some measure for the number of petty chiefs existing in each tribe, as each clan can boast of its headman. The more property a clan accumulates and gives away to rival clans, the greater number of head men it may have."

"Eighth. Another prominent use made by the natives of their heraldic symbols is, that they take names from them for their children; for instance, Wee-nay-ach—'big fin' (whale). Lee-tahm-lach-ta —'sitting on the ice' (eagle). Iksh-co-am-alyah— "the first speaker" (raven in the morning). Athl-kah-kout—'the howler travelling' (wolf)."

"Ninth. And last, but not least, the kinship claimed and maintained in each tribe, by the method of crests, has much to do with preventing blood-feuds, and also in restoring the peace, when quarrels and fighting have ensued. Tribes, or sections there-of, may and do fight, but members of the same social clan may not fight. Hence, in contests between two tribes, there always remains in each, some non-combatants who will watch the opportunity to interpose their offices, in the interest of peace and order. In case too, of a marauding party being out to secure slaves, should they find one or more of their victims to be of their own crest, such a person would be set free, and be incorporated as a member of their family, while the captives of other crests would be held or sold as slaves."

" In writing of these matters, it must be understood that I have kept in view the natives in their primitive state. The Metlakathlans who are civilized, while retaining their crest distinctions and upholding the good and salutary regulations connected therewith, have dropped all the baneful and heathenish rivalry with which the clannish system was intimately associated."

" Yours respect.,"

(Signed) " W. DUNCAN."

FRIDAY, AUGUST 7TH.

IT was perfectly lovely this morning, so sunny and bright, and at half past eight o'clock, James and I started in a hansom, for the shops of Victoria. Mr. McD. our Hudson Bay Co. friend, met us, to look about a little with us, and he is such a whole-souled lovely man, James and I enjoyed him greatly.

We skipped about from shop to shop, constantly meeting our friends and fellow-passengers, and about eleven o'clock we turned our faces toward the ship, and returned to the dear old *Mexico*, bidding our new friend good-bye, as he was about to start in a few hours, for his home in Winnipeg. We had hardly reached the *Mexico* and exchanged notes with all our friends, as to bargains, etc., when to our surprise, Mr. McD. whom we had just a half hour before bade good-bye, and left in excellent spirits, appeared before us, with red eyes, and a black-bordered letter in his hand. I saw in a moment that some sorrow had come to him, and calling Jamie and me aside, he told us that after we left him, he had received and read the letter he then held, telling him that his favorite brother—the one whom he anticipated meeting more than any one else—was dead and buried. The great strong man covered his face with his hands, and turned to go away, but James and I opened our cabin door, and took him into the little room for a few minutes. He was completely unnerved and had come to us for sympathy. He had looked forward like a boy, to his home-coming ; now anticipation and joy were crushed by this unexpected and saddest of sorrows. Only yesterday I made the remark, that I wondered if all of our passengers would reach shore, without some, or many, finding sad tidings awaiting them, and as the disciples of old asked the Master, at the Last Supper, "Lord, is it I?" so the same query went up from my heart, with a prayer for mercy. Anxiety was mine for a little, for who has nerves so strong that they can battle with such moments, and conquer every fear and dread.

We left Victoria about one o'clock, and the afternoon was spent by all, in the disagreeable duty of packing, as we land to-morrow. It was a trying operation, and not very good for the proper development of patience and sweetness of temper, as we are all agreed.

About four o'clock we reached Port Townsend, but no one went ashore until after dinner. Then Mrs. N. the Dr. and R., Commander and Mrs. C., Miss C. and Miss E., with Jamie and myself, started out and having nothing to do, or see, or buy, we took an electric car and rode around the city twice. We were merry and made fun out of nothing.

A letter was awaiting me here from Miss Thursby, asking me to advise her about going to Alaska, on the next trip of the *Mexico*. She had been singing in this neighborhood, and would have waited to greet us, if she had not been engaged to sing somewhere else. I wrote her to-night advising her to go.

There is a genuine sadness in the air to-day, a depression one cannot escape, for the pleasant life on ship-board is soon to be given up,—the familiar every-day friendships to be no more, and the life on shore, with its heat and dusty railroads, to be our lot once again. Jamie's last remark to-night, as he hurried to sleep, was—"oh, May,—don't you hate to leave the dear old ship," and I do. It has been a restful home and shelter to us for twenty-three days, and the very discomforts and trials and deprivations, have become dear to us. Our tiny room has grown to quite palatial proportions; although at first we could only dress one at a time,—now we can both array ourselves, with only occasional bumps and thumps. Fussiness is a thing of the past, order a necessity, but not requiring energy or time to produce. Our last night on our comfortable little shelves! I hope more chances may be ours in future, for the same sweet blissful rest. The wonderful scenery will then be well-known by us, and yet it will be inspiring in its greatness and grandeur.

SATURDAY, AUGUST 8TH.

WE were all up at six o'clock this morning;— breakfast was at seven, but James and Dr. N. had been up to "The Tacoma" before that meal, to secure rooms. About 8.30, we all began to leave the dear old *Mexico*, but it was hard work, and we hung around as long as we could. Finally, we made up our minds that lingering only prolonged the agony, so we made a grand rush for the carriage. With Jamie's first awakening consciousness this morning, he groaned aloud, and exclaimed with a sigh,—"Isn't it awful to think of trains, and heat, and dust again?" The heat seemed to open its arms wide to us, as we drove to the hotel, Mrs. N. and R., Jamie and I in one carriage.

As we neared the hotel, my one thought was to get somewhere, where I could read our letters from home, which Jamie had brought to me, but as we entered the doorway, whom should I behold but Aunt Mary, who immediately exclaimed, "I've been waiting three weeks for you, to finish your trip with you."

We three went to our room, and I read the letters from home aloud, which took some time. We then wandered out to find a photographer, to develop our films, and returning, after luncheon, we came to our room to rest.

The evening was spent with Auntie and the N.s, listening to the Spanish Students' delightful music, and regretting that we were not on the good old *Mexico*, for another trip.

It is no hardship to return to Tacoma, for it is the brightest of little towns. The business streets are as lively and crowded, and the stores are as good, as any in a larger and older city. To be sure, the pavements on the streets and sidewalks are of wood, but the buildings are many, and really very fine and imposing, and altogether, Tacoma impresses us wonderfully. There are about forty-five thousand people here, and they are mostly Eastern people, and full of energy and ambition. Tacoma's chief charm, as to location, is not so much its position on an arm of Puget Sound, as the great snow mountain, which guards it day and night. Mt. Ranier, 14,444 feet above the sea level, is a grand mountain, and peeps from the clouds early every morning, and stands sentinel all day in its beauty. It is all snow, and is glorious,—pink like a shell at sunset, and then amber, and sometimes violet. If one ever feels tired of buildings and streets, they have only to turn their eyes toward Ranier, and they find food for reflection for many a long day.

COLUMBIA RIVER AND MT. HOOD

THESE three uninteresting, common-place days, must be treated collectively.

Sunday morning, Jamie and I remained in our room, and did not appear until luncheon. In the afternoon, Mr. and Mrs. A., of Tacoma, called, and were with us for a couple of hours. Dinner being over, we sat quietly on the piazza. We were all feeling the reaction of our trip, and the change from cool to warm weather again.

Monday morning, after a late breakfast, we all went to see and pronounce verdicts upon the Kodak films,—which took some time. Luncheon over, we went to work at our packing, for James was anxious to get the freight box off, with our Alaska curios, chairs, rugs, etc. Company all the evening, ended a hum-drum day.

Tuesday morning was spent out with our little party until noon; then the finishing touches were put to the box, and James went to start it on its way, while I went to drive with the three N.s, seeing many views of Puget Sound and fine homes and residences. We danced in the evening, and I wrote a letter home.

WEDNESDAY, AUGUST 12TH.

WE started for Portland at 11.40 A. M., with the N.s. It was a decidedly tiresome and dusty journey, miserably warm, and we were royally glad to reach Portland, about 6.40 P. M. A brush off and dinner, then a chat with Miss H.—a resident of Portland,—and a fellow *Mexico*-ite, and a good-night to all except Miss Thursby, who had sent us word to come to her room, after her concert was over. I was with her until about twelve o'clock, and when she asked, "Shall we go to Alaska on the *Mexico?*" my enthusiasm decided her, and they left the very next morning. If stormy, so that they cannot enjoy the scenery, she can say, like a lady I heard of last night, "she went to Alaska, not to see the scenery, but for the air"

THURSDAY, AUGUST 13TH.

NO one put in an appearance until luncheon time, after which we five took a drive all over Portland, seeing the city thoroughly and some fine views. Portland has some magnificent streets, palatial homes, and is a delightful city in many respects. Mr. C., of the *Mexico*, called to-night. We found Miss C. and Miss E. at "The Portland," also Mr.

and Mrs. S., of Summit, and we had a little reunion, and all went together to call on Miss H., and had a pleasant time.

FRIDAY, AUGUST 14TH.

IN fear and trembling, without courage or enthusiasm, we five sallied forth this morning for our trip down to "The Dalles." Disappointment, and lack of anticipation were manifested, by our low spirits and our sober faces. Last night, when we returned from our drive, with the tickets for our trip bought and paid for, and every arrangement made, we met friends who had two hours before returned from the same experience. "Don't go," they cried, "it's stupid, horrid, wretched, no money would hire us to go again! Oh, how I pity you," they added. We turned to each other and tried to look as brave as lions. We thought they were tired and cross, but *we* would have a good time. While at dinner Mrs. B. passed me, and knowing they had taken a trip part way to "The Dalles" that very day, I asked them how *they* liked it. "Well," they answered, "after Alaska it is tame, in fact, it is hardly worth the time and money, unless you have plenty of both on your hands." Had the bottom gone out of the world, or had all our "Dalles Friends," or those who had taken the trip, deliberately lied? A more forlorn, dejected set were never found. A sort of gasp, and a "we're in for it" expression, settled like the shades of night upon us, and we were crushed, and had little heart in the next day's doing.

At half-past four o'clock we were awakened, and prepared for our trip by half-past five, and as Jamie expressed it, "we all wished we were just coming back, instead of starting." Reaching the boat, which seemed to our sleepy eyes to be named " Furline " but which proved to be *Lurline*, we were further discouraged, for we beheld a regular Mississippi stern wheel affair, and anything but attractive. They say "blessings brighten as they take their flight," and so as we sailed along the Willamette River, to its junction with the Columbia, we began to think we were not in such a bad place after all. Our staterooms were palatial in size, and our breakfast at 6.30 A. M. made us feel "at peace with the world, the flesh and the devil." We three, in fact all but Dr. N. turned in at seven, for a couple of hours' rest, and when about nine we emerged as fresh as daisies, the *Lurline* was steaming along between the banks of the Columbia River, in rarely beautiful scenery, and from then until we reached " The Dalles," at 5.40 P. M., we were delighted, and much surprised at the lack of appreciation exhibited by our friends. Very different indeed from any scenery we have seen before, it was still so wonderfully characteristic and bold and beautiful. Our first glimpse of any individuality in special outline, was a huge rock standing quite alone, called Rooster Rock. Next came Cape Horn, a marvelous formation of basaltic boulders. From that point, our trip up the Columbia was between great fortresses and castles, of rare volcanic formation—great black boulders, then clay deposits which produced such a brilliant contrast. The mountains and hills on each side, rose very high above us, and were covered half way up with delicate feathery foliage, the different and variegated colors blending harmoniously with the reddish rocks, and the great bare trunks of trees, which gleamed so white among the deeper evergreens. Here and there a bright branch of some maple waved conspicuously in the October tints, and made the picture perfect. A lace-like waterfall, eight hundred and thirty feet high, by twelve feet wide, shone like silver in its beauty, and was the well-known Multnomah Falls. About twelve o'clock we had dinner, then the *Lurline* stopped at " The Cascades " and we were taken on a little train, six miles around the Cascades, where we took the *D. S. Baker* to " The Dalles." We saw a flat open freight car on the little train, and quietly seated ourselves with our luggage on it, but we were no sooner settled, than a car-man told us they needed the space for two boats. We went away, but as soon as the boats were on the car, we jumped into one, and on a flat platform car, in a boat, we rode those six miles, through lovely woods and with glorious glimpses of the Cascades.

Our afternoon on *D. S. Baker's* palatial (?) deck was a most delightful one. We enjoyed every minute, because it was really rarely beautiful, such wonderful volcanic formations, unlike anything we had seen. One funny thing kept us constantly on the alert, for every time a passenger wanted to get off the boat, or one wanted to get on, all they did was to " run the boat agin the bank, till every galoot was ashore." The first time we approached the land I was alarmed, and knew something was wrong and we were going aground. Sure enough, up in the mud ran the bow, and the engines were stopped. A long plank was thrown ashore, and passengers carefully helped along. The next time we turned for the bank, I could see nothing to make such a performance reasonable or right, but as we neared the little lonely spot, on the shore sat a young woman, with a little boy, alone with their traps, and both were quickly taken on board.

We reached " The Dalles " about 5.40 P. M. and walked to the " Umatella House," where we left our bags and proceeded to see the town. Forlorn, unattractive, doleful, a barren glaring spot, with about four thousand people living there, and we were royally glad to take a train at 6.40, for Hood River. We knew nothing of our shelter for the night, but we were taking chances, and when I saw the hotel, I felt like running to the woods, but it proved better than it looked. A general search was made by each of us, as soon as our rooms were apportioned, and simultaneously we all put our heads into the hall, and asked about clean linen. I saw the nice young wife of the proprietor, and said "Our upper sheet and pillows seem clean, but the under sheet looks doubtful." "Yes ma'am, I know, and I'll change it," she answered, "I only change one sheet for gentlemen; they don't mind, you know, so I prepared that room for a gentleman, you see." We were almost too tired to care much, and at nine o'clock we were in bed, lights out, and were not disturbed until the next morning, at five o'clock.

"Why did not those people like that lovely trip?" was our query all day. It made us fear they had wearied of the wonderful and beautiful, and were not quite in tune with these surroundings.

SATURDAY, AUGUST 15TH.

LOVELY and bright, when we were awakened, at half past five o'clock this morning, for our drive up Mt. Hood. At seven o'clock we started, packed bag and baggage in the stage, and as we had been told in Portland, that we would reach Cloud Cap Inn at noon, we thought our trip would be short and sweet. We had twenty-seven miles to go; most of those miles we were climbing hills, and the man who told us that we only needed a few hours for the ascent, had never been up Mt. Hood himself, I'll warrant. At luncheon time, we were only half way up that tremendous climb, and did not reach the Inn, until half past five o'clock that night. The drive was a glorious one, through beautiful woods, with the trees thickly hung with "Grey Beard," and the wild flowers, the little streams of gray water from the glaciers, with numerous glimpses of great Mt. Hood, in its snow mantle, made it an everchanging panorama. But the dust! Never in our lives had we seen such loving, clinging, all-powerful dust, and never had we been so bountifully powdered. Although we had plenty of dust in the Yosemite, it was nothing compared to this close and intimate bosom-friend of Mt. Hood. The road is made through basaltic and lava formations, and the powdered boulders, the deep deposit of ages, has been overturned and lies upon the surface in a thick powder. As the driver said—" it's real good clean dust," and so it was, but the most inquisitive particles that we have ever met. As I thought we had given up the Mt. Hood trip, I had left our dusters behind, but as we left the Hood River Hotel, the good wife of the proprietor had offered me her duster, which, though marvelously ample, was a blessing after all. We had all left our hats there also, and wore caps, as we have learned never to have such stiff burdensome things about, when away for pleasure. The dust sifted through everything, through our veils and dusters, and plastered us from head to heels. Our faces were worse than any coal-digger's; we were smutched all over with grim shadows around our eyes, and nose, and mouth, for the slight moisture of the warm weather mixed marvelously well with the dirt, and made a plastic mud, most uncomfortable to us all. At first

we brushed every few minutes ; then a calm resignation came over us and we sat still and took our dust,
peck by peck,—like good Christians. We swallowed
more than we liked, and absolutely ground our teeth
upon it. I am not exaggerating, for nobody could
give an adequate idea of that powdered drive. We
finally came to a barn, and the driver said we would
rest there an hour, so we thought we would eat our
luncheon. Oh, how we laughed when we were on
the ground and could have a full view of one another!
Dr. N. laughed heartily when he beheld Jamie, in
all his dustiness, little realizing that he looked just
as badly himself. Mrs. N. went about, whipping the
bushes and trunks of trees with her hat, veil and
wrap, but Jamie and I were too hungry to care, and
seating ourselves,—Jamie on a box found under a
tree, and I, perching up on one end of the little
wooden table,—we opened and prepared the
luncheon. Chickens' wings and legs, hard boiled
eggs, bread, crackers, little cakes and apples, composed the repast, but as the hostess of the Wood
River Hotel was not troubled with a tremendous
stock of refinement, every article was done up in
dingy newspaper,—old pieces that looked as if they
had been through the war. But dusty, dirty beings as
we were, could not be very particular,—our appetites
were too big to be spoiled and we sat and ate our
newspaper lunch, as if served with the air and grace
of a Delmonico waiter. We roared with laughter,
between bites, at our funny little circle, and when-

ever I undertook to move, or Dr. N. who was perched on the other end of our rude rough lunch-table, it would see-saw and shake, and every one would watch some particular dainty (?) morsel, with fever-ish anxiety, for fear it would take unto itself wings and fly away. It was a party of the merriest kind.

To give some idea of our snail's pace up the mountain, we were three hours going up five miles. It was like climbing the side of a house, and of course the higher we climbed, the rarer the air be-came, and the poor horses panted, and puffed, and made our hearts ache. When we espied Cloud Cap Inn, we were glad we had faced the discomforts and trials of that trip, to find such a lovely resting place. A log cabin of one story,—tied down to the rocks by means of strong cables, it presented the most attractive appearance imaginable. Wooden within and without,—no carpets, or wall papers, or conven-tionalities, it however proved the loveliest retreat, so quiet, so lofty, so unusual; and to our dusty souls, it seemed a heaven on earth. A most excel-lent woman keeps the Inn in the Clouds, providing home-like dainties in abundance, and we found our-selves at once so comfortable that we shook the dis-agreeable remembrance of our drive from us, with the dust, and enjoyed it all in full measure. A fine sunset, and a gorgeous moon-light night, with genuine winter coldness, made us all sleepy and before ten o'clock we had started for the land of "Wynken, Blynken, and Nod."

CL UD CAP INN.

I AM sitting alone, on the floor of the little observatory, on top of Cloud Cap Inn. It is half-past " five o'clock in the morning" and the rest of our little party have returned to their beds, but I could not shut my eyes upon such grandeur; the idea of being alone to absorb and drink in this beauty, made me so wide awake that I could not resist the temptation, and so I am here, all alone with my thoughts, the great mountains, and the flood of sunshine which surrounds me, and it was never so easy to worship my God, on a Sabbath morning, as it is to-day. The mountains and hills declare His glory; the great snow monarchs proclaim His praise; the trees sing their anthems in the gentle morning breeze, and the little birds twitter their love for Him. Why should not my heart glow and give thanks why should I not be in tune with all this glory! It makes me feel awed and speechless, as in silent grandeur all nature makes homage to its Creator. Not one word, no sound, except the wind as it rustles through the tree-tops, and yet a more glorious adoration was never given than we have witnessed this morning. In awful grandeur and magnificence, the great mountains raise their heads, beholding nothing on earth to rival their beauty, but all pointing to Heaven, the home of their King, and expressing in themselves the prayer of the Ages, the anthem they have sung since time began.

By the thoughtfulness of good Mrs. F., we were awakened before five o'clock, to see the sun rise. Scrambling into our clothes, with unwashed faces and uncombed heads, we assembled on the little rustic observatory, on the roof of this artistic little log-cabin. I was alone at first, but was soon joined by four sleepy companions, all, however, awakened before many minutes, to the beauteous surroundings. At our left, in close companionship, stood Mt. Hood, on whose side we now are. Cleanly and clearly outlined against a sky of turquoise, with its great cone-shaped summit covered with pure white snow, Mt. Hood stood in such wondrous beauty, in such mysterious grandeur, its great rocks and shining glaciers making a wonderful impression upon us. We felt as if we could put out our hands and touch its glorious summit, it was so near us. Opposite us, on our right hand and on our left, stood range after range of wonderful mountains, in such marvelous numbers, with such myriads of points and peaks, of deep shadowy blue, some in the distance resembling castles and cathedrals, that we seemed unable to take it all in and properly appreciate its beauty. The most glorious, grand and marvelous sight, however, were the great Kings of the West, lifting their snow-covered heads in majesty and might, behind the numerous mountains in the foreground and middle distance. Mt. Ranier, 165 miles away from us, opposite Tacoma, stood out so distinctly before us, that we marveled at the sight of its great glacial sides and multitude of cracks and crevasses, and could not believe that so many miles were between us. Nearer us, to the right of Ranier's gorgeous rounded top, stood Mt. Adams, in such loftiness and glorious grandeur, in such a pure white mantle, it seemed to touch the heavens, and reflect the splendor of the Pearly Gates. To Ranier's left, in a haughty gloriousness, and with a great volcanic cup full of snow, as her crown, stood Mt. St. Helens, the loftiest and most aristocratic and aspiring of the quartette. We stood in an amphitheatre of grandeur, of magnificent mountain ranges on all sides of us, with these great monarchs as sentinels, rising far into the sky, above the rest, in such unparalleled loveliness, in such unspeakable magnificence.

When we first saw Mt. Hood this morning, it was outlined against the azure blue, like a genuine gem, in a molten silver setting. To enhance the picture, one twinkling star peeped at us, over the summit of snow, a good-bye to the night, for the dawn was coming. In the far east, a great band of deep red light announced the approach of the King of Day, and glowed and glistened, reflecting rose, violet, purple, then a long finger of yellow, over the scene of enchantment before us. Mt. Adams was a purple of royal hue, with violet shadows; Mt. Ranier, like a beautiful pink rose, stood out in delicate outlines; while Mt. St. Helens, like a glorious bride decked for her wedding morn, was purest gold, rare and bright, and beautiful; and wonderful beyond words was this marvelous picture. We were harmonious in our praise and enjoyment of this vision of beauty, which far surpassed any similar scene ever witnessed. Gradually Old Sol, in the brightest of Sunday attires, peeped up from behind the mountains, a little rim of gold at first, to be sure all Nature was ready to receive him and do him homage, then, as if satisfied and puffed up with pride, he came rolling forth in a grandeur and splendor of sunshine, flooding everything with his wondrous light. The little star above Mt. Hood quickly made its exit; the snow smiled back at Old Sol, as he caressed its mounds and glaciers; the trees began to wave their welcome; the birds sang a little chorus of praise, and every rock and rill, every mountain and valley sent up a little cloud of incense, their welcome to the Sun.

As I sit on this lofty pinnacle, looking over the tree-tops, to the snow-clad mountains, and realize where I am, and that I am viewing some of the grandest scenery in the world, I am depressed as well as impressed, as I realize the atom I am, in this great world of wonder and wisdom.

While I sat in such absolute stillness, drinking in the beauty on all sides of me, the little birds did not seem afraid of me; they did not seem to realize that I was a living being, and they came and perched about me, gave a little peep, sang a merry song, looking straight into my face, then they flew away to tell their neighbors, who came in turn to see me,

and I wondered what they thought of that queer little woman, crouched down on the floor of the little rustic observatory, like an Indian squaw in her usual position. Perhaps they thought I had come " To sweep the cobwebs from the sky,"—" Old woman, old woman, old woman, quoth I."

At half-past six, I saw that Mt. Hood would soon be too bright to photograph, so I ran to our room, grasped my camera and flew to the roof, to take two photos of this wondrous companion of ours. Its awful summit is only four thousand feet above us, as it stands 11,400 feet above the sea level. Then, as the people of the house began to move about, and I felt that absolute solitude could no longer be mine, I went to our room and jumped into bed for an hour's nap. About half-past eight we assembled for breakfast, and such a good one as we had, just like a home breakfast. Soon after, we were out and wandering about, but the rare air made exercise too much for any of us, and after walking a few steps, we were obliged to give up our desire to visit an immense glacier, not an eighth of a mile away from us. We reached a point of rocks, called " Artist's Point," where Bierstadt painted some famous pictures, and there we sat for an hour or two, looking deep down into the Valley and seeing the wonderful volcanic formations, and lava beds. On the opposite side of Mt. Hood from where we are, there is a crater, which often now sends forth steam in great volumes.

About one o'clock, which came all too soon, we were called to dinner, and at two o'clock we packed ourselves again in our stage, waved a good-bye to the good woman who keeps the little Inn, and began our descent of Mt. Hood. The five miles of terrible climbing, which took us over three hours yesterday, we went down in forty minutes. The trip back to Hood River was a very tiresome one, more so than yesterday, because we had not thoroughly rested from the drive and necessary fatigue. The terrible dust of yesterday attacked us again, in quite as violent a form, but we did not enjoy it as much as before ; the novelty had worn off, and we saw visions of being too late to have a good wash, before taking the train for Portland. We were a perfect sight, when we reached Hood River at seven o'clock, and as we drove up to the Hotel, the piazza was crowded with country people in their Sunday attire, and the children set up a howl, when they saw James alight. He was plastered with this basaltic powder, literally coated with it, and his face was hardly recognizable. We were all in similar condition, and were approached by the men of the Inn, with long handled dusters and brushes. A general rush for rooms and clean clothes, "a rub, scrub and a polish," a little bite of supper, and at 7.40 P. M. we took the train for Portland, five tired out but contented people. We reached Portland at 10.45 P. M. and after "a tub" we tumbled into bed, to dream of the visions of beauty we had seen.

L OVELY morning, bright, sunny and very warm. Mrs. N. was quite ill all last night and very wretched this morning. Dr. N. however, was able to leave his mother for a while this morning, and James and the Doctor and I, wandered about the streets of Portland, into the shops, hunting some trifles and some good views of Alaska and other places. We had such a late breakfast that we did not return for luncheon, but about half past two we came back to *The Portland*, and were able to visit Mrs. N. for a little. R. was so disappointed, not being able to go with us in the morning, that she begged me to go to a few shops again with her, which I did with genuine pleasure. When we returned about five o'clock, I found the Doctor with James in our room, painting a totem-pole in water colors, from my photo, and my desire to write home had to be curbed until dinner time, but was accomplished, in spite of obstacles. We five Hood-ites dined together and had our evening together also, for the thought of parting makes us sad. It is remarkable how short a time it takes to make real firm friends. Four weeks ago, we did not know the N.s, and now we hope to keep them always as friends.

TUESDAY, AUGUST 18TH.

R AINING and cool, and joy was in our hearts when we awoke, and found this condition of things. Rain is scarce in this part of the summer, seldom visiting the country for weeks and months. A rainy day for a trip to Tacoma, the dustiest of rail experiences, was a delight to us. After packing, we breakfasted at 9.30 A. M. with the N.s, and I was made happy by the farewell offerings brought me.

At eleven o'clock, we left the Hotel and our three friends, whose waving handkerchiefs were visible until we turned a sharp corner two blocks away, and Jamie and I are already wondering how soon it may be our good fortune to see them again. At 11.45 our train started and landed us in Tacoma at 6.25 P. M. We passed the uninteresting trip quickly away, by reading " Idle Thoughts of an Idle Fellow," by Jerome K. Jerome, parts of which Jamie read aloud to me, and we richly enjoyed. Aunt Mary was awaiting us, and we were quite rejoiced to get . back. Letters were our treat from home, and were thoroughly digested before we ate one mouthful of supper.

WEDNESDAY, AUGUST 19TH.

R IGHT after breakfast, James, Auntie and I wandered out to see our photographs. While shopping, afterwards, we met Miss J. and Miss D. and Mrs. A., of our *Mexico* party, and had a short interview in Gross's " Dry Goods Shop." The girls had been to call upon me. After reaching the hotel, Rev. Dr. Y. and Dr. James Y., who were awaiting our return, made us a long call, inviting us to go this afternoon to " Tea " at the Ladies' Tennis Club. Luncheon—then a change of rooms, and while struggling fifteen minutes later, to get settled, Miss J. and Miss D. appeared again. They had not gone, when Dr. Y. arrived to escort us to the Tennis Grounds, and Dr. J. Y. was there to welcome us on arrival. The Tennis Club does not occupy imposing grounds and buildings, but there is simply a corner lot, with two courts, a small building, where tea was served, and some benches and seats, arranged very ingeniously under the sidewalk. We met many people, however, saw Tacoma's belles and beauties, and they were decidedly attractive in ap-

pearance. Life in Tacoma seems like one big picnic,—a sort of holiday life and energy, and a constant round of entertainments—which is very pleasant.

As James had not been about Tacoma, we took a
drive after leaving the grounds, and Dr. Y. went
with us. The oldest part of the town is about
twenty years old, and is spoken of with great reverence, by all the inhabitants, as "Old Tacoma,"
(strong emphasis on the Old). In this ancient corner, is a tiny edifice, a little church (Episcopal),
"St. Peter's" by name. The belfry is on a huge
tree, seven feet in diameter ; the branches have
been cut away, and on top of this huge trunk, a bell-
tower has been placed. Ivy covers the trunk
thickly, and it is a unique and remarkable church
tower. Dr. Y. wanted to stop at the old Church,
which we did, and interviewed the minister, who
took us into the Church. Then we drove to Dr. Y.'s
home and went in for a short call, and to see dear
little Gretchen. After dinner, we spent a quiet
pleasant evening with Aunt Mary, and listened to the
Spanish Students.

THURSDAY, AUGUST 20TH.

M OST remarkably uneventful, and yet a pleasant, quiet, restful day, with enough company to entertain us, and enough music to make
life worth living.

ABOUT three and a half o'clock, Auntie, James and I, in an electric car, rode to what is known in these parts as "Old Tacoma," to meet Mr. G. and his Naphtha launch *Hope*, for a trip to the "Boat Club House," about six miles across Puget Sound. Naphtha launches, have seemed to me up to date, an invention of the Devil, to be avoided religiously by me and my better half, on all occasions. Imagine my horror, when informed that James had actually accepted this invitation, for himself and me. As I prepared for my pleasure (!) trip, I kept assuring myself that drowning, after all, was a pleasant death—sort of panoramic and kaleidoscopic. As I stepped into the little twenty-one foot craft, with its shining business-like funnel, and numerous little wheels and knobs, to turn on or off the gas needed or not needed, I gasped, in despair, and to my better half's infinite disgust, "Any danger in these little ships?" to which Mr. G. answered reassuringly (?) "Don't believe so, I've never had an accident, but no knowing when will be the first time." I swallowed something that would stick up in my throat, and fibbed about its being "so pleasant to go so fast and feel so safe," but for a mile or so, I kept my eye on that little "infernal machine" in the stern, to my great amusement after, for soon a sense of safety came over me, and ever since I have been an enthusiastic admirer of these little crafts. We sailed those six miles in forty minutes, and reached the boat club in ample time, for the " Naphtha Launch Race," which was called at 6 P. M. We were landed on the float, but soon to our delight, the Commodore of the little fleet, sent us an invitation to come to his yacht, which was anchored off shore, and was the starting point, as well as finish, for the race. Soon the seven launches started out on their three miles course, and it was very interesting and a pretty sight. Our *Hope* was one of the small launches, and was beaten by a bigger boat, but we enjoyed the sight very much. A supper, served to a large num ber of guests, followed, and about a quarter to nine o'clock, we started in our little craft for the shore of Tacoma. It was a glorious sail back ; the phosphorescence was exquisite ; we seemed to cut our way through diamond waves, and the moon rose like a great fiery cart-wheel, and shed a red path of light to guide us home.

SATURDAY, AUGUST 22D.

WE had callers on the piazza all the morning, the K's, of Peekskill, whom we met in the Yosemite, and who have just returned from Alaska, and the Y's. In the afternoon, Jamie and Dr. Y., with the host of the *Hope*, went again for a sail, but as we were going to dine with Mrs. Y., I refused the tempting invitation. Jamie returned in time to dress, and we went to the dinner, and had a very pleasant time.

AUNTIE and James spent the day with me in my room, as I was not feeling well. I went to dinner, however, and after it we three went to the little church in old Tacoma, with its ancient bell-tower, and ivy (which has poked its tiny tendrils through every available crack and crevice, into the sacred sanctuary, and grown everywhere luxuriously), and we heard a fine sermon, from Rev. Dr. Y., of Staten Island.

WEDNESDAY, AUGUST 26TH.

AFTER breakfast in my room, I received calls in the parlor, from Mrs. W. and her sister Miss C., whom I met at Mrs. Y.'s dinner, after which the music was enjoyed. After luncheon, by invitation from Mr. G., Auntie, James, Dr. Y. and I, also Miss R., went for a sail on the launch *Hope*. It was a terribly warm day on shore, but in our hurried passage through the water, we created such a breeze' that jackets were necessary for comfort and safety.

The great interest now in Puget Sound is the salmon fishing, and the run of salmon is so great, that we thought a sail to the traps would be of interest. Before going near enough to see through the nets, we sailed about near the spot, and never in our lives have we seen such a sight. The fish were jumping many times their length, up into the air, on all sides of us, and it was one incessant exclamation of ' look here, quick," or " look sharp," for it was a sight never to be forgotten. As if amused by some great aquatic joke, and rolling with merriment, these "pinks of propriety" would fly up out of their watery abode, give a bound through the air, and disappear as quickly as they appeared. Like pin-wheels they would roll about, and in schools of great numbers, they would hurry along, as if out for an airing. The queerest thing of all, was to see the vast mass of fish, as they swam along, for we could see them on the surface so distinctly and plainly, and they were so crowded and so closely packed in together, that their fins stuck up above the water, and made the waves quite black. We had heard of salmon "filling the streams so full, that a man could walk on their backs safely to shore," and while in Alaska, one of our number caught a fish in a stream, *between his hands*, but these fins on the surface and these aeronautic salmon, we saw with our own eyes, and can vouch one for the other, if our veracity is doubted. We finally tied our *Hope* to two of the trap-poles, shut off the gas, and lay quietly and cosily close to the nets, to see the catch. It was one vast throng of fine fish, so many in the nets, that the sides just below the water line, bulged out to their most elastic limits. Once in a while, a fine specimen of the fish kingdom would be bounced up out of the water, on the backs of its fellow companions, like some oarsman, brought home by his college mates on their shoulders, after a victory. Mr. G., our host, to do all in his power for his guests, produced a gaff, and leaning over the side-net, easily brought up a fine salmon on the hook, in gorgeous glory and pride. Seeing the fishermen preparing to haul a net on shore, we landed, and viewed the unusual sight. Slowly but surely, the meshes of that strong net closed upon its victims, and as it came closer and closer to shore, the splashes and dashes of the prisoners, produced as much commotion in the water, as a sudden squall of wind would do. They landed hundreds, nay thousands, and Dr. Y. bought eleven fine salmon, weighing each between eight and twelve pounds, for two bits, or twenty-five cents. A man, a few days ago, sold five hundred salmon for five dollars ; for several days the run had been so great, that they had to shut their trap-doors, and after filling their boats full, and giving to any who were near, they liberated nearly five thousand—"pretty big fish story" to be sure !

On our way to shore, we steamed up to see a little collection of houses, I had become interested in from my window. It seems, a certain wandering class of laborers live in floating houses, which are carried to their different objective points, on the rising tide. Nestled close by the big sawmill, opposite this Hotel, which is situated on a point of ground in a shallow channel or water-way, are several dozens of these huts, or aquatic cottages, where women and children live their lives, having bridges to bring them to the main-land, but staying always in this way on the water, avoiding land rents and having no water tax, even for their floating homes. It is a queer little gathering of houses, and some are quite pretentious, having curtains at their windows and front doors. One little square box, which stands high and dry at low tide, but is surely at sea at high water, has quite a fine stained-glass front door, and several have platforms or floats near their front entrance, with fences about them, for the tiny tots (who abound in such quarters), to have as a play-ground. Wooden soap and starch-boxes full of flowers, serve as ornaments in various places in these homes, and they seem as comfortable and happy, in their watery paradise, and as thrifty as in more secure abodes. Surely, these floating laborers know how to evade the demands of the law. For some reason a conundrum, we heard on the *Mexico*, which pleased James greatly, recurs to me now, and that is, "Who was the best financier mentioned in history? Noah, because he floated a Loan (lone) Company while all the world was in liquidation."

THURSDAY, AUGUST 27TH.

LOVELY morning, but to arise at six o'clock again, savored too much of the Yosemite and Mt. Hood trips, and yet was a joy after we were once on our feet. Breakfast at seven o'clock, and at half-past seven, Auntie, James and I started for the eight o'clock boat, the *City of Kingston*, for Seattle. We had several minutes to spare before the boat started, and had an opportunity to study a group of

Siwash laborers, who had come to town for the hop-picking. It was a goodly gathering, and more Indians collected in one group than in any we had seen even in Alaska. Just at this time of the year, the country is full of these peculiar people, and they come floating up the Sound, with their families, their goods and chattels, in their big picturesque canoes, and remind one of Robinson Crusoe or some similar exile, just coming from a long life on some far-away desert island. They come sometimes from Alaska, sometimes from British Columbia, and make long journeys to these hop-fields, stopping when night comes, on the shore, wherever they happen to be, and little bright fires may be seen all along the shore every evening, denoting the abiding-place for that night, of those wandering pilgrims. They move along the shores like born mariners, and seem perfectly at home in their little canoes. I say little canoes, but they are big, and the bow and stern are so wonderfully well cut out, in such graceful curves, that they reflect a perfect bow in the water beneath them, a semi-circle like the new moon, and they are laden with bright blanketed women, little children with bright handkerchiefs about their heads, and the omnipresent Siwash dog, with its greenish eyes and wiry hair. The heads of these families usually sit in the stern, and paddle in such a scientific manner, carrying their paddle freely above the waves, between each stroke, and yet so closely to the water, that it never seems to leave it for a moment. They use this mode of locomotion from their cradle, and are as skillful as well trained oarsmen could be. We saw many of these big family canoes to-day, and they never failed to call forth our admiration, for they were certainly wonderfully picturesque and unusual. As they glide along over the waves, the Indian women often knit, and their dark heads and hands, bending low over some child's blue or red stocking, added much to the effect. Indians, as a rule, in the old times never wore stockings, but now, the result of education is seen in the comfortably clad children, some looking quite like white children in their modern attire. This morning the squaws and children, with their clean dresses, shoes and stockings, their combed and braided hair, and neat appearance, contrasted marvelously with the old women and their filthy dirty feet, their snarled and tangled hair, their grimy faces and loathsome expressions; and although they all crouched on the ground, and were all eating their breakfasts of berries, and had very black looking mouths, anyone interested in such a study, could very easily pick out the educated Indian, at a glance. We saw fat Indians and lean Indians, clean Indians and dirty ones, little Indians and big Indians, and we were sorry to leave our study in Siwash oils, when the bell rang and communicated to the engineer of the *City of Kingston*, the Captain's desire to be off for Seattle.

Our sail to Seattle was one of little interest, for the heat of the coming hours was preceded by an ominous mist and haze, and we could see little beyond the bow of the boat. Dr. Y., who had joined us for the trip, sat outside with James, while Auntie and I snoozed in the cabin. Ten o'clock found us at the wonderful little city of Seattle, and as we walked from the boat the two short blocks to the business streets, we were all impressed by the magnificent buildings, really imposing and fine, and by the remarkably big appearance of the little City.

Three years ago, in 1888, a terrible fire wiped out all of Seattle's business quarter, and accomplished its work of destruction so thoroughly, that crackers and bacon were the only provisions it was possible to obtain, for a few days, until relief trains brought better things to the ruined city. Twelve millions of dollars worth of property was destroyed. Now the buildings are rebuilt and are as handsome as many in New York or Boston. This gives Seattle a very new and impressive appearance, especially its business quarter. The residences in Seattle are homelike and attractive, but are as much behind the homes in Tacoma, as its business portion is far superior. The jealousy between this thirty (or forty) years old city of Seattle, and the little young eight years old Tacoma, is as ridiculous and undignified as it would be, between a woman and a child, of the same respective ages.

Our first aim was to find and see Mr. B. We

heard he was in the Merchants' National Bank, and soon found our way to a magnificent building. Asking for Mr. B. we were told to step into his private office, as he would be in directly. A fine glass door, with a silken curtain, and the words "Vice-President" on it in gold, was opened for us, and we found ourselves in a handsomely furnished room, a large desk, chairs, sofa, etc., and learned that the young friend, whom we were waiting to see, who only three years ago came to Seattle, from the East, was now Vice-President of a flourishing bank, a Park Commissioner, a public-spirited, high-principled young man, whom all respected and honored in this home of his adoption. We had not long to wait, for our friend soon came in, and was most cordial in his welcome. Arranging some matters which demanded his immediate attention, he insisted upon taking us about the City, and took us first to the beautiful Washington Lake. The system of cable and electric roads is in perfection in Seattle. It is a city on a multitude of hills; each street at its corners, seems to wave and curve north and south, as well as east and west; and up and over all these hills, as if they were nothing of any account, these roads run, flying like witches in every direction. One cable road took us one mile and a half to the Lake, and there we took a little steamer and went a mile and a half up the lake, to the "Canoe Club-Boat-House, a lovely sail to a charming spot. Mr. B. belongs to this organization, and bringing out his pretty pet "Argonaut," he was photographed in it, by our "special photographer." After some time spent in looking about, in viewing the picturesque shores of this fresh-water resort, we took another cable car and went three miles and a half back to the city, stopping before we reached the Bank, at the "Ranier Hotel," for dinner. After that mid-day meal, and a quiet rest for a little while on the piazza, we wandered to the Bank again, and leaving James and the Doctor there, Auntie and I walked about, in and out of the shops, to find photos and spoons.

At last we decided to continue our sight-seeing, and as cars were the best means of moving about, we took another line, and went several miles in a different direction, to the top of Queen Anne Hill, where the view of Puget Sound was really beautiful, and the city presented a remarkably pleasing sight. It was singularly fascinating, the manner in which we glided over hill and dale, climbing precipitous ascents at a glorious gait, and having genuine to-boggan slides at some corners, with regular "Thank-you-marms" liberally intermixed. James seemed particularly amused at this car-sight-seeing of ours, and we were so pleased by our several rides, that, having an extra hour at our disposal, we hunted for an unexplored portion of the town, and taking one electric car to its limit, and transferring to still another, we went in the only remaining unseen point of the compass, and returned in time for our boat, at half-past five. We carried back to Tacoma, besides beautiful roses sent by our friend, wonderfully pleasant impressions of the industrious spirit and energy of Seattle, with its pleasant homes and its active business quarter. Surely this western country is the place for energetic business enterprises, but the newness of the place and surroundings, is almost as depressing, as it is remarkable in its growth and sure and steady development. A lovely sail back to Tacoma, with delightful music in the evening to rest our tired brains, and an early to bed, brought to an end a pleasant and enjoyable day.

FRIDAY, AUGUST 28TH.

HOT, very, very hot, but after breakfast Jamie and I mustered up courage, and went up to Dr. Y.'s to take a photograph of the house and family, and the Doctor's office, as I had promised. Before returning, we made a short morning call on Mrs. W. and Miss C., then came down town to do a few errands, and had a quiet afternoon.

About half-past six, Mr. and Mrs. A. arrived, and dined with us and we had a very pleasant evening after, with them and the Y.s who came down to hear the music and to dance. Tuesday and Friday are dancing nights, and owing to some queer freak, Friday has become "the night" of the week. This evening, the parlor was quite full of gaily dressed young women, and young men in evening dress, and our friends seemed to enjoy it so much, that they did not leave until the music stopped, at twelve o'clock.

A WARM but bright day, and a quiet rest on the piazza in big chairs, listening to the dreamy delicious music of the artistic Spanish Students. While I was dressing for dinner, a card came up from James, saying Mr. B. from Seattle had arrived; he had come to spend Sunday with us. We had a very pleasant evening, and about half-past ten o'clock, James went to the Club with him, but returned in about a half hour, as it was a deserted place,—no one there.

BEAUTIFUL, but warm. After a late breakfast, we amused ourselves looking over our photographs, and watching the big bear and pet of the Tacoma Hotel, which was brought here when a cub. After luncheon, by invitation from Mr. G., we three (Mr. B., James and I) went out in the naphtha launch again, and had the loveliest afternoon imaginable, on Puget Sound. We stopped for a few minutes at the Launch Club, but the most of our four hours on the water, were spent in steaming in and out of lovely little bays and coves, and it was simply ideal to lie there in that little boat, and dream and think. Our evening was a quiet one, sitting and chatting on the piazza.

W E spent a pleasant morning on the piazza, listening to the Spanish Students for the last time, also received calls from both Dr. Y., Mrs. and Miss Y. and their friends. One of the Spanish Students is quite a clever sculptor, and I had taken an interest in his work, having bought a little as a curiosity, and also induced Mrs. M. to do the same. The polite fellow came to me this morning, with the loveliest little trifle imaginable, and in his broken English, and with a terribly low bow, asked me to accept the gift, "with his compliments." Jamie was quite touched by his gratitude.

After a little more packing, and luncheon, Auntie, James and I started for the 2.40 P. M. train for Helena. We had a very pleasant trip the remainder of the day, and found Washington an interesting State, quite wild and unsettled, but made beautiful by its forests and trees. The chief crop seemed to be hops, for we saw acres and acres devoted to nothing else, and as this is the picking season, the great, heavy, bushy poles were laden with the light yellow-green harvest, and all through the country the bright dresses of the Indian women might be seen, in between the rows of hop-poles, picking the heavy crop into wooden cribs or cradles. It was an interesting scene, especially viewed for the first time. The lumber camps give one such picturesque glimpses, of what must be a most monotonous mode of living. It brought back to me what I had so often heard of olden times, of early settlements in a new country, and I felt as if I could see, with mine own eyes, what the pioneer used to do, and put up with, in the "good old days." It was probably more interesting to see, than to experience.

The scenery was enjoyable, but our greatest entertainment came, when we began to climb the mountains, to cross the Cascade Range. The trestles were numerous and very, very high, and finally, as we stopped suddenly in a snow-shed, and in a cloud of smoke from the engine, I asked the brakeman what was the trouble. "A trestle on fire, I believe," he answered, "we were told in the valley about it." Sure enough, it was so, but an expert had come to examine, and pronounced it safe, and over we went, but the old bridge grunted and groaned, and creaked and cracked, as if quite out of temper that we were so short a time detained, and seemed to feel so safe. At the top of the mountain, we passed through a most marvelous tunnel, called "Stampede Tunnel," two miles in length, and lighted with electricity. We all sat on the rear platform and enjoyed the sight, for the perspective lent beauty to the scene. It was like the Hoosac Tunnel, only not so long. The greatest interest of the entire evening was, however, the burning forest through which we passed. Like some great fiery furnace, the heat penetrating, sometimes even through the closed windows of the car, the forest would gleam and glare and glow in its frenzy of flames, great curling columns of fire and smoke rising upwards, as if to dim the glory of the stars. Sparks flew right and left; stumps dried and parched for want of rain, were transformed into burning blazing caldrons and caves of fire, great glaring flames sticking out at little openings and charred places, like eyes and tongues of torture. Our way was through these burning forests for an hour or more, and was so weird and wonderful in the blackness of the night, making one feel the marvelous power of the spirit of fire, and as if we were running through a corner of the Infernal Regions, just to behold, without feeling, the blistering fiend. Way up on the mountain top, in one place, the fires were kindled to the highest pitch, and one could easily imagine the destruction of Sodom and Gomorrah. Great tongues of bright red flames licked the heavens in their fury, jumping and leaping from tree to tree, as if playing tag on the tree-tops, and as one after another, of noble bearing and ancient lineage, tumbled and fell, great columns of smoke and sparks announced the downfall of these monarchs of the mountains.

WEDNESDAY, SEPTEMBER 2ND.

WE had a pleasant journey to-day, as we passed through a part of Idaho, and that is a most attractive and fertile state. Our road lay beside the Snake River, which, true to its name, winds its serpent-like and tortuous course toward the Columbia

River, through great basaltic walls. It was most picturesque and remarkable.

Soon after breakfast, we reached Hope, Idaho, which is situated on the exquisite Lake Pond Oreille, and here, to our joy, although we reached Hope about ten o'clock, we left at eleven o'clock, for it was the first change in time, on our march toward the East. At Hope, the houses are meagre and poor, and business does not seem to be particularly flourishing, for on a tiny one-room shanty were two signs, a little bright *barber's* pole, and near it on the door was also " F. W. May, *Dentist.*"

We passed through the Flat-Head Indian Reservation, and saw the buildings of the Agency, which is under Catholic control. They say it is a well-managed and interesting reservation, that the Flat-head Indians in winter live in log cabins, and have learned to raise grain and potatoes, and cattle and horses are their stock also. These Indians boast that their tribe has never killed a white man. As our train went through these lands, we could see parties of Indians, cantering across the open country, in groups of three or five, their brilliant blankets producing quite a contrast with the green of the foliage and the bronze of the grasses.

We were quite tired before we reached Helena, at 10.40 P. M., then we had four miles in a steam-motor to Hotel Broadwater. A good feast with our letters, and then we tumbled into bed and were lost in pleasant dreams.

JAMIE and I awoke this morning as the clock pointed to ten, and quickly ordered a light breakfast served in our room, knowing the iron-clad rules of these Western hotels. A gentleman in the room next to us exclaimed, just after we awoke, in most irate tones, "The idea of that darkey telling me I was late for breakfast," and to avoid that annoyance, we had coffee, etc., in our room. After that, Auntie, James and I strolled out to see the surroundings of the Hotel Broadwater.

Nobody can imagine such weary wastes, such rolling hills and mounds, utterly devoid of vegetation, or any vestige of green in fact. The Hotel Broadwater with its trees, shrubs and flowers, is a perfect revelation to these mountain people, to think that anything, with any pretentions to beauty, can be made out of such a barren wilderness. The immediate surroundings of the Hotel are, however, pretty and pleasing, and quietly restful. The greatest attraction is the fine Natatorium, really an imposing building, quite Moorish in design and finish. It is a huge building, three hundred and fifty feet long, one hundred and fifty broad, and is all one big water-tank, with numerous rooms surrounding it for bathers. It is a superb room, vaulted and well lighted by stained glass windows. On each side are twenty-four large round ones, of brilliant colors, and as many smaller ones over them, making a very pretty effect, with the colored rays of sunshine. At one end of this room is a tremendous water fall, tumbling and bubbling over rocks and stones, and some one said, "It was such a good idea to build a Natatorium over such a fine cascade." The cascade is made, however, and the spring water is carried several miles in pipes, and brought over these rocks into the Natatorium. It is a natural mineral spring, and is so very hot, that it takes 500,000 gallons a day of cool water, to make it possible to bathe in it. This Broadwater Hotel and Natatorium is a fashionable and popular health and pleasure resort, in embryo, but just now it is young and new, and needs time to bring out its salient points.

About two o'clock, we took the electric car and went into Helena, to see the richest city, for its size and number of inhabitants, in our United States. We met a friend of Auntie's, a very pleasant young fellow, who gave us much information, and showed us some pretty nuggets of gold, just as they had been found in a Montana Gold Mine. Later we went to a place right in the city, on a very prominent corner, where workmen were digging foundations for a new Club house. Down in the dirt, with little tin pans, were boys, and some men, bringing up pans full of the brown soil, which we watched them wash and sift, to find the gold deposits. It was a funny sight, to see a dozen men and boys all shaking pans of dirt in a little water-trough, crouching down in the mud, seeking gold which they found in little yellow shining lumps, and they immediately assumed such airs, with their riches and success as gold-diggers. We tried to buy a few flakes from one youth, but he said he preferred to retain them. It was a novel experience, to see gold brought out of the soil in the very heart of the city.

Helena was an unusually unattractive place to us, but there are some fine buildings, attractive houses and homes, and the society is delightful. Auntie had met Mr. and Mrs. Broadwater on the *Queen* (for Alaska) also Judge C., wife and daughter, and they made it very pleasant for us. One young lady said to me, "We all like Helena, I suppose, because we go away from it so much!"

James suggested our walking to the end of the Main Street, which being an undertaking requiring neither time nor exertion, we accomplished. We were surrounded on every side by men of all ranks and grades, and soon saw the reason, for two buildings bore the inscription "The Headquarters of Licensed Gambling House" in big bold letters. Cow-boys, in their leggins of buck-skin, their sombreros and rough jackets, were liberally sprinkled through the fortune-seekers, and faces full of hope, others of despair, were easily distinguished in the crowd.

We were on our way back in our electric car, when a genuine prairie sand-storm struck and enveloped us, and such a sudden and determined storm as it was. Not a crack or crevice that it did not seek out and go through. By the time, however, that we reached the Hotel, the storm had somewhat abated, and a rainbow stood out, arching royally across the city, which it seemed to hold in its embrace.

In the evening we visited the Natatorium, to witness a base-ball game, played in the pool, and as some seventy or eighty bathers were in the water, it gave us much merriment to watch their antics. A trapeze tempted athletes, a canoe easily capsized captivated others, while a most interesting toboggan slide made fun and frolic, as it hurriedly deposited its adventurous visitors, in wild hot haste, far out in the tank. We watched it for some time, then returning to our hotel, we listened to some music, danced, and soon retired.

FRIDAY, SEPTEMBER 4TH.

A DAY of little moment, until we left Hotel Broadwater, at three o'clock, and drove into Helena, to take the 4.40 P. M. train for Livingston. No sleeping cars were on our train, so we seated ourselves in an ordinary coach, to ride until after seven o'clock, when we were to reach Logan and take the Butte train there. It was a most desolate country through which we traveled, until we reached the Missouri River, and there a band of fertile ground stretched out as far as the eye could reach. We were startled at one place, by four quick, sharp reports of some fire arm, and when James returned from the smoking car, he told us that the " News Agent " had taken aim out of the car window, as we were moving along, and with four pistol shots he had killed four wild ducks.   Soon this remarkably plain uninteresting man came into our car, selling peaches. We spoke to him, saying we had heard he was a good shot, and he said "Oh, shooting four ducks aint anything.   Last week I fired twelve shots out of two six-shooters, and knocked down eleven ducks out of the twelve shots." I naturally asked "When did you learn to shoot?" He answered, "I was brought up in Montana, where a feller had to learn to shoot to live."   As he spoke, he pulled out a little "bull-dog pistol" (he called it), and handling it lovingly, he showed it to me, and to my remark that some men I supposed always carried such things with them, he answered, "I aint in good health, when I haven't a thing like that about me." He then told us a little of what those "old days" used to be in Montana, where a man's life was nothing and where no warning was ever given, but a life demanded and taken in one moment. He had crossed the plains in an emigrant train, composed of fifteen canvas-covered wagons, and consisting of over one hundred and fifty souls, men, women and children together. These trains often took six months to cross the plains.   The Indians attacked them when nearing Helena, and only seventy of that little company ever reached their new home.   He told us much of Gen. Miles and Gen. Custer, and waxed eloquent when speaking of the latter.   He said

"Gen. Custer warn't no white-livered chap, and there wasn't a man in the West who'd speak agin him. His only trouble was he was too *bravey!*" A couple of nights ago, at the end of the run, he was held up by a robber, but he said "I just held up my little bull-dog, and persuaded him that he'd better take a little walk he-self." After changing trains at Logan, this Montana shooter came through the car again selling something, and James said to him, laughingly "killed anybody since I saw you?" "No, but I wish you was going through to the end of my run, and I'd show you the latest *modes* for doin' it," he answered.

We reached Logan at 7.35 P. M., and our train being late, we seated ourselves on our luggage to wait comfortably. A dozen houses and an engine switch house, and about a hundred people compose the village of Logan. Our "News Agent" still entertained us with blood-curdling accounts, and soon our little group was joined by a tiny specimen of humanity, in the shape of a little boy, in trousers evidently made out of his father's old ones, for they were alarmingly ample and "bagged" about his *ankles*. A coat four sizes too big, a funny round skull-cap, a basket on his arm, and a more remarkably ludicrous specimen could not be found. He was tiny and such a character. We asked his age, "just ten,"—what he did every day, "herd cattle on horseback." Auntie, in a most impressively earnest way said, "Little boy don't you go to school?"

" No marm ! " answered the young hopeful. " But, added Auntie, " don't you want to learn something," and as if to inspire ambition in the little breast, she said " what will you do when you grow up, if you don't learn something?" Drawing his little shoulders up into their ample covering, eyeing Auntie all the time, he drawled out, with the tone and emphasis of a genuine and hardened ruffian, *"I don't know and I don't care!"* Just then some one asked him to go and bring us some wonderful petrified wood, found in that vicinity, and he showed decided disinclination to any such exertion, and pleaded " no time," but when the Agent insisted upon it, his energy came out in such a vigorous " *Gee-whiz* " and away he ran, and brought us two fine specimens, which we forthwith purchased. It was duly admired, and somebody suggested a doubt as to its genuineness, when the little fellow shouted, " Bet your boots, it is ! "

Our train came at 8 P. M., and at eleven o'clock we reached the " Albemarle," at Livingston, a big-sounding name for a little moderate hotel. We soon slept, however, and knew nothing until the next morning.

THE YELLOWSTONE.

A BRIGHT lovely morning, and glorious for our trip to the Yellowstone Park. After a seven o'clock breakfast, we started out to spend the few minutes before our train left, at a quarter past eight, in seeing some sights in Livingston, of which we had heard. At a taxidermist's, we saw one of the very few mountain goats in existence, and were right glad to get the chance.

Our trip from Livingston to Cinnabar was through lovely country, but the special feature of interest was Auntie's and my ride on the engine. Jamie made love to the engineer, and Auntie went on the engine when we left Cinnabar, and rode some twelve miles or more. I went on it then, and rode for three-quarters of an hour, with Jamie near, as he feared I would be nervous. What an unusual sensation it was! We bounded off into space at a tremendous pace, tossing and tumbling along, as if on the wings of the wind. It was awfully exciting and exhilarating, and put me all in a glow, but I never before realized how thoroughly we travelers were in the hands, and at the mercy, of the engineer. It was terrible to contemplate, and to see the careless manner in which he turned his back to the road ahead, every once in a while, and joked and laughed with us all. I think I ran that train for those few miles, for I never took my eyes off the track ahead, and never felt more responsibility than I did then. As we neared a trestle, the engineer slowed up a little, and as he did so he said,—"I go slow over those things, so that if we go through, we'll go easy." And just then, as he finished telling me of having run over six horses the other day, as we tore madly around a great curve, cut out of a tremendous rockcliff, he said,—"I slow up here a bit too, for rocks are not half so nice to run into as horses." He told me that engineers often slept at their posts at night, for, as he said,—"We are all human, and can't help it sometimes." It was quite an experience, and I never before flew out into space in such a hurry, for it gives one a queer sensation, to feel the engine throb as it puffs and groans, and to be pushed out into the world, in company with such a tremendous power. Nothing happened to harm us, but when the engineer lifted me from my seat in the cab to the ground, when stopping to take water, my little side-bag, or "valise" as Mr. H. called it, slipped from my belt, and I discovered my loss too late to search for it then and there. It completely upset me for the rest of the day, as it contained some few things of value, which I had never carried in it until that day. I hardly noticed the drive from Livingston to the Mammoth Hot Springs Hotel, although I knew it was through most beautiful cañons, and I have read that they were finely marked by, and gave strong evidence of, the Ice Age of our Continent. After luncheon I took a rest to quiet my ruffled spirits, and about half past four o'clock James, Auntie and I went out to examine the wonderful formations near this hotel, at which I had been peeping at intervals from my window. This was our——

FIRST GLIMPSE OF WONDERLAND.

STANDING below, and looking up at this small mountain of glorious formation, with its terrace upon terrace,—its steam-covered springs, all lifting their vapors in adoration to the skies,—the brilliant colors contrasting gloriously with the great masses of pure white,—one could hardly help feeling that a new world was opening for us,—a new order of things, demanding our watchful attention, and commanding our praise. We stood still to see it in its entirety, before examining it in detail, and this great and marvelous formation was glorious and grand indeed, to our eyes. At the foot of this set of terraces, stands a great colossal pyramid, rising fifty or sixty feet from a level surrounding, and as it points upward, with its layer upon layer of formation, once the seat of a powerful geyser, which has departed but left this monument to survive it, it presents a most imposing picture, and has been most appropriately named "Liberty Cap." Little by little, slowly, for lack of breath (for these Mammoth Hot Springs stand at an altitude of 6,200 feet), we climbed these marvelous terraces, and as we threaded our way between the bubbling and boiling springs, and the little rivulets which chase one another down the hill-side, we were lost in wonder and admiration, and stirred to our depths by these wonderful and marvelous sights. There are one hundred and seventy acres in this hill and plateau, over fifty terraces, and as many active springs, and it is divided into three parts, Minerva's Terrace, Jupiter's Terrace, and the Pulpit. The hot springs have formed all these, evaporating in steam and leaving the most exquisite and delicate deposits, as truly inimitable as the sunshine. These layers, or deposits, form the most peculiar fluted edges, curling and scalloping and waving like beautiful frills, and forming terrace after terrace, transforming all into magnificent pictures by the luminous colors. These springs, with their frost-like rims, their flake-like frills of coral and fret-work, set one against the other, in innumerable shapes and sizes, in terraces and layers, made us feel that we had never before beheld such grandeur in colors. Nothing we had ever seen could be compared to this beauty, all wonderful as it was, and after standing for some time, gazing and searching in my mind for something, which might be used as an example of its shapes and character of formation, a homely simile suggested itself, of colossal tarts and pies, with crimped crusts, and indented edges, only all in white, and rose-color, and deep red. In these pools or springs, which were too hot to do more than dip in our finger and withdraw it quickly, were the most delicate frost-work, and honey-comb deposits, like feathers in the many colored pools, for one pool would be a heavenly blue, the one next it, perhaps, an emerald green, then a yellowish green, until one was bewildered by the combinations and prismatic tints. Some spaces between these springs were hard, but streaked, as if some one had swept them when wet and the broom-marks were distinctly visible. Some great formations, like frosted or frozen cascades and waves, were like whipped cream in their velvety softness, and the white and glistening stalactites stood out against the clear sky, like great organ-pipes, and it seemed to me that some angel from the heavens could strike those glorious gems, and bring forth the harmony of the past, when all nature was in tune with this great glory. Perhaps the " Lost Chord " or that " Great and Last Amen " is locked up in these frozen fortresses, to swell forth on the Judgment Day. As we wandered over these terraces, we walked upon the white deposit, which crunched and creaked beneath our feet like snow in winter, or an ash-path in some marshy place. It seemed to sing a little low soft song, at least to me, as I wandered thoughtfully along, and when I exclaimed aloud, thinking audibly to my surprise," I feel as if I were walking on the ashes of the past,"a dear old gentleman who had joined us, exclaimed"I fancy that is just what you are doing."

One impressive thing to us were the waves of color, in triangles and rectangles, which were so beautifully blended and so artistically shaded, from crimson and maroon to pink and rose-color, from brown to the most delicate yellow, with grey, and white, and black, so interwoven that it was a magnificent spectacle. Over all these colors a stream of hot-water constantly coursed, which in the sunshine was like a silver sheen or veil, blending each color and shade in exquisite harmony. On the same terrace on which this marvelous coloring was visible, was a similar formation of purest white, which made a dazzling and wonderful contrast.

SUNDAY, SEPTEMBER 6TH.

WHEN James interviewed the manager of the stage line yesterday afternoon, and found we were not certain of a stage for our start into the Yellowstone, on Monday morning, we were quite perplexed and did not know what to do. Our plan to rest quietly over the Sabbath, seemed to meet obstacles on every side, for the only stage for such a small party—and the only driver, could be obtained for a Sunday morning start, and no other! After a serious consultation, and a struggle with our consciences, we found we were really obliged to do so, and at eight, or to be perfectly exact, at 8.15 A. M., James, Auntie and I started from the Mammoth

"OUR COACH AND FOUR."

Hot Springs Hotel, in "our own hired coach and four," for the tour of the famous Yellowstone Park.

Our glimpse yesterday afternoon, into Wonderland, was enough to make us truly enthusiastic and full of anticipation, and we started on our long drive, as bright as the proverbial buttons. Our way, for the first twenty-two miles, as far as Norris Basin, was beautifully wooded, through most interesting country, over hills and through valleys, which commanded extensive and exquisite views. Mountain peaks crowned with snow, escorted us in their rocky grandeur, to the "Golden Gate" of Yellowstone Park, and there left us to ponder and wonder at the great basaltic formations, the lava of ancient eruptions, which has hardened in centuries into marvelous pinnacles and pillars, and which derives its name from the golden moss or lichen, which clings so lovingly to its many shaped and multitude of formations, making a glorious gold mantle over all. Bunsen's Peak, Electric Peak, the highest in the Park (11,000 feet), Belle and Quadruple then came into view, with beautiful waterfalls to enhance the beauty of the scene, and make the contrast of light and shade perfect. Beaver Lake interested us much, because it was full of dams made by the beavers, who stopped the waters of the creek, and made this lovely little lake by their work. A beaver house was plainly visible, and is said to be inhabited now.

Our greatest interest, however, was aroused when

we reached the Obsidian Cliffs, which skirt the shore of Beaver Lake for some distance. From one hundred and fifty, to two hundred and fifty feet, these great jet black cliffs rise into the air, in almost vertical columns, like basalt in pentagonal pinnacles, and like basalt when broken, they divide into pieces having one concave and one convex surface. Obsidian is a species of lava; it is volcanic glass, and very rare. Although found in other places in small quantities, there is not a cliff like this in the Rocky Mountains, or anywhere, except in Mexico. This Obsidian Cliff is considered unequalled in the world, and it is really a grand sight. It is exactly like jet, and glistens in the sunshine like genuine glass. It is opaque. It was necessary to construct a carriage-road at its base, and this was quite a difficult operation. Large fires were built upon the largest masses, and when the obsidian was sufficiently expanded by the heat, cold water was dashed upon it, which fractured the blocks so that they could be handled. It is said that "this is the only piece of glass carriage road in the world." It is a quarter of a mile in length. It is very interesting to see the different varieties of this marvelous glass. Pure black is the rarest and best, but some of it is flaked with yellow and red, some with white, pink and blue. The Indians used to visit these cliffs for obsidian, for their arrow-heads and weapons, and it was such a sacred spot to them, that hereditary enemies used to meet here as friends, and it was neutral ground.

We had not gone far from the Obsidian Cliffs, when our driver asked us if we wanted to drink some genuine Apollinaris water, and being quite ready for drinks, we walked a short distance into the woods, and found a fine spring of mineral water, quite rivaling its namesake. As we stood near the spring, a dear little squirrel pranced about us, as tame as a kitten, and it almost came into our hands. We saw some lovely lakes, and arsenic springs, containing genuine poison, and labeled on a big board "dangerous!" Suddenly a great white side of a mountain attracted our attention, and it was puffing and steaming away up on the top, and being our first glimpse of a geyser district, or the numerous steam vents of that locality, we were much impressed. It is called "Roaring Mountain." Soon, by our roadway, singing and sizzling and sputtering away, was the Devil's Frying Pan, a hot spring rising to the surface in the shape of a frying pan. The steam and boiling process made the water dance like genuine devils and sprites, and they sang their 240° song in a very staccato treble. We were much amused by this little devilish appearance, but our driver laughed at our enthusiasm, saying we would hardly notice that on our return trip, after we had seen the greater wonders of the Basin.

After dinner at Norris Geyser Basin, a place twenty-two miles from Mammoth Hot Springs, we wandered out to get our first view of genuine and real geysers. We walked about half a mile, before

we saw any real manifestations of steam; then, all at
once coming to the top of a little knoll, we saw the
whole Basin stretched out before us, and such a
revelation, such a marvelous sight as it was. A
great stretch of land lay before us, of such pure
white formation that it was dazzling to our eyes.
Great masses of deep red appeared at intervals, where
the iron ore had been deposited ; sulphur had made
other spots a regular green and yellow, and between
these deposits, in circular, oblong, small, big and
tiny shapes were the hot pools and springs, smoking,
puffing, and pulsating, and all sending such volumes
of steam up to the skies, that the whole place reminded us of a great manufacturing town, the buildings hidden by the steam, but the roar and hum and
puff of machinery, and the power moving it, very
distinct and audible. Every minute, several geysers
near us would throw up into the air a great fountain
and spray of water and steam, play and coquette in
mid-air half a minute, then subside to accumulate
strength and material for another great outburst.
We stood silently watching this new and marvelous
sight, when we were horribly conscious of heat coming up into our faces and under our clothes, and
looking down and about us, we discovered that we
were standing *over*, and were surrounded by, great
cracks in the earth's crust, which were sending forth
great streams of steam (if *steam* can be spoken of as
a *stream*). The holes, and crevices, and cracks, were
ugly and awful, some like caves, reaching deep down

into the bowels of the earth, others great yawning openings, all cracked and split and seamed, and yellow and burned-looking, and all sending forth steam, with such grunts and groans, such sputterings and sighings, that we were quite willing to move along. The sulphurous odors were stifling, and came into our faces in great volumes. We wandered along the road which is made through this Basin, until we approached a mammoth and much noisier spring than we had seen, and being enthusiastic in our discoveries, we walked back from the road a little, in among some queer "paint-pots," which were boiling their muddy pastes in such a sing-song manner, and were wonderful indeed. We were unconscious of danger, until the heat through my cork-sole shoes brought me back to commonplace things, and feeling of the shoe, I found it so hot that I could not hold the sole in my hand. I then leaned down to touch the spot on which I stood, and my hand was nearly blistered. In an instant we were cautiously picking our way back to the road, when Aunt Mary gave a scream, and said she had burned the side of her foot badly. It pained her the rest of the day. A story came to my mind then, of an Irishman, who came into the Park with a friend, and standing and looking into one of these boiling pools one day, he called to his friend, "Bedad, Pat, let's go back, Hell's only half a mile ahead."

One great crack in a little hollow near the road, emits such a powerful steam force, that it comes forth with a growl and a roar, and is appropriately named "The Growler." It seemed like one of Hell's chimneys, and was too suggestive of the Inferno for us to remain long. The trees about it are white and dead, as if their life had been suddenly ended by the poisonous gases, which pour from this vent.

We read in a guide book of a "New Crater," which had made its appearance recently, within the last twelve or fifteen years, and which is watched with great interest by scientists. We found it in the woods near, and were looking into its awful mouth, listening to the thunder and hissing down in the depths, when, with a spurt and a dash, a great heaving and roaring, it began to play, throwing boiling water over the place we had been occupying, while we were skipping to points of safety, to watch it from afar. It was too awful to stay long near its tremendous power, and we walked along to places, where the steam showed us there were other springs. We came to one fine Mud Geyser, as it is called, its great pool being about twelve feet in diameter, and its walls about five feet high. Seeing the muddy clay-colored water quite agitated, we waited a short time and were rewarded, by seeing it play finely. The water rose in the basin until it filled the entire opening, and then threw up a drab-colored spray, and continued this operation, splashing and dashing high into the air, for four or five minutes. It leaves an inky deposit, which forms into beautiful shapes. This Mud Geyser plays regularly every twenty minutes, and we waited to see it a second time. We saw "Hurricane Spring" and the great "Monarch"; the latter is so erratic in its playful moods, that no dependence can be placed upon it, and it was not wise for us to wait, in hopes of seeing its grand display. Consequently, after two hours of familiarity with the geysers and springs of Norris Basin, we took our stage which had followed us along, and drove twenty miles farther on, to "Lower Geyser Basin." We went through Gibbon's Cañon, a most exquisite and beautiful bit of scenery, so picturesque and delightful. As we were driving along, we came suddenly to one of the loveliest springs we had seen, right close to the road, alone in all its beauty, and coming near to its circular edge, we could look deep down into its exquisite depths, for rightly called was "Beryl Spring."

We made two fords, one across Reservation Creek, another the Fire-Hole River, and at last, about 5.45 P. M. we reached the new "Fountain Hotel," at the Lower Geyser Basin. Dumping our luggage hurriedly in our rooms, although it threatened rain, we went out to see the formations here and to be in time if any of the big geysers should play. The formation here was as purely white, and as tremendous and colossal, as our wildest imaginings could have pictured, and the terraces were finely marked and colored. The great Fountain Geyser, whose crater is thirty feet in diameter, with its depth of exquisite blue water, its sides of the most dainty colored formation, and its brilliant deposits, making a crinkled edge four or five inches deep, was actively boiling and bubbling, but "a keeper of the peace," in the shape of a gallant young officer of the guard, which is placed throughout the Park, informed us that the Fountain would not play for an hour at least. He escorted us to see the Mammoth Paint Pots, and oh how fascinatingly beautiful they were! A great pool or lake of white pasty clay, forty feet by sixty (with walls of its own formation, five or six feet high, on three sides), sputtering, gurgling, rising in globular masses, making cones and rings, and throwing up jets of mud, presented a spectacle utterly new to us, and as beautiful as it was bewitching. It captivated me, and I could not take my attention from this beautiful, thick, cream-white siliceous clay, which was in perpetual and incessant agitation. Its surface was ever changing, and as the mud puffs flew up into the air, and from the nature of its composition, settled back into itself, like little circles or cones, it reminded me of a game of checkers, and it seemed as if the playful plastic material was having a colossal game with itself, and as one checker of white mud settled itself on the surface, as if to rest from its labors, the mud next it would jump up and hop over the first, as if hurrying to the end to be crowned and have double power. All over this huge caldron, this operation was repeated, over and

over, and the "plop, plop" of this pasty stuff became quite musical to our ears. Three sides were
surrounded, as I said, with walls of deposit, but the
fourth side was composed of some thirty or forty
cones or mud-puffs, three or four feet high, which
presented a cracked or seamed appearance. These
little cone-shaped hills are of the softest and loveliest shades of pink, and like velvet to the touch.
They almost all have pulsations, but one attracted
us beyond anything we had seen. It was more a
caldron than a cone, of thicker consistency than
the white, and of a delicate pink color. It heaved,
sighed and actually sneezed, then lazily opened an
exquisite lily-like flower, and up shot, four or five
feet into the air, a little stream of pink, which as
quickly settled back, and the lily became a tulip;
then doubling back its petals and leaves, an exquisite full rose was before us, and with infinite
variety this process continued, until we were driven
away by a wretched shower, which threatened to
cover us too copiously with its "little drops of
water." We left the marvelous phenomenon with
its sighs and groans, its upheavings and artistic
forms of ever changing variety, and hurried through
the mud to our "home for the night," but not until
we had seen the remarkable red feathery formations
in some springs, which flowed over the white
ground about it, like rivers of blood, which, scientists or chemists say, comes from the ferric acid,
which is in the flow, and these wonderful colors

make chemical combinations, producing the most marvelous mosaic rocks, like marble and onyx. It is merely one of the many things to marvel at.

Surely our first day's wanderings in this "Wonderful Wonderland," made us feel as if we had been fully repaid for all our journey, to see such marvels, and would have contented us if we had never seen more. Our brains and bones were tired and worn, and we were in our beds before nine o'clock was reached, thanking God in our prayers, that our Sunday had been spent among such wonders of His creation, and we could sing in our hearts: "O all ye works and powers of the Lord, bless ye the Lord; praise Him and magnify Him forever."

MONDAY, SEPTEMBER 7TH.

THIS band of formidable formations seems to extend, so I was told, about fifty miles across the country, appearing at times and places wholly unexpectedly, and proving that a tremendous power is constantly at work under the earth's crust, moving back and forth, and finding vents and holes to expend its fury and strength. It is a mysterious and awful power, terrible in its playfulness and violence, even in its quietest moments. This seems to have been the last portion of our continent to cool and become hard, making one feel intuitively that the entire crust of our earth was once in just such a state of ferment and activity, as this is now. Great cracks, and hollows, and caves, are only thinly crusted over, and some are treacherous and dangerous. The earth's crust is honeycombed at some places, and holes with steam coming forth, are met at most unexpected times and are quite hidden, making watchfulness imperative, and carelessness often pays a painful penalty.

It was densely foggy when we awoke, at half past six this morning, and it took a tremendous amount of self-control and courage to prepare for our trip, with such a frowning promise for the day. We felt as if the whole surrounding country had perhaps developed into a huge geyser, during the night, and this dense fog was after all, a cloud of steam from the new crater. But "fortune favors the brave," and when we drove from the Fountain Hotel, at ten minutes before eight o'clock, a ray of sunshine lay across our path, and seemed to follow us as we went. The whole earth's surface seemed to rise up in clouds of vapor, to kiss the sun, and as we drove away from the lower basin, it made the most perfect picture, with the white fleecy veil reaching out from the earth to the blue sky above. We drove a few miles, then stopped by the "Fire-Hole River" (I always feel as if I could smell brimstone and sulphur whenever I name that river), and after leaving our coaches and crossing the aforesaid stream, we had but a tiny walk before we stood on "Hell's Half-Acre." White soil, with such dense volumes and columns of steam, that our fellow-travelers were often enveloped and hidden from our sight, and they were not fifteen feet away,

with a great yawning geyser on our left, and innumerable pools and springs on all sides of us, such
was "Hell's Half-Acre," and after a solemn conclave
we unanimously agreed, that if Hell's *Half* Acre was
as bad as that, we did not ever care to see a whole
acre of that Infernal Region. The "Prismatic Lake"
was in this dire place, but it was so exquisite in its
beauty, that we were spell bound by its waves and
bands of prismatic tints, its brilliancy and radiancy
being something quite remarkable. "Turquoise
Spring" was near us on our right, a crystal-like
spring of exquisite blue waters, so clear that we
could see deep down into its boiling depths, and the
little rivulets which conveyed its overflow into the
river, were lines of white, with deep yellow
borders.

But this awful abyss on our left, with its terrific
hissing, and gurgling, and rumbling, was the crater of
the greatest of all the geysers, the "Excelsior,"—
whose eruptions have shaken the country for miles
around, and whose terrible volume of rising steam
never ceases, night or day, winter or summer, but
can be seen for miles. The "Excelsior" has not
been in active eruption for some time, but the destruction it has worked about and within its own
crater, is wonderful to behold. It is two hundred and
fifty feet wide and four hundred feet long, with
walls twenty and thirty feet high. At the bottom
are numerous springs, boiling and sputtering, great
boulders that have been thrown from their resting

THE GIANT.

places, into masses and dire confusion, and such a dreadful scene,—that I felt as if I had been transported into the realms of some mysterious and awful spirit. There is utter desolation about these fireholes; no tree lives near these boiling caldrons; no bird did we see, not any living insect; in fact, the siliceous deposits make great white masses about the roots of all the trees.

After leaving this marvelous " Half Acre," we drove to the Upper Geyser Basin, where the principal geysers of the Park are found, which are not surpassed by any in the known world. Iceland and New Zealand are the proud possessors of such demonstrations of the powers of the earth's central force, but nowhere are geysers found of such magnitude and magnificence as here. Some years ago, there were said to be four hundred and forty active springs and geysers in this Basin, but we saw so many that we could not count them, and must trust to our memories, to retain facts and data of a few of the many. As we drove along the Fire-Hole River, which receives most of its force from these hot-water eruptions, we were watching anxiously for some sudden symptoms of display, when the coaches in front of us stopped suddenly, and our driver electrified us by saying, " Just in time, there goes the Mortar!" Sure enough, as we drove up, this beautiful geyser was sending up its stream of water and steam, and was a most inviting invitation and initiation into the mysteries of the Upper Geyser

Basin. Then some one shouted, "The Grotto, quick!" and one after another the horses tore along, but an eruption was just over, as we discovered to our sorrow. We left our coach here, and walked the mile between us and the hotel, in order to see all we could. "The Grotto" was exquisite to examine, encrusted with a geyserite deposit like glorious pearls, and some portions were like frost and exquisite white coral. As we stood before this grotto of gems, some one said, "The Splendid is going off," and like a flock of sheep, we all ran toward the geyser, which was said to be ready to play. But we watched and waited for some time, then in a line, we wandered to see the great "Giant," one of the most powerful in the Upper Basin. The numerous clouds of vapor and steam, between us and the hotel, began to attract us in that direction, and as we met a young soldier, who escorted us all over,—everywhere,—we were soon viewing the springs and geysers, in their order and regularity, and under "military escort." To our right and to our left, behind us and before us, were spouting geysers, and that whole portion of the earth seemed to be in active motion,—the entire surface was covered with clouds and veils of vapor.

"Economic," a geyser which plays every five minutes (as regular as a clock), attracted us much, as we watched the small apperture through which the water bubbled up at first, then flew out into space with a roar and a dash, and as quickly crept back into the same hole again, to get ready for the next uprising. "The Grand" and "The Turban," —both geysers,—next charmed us, and as we gazed into their wonderful depths, it seemed as if some fairy had touched the formations with a magic wand, for all was so exquisitely shaped and with such marvelous variety! A most curious effect was witnessed, as we all gazed deep down into "The Turban's" blue waters. From openings in the white geyserite deposits, deep down at one side, shot out great tongues of blue flames, licking the water as if to quench some distressing heat or thirst. Like monsters, these blue flames lapped against the geyser's sides, and as they touched the water, a combustion resulted, the reports, which were incessant, being distinctly audible where we stood, and after each, bubbles of air rose to the surface, keeping a romping ripple playing across the water. Of course, we knew water would extinguish flames, and they could not be what they seemed, but some scientist explained to us, that a certain gas coming out of the earth at that outlet, meeting water, produced combustion, and then the gas rose to the surface like an air-bubble. It was singularly beautiful. A "Crested Pool,"—so named on account of the glorious masses of ornamentation about its rim, which was raised in beautiful cushioned puffs,—"The Castle,"—a magnificent and glorious fortress of deposit and formation, with a great crater-cone, many feet high,—both were examined, and admired.

We were nearing the little hotel, having walked a good long two miles, and although we had seen the trusty "Old Faithful" twice, at a distance, we determined to have a nearer and more intimate acquaintance. This geyser, all of wonderful formation and deposits, is raised above the surrounding ground, —but although "Old Faithful" was roaring and hissing, and showing strong symptoms of an approaching display, we knew it would not be until the proper and regular time, so Auntie and I climbed up to the crater's mouth and gazed down into its steaming and gurgling aperture. This formation was like gems, too, being in terraces with beaded and fretted rims and beautiful colors, and it was exquisite. Just on the moment,—for Old Faithful plays every sixty-five minutes, regularly (it plays five minutes, with sixty minutes interval),—it began its magnificent eruption, sending a column of water, two feet in diameter, up one hundred and fifty feet into the air, the steam going half again as high. It was grand, marvelous, wonderful !

After luncheon, we thought another display by "Old Faithful," although our fourth, would please us, so we waited until it was time, and while we waited, the geysers just in front of us, "The Lioness" and "The Cub," gave fine exhibitions of their strength and power, and were beautiful to behold. James was feeling too tired to walk any more, so Auntie and I, with our military escort (for he had returned for us), started out again, and saw so many springs,

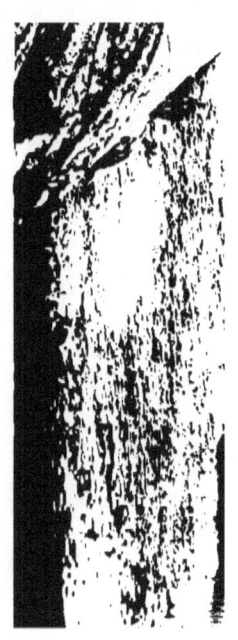

THE CHIMNEY AND OLD FAITHFUL.

and pools, and geysers, that we were almost bewildered. "The Bee-Hive," a glorious geyser, did not play for us, it being very irregular,—but it is most appropriately named, as is also "The Butterfly," merely a boiling spring, and "The Sponge," a formation exactly resembling the article for which it is named. "The Bee-Hive" throws water two hundred and twenty feet into the air. "The Run," "The Vault," "The Infant," "The Chromatic," "Wave," "Tea-Kettle," are all exquisite, with crystal waters and marvelous formations in their basins. "The Beauty" is rarely exquisite, and blue as the heavens above, while the "Oblong," with an opening fifty by thirty-one feet, is a most glorious and magnificent geyser. We were hovering about "The Grotto," looking at its glorious great aperture, when James came in the coach, and as steam was appearing from further down, we drove to see from whence it came, and found one of the finest geysers of the Upper Basin was playing. We were just in time, and the great "Riverside" displayed its gigantic strength and power for full fifteen minutes, by our watches. It sent up two great streams, ninety feet high, and roared, and hissed, and rumbled, and quaked so heavily that the ground under our wheels shook violently, and we could feel it distinctly, sitting in our seats in the coach.

We were quite satisfied after this display, having seen many geysers play, so we drove along to examine some springs and pools. The beautiful and unsurpassed " Morning Glory " received from us a lengthy visit. Its great circle, twenty feet in diameter, is surrounded by the most beautiful white deposit, which crinkles and curves with exquisite irregularity, and is beautifully encrusted. From this crisp edge, shade the morning glory tints; rose-color creeps from the white and yellowish band, then blues from light to dark, until all is concentrated in a royal purple! Water, clear as crystal, covers all these waves of color, and through the water, as we looked, the sun shone brightly, the rays of light bending and blending, crossing and recrossing, making little golden squares over all, which produced a harmonious union, a beautiful whole.

One of our Alaska friends, who had visited the Park, before the trip on the *Mexico*, begged us not to fail to see " Biscuit Basin," which is not in the regular route, and it was with difficulty that we persuaded our driver to take us there. We had to make a dangerous ford, but it repaid us. A glorious " Sapphire Pool " pulsated constantly, and was surrounded by formations, resembling biscuits of all sizes, in rows. The pool was deep blue, and these formations were all olive-green! A spring, called the " Silver Globe," was near one, called the " Black Pearl," both true to their appellations. " Avoca " was in perpetual commotion, and " The Jewel " played every three minutes, and was such a rollicking jolly little affair.

We reached the Fountain Hotel about 4.50 P. M.,

THE CASTLE.

for we were to spend another night there, but no sooner had we deposited our things in our room, than we rushed to see the " Mammoth Paint Pots," which had fascinated us so much yesterday. They seemed more beautiful—the rose ones especially—and we vowed that they really sobbed and sighed, and as the beautiful rose-colored lilies unfolded and developed into one lovely form after another, it seemed as if Dame Nature was moulding and fashioning forms, for a sculptor to fire in her furnaces, when modeled exactly true ; but she seemed in a dissatisfied mood, as if nothing was ever quite as lovely as she wished it. We mortals stood bewildered by the multitude of creations, and marveled at the beauty of each.

TUESDAY, SEPTEMBER 8TH.

A T 8.15 A. M. we left the Fountain Hotel, at the Lower Geyser Basin, and started on our all day drive to the Yellowstone Cañon. We felt that we had had the most unusual and interesting part of our trip, and we quite settled ourselves for a monotonous and hum-drum day. We had no more geysers to see, except a straggling one, now and then, by the road-side, and when somebody said " You will have beautiful scenery," a query arose in our minds, if we had not already seen the loveliest scenery in our country. The Yosemite was grand and magnificent; Alaska was interesting and unusual ; Mt. Hood was decidedly novel and inspiring ;

the Yellowstone geysers had been phenomenal and most weird and fascinating; and *could anything* come now, to surpass any of these? Our day began well, as we had the fun and excitement of making many fords, and in the middle of one small river our driver lost his hat, and had to run down stream, and fish it out with the whip. We drove through most fertile and beautiful valleys, going for miles through the most glorious green and gold grasses, with here and there a patch of bronze or red, to illuminate the entire fields. We then climbed a great mountain, the trees being numerous at first, but we came to many places where a fire or some destructive agent, had laid the trees low, and for miles fallen trees, criss-cross, at angles, in piles and every kind of a heap, surrounded and outlined our path. It was an uninteresting sight, but it seemed to me that the giants of the forest must have been having a gigantic game of Jack-straws, and left their mammoth game in a pretty tight place, where no one could "play without moving."

We passed over "Mary's Mountain," a very precipitous climb, one bit of road being so narrow and rough, that Jamie and I walked up it, and found afterwards that we had climbed, not "the golden stairs," but the "Devil's Ladder." It was on this mountain, about a year ago, that a buffalo appeared in front of a stage-load of people, frightening the horses so terribly, that they ran away and upset the stage. Fortunately only one person was injured.

After driving about sixteen miles, we came to a hollow in between the hills, and there found a little collection of tents, and were informed that it was "Larry's Lunch Station!" It was a most remarkable place, one tent for a dining-room, one for a waiting-room, a kitchen, and all the necessary requirements; and elk-horns, with their great branches, ornamented every available space in front of the entrance to this remarkable abode. On the white canvas were grotesque drawings, two of which we photographed. The owner of this quaint lunch-station, was a roaring Irishman, with a fund of ready wit and humor, really remarkable and truly amusing. He acted the part of host to perfection, in his shirt-sleeves and little round skull cap, and although "his guests" sat down at his bountiful board as strangers, they arose as friends, for his remarks, as he walked back and forth from one to the other, to see that all were waited upon, produced such an uproar, that we lost all formality and ceremony while in that tent. A long wooden bench stretched down each side of the table, and one either had to go in at the end, or climb over. As one lady climbed to her place at the table, Larry exclaimed "Please, lady, don't soil the upholstery," and soon perceiving some haste on the part of one person present, he shouted, "You have one hour and a half to eat; this ain't no twenty minute lunch counter." Just as we were all seated and had opened our Japanese napkins, and prepared for our meal, Larry electrified us all, by shouting at the top of his decidedly loud voice, "Let her go, coffee," and to our surprise, from another tent near by, there came a young man, with an earthenware pitcher full of really excellent coffee. It was surprising how good things did taste to us all.

After leaving Larry's, we drove through a long stretch of desolate country, owing to the loss of trees, but were surrounded by mountains; and as we crept along, we kept coming nearer and nearer to such a peculiar mountain, so white and green and yellow all over, and discovered that we were viewing the famous Sulphur Mountain, a most remarkable formation of almost pure sulphur. A boiling spring lies right at the foot, on the road-side, and was in a very active bubbling state.

About four o'clock, we were climbing a very steep ascent, when a sudden glimpse from a place called "Grand Point," gave us a little idea of the beautiful scenery before us, of the marvelous Cañon we had come so many miles to see, and hurrying our horses to the hotel which was near, we lost no time in obtaining a little "rattle-trap" of a carriage, and drove rapidly to see the two most extensive views into the Cañon, from " Point Lookout," and " Inspiration Point." Point Lookout was reached by driving to the edge of the woods, and walking in. And as we neared this high point, and saw the vision of beauty which met our eyes on every side, in that sunset hour, when all was bathed in floods of exquisite light, we felt as if nothing so beautiful in nature, had we ever seen before. Kneeling on a little stone near the edge, looking down hundreds of feet into that vast abyss, gazing ahead at the wonderful sheet of water falling over the Yellowstone Falls, three hundred and sixty feet without a break, then turning and looking backward, into that glorious coloring, made us feel as if we had seen God's Heaven at last!

Supreme and sublime emotions come to us all, at times and seasons when we least expect them; they do not come at will, but overpower us when we know not of their approach. Twice before in my life had I been so deeply moved, once by Mt. Blanc's superb serenity and golden glory, and again when the grand organ in the Cathedral at Freiburg, pealed forth into the dimly lighted edifice; and now the same emotions overwhelmed me, and I sank on my knees, and the tears chased themselves down my cheeks, unbidden and unnoticed, until Jamie's alarm lest I should fall or faint, brought me to myself.

If words or pen could describe that scene! The great sides of the Cañon were wide apart at the top, but sloped gradually together at their base, leaving a small space through which the river ran, like a beautiful band of green, or a strip of moss-agate. Rising on each side, as if a great sea of prisms had been frozen side-wise into a perpetual formation, the great points and waves of color rose, broken off jaggedly into pinnacles of all sizes and ragged edges, some standing alone, others in companies of twos and threes. Over all these formations and groups were the tints of beauty, red and deep crimson shading into palest pink and rose-color, browns and orange tints to lemon-color, purple of a most royal hue, and violet of such exquisite tint, of such distinct and yet soft shades, green too, and olive, and purest white, and such richness of color, such blending and harmonious combinations, such mellow tints, that not one harsh line was visible, not one unpleasant impression to mar the whole. It seemed as if the entire world had been transformed, as if we had been gazing into " Hades Holes," and now we were looking into the "Heavenly Gates," at the amethyst walls, and streets of pearl. It seemed as if the autumn tints had all been gathered here, as if it was the store-house of Dame Nature's paints and palettes, as if these blending and mellow prismatic walls were nature's copy and inspiration, for all the beauty of the trees in autumn. It impressed us all, and we came away reluctantly. It left in our hearts the peaceful exaltation and ecstasy of a beautiful prayer, or hymn ; and it seemed as if we could not but be better in the world, because of this blissful and perfect vision of natural beauty. It was the same scene of loveliness on Inspiration Point, and over all, the mellow twilight spread a golden veil, adding the last touch to that perfect scene. We were two hours in this paradise of color.

SUCH a sunshiny morning inspires any one, and life seems worth living, when such floods of golden light cover the earth. Some rays must peep into our hearts, on such days as this, I think, and it is only when our hearts and minds are too full of something else, that the sunshine cannot enter, and we wonder then, why we are not in tune with such glorious surroundings. Auntie, James and I were in full harmony with the beauty of the morning, and as soon as our breakfast was over, and our luggage ready for the coach, we started for " Point Lookout," to see in the morning light, the beauty which had so enthralled us in the last sunset hour. It was a twenty minutes' walk, but as we started before nine o'clock, we had plenty of time before us and were able to stay there a full half hour. Reaching Point Lookout, by the path of rare beauty through the woods, we immediately isolated ourselves, one from the other, to drink in silently and to meditate alone upon that rarest of rare beauties in nature. All before us, in the morning glory, lay the greatest of natural wonders, and the longer we lingered and looked, the more speechless was our admiration,— the more marvelous it seemed to us. It was a different aspect in the morning,—the sunlight came from such a different angle, and the mellow dreaminess and exquisite pathos of the sunset, had given place to the hopefulness and brightness of the morning glow. New beauties attracted me, new colors which shadows had deepened in the twilight and which I had not seen distinctly, and new and beautiful combinations of the prismatic tints, stood before me, in such rare radiance, that I was fascinated anew, and loath to leave this Point of Enchantment, as I love to call it, when Jamie brought my wandering thoughts back to terra-firma, by the suggestion that our half hour was up, and our coach was ready for us. Silently, in single Indian file, we reluctantly retraced our steps, and found all ready for our day's drive. In that little walk, neither Auntie, Jamie nor I exchanged a single word, and it seemed as if we felt the need of silent meditation, to bring us back to every day things again, and to print indelibly upon our hearts and minds, that scene of grand and exquisite beauty. The beautiful Falls had been like sparkling crystals and diamonds in the sunshine, great bands of emerald green, and a beautiful rainbow in the mist and spray, and it was like the mystical beauty of the heavenly land.

Our thirteen-mile drive was a fine one, over a pass in the mountains, through great forests and along splendid roads, and we reached Norris Geyser Basin, about half past twelve. It was old ground to us this time, but we fancied a second view of the geysers and great smoke-holes would be valuable to us, so after our luncheon, we wandered again through that marvelous formation, which had been our first introduction to the "Wonders of Wonderland.

On this visit, I noticed more caution,—greater pru-
dence in investigating hot places, and we kept mostly in the roadway and wandered little, in among the
boiling pools and caldrons. But our interest was
not lessened, but rather strengthened, by further
familiarity with these volcanic forces, and we came
away reluctantly, wishing our trip had just begun,
instead of about to end.

When we started, at about 2.15 P. M. for our return
trip to the Mammoth Hot Springs, we were informed
that we would meet, half way in our twenty-two
miles, a stage with five people in it, who would
change there with us, and take our driver and his
poor horses back into the Park. We drove along
pleasantly over the same ground that we had covered
in our start, but when we reached the Obsidian
Cliffs, we felt such interest in the deposits and the
glass boulders, that we thought it well to let the
horses rest, and we amused ourselves for a half hour,
wandering about those great cliffs, upon the pieces of
all sizes, which creaked and cracked and rattled and
chatted to us, as we walked over them. The glitter
of the obsidian is its chief beauty, and as we watched
it in the sunshine, it was like polished jet in the
bright light.

Finally, the stage from the Hot Springs arrived,
and the transfer of passengers and luggage took
place, and our final move towards the end of this
part of our journey was made. Imagine our horror,
when we discovered that our new driver was intoxi-

cated, and showed the symptoms so seriously, that we were quite alarmed. He had a man on the box with him, to whom he handed the reins, for about nine miles, and then to my horror, he came into the stage and sat with me,—an unprecedented proceeding. I was not half so much afraid then, as when he held the reins, and did my best to keep him good-natured, smiling at his silly jests, and letting his foolish remarks pass unnoticed. Jamie and Auntie watched me anxiously, but I carried out my part of the comedy, and acted as if I enjoyed my drunken companion. Finally, when the steepest part of the road lay before us, our driver stepped out of the stage, took a bottle of whiskey, and inviting James to join him (which he of course refused), turned it up and drank freely; then taking the reins, we went like the wind, down those three miles, through the steepest and narrowest of the passes, rolling round the curves and corners, as if the laws of centrifugal forces could not catch us, if we flew fast enough. Riding on an engine, was nothing to this excitement, with a man at the reins, who could not have sat straight, or remained on the coach, but for the break at his side, on which his foot was braced. Jamie, Auntie and I said nothing, but pressing our lips tightly together, and watching the lay of the land, if a jump was necessary, we resigned ourselves to our fate, not knowing which way it might go, at any moment. When a person is in a bad scrape and cannot get out of it, a calmness and resignation come, which are perfectly inexplicable, and help one through. Such was our experience.

We reached the hotel at 6.40 P. M., having had a most glorious and enjoyable trip through the National Yellowstone Park.

THURSDAY, SEPTEMBER 10TH.

A UNTIE, James and I walked a little in the morning. There is a spring among the Mammoth Hot Springs here, which coats any article that is put into it, with a heavy glistening white deposit. We walked to the little house where these "Coated Specimens" from Cleopatra Spring, are sold.

At 2 P. M., in a heavy shower which had just reached us, Auntie started on her journey to Salt Lake City. Our afternoon was spent quietly, resting and writing, and watching the succession of showers, chasing one another across the mountains near us. In the evening, we received some calls from those to whom we had letters of introduction.

FRIDAY, SEPTEMBER 11TH.

L OVELY day,—really too chilly for comfort. My morning was spent writing and packing, and we left the Mammoth Hot Springs Hotel, at two o'clock, truly sorry that our pleasant trip was ended. Our drive to Cinnabar was interesting, and the wonderful volcanic action, as well as the glacial cuttings, were plainly marked and easily recognized, and the stranded boulders were a source of constant remark, at least to anyone interested in such things. One could easily trace the slow but steady advance of the great ice sheet, which had covered the earth, so long ago, and see the keen and sharp outline of its work, in the cañons through which we drove, on those eight miles to Cinnabar. We had a half hour when we reached there, before the train started, and one of the baggage-men constituted himself our guide, and took us to see a few curiosities, live ones, too, owned by the people about there, which were trotted out for our special benefit, while an admiring crowd stood around us. There were two baby antelopes, dear tame little creatures, a great black bear, and a wolf; then a rattle-snake was poked out of his cage, to rattle for us, and let us take his picture, and our half hour passed pleasantly and profitably.

At 4 P. M. the train started, landing us in Livingston at six. The M— family,with James and myself had dinner at the "Albemarle Hotel"; then we took little Philip to see the Mountain Goat, and after looking in the few shops of interest, we returned to the hotel. Mr. M. left his family with James as protector, and took a train for the West, so after writing some letters, we joined our new charges in the sleeper, and long before the train started, we were in bed and asleep.

HOMEWARD!

THE day was beautiful, and we spent it quietly and pleasantly, resting, reading, and watching the varied scenery from our car windows. We were much interested in seeing Miles City, and Fort Keough, in Montana, and especially curious about the Camp of Indians, near the latter place. Col. Page, an officer from that fort, told us that those Indians were the Cheyennes, whom the soldiers brought last winter from Pine Ridge, where they were held and badly treated by their enemies, the Sioux. It was a curious village, the queer Indian tents being seen by the dozen, and such squalor and filth was visible, even from the train. We also saw two cattle round-ups, and the whippers-in were very busy, keeping refractory animals from making breaks and succeeding in fleeing from their enforced captivity.

We anticipated the Dakota "Bad Lands" very much, but were disappointed when we finally saw them. They are a most marvelous formation, in points and pinnacles, turrets and domes, in every remarkable and unusual form and size, many of them brilliantly colored, the brightest bands of red and yellow, being at the top of these mounds and hills. They interest one at first, but soon grow monotonous and wearisome. These unusual lands were once at the bottom of a great sea, for the rocks in them record the fact, and make it positive and beyond a doubt, as they are full of the most interesting and marvelous fossils. Truly it is an education in itself, for one to travel through this wonderful country of ours, and if one's eyes are open to all the interesting sights and scenes, a store of information can be tucked away, to be properly developed when time and opportunity allow. Jamie and I are returning home, with a firm determination to read and digest the many books we have heard of, and to look well into the continent building forces, which have interested us so much of late.

The Dakota wheat fields were a marvel in their wonderful harvest, as we steamed through them today. For miles on every side of us, as far as the eye could reach, were these yellow mounds, bearing such a harvest as Dakota has never known before. A prairie sunset of marvelous beauty, finished a really interesting day, on our journey.

SUNDAY, SEPTEMBER 13TH.

SOMETIMES "common-place days" are a treat, the very idea of having nothing to do, being restful, and after a feast in mysteries and wonders and color, such as we have had, in the Yellowstone, we are quite ready for the dusty railroad again. Having the Drawing Room last night, we slept very well, and were hardly ready to waken when the porter knocked, at 7.30 A. M. We lost our travelling companions, Mrs. M. and little Philip, and Miss M. when we reached Staples, in Minnesota, about breakfast time.

Minnesota is a beautiful state, and coming out of Dakota, with its broad expanse of treeless prairies, it was a delight, in the lovely autumn tints, and as we watched the varied and brilliant colors, it seemed as if the Grand Cañon of the Yellowstone had been brought to this region and distributed liberally over the land. We reached Minneapolis all too soon and unexpectedly, feeling bright and more refreshed than after any trip before, of similar length. Our day was uneventful. A rest, some writing, dinner in our room, and a lovely quiet evening, and then to sleep.

MONDAY, SEPTEMBER 14TH.

VERY warm, beautifully bright. After strolling about the city, looking into the shop windows and enjoying some fine pictures, we were so warm and so tired, that we returned to the West Hotel, and rested awhile before luncheon, and as we were on our way to the dining-room, Jamie's Aunt Annie, with her daughter and son, came to call upon us. Jamie had never seen these cousins, and it was the principal reason that brought us to Minneapolis. They took us to drive, for three hours or more, and we saw the famous Minnehaha Falls, where they

> "Flash and gleam among the oak-trees,
> Laugh and leap into the valley."

One could easily picture the beautiful maiden and Hiawatha her lover, in that exquisite spot, as she placed her hand in his, and her promise "I will follow you, my husband," seems to have been the song of those water witches ever since.

We drove about two beautiful lakes, with fine boulevards surrounding them, which, with the arched roadways of exquisite shade and natural beauty, make a drive any city might view with envy. Lake Harriet and Lake Calhoun are indeed gems of beauty, and well deserve their popularity. We went home with our newly found relatives and remained to supper with them, meeting all the cousins whom we are so glad to know at last.

TUESDAY, SEPTEMBER 15TH.

JAMES' cousin Mamie, came early this morning and took me for a long and very beautiful drive. Truly Minneapolis is a charming city, and so eastern in appearance, we are delighted with it.

Our afternoon was spent writing and resting, and we made a few visits in the evening. It is a relief to us sometimes to have a quiet day.

WEDNESDAY, SEPTEMBER 16TH.

A DAY without an event to chronicle, is indeed a rarity in our present wandering existence, and yet it was restful and sweet to us, "to pause and ponder by the way." Needful are these periods of quiet repose to us, and we always enjoy an undisturbed day together.

We made a little call in the afternoon on the cousins, and aunt, and took a few views with our camera.

THURSDAY, SEPTEMBER 17TH.

A S James had some important business to attend to in Minneapolis, he asked Aunt Annie and Mamie, to accompany me to St. Paul to-day. We had planned to spend several days there, but *an ungovernable desire to get home* suddenly seized James, and he wanted to start at once.

St. Paul is a wonderfully beautiful City, and I suppose would be pronounced far ahead of Minneapolis, by anyone having no particular interest in either place to influence them. The houses are certainly most palatial and inviting, and with a few exceptions on Fifth Avenue, in New York, are far ahead of our city, in number and architectural beauty, but, I came back with pleasure to Minneapolis, and decidedly prefer this city to her rival, St. Paul.

I returned in time to pack, and was ready to start for the east at seven o'clock, when we took the train for Chicago. Homeward bound in reality! Jamie is like a little boy in his anticipation!

WE reached Chicago about nine o'clock, having had a pleasant and comfortable trip from Minneapolis. We went at once to the Auditorium Hotel, and expected to stay a few days, to again see our friends. Jamie, however, felt so impatient to get home that he could not hear of any delay, and we decided to start for home to-night at five o'clock.

It had always been James' desire to take me to Mr. K's store, to see the working of that large establishment, and to meet some of his friends whom I did not know. This morning, he insisted upon my going, and we had such a pleasant time, seeing the entire process of the work and meeting such a host of friends, who welcomed us most cordially. Two sad items of news, however, greatly depressed us. We learned this morning of the sudden death of our new but dear friend, Mrs. J. in Salt Lake City, and we feel deep sympathy for that young husband, and his motherless little ones. Then trouble has come to another friend, whom we left in Chicago in May, in such health, and full of promise. As Jamie and I drove along on our return to the Hotel, he comforted me, in the sudden shock which had come to us both, and said, " We are sad, May, and I do not see how we can help it, but we must not let it depress us too much, *for we are spared to each other yet*, and are so happy and well, and I am so thankful for that."

Stopping at the photographer's studio, to order more of Jamie's pictures, the artist urged us to let him make a large crayon head of him for me, at which he exclaimed, "Who wants a large crayon of me hanging about? *No, people do that after one is dead!*" As we stepped into the carriage again, Jamie turned to me, asking if I "really wanted that crayon very much," and when I said that it would be a pleasure to have it, he hurried again into the studio. In five minutes he joined me saying, "There, May, the crayon is ordered for you, but *don't have it framed till I am dead!*"

At five o'clock, we took the Pennsylvania Limited for New York, and meeting our friend, Mr. I. from Brooklyn, we spent a pleasant evening, chatting with him.

SATURDAY, SEPTEMBER 19TH.

THE slowest of slow days! It seemed as if the time could not go fast enough, to keep pace with our impatience and eager desire to get home.

"We're four hours late!" exclaimed Jamie this morning, "but perhaps we'll make up some time." All this day, the time-table for the Staten Island boats, was constantly studied, and much anxiety expressed for fear we could not catch the midnight boat from New York. At a quarter past eleven o'clock, we rolled into the depot at Jersey City, being over four hours late. We easily caught the last boat to the Island, and at half past one o'clock Sunday morning, September 20th, we reached the home and loved ones so dear to us. How good it was! All the way, as we drove from our little station to the house, in a beautiful path of moonlight, Jamie kept exclaiming, " Isn't it lovely to get home! The best part of going away is the coming home," etc., etc., but although I was overjoyed to see the dear ones again, a nameless something made me sad, as well as glad. Was I too tired?

EIGHT days of unspeakable happiness followed, days of joy in everything about us, such perfect pleasure and serene content; and the home was never so lovely to us. Jamie exclaimed, the morning after our arrival, "Although we have seen many beautiful places in our own country, May, there is no spot so lovely and beautiful as this home of ours, after all." Jamie had found that "Be it ever so humble, there's no place like Home."

Many times, during those few days, Jamie spoke of the wonderful good fortune, that had followed us in all our trip, and how remarkable it was that we had always been either just ahead, or just behind, the numerous railroad accidents, on the roads over which we had passed, having had no annoyance save one or two short delays, in reaching our destination. "I hope you give thanks daily May, for I do, for we surely have been guided and watched over by a Divine Providence."

And we had been! That same Guiding Hand had brought us home, just when we should have come, and granted us more happiness, so that we thought we felt strong in heart and body, for whatever might come; and when, only four days later, the Father took one of us gently by the hand, and led him to that Better Land, where his eyes should behold more wonderful wonders and greater beauty, than together we had seen, it seems as if his lips must have whispered again, "There is no place like *this* Home."

"I can not say and I will not say
That he is dead.—He is just away!

With a cheery smile, and a wave of the hand,
He has wandered into an unknown land,

And left us dreaming how very fair
It needs must be, since he lingers there.

And you—O you, who the wildest yearn
For the old-time step and the glad return,—

Think of him faring on, as dear
In the love of There, as the love of Here;

* * * * * *

Think of him still as the same, I say:
He is not dead—he is just away!"